I0829666

THE
RESONANCE
BREACH

Victoria E. Charles

GODDESS
& GLYPHS
PRESS

For the ones who remember what they were never taught, who feel
homesickness for places they have never been, and who know that some
loves do not belong to a single lifetime.
This is for you.

Some souls do not end when their bodies do.
They wander. They remember.
They return.

I

THE VEIL TEARS

The forest didn't scream when the rift opened. It exhaled—slow, heavy, and wrong—like the world had been holding something in its lungs for centuries and finally couldn't keep it in.

Light bent. Not in a way the human eye would call magic, but in a way that made the air look briefly liquid, as if reality had thinned to a membrane and someone on the other side had pressed a palm against it. The wind stilled. Birds stopped mid-thought. Even the insects went quiet, as though they recognized a rule had been broken and didn't dare be the first to testify.

Then the veil tore.

A seam of silver cut open between the trees, bright enough to bruise the dark, and a body fell through it like a thrown star—fast, spiraling, desperate—until moss and earth caught her with a wet, muffled impact. She didn't land like a person. She landed like something that had never been meant to touch this world.

Isorae's breath exploded out of her in a strangled sound, a broken gasp that tasted of iron and cold sap. Her bones rang with the force of gravity—heavy, blunt, claiming. The air here was thicker than it should have been; the sky pressed down like a lid.

Her fingers dug into the moss, seeking the familiar pulse of Aelinthar beneath it.

Nothing answered.

The ground was mute—not dead, no, she could feel life all around her, frantic and small and wild in the roots and damp—but it didn't sing to her the way her realm did. This soil had no ancient cadence, no resonant language. It was a different instrument entirely, and her body, tuned for another symphony, trembled with the shock of it.

Isorae tried to rise.

Her muscles rebelled.

A sharp pain cut across her ribs. Another lanced down the length of her spine. She managed one shaky elbow, then collapsed again, cheek pressed to cool earth, hair spilling across the moss like pale smoke.

The air vibrated with something harsh and invisible—electricity, metal, signal, human. It wasn't just the gravity that made her sick; it was the frequency of this place. This world buzzed with unnatural currents and sharp, constant noise, like a thousand invisible wires strung through the air, humming their private song.

Her magic recoiled instinctively, folding inward to seek shelter behind bone and blood.

And yet—beneath the pain and confusion, beneath the wrongness of the air—there was something else.

A pulse.

Not the world's.

A presence.

It rolled through her like a low drumbeat she hadn't heard in lifetimes, familiar and impossible, a scent-memory of smoke and salt, a touch remembered by her skin though her skin was new. A name her tongue had never spoken in this body yet could not forget.

Her heart stuttered.

No.

It couldn't be.

Isorae swallowed, throat raw, and pushed herself upright again, shaking. The trees loomed above her in dark vertical lines, their branches tangled like ribs, moonlight—or something close to it— spilling between leaves. The forest was dense, damp, alive.

But it wasn't hers.

She tried to focus on the rift, to find the tear she'd fallen through, the seam she could slip back into like a needle returning to cloth.

There was nothing.

Only ordinary night.

And the quiet horror of being somewhere she did not belong.

Her breath came too fast, panic threatening, hot and animal.

Isorae pressed a hand to her sternum as if she could physically hold her soul in place.

Think.

You are not prey.

You are not lost.

She steadied herself, eyes closed, reaching inward for the old skills: feel the water in the air, taste the roots beneath the soil, listen for the heartbeat of the land.

She found heartbeat, yes—but it was scattered, wild, untrained, unsanctified.

She could not weave it the way she could at home.

Aelinthar had always responded to her like a lover—slow to rouse, loyal once touched.

This world did not know her.

This world did not recognize her authority.

Her hand shook against her chest.

The presence came again—a tug so intimate it felt like fingers curling around the thread of her ribcage, a pull, a summons.

Isorae's throat tightened.

She didn't say his name aloud. She couldn't afford to. Naming was a kind of calling, and she didn't yet understand what rules governed this realm.

But her mouth formed the shape of it anyway.

A sound softer than breath slipped out.

"…Caelith…"

For a moment, nothing happened.

Then—far away, somewhere deeper in the forest—something answered.

Not with words.

With attention.

The hair on the back of Isorae's neck rose. Her gaze snapped toward the darkness between trees.

A branch cracked.

Human footsteps.

Not one person.

More.

Her blood went cold.

Isorae tried to stand.

Her legs buckled.

She caught herself against a tree trunk, bark rough under her palm, vision swimming as the world tilted like a slow wave beneath her feet.

No.

She couldn't be found.

Not yet.

Not before she understood where she was.

Not before—

The invisible buzzing in the air sharpened abruptly, like a blade dragged along bone.

Her magic shuddered.

A faint bioluminescent flicker sparked beneath her skin—betraying.

She pressed her hand over her wrist, forcing her breath slower. Quieter.

The footsteps came closer.

A soft mechanical whirring threaded the night.

Something in the air tasted like cold glass.

She didn't know what a drone was, but she felt it like a predator with no heartbeat.

Isorae stepped backward into shadow, weak and dizzy, out of tune.

Her fingers brushed a vine trailing along the tree trunk—nothing sacred, nothing vowed, just a common thing, alive and simple.

She whispered in her own tongue, not quite a spell, more like a plea.

The vine twitched, sliding across her wrist and tightening slightly, as if trying to hide her pulse.

A light swept between the trees—white, focused, searching.

She froze.

The beam skimmed her shoulder.

Her skin crawled. Her breath caught.

But she did not move.

The light passed.

Isorae exhaled, trembling, and pressed herself deeper into shadow.

Somewhere beyond the trees, human voices murmured, low and clipped, carrying the cadence of authority and protocol.

Not hunters for food.

Hunters for possession.

Her heart hammered.

Her magic, caged inside her, pulsed against her ribs like something trapped in a jar.

She turned and ran.

Not gracefully.

Not like the stories humans told about fae gliding through moonlit forests.

She ran like an injured animal—branches lashing her face, mud sucking at her feet, lungs burning with the wrong air while the buzzing lines of human frequency tangled around her like invisible thorns.

She stumbled.

Caught herself.

Stumbled again.

The pull tightened—not from behind, but from ahead—drawing her onward like a thread tied to her sternum.

It felt obscene and intimate, too familiar, like being touched by someone you haven't seen in a thousand years.

Her eyes watered.

She didn't know whether from pain or something else.

She ran toward it anyway.

Because she had once died for it.

Because she had spent lifetimes searching for it.

Because her soul recognized the taste of home in the dark.

And because she had no other choice.

Rowan Hale didn't believe in anything that couldn't be measured.

That wasn't an insult to wonder. He loved the forest because it was measurable in the ways he understood—wind direction, animal tracks, seasonal shifts, the quiet physics of survival. If you listened closely enough, the world told you what it was doing.

You didn't need angels or omens.

You needed attention.

Still, some things had never fit neatly into his explanations.

For as long as he could remember, Rowan had dreamed of a woman with pale hair and eyes that looked like moonlight caught in water. She was always just out of reach, always half-hidden by mist. Sometimes she smiled at him like she knew his name. Sometimes she bled. Sometimes she died in his arms and left him waking with a scream stuck behind his teeth.

Rowan had done what any reasonable man did with something like that.

He had built a life sturdy enough to hold the strange.

A small cabin on the edge of protected woods.

Work that kept him outdoors.

Quiet routines.

Long hikes.

The kind of solitude that didn't ask too many questions.

And a dog—because some part of him had always needed another heartbeat nearby.

Tonight, the forest felt off.

He told himself that as he rested a hand briefly on Bramble's collar and stepped out into the cold.

Bramble didn't need a leash.

He never had.

He stayed close because he chose to.

The air smelled of damp leaves and pine. The ground was dark with recent rain. The sky was a bruised indigo, the moon hidden behind cloud.

Bramble—a rangy mutt with too much intelligence in his eyes—paused at the edge of the yard.

Rowan frowned.

"What is it, buddy?"

Bramble's ears pricked forward. His nose lifted, scenting. A low, uncertain sound vibrated in his chest—not a bark, not a growl.

Something between.

Rowan followed the dog's gaze.

The treeline stood perfectly ordinary.

And yet—

There was a tension in the air, like someone had drawn a bowstring and left it pulled.

Rowan felt it in his skin.

He shook off the thought and started down the path, boots crunching softly on gravel.

They had barely made it fifty yards when Bramble stopped again.

This time, the dog refused to move.

Rowan gripped the collar.

"Hey. Come on."

Bramble's hackles rose.

Rowan's pulse ticked faster. He scanned the trees. No eyes reflecting. No movement. No scent of bear.

But the forest was too quiet.

The usual chorus of small sounds—crickets, distant owls, the restless whisper of leaves—had thinned, as if someone had turned the volume down.

Rowan swallowed and stepped forward cautiously.

Bramble pulled back.

"Okay, okay."

Rowan crouched, fingers brushing Bramble's neck in a calming stroke.

"It's alright. It's just the woods."

Bramble stared at him like he'd said something profoundly stupid.

Rowan straightened, unease creeping deeper now, and listened the way he always did.

At first, nothing.

Then—faintly—something like a low mechanical whirring.

Distant.

Almost swallowed by the trees.

Rowan's brow furrowed. The park service sometimes used drones for survey work—but not this late, and not this quietly.

Then he smelled it.

Not smoke.

Not rot.

Something sharper—like cold metal after rain.

His chest tightened in a way that had nothing to do with logic.

Bramble suddenly veered to the right, stepping off the main path with quiet insistence and into a narrower trail Rowan rarely took.

Rowan hesitated only a moment before letting the dog lead.

They moved between dense pines as the path narrowed until branches brushed Rowan's shoulders.

The forest swallowed them.

Behind them, the cabin might as well have been a myth.

Bramble's pace quickened.

Rowan's breath fogged in front of him.

His pulse kept time with Bramble's steady pull forward.

Then he saw it.

A faint shimmer on the ground—not light exactly, but a residue that caught moonless darkness and made it briefly… wrong.

As if the air itself had been scraped raw and left sensitive.

Rowan crouched, his fingers hovering just above it.

His skin tingled as if he were holding his hand near static.

"What the hell…" he murmured.

Bramble whined.

Rowan straightened slowly and looked deeper into the trees.

A sound carried on the wind—barely audible.

A woman's breath.

A soft, broken gasp.

Rowan moved before thought could catch him.

He pushed through brush, following the sound.

Bramble strained beside him, eager and frightened at once.

The forest opened just enough—

—and Rowan saw her.

She was half-kneeling against a tree, one hand pressed to her ribs, the other braced against bark. Her hair—pale, too pale—spilled across her shoulders like spilled milk under starlight. Mud streaked her luminous skin.

She wore clothing Rowan couldn't place: gossamer layers that clung and fluttered like mist, torn and dirtied as though she had fought the woods themselves.

She lifted her head.

And the world tipped.

Rowan knew that face.

Not from memory—he was certain he had never seen her—but from the dreams.

From the ache that had followed him since childhood like a quiet shadow.

Her eyes locked on his.

They were wrong in a way that sent cold down his spine—iridescent, shifting, as if light lived beneath them.

Violet.

Silver.

Something between.

For a suspended moment, they stared at each other as if the forest had narrowed the world down to only two living things.

Her body swayed.

Rowan stepped forward.

"Hey—hey, are you okay?"

His voice sounded too loud.

Too human.

She flinched, gaze darting toward the trees like a hunted animal.

He raised his hands slowly.

"It's okay. I'm not going to hurt you."

Her throat bobbed.

She whispered a word—soft, sharp—in a language Rowan didn't recognize.

But it struck him like a memory in his bones.

Then her knees buckled.

Rowan lunged and caught her.

She was lighter than he expected—and too warm, as if fever lived beneath her skin.

Her body trembled against him, shock or cold or something deeper.

And when his arms wrapped around her, something in Rowan's chest cracked open.

Heat surged along his nerves.

His heart stumbled.

She smelled of rain and crushed leaves and faint night flowers—and beneath it, smoke and salt, like a memory he didn't know he carried.

"Hey," he whispered, instinctively lowering his voice. "Can you stand? I can help you."

Her eyes sharpened—recognition and terror tangled together.

Her trembling fingers lifted to his jaw.

The instant her skin touched his, Rowan's vision flashed white.

A luminous tree.

Roots glowing like veins.

Her laughter beneath alien stars.

His own bloodied hands cradling her face.

A vow spoken under a sky that was not this sky.

Rowan gasped.

Dizziness slammed into him.

He nearly dropped her—but his arms tightened instinctively.

"What the hell is happening?" he rasped.

She recoiled as if burned.

Her breath broke.

Her body went slack.

Rowan swore softly and shifted her carefully into his arms.

"Okay," he whispered. "Okay. We're going to my place."

She tried to protest—her head turning sharply toward the trees.

And then Rowan saw it.

A white beam of light swept between trunks.

Not a hiker's flashlight.

Bramble growled low.

Rowan's instincts snapped into place.

He lifted her fully and moved—fast, silent—Bramble close at heel.

Voices murmured behind them, too distant to make out, but close enough to sharpen his veins.

He didn't know who they were.

He only knew they were not here to help her.

In his arms, her eyes fluttered open again.

Her lips shaped a word.

"…Caelith…"

Rowan stumbled, breath catching painfully.

No one had ever called him that.

And yet something deep inside him answered like a struck bell.

He kept moving.

Because whatever she was—whatever this was—he could not leave her here.

Not when his body knew her.

Not when the forest itself had gone quiet to listen.

Not when the word she spoke sounded like a key turning in a lock he had never known existed.

He didn't know it yet—but the moment he carried her across his cabin threshold, his life would split cleanly in two.

Before her.

And after.

And somewhere in the bones of the world, the veil shivered again.

Not torn.

Recognizing.

Remembering.

2

THE PLACE HE BRINGS HER

Rowan does not remember deciding to run. He remembers the pressure in his chest—the same sharp, breath-stealing pressure that used to follow his worst dreams—and the way his arms tightened instinctively around the woman's light, trembling body, as if his bones had already chosen her before his mind caught up.

Branches tore at his jacket as he moved fast through the trees. Bramble ran low and silent at his heel, ears pinned, occasionally glancing back as if checking that the forest itself was still following them. Behind them, the white beam cut through the trunks again.

Rowan veered sharply off the trail and didn't stop until the dark shape of his cabin rose out of the trees like a held breath finally released. He fumbled the door open, carried her inside, and kicked it shut behind him.

The cabin was small—one room, a wood stove, a narrow kitchen counter, shelves heavy with dried herbs, jars of plant specimens, notebooks stacked in quiet chaos. The windows were already shuttered for the night. He slid the bolt home and stood there for a half second longer than necessary, heart slamming against his ribs.

Only then did he look down at the woman in his arms.

She was breathing—shallow and uneven—her lashes trembling faintly against pale skin. Her hair clung damply to her temples, mud streaking her cheek and collarbone. She did not look real enough to be here.

Rowan swallowed and carried her to the couch, lowering her carefully onto the blankets. His hands hovered for a second after he released her, reluctant—as if letting go might make her vanish. Bramble circled once, then sat at the foot of the couch, eyes fixed on her with unwavering intensity.

Rowan rubbed a hand over his face. "Okay," he muttered softly. "Okay."

He fetched water, a clean cloth, and a small first-aid kit from beneath the sink. His hands shook—not badly, but enough to annoy him. He forced his breathing to slow and knelt beside her.

Her eyes fluttered open as the cool cloth brushed her forehead. She startled slightly, breath hitching, gaze darting—until it found him. Her stare locked on his face like she had found a star she'd been looking for in the wrong sky.

He froze.

"It's okay," he said quietly. "You're safe. You're inside."

She searched his face slowly, as if mapping him. Her lips parted. "…Caelith…"

The word slid into him like a key into a lock that had never had a name.

Rowan swallowed. "My name is Rowan," he said gently. "Rowan Hale."

She frowned faintly—not confused. Worried. She lifted one trembling hand and brushed her fingertips over his wrist, where his pulse thudded visibly beneath his skin.

"You are… louder than you were," she murmured in a soft, unfamiliar cadence.

Rowan blinked. "What?"

She withdrew her hand, wincing as pain flared through her ribs. Her fingers curled into the blanket, and he noticed the movement instantly.

"Hey—don't move too much," he said, shifting closer. "You're hurt."

She nodded faintly. "Your world is heavy."

He exhaled through his nose. "Yeah. Gravity's kind of a jerk."

She studied him again—not smiling, simply trying to place him. Rowan began carefully cleaning the mud from her hands and arms. Her skin was warm—warmer than it should have been—and faintly luminous, as if moonlight lived just beneath it.

"You fell pretty hard," he said quietly. "Can you tell me what happened?"

Her gaze drifted toward the dark window. "The veil tore," she whispered.

Rowan's hands paused. "...Okay," he said slowly. "Let's pretend I know what that means."

Her lips curved faintly, briefly—something almost like sadness. "It is the place between breaths."

He nodded like that helped. "Can you tell me your name?"

"Isorae."

The sound settled into his chest in a way his name never had.

"That's... not common around here," he said.

Her eyes flicked to the shelves of jars, books, drying herbs. "You tend the quiet sciences," she murmured.

Rowan frowned. "Botany. Ecological survey. Mostly. I write research articles. Sometimes field guides."

She nodded as if that explained something important.

He eased her torn outer layer of gossamer fabric aside just enough to check the bruising along her ribs. Dark marks were already blooming beneath her skin. She flinched—but didn't pull away. His jaw tightened.

"You're lucky nothing's broken," he murmured. "But you're going to be sore."

"You bind wounds like a kin-keeper," she whispered.

Rowan snorted softly. "I bind wounds like a guy with YouTube."

She didn't understand the words—but she smiled faintly anyway.

He wrapped her ribs, careful and steady. She watched him the entire time, eyes following his hands like they were something familiar. When he finished, he hesitated.

"You're soaked," he said. "You need dry clothes."

She tilted her head slightly. "Are they... safe?"

He met her gaze. "They won't hurt you."

She considered that carefully.

He stood and rummaged through a drawer, returning with a soft cotton shirt and sweatpants. "These are clean. They're… normal clothes."

She accepted them slowly, fingers tracing the fabric with wonder. "This is woven very quietly," she murmured.

Rowan smiled despite himself. "I'll, uh—I'll turn around."

He did—but not before Bramble stood, walked closer, sniffed her gently, then sat again with his back against the couch like a sentry. Isorae watched the dog with wide, cautious eyes.

"He guards the threshold," she whispered.

Rowan froze mid-step. "…Yeah," he said softly. "He does."

While she changed, Rowan stared at the far wall, listening to every sound, every shift of breath. Something was still out there. He felt it the way you felt weather coming before clouds appeared—a pressure beneath thought, beneath fear.

Not the veil.

Not the forest.

Something that had noticed the tear.

Something that had followed it.

And for reasons he could not explain, he already knew:

Whatever had found her…

was still searching.

3

THE THINGS HE LEARNS WITHOUT MEANING TO

Rowan kept his back turned while she changed. He told himself it was politeness. He told himself it was respect. But the truth was simpler and more uncomfortable: he didn't trust what his body would do if he looked at her too long.

Behind him, cloth whispered. A small intake of breath—sharp, uncertain—like she'd put her hands on something unfamiliar and didn't know whether it would bite. Rowan stared hard at the far wall, jaw tight, listening anyway.

Bramble sat close by the couch, a silent sentry, ears angled toward every sound she made. When she shifted, the dog's tail gave one slow thump against the floor—approval or reassurance, Rowan couldn't tell.

Then her voice—soft, careful.

"This… is yours?"

Rowan turned slowly.

She stood beside the couch in the oversized cotton shirt, sleeves falling past her wrists. The sweatpants sat awkwardly at her hips, tied too tight in the front because she hadn't understood the drawstring until he'd demonstrated it with his own hands, facing away. The clothes looked wrong on her—not because they didn't fit, but because she didn't belong to anything made in this world. She looked like something ancient wearing modern fabric like a disguise.

Her hair still hung damp and pale over her shoulders. The bruising along her ribs was darker now, blooming beneath skin that held that faint, impossible inner glow.

Rowan's throat tightened. "Yeah," he managed. "They're mine. They're… clean. They won't hurt you."

She looked down at her own hands, fingers flexing in the sleeves as if testing the quiet softness of the fabric. "Woven quietly," she murmured again, almost to herself.

Rowan huffed a short breath that might have been a laugh if he hadn't been too tense to let it fully exist. "Cotton," he said. "Normal."

She lifted her gaze, eyes bright and unnervingly aware. "Nothing here is normal." The English came out halting, but intentional—like she was assembling each word from memory she hadn't earned.

Rowan stared. "You speak English."

"A little," she admitted. "Not… yours. Not the same." She swallowed. "But the shape of it is near."

His mind snagged on that. The shape of it. He should have asked a hundred questions right then.

Instead, he said, "Sit down. Please."

She did—carefully, like her ribs were made of glass.

Rowan grabbed the first-aid kit again and knelt in front of her. His hands were steadier now—not calm, exactly, but precise. The kind of precision he used when handling delicate specimens in the field. The kind you used when you didn't want to lose something rare.

He reached for the edge of the shirt. "May I?"

Her eyes flicked to his face, then down to his hands. "Yes," she whispered.

Rowan lifted the hem only enough to see the wrap he'd already placed and the bruising that had darkened beneath it. He adjusted the bandage, tightening pressure carefully, making sure it didn't steal her breath.

She flinched once.

Rowan's hands froze instantly. "Sorry."

"It is not you," she murmured, breath shallow. "It is… the weight. Your realm presses like stone."

Rowan swallowed. His gaze lifted to her face. "What are you?"

A pause. The air between them felt full, as if even the cabin was listening.

Isorae's gaze drifted toward the window as if she expected the walls to become transparent. "I am—" she started, then stopped, as if the words didn't translate cleanly. Her brows drew together. "I was… a bridge-keeper."

Rowan's expression didn't change, but something inside him went colder. "A bridge," he repeated.

"Yes." Her fingers tightened around the shirt fabric at her thigh. "Between places that are not meant to touch."

Rowan's eyes narrowed. "And you fell through one."

Isorae nodded once.

He tried to keep his voice even. "From where?"

She hesitated, eyes flicking away like the answer hurt. "Aelinthar," she said softly.

The name landed in the cabin like a stone dropped into still water. Rowan didn't know it. And yet his body reacted as if it did.

A pressure gathered behind his sternum—the same ache he'd carried through too many dreams, the same sensation that had seized him the instant he'd seen her in the woods. He forced himself to breathe.

"And why do you keep calling me Caelith?" Rowan asked, careful, like he was walking toward something that might break.

Isorae's throat bobbed. Her gaze snapped to his face, sharp and searching. "You do not remember," she whispered. It wasn't a question.

Rowan held still, every muscle tight. "I don't know what you mean."

Isorae stared at him like she was staring at a door that should have opened and didn't. Slowly—very slowly—she lifted her hand and reached toward him again.

Rowan didn't flinch. He should have. But he didn't.

Her fingers hovered near his jaw—the same place she had touched him before. Rowan's pulse jumped hard enough to blur his vision.

"Don't," he rasped, not unkindly. More like warning himself.

She stopped. Then, with careful restraint, she lowered her hand and instead rested it lightly over his wrist, feeling the pulse there. Her eyes widened slightly at the strength of it.

"You are alive," she whispered. "But… loud. Anchored. Dense."

Rowan's mouth went dry. "What does that mean?"

"It means your body is more here than it was," she said, swallowing. "More trapped into matter."

Rowan stared at her. "More trapped," he repeated.

Isorae nodded faintly, voice softening. "In Aelinthar, you were… thinner. Like flame. Like wind through stone."

His chest tightened painfully. He heard himself ask, "And in Aelinthar… you knew me?"

Isorae's lips parted, but no sound came for a beat. Then she whispered, "Yes."

The word didn't feel like an answer. It felt like a blade sliding into place.

Rowan leaned back on his heels, trying to force logic into his bones. "This isn't—" He stopped, voice rough. "Is this some trauma thing? Are you concussed? You hit hard. You're in shock."

Isorae's gaze didn't change. It stayed steady. Almost sad. "No," she said quietly. "This is not confusion."

Rowan's hands flexed. He needed something solid. Something measurable. He reached behind him, grabbed the glass of water he'd poured, and offered it.

She accepted it with both hands, like the weight of it required reverence. She sipped—then winced, as if even the taste was unfamiliar.

"Too sharp," she murmured.

Rowan frowned. "It's just water."

Isorae lifted her eyes. "It tastes like… wire."

Rowan stared, mouth opening and closing once without sound. Of course it would. Chlorine. Minerals. Modern filtration. All the little things his life ignored. He suddenly hated how normal his cabin was— hated the electric hum in the walls, the invisible signals, the way everything in his world buzzed without ever being quiet.

He moved to the kettle on the stove, filled it, lit the burner. "Tea," he said. "Maybe… better."

Isorae watched him like boiling water was unfamiliar magic. Bramble padded closer and pressed his shoulder against her shin. She startled, then softened, fingers sinking into the dog's fur.

"He likes you," Rowan said, trying for lightness.

Isorae's lips curved faintly. "He does not fear me."

Rowan's gaze flicked up. "Should he?"

Isorae hesitated. Then something older passed behind her eyes. "No," she said softly. "But others would."

Rowan's hands stilled over the kettle. "Others," he echoed.

Isorae's fingers tightened in Bramble's fur. "The ones with cold light," she whispered.

Rowan's stomach dropped—the searchlight, the hum, the metallic smell. He forced his voice steady. "You saw them?"

Isorae nodded once. "They followed the tear."

Rowan's jaw tightened. "ARIS?" She blinked at the acronym. Rowan swallowed. "Never mind."

He poured hot water into a mug, dropped a tea bag in, added honey, then brought it to her and crouched again, holding it out. "It's warm. Sweet. Drink slowly."

Isorae took it, careful around the heat, and sipped. This time she didn't wince. Her shoulders loosened by a fraction, and Rowan watched that tiny shift like it mattered more than it should.

He cleared his throat. "What happened to you... before you fell here?"

Isorae lowered her eyes to the mug, as if staring into the steam kept the memories from slicing too cleanly.

"The bridge broke," she whispered.

Rowan waited.

"It was not an accident," she said quietly. "The bridge did not simply fail. It was pressed. Something was reaching across it — something that could not cross, but could pull."

Her eyes lifted.

"They learned my name before I fell."

Rowan's stomach turned cold. "You mean something attacked you."

She didn't answer.

"They wanted the door," she whispered. "They could not take it. So they took the hinge."

Rowan's fists clenched. "What do you mean by hinge?"

She swallowed.

"I fell," she said. "But I did not fall alone."

His breath stuttered. "You weren't alone?"

"You were there," she whispered. "You caught me."

Rowan's vision dimmed at the edges.

"You held me," she said. "But my light was already failing. Your hands were red. Not with harm. With holding."

Rowan swallowed hard. "Blood?"

She nodded once.

"You did not let me fall through alone."

Rowan's breath came shallow. "And then?"

"And when my body failed," she said softly, "you tried to anchor me."

His voice barely formed. "Anchor you."

"You tried to keep me there," she said. "But my form could not remain. Only my pattern could."

Rowan whispered, "Your pattern."

"I crossed as memory before I crossed as matter," she said. "You called me through the fracture."

His head lifted sharply.

"I did not know your voice by sound," she continued. "I knew it by shape. And I followed it."

The cabin felt suddenly too small for the weight of that.

"You didn't fall here by accident," Rowan said hoarsely.

She met his eyes.

"You brought me through."

Silence pressed thick around them.

"They followed me," she added quietly. "Because I am still shaped like the breach."

Her fingers brushed the place over her sternum where the mark would later live.

"They do not hear worlds," she whispered. "They hear hinges."

Rowan drew a slow, steady breath.

"You're safe here," he said again. This time it sounded less like reassurance and more like a vow.

Isorae lifted her gaze. Her eyes were too bright in the cabin light. "You do not understand what you are saying."

"Try me."

Her mouth trembled faintly. "If they find me… they will not stop."

"Then we make sure they don't," Rowan said quietly.

"You cannot hide me from machines."

"I can hide you from anything that bleeds."

Her gaze softened — like she had heard the same words once before in another life.

Her grip on the mug loosened. Her shoulders sank as exhaustion finally claimed her.

Rowan took the mug gently from her hands.

"Sleep," he murmured.

Her lips parted once. "Caelith."

He didn't correct her.

He covered her with the blanket. Bramble lay at her feet like a sentry that did not question orders.

Rowan took the armchair across from her.

He listened to the cabin settle.

To the wind.

To her breathing.

And beneath it all —

the thin, distant mechanical whirring in the trees.

Rowan's fingers laced until his knuckles went pale.

Because whatever had detected the tear had not left.

It was only widening its search.

4

THE QUIET BETWEEN BREATHS

Rowan didn't remember choosing stillness. He only remembered the moment his hands stopped moving, the kettle forgotten, the tea cooling on the counter—like his body had finally run out of places to put its panic.

A woman had fallen out of the woods. She had looked at him like she'd been looking for him for lifetimes. She had spoken a name that wasn't his. And now she lay on his couch, asleep, breathing, warm and impossibly real in his cabin.

Rowan sat in the old armchair across from her with his forearms braced on his knees, hands loosely clasped, posture tense in a way that looked almost prayerful if you didn't know him. His shoulders stayed set like he was prepared to lunge to his feet at the first wrong sound. His gaze kept cutting to the curtained windows, then back to her, then back to the door, the bolt, the walls—checking, rechecking, as if the cabin had suddenly become something fragile he couldn't afford to trust.

Bramble lay stretched out in front of the couch, head on his paws, but the dog wasn't sleeping. His eyes were open to slits, ears flicking toward every creak of wood or sigh of wind. When Rowan shifted, Bramble's gaze lifted briefly—an unspoken question—and then returned to the woman like even the dog didn't know what, exactly, she was… only that she mattered.

The cabin itself felt different. Same cedar walls. Same worn floorboards. Same faint smell of coffee grounds and pine resin embedded into old wood. But there was a new scent braided into it now—rain-wet leaves and night flowers and something pale and strange, like the ghost of a garden that didn't grow in this world.

23

Rowan couldn't stop breathing it in.

He told himself it was instinct. Tracking. Survival. He told himself he was cataloging details in case he needed them later.

But his gaze kept returning to her face with an intensity he couldn't justify.

She lay on her side beneath the blanket he'd pulled from his bed, the fabric tucked under her chin the way you tucked in someone you didn't want to wake. Her hair had dried in uneven strands, pale as moonlight on snow, fanned across the couch cushion and armrest like it had a life of its own. Mud still clung faintly at her temple and along the edge of her cheekbone. He'd wiped most of it away with a damp cloth, but not all of it, and the part of him that noticed those details—the part that wanted to lean closer and fix them—made his throat go tight.

She looked too soft for the way she'd run. Too delicate for the wildness in her eyes when she'd seen the searchlight between the trees. And the bruising on her ribs—darkening beneath skin that held a faint, subtle glow—had made something cold and violent flicker behind Rowan's calm.

He'd seen injuries. He'd treated his own. He'd helped lost hikers. He knew how bodies worked.

But her body didn't feel like it belonged to physics the same way his did.

Even asleep, she was… humming.

Not audibly. Not like a sound.

Like a sensation.

Rowan's skin prickled when he looked at her too long, as if the air between them had taken on charge. He shifted in the chair and exhaled slowly through his nose, trying to bleed off the restless energy in his limbs.

His gaze drifted again. Her lashes were dark and thick against pale cheeks. Her mouth was slightly parted as she slept, the softest line of breath moving in and out—in and out—the kind of breathing that made you instinctively lower your own voice, even when you were alone.

Rowan's eyes traced the curve of her lips once, then he forced himself to look away like he'd been caught doing something indecent.

Get a grip.

You found an injured woman in the woods. That's it. That's all.

Except it wasn't all. Because every time his mind tried to file this into a category that made sense, his body rejected it. His body had known her the instant he saw her—not like recognition of a face from memory, but like gravity. Like the way you knew the taste of your own name.

Rowan's fingers flexed unconsciously as if he could still feel her skin against his—warm, too warm—and the moment her fingertips had brushed his jaw. The flash of white. The tree with glowing roots. Her laughter under violet stars. His own hands cupping her face, blood on them that wasn't his—except it had been.

Rowan swallowed hard and lifted a hand to his mouth, dragging his knuckles over his lips as if he could wipe the memory away.

He didn't want to forget it.

That was the problem. That was the worst part.

The part of him that should have been freaked out, rational, suspicious—run your questions, lock your doors, call someone—had been replaced by something older, quieter, and terrifyingly certain.

Protect.

It wasn't even a thought. It was a command written into his bones.

He shifted again, eyes flicking to the corner where his phone sat facedown on the table, dead silent. No service out here most days. Sometimes he could get a bar if he climbed the ridge behind the cabin and held the phone up like an offering to the sky.

He hadn't tried.

He didn't want to.

Because calling for help felt like calling for someone to take her.

Rowan sat in the hush of his cabin, listening. Outside: wind through pine needles. A distant owl. The faint drip of melted frost from the roof edge. Inside: the crackle of the small woodstove he'd lit earlier. Bramble's slow breath. Her breathing.

Her breathing was the loudest thing in the room. It was the only thing Rowan trusted.

She shifted, barely—a small twitch of fingers at the edge of the blanket, as if her hand was looking for something in sleep. Rowan's spine went rigid. His eyes snapped to her. Her brows drew together, mouth tightening. A sound slipped out of her throat—soft, broken, not quite a word.

A dream.

Rowan leaned forward without realizing he'd moved, elbows on his knees now, shoulders hunched as if his body was trying to close the distance without letting itself stand. "It's okay," he murmured, barely louder than breath. "You're safe."

The sound of his voice seemed to reach her in some hidden place. Her expression eased a fraction.

Then her lashes fluttered and her lips moved.

Not English.

A soft string of syllables that slid together like a prayer said in water. Rowan didn't understand it, but the sound tightened his throat anyway. His heart slowed, deepened, like it was listening.

She spoke again, quieter now, one word repeated, rough with emotion.

Rowan stared at her mouth, trying to catch the shape of it.

Trying to learn her.

Bramble raised his head, ears lifting.

Rowan didn't look away. He couldn't. Her whisper broke into a faint, trembling exhale, and then her hand drifted free of the blanket, sliding across the cushion until her fingers brushed air—searching.

Rowan stood so fast the chair creaked. Bramble's head snapped toward him.

Rowan didn't even think. He moved to the couch and knelt beside her, one hand hovering over her wrist like he was afraid to touch her and terrified not to. Her fingers curled, almost grasping nothing—the same way they had earlier, reaching for his pulse like it was an anchor.

Rowan made the decision the way you made a decision when your body was already halfway there. He slid his hand beneath hers. Not gripping. Just offering.

Her fingers curled around his like she'd been waiting for it.

The contact sent a low ripple up Rowan's arm—not pain, not shock, just awareness. Like a door opening quietly in a room he hadn't known existed. His breath caught.

He stayed still, afraid that if he moved he'd break whatever fragile thread had just formed between them. Her grip tightened slightly, and then her breathing eased. The tension left her mouth. She slept deeper—still curled inward, still guarded, but no longer teetering on the edge of waking fear.

Rowan stared down at their hands. His was rougher—callused, scraped, knuckles nicked from years of work and wilderness. Hers was slender, pale, warm—too warm—with faint, almost luminous veins threading under the skin like moonlit rivers. He could see the curve of her nails, clean and slightly pointed, as if shaped differently than human nails… though that might have been his mind looking for proof of the impossible.

Her hand looked delicate.

But it had held power.

It had touched his face and cracked open a lifetime.

Rowan swallowed and—very slowly—let his thumb brush the back of her hand once. A grounding motion. A test.

Her fingers flexed around his. Not startled. Not pulling away.

Accepting.

Something in Rowan's chest loosened in a way that scared him more than the drones.

He looked at her face again, close now. He could count the faint freckles scattered across the bridge of her nose—so light they were almost invisible unless the lamp hit her just right. A small cut at her hairline had already scabbed. His shirt hung on her like a truce between worlds, but the bruise beneath it kept forming anyway—dark ink rising under skin that didn't feel like it belonged to this realm.

He noted all of it like his attention could keep her alive.

He told himself he was checking injuries.

But the truth was heavier.

He was memorizing her.

Because some part of him believed—without evidence, without logic—that he'd been trying to memorize her for lifetimes.

Rowan leaned back slightly on his heels, careful not to jostle her. Even kneeling, his posture stayed angled toward her like a guard dog's body language, like he needed to be ready.

He listened again. Outside, the forest remained too quiet. He stood, crossed to the window, and lifted the curtain a fraction.

Darkness pressed against the glass. Pine trunks stood like sentries. The clearing looked empty.

Too empty.

Rowan held still.

At first he saw nothing. Then—faintly, far between the trees—a pale sweep of light moved. Not moonlight. Not a flashlight beam from a hiker.

A search pattern.

Rowan's stomach dropped. He let the curtain fall and turned sharply, pulse roaring in his ears. Crossing back to the couch, he crouched low beside her again, lowering his voice to near-breath.

"Isorae," he whispered, using the name she'd given him earlier like a fragile thread. "Hey. Isorae. Wake up."

Her lashes fluttered but didn't open.

Rowan's eyes flicked to the door. The bolt. The windows. The walls. His mind ran through options in a harsh, fast calculus. If they were searching, they would sweep the clearing. If they found the cabin—

He looked down at her hand still curled around his.

He couldn't leave her asleep.

He wouldn't leave her.

He tightened his fingers gently around hers, not waking her, just anchoring her, and then—quietly, carefully—began gathering what he needed without standing: his jacket draped over the chair, the small pack hanging by the door, the flashlight, the first-aid kit, his keys.

Bramble rose without being told, nails clicking softly on the floor, posture alert. The dog's gaze snapped between Rowan and the windows.

Rowan swallowed. His gaze returned to Isorae's face. Her breathing was steady, but her brow furrowed faintly again, as if she could feel the shift in the room even in sleep.

Rowan leaned closer, mouth near her ear, voice as soft as he dared. "Wake up," he murmured. "We have to move."

Her lashes fluttered again.

This time, her eyes opened.

For a moment they were unfocused—caught between dreams and waking. Then they found him, and the change in her face was immediate. Not confusion.

Recognition.

Like seeing him steadied her.

Her lips parted. She whispered something in her language—one short, urgent phrase.

Rowan shook his head once, just enough. "I don't understand. But—listen to me—someone's out there."

Isorae's gaze snapped toward the window. Her pupils widened. The faint shimmer beneath her skin flickered like a threatened flame.

"They… are near," she whispered, her English thick and careful, as if each word had to be shaped by intention.

Rowan nodded. "Yeah."

Her fingers tightened around his hand, then loosened as she forced herself to sit up, wincing at her ribs. Her movements were careful in a way that spoke of memory—not of this injury alone, but of bodies that had learned to move around restraints.

Rowan steadied her instantly, palm hovering near her back before settling lightly when she didn't pull away. He watched her swallow the pain like she'd done it a thousand times.

She looked up at him again, eyes bright and too old for her face. "They followed," she said softly. The words weren't fearful. They were resigned—shaped like something she had already survived.

Rowan's jaw tightened. "Looks like it."

She stared at him a heartbeat longer, something trembling behind her expression that wasn't just fear. Then she reached—slowly, deliberately—and brushed her fingertips against his wrist again, the place where she'd felt his pulse earlier like it mattered.

Rowan's breath caught.

Her voice dropped to a whisper. "You stayed."

Rowan swallowed. "Yeah."

He didn't say the rest—*I couldn't leave*—because it sounded too intimate, too insane, too true.

Outside, the sweep of light moved again.

Closer.

Rowan stood and held his hand out to her. Isorae looked at it like it was both an offer and an oath. Then she took it, and the moment her fingers threaded through his, the shimmer beneath her skin steadied again—like contact with him tuned her back into herself. For the first time since he'd found her, she looked less like prey and more like something that remembered how to stand.

Rowan felt it: the way her pulse calmed, the way his own body locked into protective readiness like it had been trained for her. He leaned in, voice low, fierce, certain.

"We're leaving. Quiet. Fast. Stay close to me."

Isorae nodded once.

And in the hush between breaths, with Bramble poised like a shadow at their heels and the woods outside sharpening into a hunt, Rowan realized something with a cold clarity that made his spine go rigid:

This wasn't just a night gone wrong.

This was the beginning of something the world had been trying to prevent.

And whatever she was—whatever he was—they had already found each other again.

Now they just had to survive it.

5

THE FIRST SHELTER

The forest swallowed the cabin's glow within ten steps.

Rowan did not stop moving.

Branches tore at his jacket and wet ground slid beneath his boots. The narrow beam of his flashlight jittered uselessly between trunks while Isorae's breath stayed shallow against his throat — too warm, too light to be human, too real to be imagined. Bramble ran low and silent at his heel.

The woods were wrong.

Not dangerous — not yet — but listening.

Sound bent around them. Leaves brushed his shoulders like fingers hesitating before touch. Even the wind seemed to hold its breath as he moved. Fear pressed the forest inward — not loud, not panicked, but deliberate — as if the land itself leaned closer to witness their passing.

His lungs burned. His legs trembled. His arms began to shake — not from exhaustion, but from what he was holding.

She was too light.

Too warm.

Her body curved against his as if it remembered this shape — his shape — as something it had once trusted with its life.

He did not know how long he ran.

He only knew the moment his body refused to go farther.

He slowed near a stand of cedar, breath tearing loose in sharp, wet bursts, and finally lowered her carefully to the moss at the base of a wide trunk. He stayed crouched over her for a moment, hands hovering uselessly, pulse hammering in his ears.

She was still breathing.

Still warm.

Still impossibly real.

And nothing in his life had prepared him for the truth settling into his bones:

If he walked away now, he would never come back from it.

Rowan pressed his palm flat to the earth, grounding himself.

"I don't know what you are," he whispered. "But I am not leaving you."

The words did not echo.

They sank.

And something in the forest leaned closer to listen.

They moved again — slower now — until pine gave way to alder, and alder to a shallow hollow where moss swallowed sound and pale stone ribs curved upward like the remains of something ancient and sleeping.

He guided her beneath a shallow rock overhang veiled in hanging fern. Shadow gathered around them like something protective. He shrugged out of his jacket and draped it around her shoulders.

She hesitated.

Then allowed it.

Her hands clutched the fabric as if it remembered her.

"You hurt?" he asked quietly.

"Not… that way."

Her gaze lifted to his — searching, luminous.

"You feel heavy," she whispered. "Anchored. Like you are standing inside me."

Rowan blinked. His mouth twitched faintly.

"That probably sounded different in your head."

"It sounded like truth."

He studied her for a moment — not unkindly, but with quiet bewilderment. The kind of look you gave someone who had just said something that landed deeper than it should have.

He shifted slightly.

Realized then how he stood — not beside her, but half in front of her.

Shielding.

"You still do that," she murmured.

"Do what?"

"Place yourself where the danger would come from."

His jaw tightened.

She looked at him like she was reading something written into bone.

"You were always my wall."

Rowan's brows drew together slowly — not offended, not dismissive — just… caught.

"That's a strange thing to say to someone you've known for—"

He stopped. Exhaled.

"—however long we've known each other."

Her lips curved faintly.

"Strange does not mean untrue."

The forest tightened.

A pale mechanical hum slid between trunks.

Rowan stepped forward without choosing to, angling himself fully in front of her.

"They sweep like insects," she whispered. "They cannot feel. Only count."

He waited until the hum slid past before easing his breath.

"You're shaking," he murmured.

Without thinking, he rested his hand gently at her waist.

Her breath slowed.

Her faint shimmer dimmed.

She leaned closer — not collapsing. Fitting.

"You calm the crossing," she whispered. "You always did."

"I don't know what that means," he said quietly.

But something in his ribs answered anyway.

They moved deeper into folds of land where sound thinned and stone curved upward like pale ribs. Moss swallowed their steps. Fern draped the air.

The forest did not push back.

It bent.

They reached a shallow basin veiled by alder and shadow. From the outside it looked like nothing. Inside it, sound fell into a hush so complete it felt padded.

"This place forgets," Rowan murmured.

"Then it will keep us."

He knelt and unpacked water, gauze, a blanket — ordinary anchors. He hesitated with the protein bar before offering it.

"Food," he said. "It's… not good food."

She sniffed it once. Then again. She took a cautious bite.

Her face went still.

Rowan waited.

"It tastes," she said slowly, "like bark that forgot it was alive."

A short breath left him — not quite a laugh, not quite a huff.

"Yeah," he murmured. "That's… probably the best description I've ever heard."

She swallowed politely anyway and set the rest aside.

He cleaned her ribs carefully. His movements were quiet, steady.

Her breathing slowed.

Her shimmer dimmed.

"That helps," she murmured. "Whatever you're doing."

"I'm not doing anything special."

"You are."

They sat as the forest cupped them like a held breath.

Three nights passed.

The hollow no longer felt like a place they were hiding.

It felt like something that had closed itself around them.

Rowan sat with his back to stone. Isorae lay beneath the blanket, watching him like someone standing on the edge of a memory.

"You are tired," she said softly. "But you do not rest."

"Someone has to listen."

She shifted. Rowan was kneeling beside her before the sound finished forming.

His hand hovered — then settled above her ribs.

Warm.

Her breathing smoothed.

"That steadies it," she whispered.

"Steadies what?"

"The echo I carried through."

His throat tightened.

"Your hands speak a language my body still knows."

She lifted her hand slowly, fingers hovering near his jaw — waiting.

When her skin brushed his, warmth rippled down his spine like something long asleep shifting.

The forest leaned inward.

Then the faint mechanical whine threaded the night again.

Isorae moved behind him.

Rowan widened his stance — not defensive.

Declarative.

"They are learning my shape," she whispered.

Cold slid under his ribs.

They slipped deeper into ravines where sound fractured and light bent. Rowan moved as if the land whispered paths only his body could hear.

By the fourth morning, her breathing no longer shook.

They stood in a narrow ravine veiled in hanging fern, cool shadow gathered close around them, her warmth brushing his collarbone — steady now, real, no longer brittle with pain or fear.

"You make the crossing quiet," she whispered.

"I don't know how," he replied. "I just… move."

"You don't have to know."

She tipped her forehead gently to his, breath to breath.

"I know what I am choosing," she said softly.

"And you are already remembering."

Rowan didn't answer at first.

His chest rose once — slow. Heavy.

Not because he was afraid.

But because he understood what she had just placed into his hands.

He lifted his forehead from hers just enough to look at her.

Really look at her.

Not as something he had found.

Not as something he was hiding.

But as someone who had just stepped willingly into his keeping.

"You don't owe me that," he said quietly.

Her lips curved faintly. "I am not paying a debt."

Something in his ribs shifted — not breaking.

Locking.

He nodded once. Small. Final.

"Then I won't fail you," he said.

Not a promise.

A placement.

He turned slightly, angling his body the way he always did — already creating the line the world would have to cross first.

And as they moved deeper into shadow, Rowan understood with cold clarity:

He was not only protecting her.

He was becoming the way forward for her.

Whatever came next would not reach her first.

It would reach him.

And it would have to decide what to do about that.

6

LEARNING EACH OTHER

They did not move far after the ravine—not because the danger had passed, but because their bodies had.

Time loosened into shared silence. Mist clung low to the ground, coiling around roots and fallen needles like breath resting on sleeping lungs. Pale dawn threaded itself between branches, thinning the dark without breaking it.

Rowan slowed first. His senses were still stretched, still listening for mechanical wrongness in the air, but his steps eased as gray light softened the forest. Isorae stayed close at his side, her sleeve brushing his arm when the trail narrowed.

She did not pull away.

Neither did he.

They found a shallow hollow between two ancient firs where the earth dipped and flattened—naturally shielded, naturally quiet. Rowan crouched, brushing pine needles aside and reading the soft story the ground carried.

"Nothing crossed here overnight," he murmured. "It's clean."

Isorae watched him, head tilted faintly, silver hair slipping over one shoulder. "You read the ground like water," she said softly.

"Old habit."

Rowan cleared a space beneath the low boughs and set his pack down, the motion easy and practiced. He struck a small smokeless flame, cupped it against the night air, and warmed water in his steel cup. He had done this a thousand times — but the care in his hands was not mechanical. It was intimate. Safety shaped by muscle memory.

Isorae crouched nearby, watching him. His scarred hands. Their steadiness. Their gentleness.

When he passed her the cup, their fingers brushed. The warmth rippled beneath his skin — not sharp, not startling — but slow, like something recognizing its way home.

"This fire does not sing," she murmured after a moment, tilting her head as if listening.

Rowan huffed softly. "Yeah. We're not great at poetry."

"But it listens."

They sat together as the mist thinned and the hush of the hollow subtly changed its texture — less guarded now, more curious. Rowan leaned back against the trunk of a pine, one knee bent, one arm resting loosely across it. Without realizing she was doing it, Isorae mirrored his posture and settled close enough that her shoulder brushed his thigh.

Rowan noticed.
He did not move away.

"You are quieter when you rest," she said.

"Usually means I'm finally thinking."

Her smile was faint, but it reached her eyes.

Rowan found himself studying the details he had been pretending not to see — the pale freckles across her nose, the soft glow beneath her skin, the way her breathing loosened when she was no longer bracing herself against the world.

"You're not going anywhere," he said quietly.

Her breath caught. She nodded once.

The words were enough.

Light rose higher through the branches.

The forest did not hurry it.

Mist thinned in pale ribbons. Dew gathered along fern tips and pine needles, catching early gold like the world was remembering how to glow gently instead of defensively.

They stayed.

Not because they had nowhere else to go.

Because neither of them felt the quiet asking them to leave.

Isorae's weight settled more fully against the trunk beside him, her shoulder resting lightly into the line of his thigh. Her breathing had slowed into a deeper rhythm — not sleep yet, but the soft edge of it. Rowan became aware of the way her warmth lingered in the narrow space between their ribs, how his own breath seemed to adjust itself around hers without his permission.

He shifted slightly — not away, but to give her more room — and she followed the movement instinctively, curling closer, her head tipping faintly toward his shoulder.

Rowan froze for half a breath.

Then he let himself breathe again.

She did not wake.

Her body simply fit.

He rested his forearm loosely along his knee, his hand close enough that if she moved again, he would feel it before he saw it. The forest cupped them — not hiding, not warning — just holding the shape of two people who were no longer in motion.

Time loosened.

Birdsong began again in small, tentative threads. A squirrel crossed a fallen limb above them, pausing to stare down like it was trying to decide whether they were scenery or story.

Isorae exhaled softly in her sleep.

Rowan felt it in his bones.

Later, she fully slept.

Curled on pine needles and his spare jacket, her body finally surrendered to rest — not collapsed, not guarded — but folded into itself like something that trusted the space it was taking up.

Rowan brewed coffee nearby, posture still alert but no longer sharp — less like a man waiting to flee, more like someone who had chosen to remain.

He watched her breathe.

Not to count it.

To believe it.

The faint shimmer beneath her skin was steady now — no longer flickering, no longer flaring — just present, like moonlight that had finally found still water.

He crouched beside her after a while, his knuckles brushing lightly along her hairline — barely more than a whisper of contact.

She stirred.

Lashes fluttered.

Her eyes opened — luminous with sleep and immediate recognition.

"Hey," he murmured.

Her lips curved faintly.

His hand stayed where it was — not claiming, not retreating — just present.

"You're trouble," he said quietly.

Her smile deepened. "And you're loud."

He huffed softly.

The moment settled around them — domestic, strange, and sacred all at once.

Far beyond the trees, unseen instruments recalibrated.

Not toward her alone.

But toward the quiet, luminous space that only existed where the two of them met.

Because whatever Rowan was becoming… only existed when she was close enough to be felt.

7

THE FIRST PLACE
HE EVER STOOD

They did not move for a long time after she rose—not because there was nowhere to go, but because the hollow itself seemed to be listening.

Mist rested low among roots and stone. Light filtered through the canopy in pale ribbons that did not quite reach the ground, leaving the air suspended between night and morning. Even the birds had gone quiet, as if the valley had decided something old and careful was being reassembled.

Isorae stood barefoot in pine needles, silver hair loose down her back, faint light pulsing just beneath her skin like breath inside crystal. She did not look fully of this world. She looked… borrowed.

Rowan leaned against a cedar trunk, arms crossed loosely, weight settled into one hip—the unconscious stance of someone who had lived his life reading rooms, reading forests, reading exits. He realized suddenly that his body had always stood this way.

Like it had learned long ago how to become a wall.

Isorae lifted her gaze. "You are standing the way you did before."

He shifted slightly. "Feels… right."

She stepped closer. Not hurried. Not hesitant. Deliberate.

"You always stood where danger would arrive first."

"Guess I've got a bad habit."

"It kept me alive."

Her hand lifted and hovered before his chest. Rowan did not move.
When her palm settled over his sternum, warmth flared instantly
beneath his skin. His breath stuttered. Her eyes closed.

"This place," she whispered. "Your body remembers it. It is where
you first chose me."

Pressure swelled beneath his ribs—not pain, not fear, but
something opening.

"I don't remember."

"You will."

Her fingers flexed faintly. "You stood beneath a tree that glowed
like veins of light," she murmured. "You placed your hand here—"

Her palm pressed more firmly.

"—and you said that where my soul walked, yours would follow."

Light tore through his vision.

Luminous roots. Violet stars. Her laughter under falling petals of
radiance.

Rowan inhaled sharply and caught her wrist gently, grounding
himself. "Isorae…"

Her eyes searched his, unafraid. "You are waking."

His thumb brushed along the inside of her wrist, finding her pulse.
"I don't know what I am yet," he said low. "But I know I won't let them
take you."

Her lips curved faintly.

They stood close enough to feel the heat of each other's skin, the
faint shimmer beneath hers aligning unconsciously with his breath.

Far beyond the trees, something quiet and mechanical
recalibrated—not toward her.

Toward the hollow.

Toward him.

Night returned softly. The fire had collapsed into pale coals.
Shadows breathed across stone and fern.

Rowan sat beneath the cedar again, jacket folded beside him,
posture loose but alert. Across the hollow, Isorae slept. She lay curled on
pine needles and woven fern, blanket tucked carefully around her ribs,

silver hair spilling across a moss pillow he had shaped for her. Moonlight traced her cheek, her throat, the faint glow beneath her skin—something not quite flesh and not quite light.

She looked impossibly still.

Rowan had been counting her breaths for nearly an hour.

In.

Out.

Slow.

Alive.

His chest eased slightly every time her lungs completed the cycle.

He leaned forward, forearms resting on his knees, shoulders rounding into the posture of someone who did not wish to disturb something sacred. He rose slowly and knelt beside her—close enough to feel her warmth, close enough to smell rain, leaf, and something pale and unearthly.

His fingers hovered near her temple.

He did not touch her.

The light beneath her skin pulsed gently, matching his breath. His heart stumbled.

"You look like a dream that forgot it was dangerous," he murmured.

Her brow twitched faintly.

"You're going to get me killed," he whispered. "Or saved. Or both."

He drew back before he could touch her — because he knew: the first time he touched her while she slept without needing to protect her, without needing to anchor her, without needing to keep her from breaking would be a vow. And vows shape worlds.

Rowan returned to his place beneath the cedar. He did not sleep. He listened to the forest. He listened to her breath.

And the land—quiet and ancient—recorded the moment…

…as something inside his blood finished standing upright.

8

THE FIRST BOUNDARY

Isorae woke slowly, not the way humans woke — dragged unwillingly out of sleep by sound or light — but as if she were surfacing through warm water, her awareness rising in gentle layers until sensation returned before thought. The first thing she felt was warmth. Not the fire. Not the earth. Something closer. Something alive.

Her lashes fluttered open.

Rowan sat beneath the cedar exactly where he had been when she fell asleep, one knee drawn up, his forearms resting loosely across it, his body angled unconsciously toward her as though he were still guarding a threshold that did not exist anymore. He was watching her — not staring, not intruding — simply present in that quiet way that made the difference between being observed and being held.

Mist hovered in pale threads between fern and stone. The fire had collapsed into low coals, their amber glow brushing along his jaw and shoulders, anchoring him in the hollow like something the land itself had quietly decided to keep.

Something inside her loosened.

"You're awake," he said softly.

"Yes." Her voice came out thin, brushed with sleep and with something deeper she did not yet have words for.

He didn't move. He waited.

She pushed herself upright slowly, careful of her ribs, the blanket slipping from her shoulder and revealing the faint shimmer beneath her skin. Rowan noticed — not with alarm, but with a tightening restraint — and crossed the hollow in three quiet steps before kneeling beside her, close enough to feel her warmth without crowding her space.

"Does it still hurt?"

"A little."

His hand lifted, paused. "Can I?"

She nodded.

His fingers brushed lightly over the bandage, gentle and precise, his touch carrying more than temperature — something that settled beneath her ribs like gravity finding its center again. Her gaze never left his face.

"You stayed," she said softly.

"Yeah."

"You kept watch."

"I always do."

Her lips curved faintly. "You did before too."

He didn't argue.

Silence settled between them — not empty, but dense with something careful and held. She studied him in that quiet: the scars on his hands, the calm strength in his shoulders, the unconscious way his body still angled toward hers even as he knelt.

"You stand like my shelter," she murmured.

His breath caught. "That's… oddly specific."

"It is not a compliment," she said gently. "It is a remembering."

Her fingers hovered near his sleeve for a heartbeat, then drifted forward and brushed lightly against his forearm. The contact sank deeper than skin — slow, warm — like heat finding its way into bone.

Rowan didn't pull away. He didn't lean closer. He simply let the touch exist.

The hollow responded.

The air thickened by a breath. Moss along the stone edge curled inward. Something deep beneath the soil shifted — not roots, not stone, but a quieter architecture, as if the land itself had felt the contact and adjusted the way it held them.

Not command.

Not force.

Recognition.

Two presences easing into the same gravity. Two rhythms remembering how to breathe in the same shape of time.

Rowan's chest rose and fell more slowly. Isorae's hand remained where it had landed — warm, steady, real. Neither of them moved, and yet something between them did, settling into place like a promise the world had been waiting to keep.

And far beyond the trees, unseen instruments recalibrated again — not toward Isorae alone, but toward the quiet, luminous space they were beginning to make together.

The forest shifted before Rowan heard it—not with sound, but with pressure. A subtle tightening in the air, a quiet inward draw, like the world pulling breath into its lungs and forgetting to release it.

Rowan straightened instantly. His shoulders squared, his stance widened, his weight settling through his heels as if the ground itself had cued his body into position.

Isorae felt it too.

"They are closer."

"Yeah."

The birds were gone—not scattered, but erased. The canopy held unnaturally still. Even the moss beneath Rowan's boots felt slightly angled, subtly contoured, as if the land were already shaping paths before he chose them.

He crossed back to her and knelt, his presence lowering the tension around her like something stepping into a field of static. "We move soon," he murmured. "But not rushed. We wait until the woods give us deeper shadow."

"You are already choosing paths," she said softly. "Before I ask."

"That a bad thing?"

"No." Her gaze lifted to him. "It is what you did before."

Something stirred beneath his sternum—low, familiar, old.

"You really think I was like this before?"

She rested her fingers lightly against his forearm. "You were my shelter," she whispered. "My shield. My compass. You were how I stayed."

The words struck somewhere beneath bone.

"Well," he murmured, "guess I haven't changed much."

"Not in the ways that mattered."

Movement whispered through branches beyond the hollow. Rowan rose in a single fluid motion, angling unconsciously between Isorae and the open forest. His posture was no longer only defensive.

It was declarative.

He did not look like prey.

He looked like a boundary.

"You look like a vow," Isorae whispered.

"That's a dangerous way to describe someone."

"You were always dangerous."

The mechanical hum brushed the air like cold breath through wire.

"That is them."

Rowan was already moving. He crossed to her, gathering her gently but firmly, wrapping the blanket tighter around her shoulders and lifting her into his arms with careful, practiced strength. She fit against him as if her shape had always belonged there.

"They track my echo," she whispered. "The place where I crossed scars the world."

"Then we don't give them a clean trail."

He stepped into slope and shadow, boots silent on moss, choosing ground that fractured sound and swallowed lines of sight.

"You do not fear them," she murmured.

"I do," he said quietly. "I just fear losing you more, even though I don't know why."

Her fingers curled into his jacket. The hum faded behind them.

But the forest did not relax.

It leaned inward.

Because something inside Rowan had crossed its first invisible threshold—and the world had begun to notice.

Not as a man.

But as a moving line the hunt would now have to reckon with.

9

WHAT HIS BODY REMEMBERS

The forest did not sleep. It leaned—as if something old had recognized the shape of him again.

That was the first thing Rowan felt as he guided Isorae into the shallow ravine. Not sound. Not movement. Pressure—the sense of something vast shifting its weight to listen more closely. They were hidden as well as any place could hide two living heartbeats, yet his bones hummed with the knowledge that the hunt had not ended, only drifted farther away.

Isorae swayed as he eased her down onto a bed of pine needles and folded leaves he had gathered quickly but carefully. Her breath trembled with the effort of staying upright, and Rowan dropped to one knee in front of her without thinking, his hands hovering just long enough to make sure she was real before he touched her.

"You're shaking," he murmured.

"The crossing always takes something from me," she whispered.

And gives something back, his body answered without words.

His jaw tightened. "Then let me hold what it took."

She tried to smile. It faltered.

That was enough to wake something ancient and dangerous beneath his ribs.

He slid off his jacket and draped it around her shoulders, tucking the fabric carefully—reverently—around her frame. His fingers lingered longer than necessary. Her breath ghosted faintly against his throat.

"You are very gentle for someone who walks like a storm," she whispered.

"You should see me when I'm not terrified."

Her lips curved faintly—but her eyes were heavy.

Rowan hesitated only a second before sitting beside her and opening his arm—not asking, not demanding—simply making space.

Isorae studied him.

Then she leaned into his side, her head resting against his shoulder, her weight settling into him like something his bones had been carved to receive.

His breath hitched.

He wrapped his arm around her—firm enough to promise gravity.

They sat that way while the forest whispered, while distant hums faded, while night cooled around their skin. Her breathing slowed. Her body softened against his.

And without realizing it, Rowan found himself counting her breaths, as if the rhythm itself were the thread holding his heart together.

Her lashes fluttered. She murmured something not English and shifted closer, her hand curling faintly into the fabric of his shirt.

Rowan went very still.

He lowered his head, resting his cheek lightly against her hair. "You're safe," he whispered—not just promise, but binding. "Even if the world burns, I've got you."

The vow surprised him with how easily it came.

He meant it anyway.

Isorae slept.

But Rowan didn't.

He watched the pale line of her throat, the soft curve of her mouth, the faint shimmer beneath her skin rising and falling like a hidden moon.

For a long while, she did not sleep.

She rested — suspended — as though her body were deciding whether it was finally allowed to let go.

Her breathing slowed by degrees. Not collapse. Not surrender. Just the gentle recalibration of a system learning it was no longer being hunted in this exact moment.

Rowan stayed utterly still, afraid that even breath might unmake the fragile quiet her body was beginning to accept.

His thumb brushed once — barely — across her knuckles.

She inhaled softly, unconsciously, and shifted closer. Her fingers tightened faintly in the fabric of his shirt — not clinging, not waking — simply choosing where gravity lived.

He did not move.

He let her choose him.

Minutes passed. Then more. The forest exhaled its night slowly around them — insects resuming their low hymn, the stream lowering its cadence, leaves loosening their held tension.

Isorae's breathing finally tipped into the deeper rhythm of true sleep.

Her weight settled fully into his ribs.

And Rowan understood — not suddenly, but with terrible gentleness — that she had fallen asleep inside him.

Not beside him.

Not near him.

Inside.

Something old loosened in his chest.

He lowered his cheek to her hair, breathing her in — leaf and rain and that faint luminous note beneath her skin that did not belong to this world but had always belonged to him.

"You're safe," he whispered — not as comfort.

As structure.

As law.

"I've got you."

Her lashes fluttered faintly. She murmured something not English — soft and distant — and her hand curled once more against his chest.

Rowan did not sleep.

He remained — unmoving — while the night thickened around them, while distant hums faded farther into the forest, while dew gathered on fern tips and stone edges like quiet witnesses.

And sometime in that long, held stillness —

a memory not his slid behind his eyes.

Violet stars.

Silver flowers tangled in her hair.

A vast luminous tree, its roots glowing like veins of light beneath crystal soil.

Her body cradled in his arms — heavier than she was now — blood warm against his hands.

A promise spoken beside that tree.

A promise he did not remember learning — but which his bones obeyed anyway.

"I remember you," he whispered into her hair. "Even if I don't yet."

The forest leaned closer.

Something ancient listened.

Isorae murmured his older name in her sleep.

"Caelith…"

The sound struck him like a bell underwater.

His jaw set.

If they came again, he would not run.

He would stand.

He would tear open every gate that ever tried to cage her light.

Time loosened.

Dawn had not yet decided to exist when she stirred against his chest — that fragile hour when night still owns the world, but light has begun its quiet negotiation.

Blue shadow wrapped the ravine.

Her lashes fluttered.

"Isorae," he murmured.

Her eyes opened — unfocused at first — then found his.

Recognition crossed her face like dawn touching a ruined temple.

"Caelith," she whispered.

His hand lifted, brushing slowly along her jaw.

She leaned into the touch — not in urgency.

In memory.

"You came back to me."

"I never left."

Her palm slid over his heart.

His pulse answered her — slow, deep — as if something inside him had finally remembered its own rhythm.

The air thickened — not brighter — denser — as if the space itself leaned in to witness.

"I remember your soul," she whispered. "Even when my body was gone."

"Then remember me now."

She did — with breath, with trust, with the slow way her body softened fully into his.

Their foreheads rested together, breath mingling, the world narrowing to the charged space between their ribs.

But he did not kiss her.

Not yet.

Instead, his thumb brushed her jaw once more — reverent. Grounding.

"We move," he whispered.

"Yes," she breathed.

Rowan rose slowly and offered his hand.

Isorae took it.

Their fingers threaded together like something inevitable.

Before they left the ravine, Rowan glanced back once — at the shallow dent in the pine needles where she had slept against him, at the faint warmth still held in the place where they had been still.

Then he turned forward.

Because the forest was listening again.

And this time, he was no longer just hiding her.

He was becoming the place she stayed.

IO

WHERE THE OATH BREATHES

They did not move far—not because Rowan lacked urgency, but because the land had begun to speak to him differently.

Where once the forest had been a map he navigated by memory and instinct, it now felt responsive. Not guiding him outright, not commanding, but subtly tilting around his steps—softening where he needed passage, tightening where the world wanted him to pause. The ground no longer simply held him.

It answered him.

Isorae felt it too.

"You walk like the veil bends for you," she murmured as they followed a narrow deer run along a moss-slick ridge.

Rowan glanced back. "It doesn't feel like bending."

She tilted her head slightly. "Then it is remembering."

They descended into a shallow bowl of earth where ancient stones rose in a loose circle, half-swallowed by moss and vine, their surfaces smoothed by centuries of rain and forgotten hands. The space was quiet in a way that felt deliberate, as if sound itself paused before entering.

Isorae slowed. Her fingers curled faintly into his sleeve.

"This place," she whispered. "This is where your oath was first spoken."

Rowan's chest tightened.

He had never seen these stones before. And yet something in his bones leaned toward them—like breath held too long, finally allowed to release.

He guided her gently into the ring.

The air changed.

Not colder. Not warmer.

Deeper—like sound traveling through thick water. Time itself seemed to stretch, not forward, but inward.

Isorae stepped to the center and knelt, pressing her palm flat to the earth. Rowan followed without hesitation, lowering in front of her.

"What did I say?" he asked quietly.

Her gaze lifted, luminous and steady. "You said: *Where your soul goes, mine will follow—across worlds, across death, across forgetting.*"

The words struck him cleanly.

"I somehow remember that," he breathed—and realized it was true.

Her breath hitched faintly.

"You were never meant to be human only," she said softly. "You were born close to the veil — not anchored fully to either side."

Rowan searched her face. "Is that why they're hunting you?"

She shook her head slowly.

"They hunt me because I am a crossing," she whispered. "But they fear you… because you are becoming a boundary."

Silence settled between them.

Not empty.

Heavy.

Alive.

The stones around them seemed to lean—not physically, but attentively.

Rowan reached for her hands. They fit into his as if they had been waiting there since before language.

"If this oath still lives," he murmured, "then we do not belong to their cages."

Isorae's eyes shimmered faintly. "It does. It never died. It only slept."

He leaned closer, resting his forehead against hers, breath mingling. "Then wake it."

Her hands slid slowly up his arms, resting over his shoulders—not clinging, not claiming, but aligning.

The stones beneath them thrummed faintly, not with sound but with pressure, as if the earth itself had drawn breath around their vow. The hollow of the circle deepened. Wind softened. Light bent slightly along mossed stone edges.

Rowan felt something shift beneath his ribs—not power, not heat, but position.

Like the world had just moved him into a place it remembered him belonging.

And for the first time since the veil had torn, he did not feel like he was hiding.

He felt like he was standing inside something sacred.

They remained inside the stone ring long after the forest had finished holding its breath. Light slid down through the canopy in pale, drifting shards, touching the smooth blackened stones like fingers learning a body. Moss breathed damp green against ancient edges. Somewhere far away, a bird dared to sing—one tentative note, then another—as if the land itself were testing whether it was allowed to be alive again.

Rowan stayed where he was, crouched in front of Isorae, close enough to feel the warmth of her through the space between their knees, close enough that her breath stirred the fine hairs along his forearms. His hands still held hers—not tight, not loose—simply present.

Neither of them had let go.

"You are standing at a door," she said quietly.

"Feels like it."

"You stood like this once," she said softly. "In another place. In another life. Your body remembers the shape of choosing."

Something warm and steady opened beneath his ribs.

"I don't know what I am yet," he murmured. "But I know what I'm not."

Her fingers curled gently around his. "Tell me."

"I'm not letting them take you," he said quietly. "Not in any world."

Her breath caught—barely—but he felt it like a held note vibrating inside his chest.

"You are choosing me," she breathed.

"I already did. I'm just saying it out loud now."

The forest leaned inward.

Rowan lifted one hand slowly, giving her time to stop him, and rested his thumb lightly at her jaw. He felt the warmth of her skin, the faint answering pulse beneath.

Her lashes fluttered. She leaned into his palm without hesitation.

The motion unmade something ancient in him.

He leaned forward—not rushing, not claiming—simply closing the last quiet distance between them. Their foreheads brushed. Their breath mingled. The moment stretched thin and trembling.

Isorae lifted her hand to his chest, palm flattening over his heart, listening.

It answered her.

Deep. Steady. Alive.

"You are waking," she whispered.

"And you are dangerous," he murmured faintly.

Her lips curved. "You always liked dangerous."

His forehead rested gently against hers, breath unsteady.

"Yes," she said softly.

The word rang like an oath.

He nodded once. "Yes."

The stones beneath their feet thrummed faintly—not with sound, but with pressure—as if the earth itself had leaned closer to witness. Wind softened around the ring. Light bent along mossed edges.

They stayed there, breath tangled, hands linked, letting the world remember them again.

Until—faint and unwelcome—the mechanical hum threaded the trees.

Isorae stilled.

Rowan did not release her. "Not yet," he murmured. "Just… stay right here."

She nodded.

And for a few more stolen heartbeats, nothing else in the world existed but the space between their ribs—and the first yes that had just been spoken back into the bones of the land.

II
WHEN THE NET TIGHTENS

The scream did not belong to any animal Rowan had ever known. It ripped through the trees like metal dragged across bone — too high, too piercing, too wrong — and shattered the fragile hush that had settled over the stone ring as if the forest itself had been struck in the throat.

Rowan's entire body coiled tight in a single breath.

Isorae's fingers dug into his sleeve. The faint shimmer beneath her skin drained pale, her eyes widening as something ancient inside her recognized a predator older than fear.

"They are deploying," she said, breath uneven. Her voice shook, but her certainty did not. "This is no longer search. This is containment. They are preventing convergence."

Rowan didn't ask what that meant.

He was already moving.

He pulled her up with him in one fluid motion and angled his body between her and the sound before the last word left her mouth. "Run," he said quietly. "Stay with me."

They didn't flee blindly. Rowan chose terrain the way a hunted animal chose it — slipping them between root-choked slopes, cutting across narrow rock shelves, ducking beneath hanging moss and thorned branches that tore at his sleeves and dragged against his shoulders. Bramble ran beside them like a shadow, breath ghosting in sharp bursts.

Behind them, the forest began to glow.

Not moonlight.

Sweeping white beams slid between trunks in mechanical arcs, washing bark and leaf in sterile brilliance. A layered hum vibrated through the soil — deep enough that Rowan felt it in his teeth, in the marrow of his legs, in the hollow beneath his sternum.

"They're triangulating," he muttered.

Isorae stumbled.

Rowan caught her instantly, hands sliding to her waist and shoulders, pulling her against his chest. Her breath came fast and shallow, trembling against his collarbone.

"Their compression fields are closing," she gasped. "They are folding space around my echo."

He cupped her face gently but firmly. "Isorae. Look at me. Stay with me."

Her glow flared violently — bright, erratic — like something trying to claw its way back through her bones. Rowan pressed his forehead to hers.

"Don't go anywhere I can't follow."

Her eyes locked on his.

The shimmer steadied — not gone, but contained — like a storm forced into a narrower sky.

Rowan didn't wait.

He scooped her into his arms and ran.

Muscle burned. Lungs screamed. The world narrowed to pounding blood and tearing breath. He did not slow.

A beam sliced across the ground just behind his heels. A sharp discharge cracked the air — not a gunshot, but close enough to rattle his skull.

"I've got you," he growled.

They burst through brush into a narrow rock chute plunging into darkness.

Rowan didn't hesitate.

He slid.

Stone tore at his boots. His shoulder slammed into rock. He twisted instinctively, turning his body so Isorae was shielded by his chest. They crashed into the bottom in a spray of wet leaves and dirt.

Rowan hit hard. Breath punched out of him. White light burst behind his eyes.

But Isorae was still in his arms.

She pushed up shakily. "Rowan — your shoulder—"

"I'm fine," he lied through clenched teeth.

Above them, beams cut across the mouth of the chute. Footsteps crunched. Voices filtered down — clipped, professional, unhurried.

"Thermal anomaly confirmed."

"Bioenergetic instability escalating."

"Deploy capture net. Nonlethal compliance only."

Isorae's face drained of color. "They will open me," her voice trembling. "They will unmake me."

Rowan rose slowly, pain flaring hot and blinding in his shoulder, and stepped fully in front of her.

Blocking the light.

Blocking the path.

The way his body had once learned to do before memory.

Isorae inhaled sharply. Recognition flashed through her like lightning. "Rowan…"

He raised his hands slowly, palms open. "Hey! You've got the wrong person!"

A beam locked onto his chest.

"Sir, step away from the anomaly."

"No!"

Behind him, Isorae's fingers curled into his jacket. Her glow surged — unstable, frightened.

The air thickened.

Leaves lifted.

Stone vibrated.

The ground shuddered beneath their feet.

Isorae screamed his name —

and the world lunged toward catastrophe.

Pressure slammed inward from all sides, compressing air and space alike. Rowan's ears rang violently. His vision tunneled as if the forest itself were being shoved into a smaller shape.

"Subject confirmed," a calm voice said.

"Energy spike escalating."

Something detached from the darkness above.

A narrow black cylinder dropped soundlessly through the beams of white light and unfolded midair — not opening, but becoming — splitting into a lattice of vibrating filaments that shimmered like stretched glass.

"That is not a net," Isorae cried. "That is a cage!"

Rowan lunged.

The field snapped outward faster than thought.

Filaments surged around Isorae in a seamless cocoon, swallowing her glow, compressing her resonance inward like breath forced from lungs.

Her cry tore out — not pain.

Terror.

Rowan hit the lattice full-force.

Electric agony ripped through his arms and hurled him backward into mud and leaf rot. Breath tore from his chest.

But he was already rising.

Already reaching.

"Isorae!"

She pressed both palms to the inside of the cage. "Caelith—!"

The name detonated through his veins like lightning finding old wire.

The lattice warped.

Shuddered.

Recoiled.

For one impossible heartbeat, the geometry itself hesitated around him.

He almost had her.

Then boots hit the ground.

Three armored figures emerged, visors mirrored, movements unhurried.

"Sir," a calm amplified voice said, "step away from the containment field."

Rowan stepped toward it.

The pulse hit him like a freight train.

He was hurled backward, spine slamming into stone, breath ripping from him in a strangled sound.

They lifted the cage.

Isorae rose smoothly into the canopy, suspended inside like something sacred and stolen.

Rowan pushed up on shaking arms. "No—"

Mud coated his palms. His lungs burned.

Isorae turned.

Her eyes found his.

Fear.

Grief.

And something that refused to die.

"Remember," she cried, desperate.

The cocoon vanished.

The forest went silent — not peaceful, but vacantly, as if something essential had been cut out of it.

Rowan dropped to his knees in the mud.

His hands sank into the earth.

His chest heaved.

And he whispered into the soil that had failed him, "I will tear every gate you built. I will burn every cage you made. I will bring her home."

Something ancient and enormous finished waking inside Rowan Hale.

And it already knew the way back.

12

WHAT WAKES IN HIS BLOOD

Rowan did not remember standing. He remembered the forest. Not as trees and earth, but as a body that had just lost a limb. The air felt hollow. Wrong. As if something vital had been torn out and the wound had not yet realized it was bleeding. He moved through the place where Isorae had been taken like a man walking through the outline of someone who had just vanished—boots sinking into wet leaves, fingers brushing bark that still trembled faintly with her absence. Every step felt misaligned, as though gravity itself had lost its reference point.

Her echo had not faded.

It ached.

The world did not feel empty so much as amputated, as if something vital had been cut cleanly out of it and the wound was still burning open to the air. Rowan's chest burned with it. His jaw locked. His hands curled until his knuckles went pale.

They took her.

They cut her out of the world.

He dropped to one knee without knowing why, instinct dragging him downward, and pressed his palm into the soil. The ground was warm beneath his hand — not sun-warm, but alive — and something deep within it shifted in answer. It wasn't movement. It was resonance. A low, ancient hum climbed his spine and settled behind his sternum like a second heart beginning to beat.

The forest did not recoil.

It leaned.

"You remember her," Rowan whispered, and it was not a question.

The earth answered — not with language, but with vibration. A slow, deep pulse rolled through him, shaking his ribs from the inside out. Moss bent inward. Roots tightened. The land bowed its invisible spine toward him.

And then memory did not return.

Memory detonated.

A luminous tree rose behind his eyes, its roots like veins of light threading through dark soil. Violet stars fell like petals through endless sky. He heard her laughter — bright and broken and sacred — and felt his own bloodied hands cradling her face. A vow flared through him, spoken in a language his mouth no longer remembered, but his bones still did:

Where your soul goes, mine will follow.

Rowan gasped and folded forward, breath tearing from his lungs as if he had been struck through the chest. This was not remembering. This was position snapping violently into place — a door inside him grinding open after lifetimes of rust.

He had been the Bridge.

Born near the veil. Never bound fully to either world.

He had been the one who could stand where realms touched without breaking.

He had not simply loved Isorae.

He had been built to find her. Built to anchor her. Built to keep her alive when worlds collided.

Rowan staggered upright, and something in his posture changed — not his silhouette, but his architecture. His spine lengthened. His weight grounded. His bones locked into the shape they had always been carved for.

He lifted his gaze to the black canopy where the cocoon had vanished.

His voice did not shake.

"I am not done."

The forest answered him.

Leaves trembled. Roots tightened. The ground beneath his boots firmed subtly, recognizing him, supporting him as a wind passed through the trees that did not belong to weather.

Far beyond the woods, unseen machines recalibrated.

But something far older than machines had fully woken inside Rowan Hale.

And it was no longer waiting.

It was hunting the way home.

13

THE MAP THAT BREATHES

Rowan did not chase blindly. He remained where Isorae had been taken, one hand pressed flat to the soil that remembered her—because it did—and closed his eyes.

The forest no longer felt empty.

It felt attentive.

As if something vast had just sat up and turned its face toward him.

The hum beneath his palm remained, faint and steady, a second heartbeat answering his own. Rowan breathed in slowly.

Not the air.

The land.

"Show me," he murmured.

The earth answered—not with sound, but with recognition. Pressure bent beneath his ribs—eastward, deeper, away from the torn place, toward older shadow and heavier stone. His body obeyed before thought could interfere.

He moved faster now — not running, not hiding, but certain.

The forest altered itself around his passage. Thickets parted. Roots curved. Ravines that should have ended softened into slopes that accepted his weight.

It was not guiding him.

It was remembering him.

Pain flared briefly behind his eyes and he halted.

A drone passed soundlessly through the path his body had been choosing.

The forest had already bent him out of its reach.

By dusk, Rowan crested a narrow ridge and froze. Below him, carved into a valley that should have held nothing but stone and fern, stood a structure that did not belong. Matte black. Modular. Temporary in build—permanent in intention. Antennas rose like ribs. Blue light bled faintly from seams that should have been dark.

The ARIS facility hummed like a wound stitched into the mountain.

Rowan crouched at the edge of the slope, forcing his breathing to slow even though his heart refused to follow. It beat hard and fast against his ribs, not with fear, but with something deeper — a pull that felt less like urgency and more like inevitability.

He could feel her.

Not as a direction.

As gravity.

"She's here," he whispered into the fog, the words barely disturbing the air.

Something answered deep beneath his sternum — not a sound, but a pressure, a quiet certainty that settled into his bones.

Rowan began his descent, sliding down the incline in smooth, deliberate movements. He let the fog and the shadows fracture his outline, letting the land itself soften his absence as motion sensors swept the tree line and heat arrays blinked blindly above him. Drones drifted through the upper canopy, their paths precise and searching — and yet leaf and root shifted subtly as he passed, bending presence away from him like water around stone.

He reached a forgotten culvert half-swallowed by lichen — a stone artery carved into the mountain long before ARIS had learned how to name it. Rowan slowed without meaning to. Something in his chest pulled — not a direction, but a pressure — like breath held too long behind his ribs.

He knelt and placed his palm against the rock.

The stone did not crack.

It shifted.

A narrow seam widened like a held breath finally released, and cold mountain air exhaled into the fog.

Rowan froze.

For a heartbeat, he only stared — waiting for alarms, for lights, for something to prove this was a trap or a trick of exhaustion.

Nothing happened.

The opening remained.

Slowly, cautiously, he stepped forward.

Metal and damp stone folded around him as he moved deeper into the mountain. Status lights blinked quietly — green, amber, blue — painting faint color across rough walls as he followed the tightening pull beneath his ribs instead of any marked corridor. He didn't know why he was turning when he did.

Only that not turning felt wrong.

A sealed hatch stood in his path.

Rowan hesitated.

Then he stepped closer.

The hatch did not open.

It… waited.

His breath caught.

A faint vibration moved through the metal — not mechanical, not error — something like a listening held between states.

Rowan didn't touch it at first.

Then — uncertain, slow — he lifted his hand and rested his palm against the cold surface.

The hatch parted.

Not in malfunction.

In recognition.

Rowan swallowed hard and moved through.

He descended farther, deeper, until the pressure in his chest sharpened into something unmistakable — not pain, not fear —

her.

Thin. Restrained. Alive.

His jaw tightened. "Hold on," he murmured, his voice barely more than breath.

The corridor curved into a reinforced chamber rimmed with glowing containment seals. Rowan stopped in front of the door, pulse loud in his ears.

He lifted his hand again — slower this time — as if the mountain itself might change its mind.

The metal vibrated faintly beneath his palm.

Listening.

Rowan inhaled — not air, but memory — and let it settle through his ribs and spine like something ancient remembering its shape.

"Open," he said softly.

The mountain leaned with him.

The seals dimmed.

And the door did not open.

It recognized him.

It slid aside without sound — obedient, ancient — answering an authority older than circuitry.

Cold blue light spilled across his boots. The air turned metallic, sterile, loud to his skin.

The chamber was circular and sunken, its walls layered in translucent containment membranes that pulsed like artificial lungs. Cables webbed the floor. Floating glyph-displays slid through the air in geometries that made his ribs ache with recognition.

The room was not merely holding something.

It was listening to it.

In the center—

Isorae.

Isorae was suspended inside a vertical containment column, her body floating weightlessly in pale resonance-light. Silver hair drifted slowly around her face like moonlight submerged beneath water. Fine filaments traced the delicate lines of her throat, her wrists, her sternum — not restraining her, but mapping her. Reading her. Learning the architecture of what she was.

Her glow was muted.

Quieted.

Wrong.

Rowan's breath fractured in his chest. "Isorae."

Her lashes fluttered. Her eyes opened slowly, unfocused at first — and then they found him.

Her breath caught.

"…Caelith?"

The name rang through his bones like a bell struck underwater, sending a low vibration through his ribs that made his vision blur for a heartbeat.

"I'm here," he said hoarsely. "I crossed."

Her gaze searched his face like she was afraid he might fade if she looked too long. "You remembered," she whispered.

Rowan stepped closer. The air thickened around him — not resisting, but measuring — as if the field itself were trying to decide what he was. He ignored it, eyes never leaving her.

Up close, he could see the lattice of invisible structures threading through the column — layers of harmonic containment, diagnostic resonance, temporal indexing. They were not cages.

They were instruments.

"They don't get to name you," he murmured. "You are not theirs. You are not a specimen."

He lifted his hand and placed his palm against the field.

The hum deepened beneath his touch.

Not rejecting.

Listening.

Rowan closed his eyes and inhaled — not air, but memory — breathing the way his bones remembered, drawing breath through the sternum, anchoring himself in the place where worlds leaned toward each other.

The pitch shifted.

The column brightened faintly.

Isorae inhaled sharply. "The gate hears you."

The field parted around his fingers like water around stone. Inside the column the air was warmer, saturated with her frequency.

Alive.

He reached for her wrist.

The instant his fingertips brushed her skin—
The filaments convulsed.
Red glyphs detonated across the chamber.
Alarms ripped through the quiet.
CONTAINMENT BREACH DETECTED.
RESONANCE DESTABILIZATION — ESCALATION
PROTOCOL ARMED.
Isorae gasped.
Rowan closed his grip around her wrist—firm, grounding.
"I've got you," he whispered.
And the mountain held its breath.

Rowan did not move immediately. He remained inside the ruptured containment field long after the alarms collapsed into warped echoes, long after the crimson emergency light dimmed into a slow, breathing haze, long after the mountain itself seemed to draw a deep and settling breath around them — as if the world were waiting to see whether he would stay.

Isorae was still in his arms.

Not suspended. Not measured. Not claimed by anything that hummed or blinked or watched.

Real.

Her breath brushed his collarbone — shallow but steady — and her silver hair spilled across his shoulder like moonlight poured into shadow. She smelled of rain, crushed leaves, and something ancient that had never belonged to machines, something that made his bones recognize the weight he was holding as correct.

He held her the way foundations hold cathedrals — not cradling, not careful — but anchored. His forearms were braced beneath her knees and back, his chest aligned to her ribs, his stance wide and immovable, as if the mountain itself had shaped him for this moment and this weight.

Her lashes fluttered.

Her fingers curled weakly into the fabric at his collar.

"Caelith," she whispered — not a name, but a place to rest.

Rowan bowed his head, pressing his brow into her hair. "I'm here," he murmured. "You're safe."

Her breath trembled. "I am home."

The words slid beneath his ribs and locked into place.

Not poetry. Not metaphor.

Truth.

Something ancient inside him — something fractured by forgetting — settled fully back into its proper shape. And the mountain felt it. The alarms faded completely. The facility did not resist.

It listened.

Rowan turned, not toward exits marked by light and warning, but inward — following the quiet pull beneath his sternum, the same resonance that had guided him into the mountain now opening the older paths back out.

When he stepped, space yielded.

Not visibly.

Directionally.

Corridors softened. Angles unknotted. Passages opened where sealed wall had existed moments before. Doors parted like breath leaving lungs. Emergency glyphs dimmed as he passed, unwilling to confront him.

Isorae stirred faintly in his arms.

"The mountain remembers you," she murmured.

Rowan swallowed. "I think… I remember it too."

They entered a vein carved not by machines but by time — older than concrete, older than steel. Stone pressed close around him. Moisture beaded along mineral seams. The tunnel smelled of cold earth and centuries of breath.

He shifted her gently higher against his chest. Her hand slid instinctively to his sternum — over the gate — and her thumb brushed faintly, grounding him.

"You are fully awake now," she said low and certain.

He exhaled slowly. "Feels like my bones finally fit my body."

Her lips curved faintly.

He carried her upward.

The tunnel narrowed. The mountain leaned toward moonlight.

They emerged through a seam that had not existed moments before, and cold night air poured over them — clean, wet, alive.

The valley lay below like a sleeping animal.

Rowan stepped onto a stone ledge and finally stopped.

Isorae blinked against open sky. "No walls," she said faintly. "No containment."

He lowered her carefully to her feet, his hands remaining at her waist until she steadied. She swayed, and he stepped closer without thought.

"You're not falling," he murmured. "Not on my watch."

Her fingers slid into his jacket, anchoring herself to him. "I am not afraid," she said quietly. "As long as you are touching me."

The truth of it tightened something sacred beneath his ribs.

He did not answer.

He drew her close and rested his forehead against hers.

Rain began to fall — soft, quiet, reverent.

And behind them, the mountain — once cut open to cage her — sealed itself again like a wound finally allowed to heal.

14

THE SHAPE OF SHELTER

They did not go far.

Not because Rowan lacked strength.

But because the land itself leaned in.

The valley answered the instant they crossed its threshold — not with sound, not with movement — but with alignment. Pressure eased beneath Rowan's boots. Wind softened. The air thickened faintly around their ribs, as if the space itself had drawn breath to hold them.

The forest did not feel empty.

It felt appointed.

Mist drifted low through the trees, threading between trunks like pale silk. Ferns bent inward — not collapsing, but curving — wet fronds brushing Rowan's sleeves as if the valley were quietly closing ranks around them. The earth beneath his steps swallowed sound, leaf-rot and rain working together to erase the fact that two heartbeats had just entered its body.

This place did not echo.

It kept.

Isorae leaned into him as they walked, one arm looped loosely around his waist, her head resting against his shoulder. Her steps were slow, careful — but steady. Her breathing had deepened into something free again. Her glow no longer flared. It had settled into a quiet inner tide, resting instead of reaching.

Rowan kept his arm firm around her back, palm spread wide between her shoulder blades — not gripping — anchoring.

"You are holding me like you think I might vanish," she murmured softly.

His jaw tightened faintly. "I'm not letting that happen again."

They followed a narrow stream that curled through stone and fern, its water whispering over moss-slick rock. Fireflies hovered low above it — pale lights trembling like breath learning to exist again.

Rowan slowed.

Not because he saw shelter.

But because his body recognized jurisdiction.

A shallow hollow rested beneath a stone outcrop — naturally shielded, dry beneath the overhang, invisible from three sides by brush and root. The air inside it was deeper, heavier — as if the valley had drawn its walls closer around this pocket of earth.

He stopped.

Isorae lifted her head slowly.

"This place…" she said calmly. "It is listening."

Rowan exhaled. "Then it's ours."

He guided her inside.

He laid down his jacket, then his spare shirt, then shaped pine needles and fern fronds into a careful bed — not hurried, not frantic — but reverent, like building an altar out of what the land allowed.

Isorae lowered herself carefully, eyes closing — not from pain — but from release.

Rowan crouched beside her, studying her face in the low firefly glow.

Her lashes lay dark against pale skin.

Her lips parted faintly as she breathed.

A faint smear of dried mud still marked her cheek.

Without thinking, he brushed it away with the back of his knuckles.

She leaned into the touch.

His hand stilled.

Something deep and tender unknotted in his chest.

"You are looking at me like you're relearning my shape," she murmured.

"I think I am," he said quietly.

He poured water into a thermos cap and lifted it to her lips.

"Slow," he murmured. "Your body's still shaking on the inside."

She drank carefully — watching him over the rim — her eyes shimmering faintly.

"You are gentle with me," she said.

He huffed softly. "Only you."

Later, when exhaustion finally claimed her, Isorae lay curled on the jacket and spare shirt, knees drawn in, silver hair spilling loose across dark fabric like moonlight poured into shadow.

Rowan sat beside her, back to stone, one knee bent, one leg stretched — not watching the woods.

Watching her.

The slow rise and fall of her chest.

The quiet glow beneath her skin.

The way her fingers curled into his jacket as if her body refused to let go of him even in sleep.

He reached out and gently tucked a strand of hair behind her ear.

She shifted faintly.

Did not wake.

Rowan leaned his head back against the rock and closed his eyes for a single breath.

"If the world comes apart," he whispered into the dark, "at least we found each other again."

The valley did not answer.

It closed around them.

And kept them.

15
THE WAY HIS BODY KNOWS

Night did not fall into the hollow so much as it eased into it.

Mist threaded low through stone and root, sliding between fern fronds and pooling in leaf-rot hollows like breath returning to lungs that already knew how to hold it. The stream whispered nearby — not breaking the hush, but reinforcing it — a steady murmur that made the silence feel intentional instead of empty.

Rowan remained awake, not because he feared the dark, but because his body had settled into position.

He sat with his back against the stone wall, knees bent, one forearm resting loosely across his thigh while the other hovered close to Isorae's shoulder — not touching her, but shaping the space around her by instinct alone. He was no longer simply guarding. He was stabilizing, the way a keystone stabilizes an arch simply by remaining exactly where it belongs.

Isorae slept on her side beside him, curled inward. Her silver hair spilled across pine needles and brushed his knee. One hand rested beneath her cheek. The other still clutched a fold of his sleeve — not with tension or need, but with the unconscious certainty of something that knew where it belonged.

Her breathing had settled into a deep, even rhythm, and the faint shimmer beneath her skin no longer flared. It pulsed softly — quiet, regulated — like something finally allowed to exist without being hunted.

Rowan watched her with the still attention of someone memorizing a map he would have to protect. The curve of her cheek. The shadow beneath her lashes. The soft parting of her lips as she exhaled. She was not simply safe. She was placed.

He shifted slightly, careful not to disturb her, drawing one knee closer and angling his torso so his shoulder and chest formed a natural barrier between her and the open edge of the hollow. He did not choose the position. His body remembered it.

A faint sound slipped from her throat — breath caught between dreams.

Rowan leaned forward without thinking. "Isorae," he murmured.

She did not wake, but her fingers tightened slightly in his sleeve. His chest locked.

He lowered his hand and laid his palm gently over hers. Her skin was warm — alive — present. His thumb brushed once across her knuckles, not as comfort, but as a quiet correction, a grounding that her body answered instantly. Her breathing deepened. Her shoulders softened.

And the valley responded.

Pressure gathered faintly around the hollow — not sound, not motion, but structure. Mist settled closer to the ground. Fern fronds curved inward. Even the stream smoothed by a subtle degree, its whisper gentling as if the land itself had accepted a new center of gravity.

Rowan inhaled — not simply air, but orientation — and the breath traveled down his spine, into his sternum, into the hidden gate beneath his ribs. When he exhaled, the hollow exhaled with him.

The land did not relax. It settled.

Not because it was calm — but because it had just been placed.

Rowan did not move. His bones did.

Something ancient inside him tested the shape of his breath and found the valley responsive — not as worship, but as law.

"I don't know how you did this," he whispered to her sleeping form, his voice rough not from cold, but from gravity. "How you walked into my life like you were already written into it."

He leaned back slowly, lifting his gaze to the narrow slice of stars threaded between the branches overhead. "You feel like home," he breathed, the words barely stirring the air. "And I don't even know how that's possible." After a moment he added, more softly still, "I won't lose you again." The words did not rise. They settled — and the valley accepted them, not as hope, but as jurisdiction. Rowan kept watch afterward, not because he feared the dark, but because the land had begun to recognize him as the place where Isorae stayed. And that meant the world would now have to ask.

Rowan did not sleep. The hollow had settled into true night — not simple darkness, but compression, distance folding inward and sound thickening as the valley's edges drew closer around a quiet, deliberate center. Mist lay low across stone and root, curling softly through fern-shadow, and the nearby stream whispered steadily, not breaking the hush but reinforcing it, making the silence feel intentional instead of empty. Isorae slept on, her breathing deepened into the slow, even rhythm of a body that had finally been granted permission to rest.

Rowan sat beside her with his back braced against stone, one knee bent, the other extended slightly, his torso angled in a way that unconsciously placed his shoulder and chest between her and the open mouth of the hollow. He had not chosen the posture — it had chosen him. Her silver hair spilled across pine needles and brushed his thigh. One hand remained curled into his sleeve, not gripping, not clinging, simply placed there, as if her body had already named him as something it did not need to question.

He did not move. He was not guarding. He was maintaining. The faint shimmer beneath her skin no longer flared, but pulsed softly — stable, regulated — like a system returned to its proper field. She shifted faintly in her sleep, a quiet breath slipping from her lips, and Rowan leaned forward without thinking. His hand hovered, then settled warm and steady between her shoulder blades. The instant his palm touched her, pressure released beneath his sternum — not tension easing, but alignment — and her breathing smoothed as if her body had recognized his touch as instruction rather than comfort.

The valley responded. Mist thinned. Fern fronds curved inward. Even the stream gentled its cadence — not quieting, but recalibrating —

as though the hollow itself had accepted him as its new center of gravity. "You're safe," he murmured — not as reassurance, but as confirmation.

When the fire burned low, Rowan fed it one careful branch. Light brushed Isorae's face, and something in his chest eased in a way that had nothing to do with exhaustion. She looked unbearably real — placed. He leaned closer, his forehead hovering near her hair, as if the warmth of her breath might anchor him to the moment. "You're my home," he murmured. The words did not rise. They settled. Isorae stirred faintly in her sleep, her fingers tightening once in his sleeve before loosening again, falling open as her breath evened. Rowan stayed still, listening — to her breathing, to the forest, to the quiet pressure beneath his ribs that had begun to feel like direction rather than warning.

They could not remain here. Not yet. Not safely. The valley was holding them — but not forever. Carefully, Rowan slid one arm beneath her shoulders and the other beneath her knees, testing her weight before lifting, as if the world might object. It did not. He gathered her into his arms — not lifting her so much as reorganizing the space around her — and rose. The valley exhaled behind him, not in farewell, but in transfer. The forest adjusted as he moved. Roots flattened. Ferns curved. Stone ribs altered their angles to receive his weight. A low inward pull beneath his sternum — not distance, but placement — oriented him forward like a directive written into bone.

They crossed a narrow glowing stream, slipped through a shallow ravine, and entered older forest where the air warmed as if drawing breath around them. There — root-shadowed and fern-veiled — stood a cabin. Not his. Older. A remembered sanctum.

Isorae stirred faintly against his chest, not fully waking — just enough that her breath changed, her fingers flexing once against his collarbone. Her eyes fluttered, unfocused, catching only shape and warmth. "It… knows us," she murmured, the words barely forming, more breath than sound. Rowan tightened his hold. "Good," he whispered back. Her lashes fell again. He stepped inside.

And the forest sealed — not behind them, but around them. As boundary.

The cabin settled the way old things do — not with silence, but with breath. Beams sighed softly. The hearth whispered low. Outside, the valley released the day in long, patient cycles, learning how to rest again. Rowan sat on the floor with his back against the couch. He had meant to take the bed, but his body had chosen this place — close enough that he could feel the shape of her breath in the room without seeing her.

Isorae lay curled beneath wool, silver hair spilling like moonlight poured into shadow. One hand rested near her collarbone, fingers faintly curved — already knowing where safety lived. Her breathing was slow, anchored. Rowan found himself counting it. In. Out. The rhythm did not calm him. It confirmed him.

He told himself he was keeping watch. The truth was quieter. He was maintaining her field. Firelight traced the faint shimmer beneath her skin — no longer defensive, but settled, contained, correct. A bruise shadowed her ribs. Something ancient tightened beneath Rowan's sternum — not anger, but jurisdiction.

He reached forward slowly and drew the blanket higher over her shoulder. She leaned faintly toward his warmth, and his posture adjusted without thought — aligned. Her breathing deepened. Something inside him did not crack. It locked.

Rowan studied her face — the scar at her brow, the softness of her mouth, the quiet glow beneath her skin. "You don't belong here," he whispered, not as doubt, but as truth. Her hand lay open near the couch edge. Rowan brushed his pinky against hers — feather-light. The cabin answered. Her fingers curled faintly around his.

He did not move. He did not withdraw. He allowed reality to accept the contact.

"You're my home," he whispered.

And the room recorded it.

Outside, the forest adjusted its breathing. Inside, something ancient and immovable took root. And Rowan kept vigil until morning — not watching for danger, but holding the shape of her being in place.

As law.

16

THE SHAPE OF MORNING

Dawn did not arrive with light. It arrived with breath.

A pale hush slid through the trees, lifting mist from fern tips and tracing silver threads across the narrow cabin windows. The fire had collapsed into a low cradle of coals, glowing faintly like something alive but finally at rest. Outside, the forest did not stir. It seemed to be listening — not for danger, but for position.

Rowan had not slept.

Sometime before morning he had shifted, his back braced against the couch, one arm bent beneath his head, the other still threaded loosely with Isorae's fingers. She had drifted closer in the night — not cautiously, not consciously, but with the slow certainty of something returning to where it had always fit. Her head rested against his shoulder now, pale hair fanned across his chest, her breath warming the hollow of his throat. His body had learned the geometry of holding her without disturbing the shape of the world.

The first bird sang.

Isorae stirred.

Rowan felt it before he saw it — the subtle change in her breathing, awareness returning like tidewater to a remembered shore. Her eyes opened and found him instantly.

"You stayed," she murmured.

"Yeah."

Her gaze traced his face slowly, memorizing him like something precious and fragile at once. "I knew you would."

"You talk like we've done this before."

Her lips curved faintly. "We have."

She shifted carefully, wincing faintly, and Rowan's hand was already at her ribs, steadying her before thought could reach it. "Easy."

She leaned into him with a soft sound — relief, not pain. "You feel like a fixed point," she murmured. "Like gravity."

"That sounds dangerous."

"It is."

They remained close, breath mingling in the quiet between their ribs. Her fingers brushed slowly along his jaw — not testing, not claiming, remembering.

"You watched me all night."

He didn't deny it. "I was afraid if I stopped, you'd disappear."

Her eyes softened — ancient and sure. "I am not going anywhere." It wasn't promise. It was truth.

Rowan rested his forehead gently against hers. "Good," he whispered — and the hollow answered. Not with sound, but with adjustment.

Somewhere beneath the cabin floor, stone drew closer lines. Roots pressed deeper into earth. The valley did not lean toward them anymore. It centered on them.

Morning did not hurry them.

Light filtered through the narrow windows in thin gold bands. Wind slid softly through pine needles outside — not passing through, but around — as if the land itself had recalibrated where its center now lived. Isorae remained curled into him, her weight quiet and anchoring against his ribs, his body shaping itself around hers without asking permission from thought.

He had memorized her — not as memory, but as map.

She stirred again, settling closer, her knee brushing his thigh, her forehead tucking beneath his jaw. She fit. Something in his chest loosened — not fear, but recognition sharp enough to ache.

Her eyes opened. "You're here."

"Yeah."

She lifted her hand and rested it over his heart. "It is loud," she murmured. "But steady."

"You feel like shelter."

Her words struck low and irrevocably true.

She leaned closer, breath ghosting his throat. "You feel like the place my soul remembers how to breathe."

"You can't say things like that."

"Why?"

"Because I might start believing you."

She studied him quietly. "You already do."

He did. He just hadn't named it yet.

Rowan brushed his thumb along her cheek, slow and reverent, feeling the warmth of her skin and the faint shimmer beneath. "Stay," he said quietly.

She nodded. "I was never meant to leave."

The valley drew a deeper breath — not sheltering, but sealing.

Rowan shifted slowly, not because he wanted to move, but because his legs had begun to ache beneath the stillness. He eased his shoulder back against the couch and drew a careful breath. The land inhaled with him — not as witness, but as boundary.

Isorae stirred faintly but did not pull away. Her hand remained over his heart.

"You're thinking too loud," she murmured — not fully awake, not fully asleep — her voice slow and low, as if it had risen straight from her ribs. "It makes the air feel tight."

She shifted faintly, her brows knitting for just a moment.

"My ribs ache," she added softly. "But the place where the world hurt me feels quieter when you're close."

Rowan lowered his forehead to her hair, breathing her in once, grounding both of them. "Then we keep it quiet."

She made a small sound — neither agreement nor protest — and her fingers curled faintly into his shirt as her body began to sink back into rest. Her breathing deepened, lengthening into the slow rhythm of sleep while her weight settled more fully against his side.

Rowan waited until he felt it — the moment her muscles released, the moment her breath evened — before carefully sliding his arm from beneath her. She shifted with a faint, displeased murmur but did not wake, only settling so her warmth remained near his.

He stayed there another quiet minute, watching her breathe, listening to the faint shimmer beneath her skin.

It was steady — but thin.

Something in his chest tightened.

He rose reluctantly, moving toward the stove more out of restlessness than hunger. He poured tea, added honey, and let the cup warm his hands — something small to keep himself anchored in the room while the rest of him remained beside her.

Only when he turned back did he notice her lashes flutter.

She did not fully wake — just enough for her eyes to find him again, unfocused but certain.

He hesitated — then knelt and offered the cup.

Their fingers brushed. Heat moved steadily between them.

Neither pulled away.

Later, he rested his forehead against hers. "We move today."

Not fleeing. Not hiding. Becoming.

Outside, the forest leaned inward — not to watch, but to re-index.

And far beyond the trees, machines quietly recalibrated — already too late to understand that what had just come home was no longer a target…

…but a boundary.

17

THE HOLLOW THAT
REMEMBERS THEM

The forest did not welcome them. It weighed them. Not with sound — but with pressure. A quiet inward draw that settled behind Rowan's sternum, like the land itself was deciding whether to accept his spine back into its gravity.

Rowan moved first.

Not hurried.

Not hesitant.

Deliberate.

He angled their path sharply off the deer run, choosing ground that swallowed sound and fractured clean trails. His steps were light but precise, his head tilting slightly with each pause — listening not for noise, but for imbalance.

Isorae followed half a step behind him, wrapped in his jacket, fingers twisted into the fabric at his back like she was holding onto the last stable thing in a shifting world.

They didn't speak.

They didn't need to.

The forest required attention, not language.

She learned his movement pattern within minutes — too fast.

Her feet began landing exactly where his had: same stones, same shallow dips, same slight forward lean when the ground sloped.

Rowan glanced back once.

"You're already tracking my stride."

Her lips curved faintly. "My body remembers yours."

The words slid straight under his ribs.

He faced forward again.

The hollow revealed itself only when Rowan cut sharply through a curtain of fern and wet root. The land dipped suddenly — stone giving way to a bowl-shaped recess ribbed with pale limestone and ancient root-veins threading the rock like something half-buried and still alive.

The air thickened instantly.

Cooler.

Quieter.

Dense.

Listening.

Rowan stopped at the rim.

Isorae stepped beside him, her breath leaving her slowly.

"This place has held crossings before," she said, like something remembered out loud. "It remembers how to shelter what doesn't belong to one world."

"Then it'll remember us," Rowan said.

They descended.

The moment his boots touched the limestone floor, the hollow settled — not visibly, but with pressure — the way ground shifts beneath something it recognizes as weight-bearing.

Isorae felt it.

Her shoulders eased.

Rowan dropped his pack and began clearing space, stacking loose stone into a low windbreak that didn't scar the land — only completed it. He moved with quiet intensity, reverent but fast.

Isorae knelt beside him, fingers brushing the root-veins etched into the stone.

"These veins once held other bridges," she murmured.

"Did they live?"

"Some," she said. "Some became the land."

They worked in silence.

Their shoulders brushed.

Their knees bumped.

At one point Isorae slipped on damp limestone.

Rowan caught her instantly.

His hands locked around her waist and lower back, pulling her hard into his chest before she could fall.

They froze.

Her breath left her in a soft, startled sound — not fear.

Awareness.

His grip was solid. Feral. Protective in a way that didn't ask permission.

"You still hold me like this," she said softly.

His jaw flexed. "Feels like muscle memory."

"Your bones remember."

He eased her down carefully, hands lingering at her hips longer than necessary.

"Sit," he said low. "Let me see your ribs."

He knelt in front of her, lifting the hem of her shirt just enough to examine the bruising. His thumb brushed her skin unconsciously, tracing heat and shape like his hands already knew the map.

"You look at me like you're remembering something," she said low.

"My hands do," he said.

She reached out and laid her palm flat over his heart.

"You are my shelter."

Something in him broke open — not gently.

He slid his hand to the small of her back, palm flattening there, fingers spreading — claiming contact. Present. Real.

Her breath hitched.

She softened toward him without falling — opening instead of collapsing.

She lifted her face toward his.

"You're choosing me," she whispered.

Rowan swallowed. "I already did."

The hollow tightened.

Not visibly.

Protectively.

The land leaned inward.

Then —

A mechanical hum threaded the trees.

Rowan moved instantly — pulling Isorae deep into the curve of the hollow, bracing one hand to stone, the other locked at her back.

White light swept distant trunks.

The air compressed faintly at the rim.

The beam hesitated.

Bent.

Slid away.

The hollow exhaled.

Rowan did not release her.

His thumb traced slow arcs against her back — unconscious, grounding.

Her hand slid up his chest, fingers resting over his heart.

"You're louder here," she murmured.

"Then stay," he said.

Night fell in silver layers.

They built a low fire.

Isorae sat beside him, bare feet tucked beneath her, glow faint and steady.

"You've stopped holding yourself apart," she said quietly.

The words struck low — not as observation, but as recognition.

Rowan felt them settle beneath his ribs, loosening something he had been bracing since long before he had words for it.

He did not answer.

He simply stayed — closer than before, but not crowding her, his body no longer angled to shield or withdraw, only present.

No wall.

No distance.

No readiness to flee.

Just him.

He lifted his hand slowly, giving her time to stop him, and brushed his knuckles along her cheek — not to claim, not to test — but to learn the shape of her being here.

She leaned into the touch without hesitation.

Her breath caught — not in surprise, but in recognition.

Because she could feel it.

The shift.

The choosing.

The moment he stopped standing near her and began standing with her.

Her gaze searched his once — steady, luminous — as if confirming what her body already knew.

Then she said it.

"I crossed worlds for you. There is nothing I am not choosing."

Something quiet and irrevocable settled beneath his ribs.

Rowan leaned in — not remembering.

Only deciding.

Their mouths met slowly, deliberately — not searching, not tentative — but claiming the small, breathing space between them as something that had been waiting for them all along.

His hand slid to her waist — not to restrain, but to anchor — drawing her fully into the place his body had already decided was hers.

Her breath broke softly against his mouth.

Her hands rose to his chest, fingers spreading there — not gripping — resting against him as if she were grounding herself in the only thing in the world that was not moving away.

He drew her into his lap without breaking the kiss.

Not hurried.

Not careful.

Certain.

She fit against him with a quiet, devastating perfection — bone and breath settling as though her body had reached the end of a long remembering. Her weight sank into him, the line of her spine softening, her breath slipping warm and steady along the side of his throat like it had always known where to land.

Their breathing tangled — slow, deep, shared — heat and gravity pulling them inward instead of apart.

For a moment their foreheads rested together, eyes closed, the world narrowed to pulse and warmth and the quiet thunder moving beneath skin.

"You're not leaving me," she whispered — not as fear, but as something that needed to be spoken aloud to finish becoming true.

His voice was low.

Rough.

Steady.

"Never."

Not promise.

Truth.

She stayed exactly where he had drawn her — weight settled into him, breath warming the curve of his throat, the soft thunder of her pulse answering his through the thin space of skin to skin.

Rowan's hands traced slow, deliberate arcs along her waist and back — grounding, claiming — his palms memorizing the shape of her like his body had waited years to relearn this exact geometry. Then one hand slid to her jaw and held her there — firm, steady, unavoidable — his thumb pressing beneath her cheek as he drew her mouth closer like restraint was the only thing keeping him from breaking apart.

His breath shuddered once against her lips.

Not with uncertainty.

With control barely held.

His jaw tightened — a visible flex of muscle — and when he kissed her again it was slower, deeper, weighted with intent, like he was staking something wordless and permanent into the space between them. His grip around her waist tightened just enough to make his meaning unmistakable — stay. here. with me.

His voice, when it came, was low and rough — not loud, not gentle — but grounded with something that sounded like inevitability.

"Look at me."

She did.

His eyes were dark — not with shadow, but with focus — locked on her like he had already chosen the shape of the rest of his life.

"This," he murmured, breath warm against her mouth,

"is where you belong."

Not a promise.

A placement.

His thumb traced once, slow and grounding, along her jaw — not soothing, not asking — sealing the space he had already claimed as hers.

Her breath caught — not sharply, but in a slow, startled pull — as if her lungs had forgotten their rhythm the moment his hand closed around her jaw. A faint sound slipped from her throat, soft and unguarded, and her body leaned into his hold before her mind could decide anything at all.

Her arms wrapped around his neck, pressing herself fimrly against him like she was grounding herself in something solid and real and chosen, her weight shifing more into him — more than balance required — her breasts brushing his chest, her breath warming his neck like something finding its center of gravity again.

The faint shimmer beneath her skin brightened — not flaring, not defensive — but deepening, like moonlight thickening into something denser and more alive. Her shoulders softened. Her spine curved just enough to fit into the line his hands had already drawn for her.

When he kissed her again, her breath broke against his mouth — slow, unsteady — and she followed him into it without hesitation, her body answering the pressure of his hands like it had been waiting for permission to exist fully again.

Her forehead rested briefly against his, lashes fluttering, breath tangled with his — not escaping him.

Staying.

Her voice came out softer than breath, almost lost between their mouths.

"Rowan…"

Not calling.

Claiming.

Her body settled more fully into his, as if the space between them had finally learned the shape it was meant to hold.

The sound she made — soft, startled, real — went through him like a strike of heat beneath the ribs.

Rowan's breath left him in a low, unguarded exhale, something close to a growl before he could stop it. His grip on her tightened — not enough to hurt, just enough to say *stay* in a language older than words —

and his forehead dipped to hers as if he had to anchor himself to keep from being pulled completely off balance.

For a heartbeat he simply stayed there, breathing her in, feeling the way her body had leaned into his without hesitation, the way her weight had shifted toward him like gravity had chosen sides.

Something in his chest gave — not breaking, but opening.

His thumb brushed slowly along her jaw, grounding and reverent at once, and he let his breath settle against her temple.

"You have no idea what you do to me," he murmured — not as a confession, not as a warning — but as something closer to awe.

His other hand drew her closer again, instinctive, certain, as if his body had already decided the world made more sense with her right there.

Not holding her.

Claiming the space she belonged.

His mouth hovered just near hers — not touching — breath warm, steady, restrained only by intention.

And in that narrow, humming space between them, the forest leaned a fraction closer.

Not to watch.

To remember.

And the valley did not move.

It simply adjusted — quietly — around the new center of gravity they were becoming together.

18

THE NIGHT THAT HOLDS THEIR NAMES

Night did not arrive. It settled. No wind stirred the upper branches. No birds called. Even the insects seemed to hesitate, as if the forest itself had folded inward to listen to the sound of two heartbeats learning how to exist in the same quiet.

Only the stream beyond the rock wall whispered — low and steady — a memory looping itself so it would not be lost.

Rowan shaped the fire pit with unhurried care, coaxing flame from damp kindling until amber light breathed softly into the hollow. He kept it small — not out of fear, but because this place asked for gentleness.

The fire did not roar.

It hummed.

It did not expose the hollow — it softened it.

Isorae sat nearby on the bedding of moss and fern, wrapped in his jacket, knees drawn in. Firelight threaded pale gold through her silver hair. The glow beneath her skin no longer flared — it rested, quiet and alive.

Her eyes followed him.

Not idly.

Attentively.

When Rowan finally sat beside her, their shoulders brushed — and warmth slid through his ribs like something recognizing where it belonged.

"You look like you're still braced for impact," she murmured.

He huffed faintly. "Body hasn't caught up yet."

"

She studied the tension in his jaw, the way his shoulders never quite lowered — then reached out and rested her palm against his forearm.

"You can stand down," she said softly. "I am here."

The words went straight through him.

They lay down together on the bedding, facing one another at first — knees brushing, breath mingling in the low gold light. Rowan shifted instinctively, angling his body — and Isorae moved just as naturally, closing the space between them until her forehead rested at his collarbone.

His arm curved around her.

Her breath trembled once — then softened.

"You're cold," he murmured.

"A little."

He drew her closer slowly, deliberately — chest to ribs, thigh to thigh — until her body fit fully into the space his had already made for her. She exhaled against him — not weakness, but release — the sound of a body finally unbracing.

He stayed still, memorizing the weight of her, the quiet certainty of her warmth.

Time loosened.

Her hand drifted across his stomach — slow, absent — and settled there with quiet inevitability, as if it had always known this was where it belonged.

Rowan's breath deepened.

Not sharply.

Something lower.

He did not move her hand.

"You went very still," she murmured.

"If I move," he said quietly, "I won't be choosing whether I stop."

Her fingers curled faintly — not questioning.

Anchoring.

"You won't lose me."

The words were not fragile.

They were structural.

His voice came rough, steady, threaded with something older than fear. "Promise?"

Her lips brushed his collarbone — not asking — sealing.

"I am not leaving."

The forest leaned inward.

Not to watch.

To settle.

Fire whispered lower in its cradle. Stone drew its lines tighter. Something deep beneath root and earth adjusted — not as warning, not as defense — but as recognition finding its center.

Rowan stared into the dim stone above them and understood — not as thought, but as something written directly into his ribs —

Even if the world took everything else from him…

This would remain.

He bent and pressed a slow, steady kiss into her hair — not asking for more — acknowledging what already existed.

She exhaled softly, her body easing fully into his.

And sleep finally found them.

Not as exhaustion.

As completion.

Wrapped around each other like a vow the land itself had already learned how to keep.

19

THE MORNING
THAT FINDS THEM

Dawn did not wake them all at once. It crept.

A pale hush slid into the hollow, lifting mist from fern tips and laying thin threads of gold along the stone ribs of their shelter. Dew caught the faint light and released it slowly, as if the valley itself were waking with deliberate care. The fire had burned down to a cradle of embers — not extinguished, only resting — its warmth still lingering in the bones of the stone.

Rowan woke before the world finished changing.

He did not move.

Isorae lay curled against him, her cheek tucked beneath his chin, silver hair spilling across his chest like moonlight that had decided to stay. One of her hands rested over his heart, fingers curved faintly — not gripping, not clinging — simply placed, as if she had fallen asleep listening to its rhythm and forgotten to let go.

Awareness returned to him slowly — the ache in his arms, the stiffness in his shoulders, the deep pull in his legs from holding himself still through the long dark hours. He welcomed all of it. The discomfort felt like proof.

She was real.

She was here.

Her breathing had deepened into something whole — no longer shallow, no longer guarded — and the faint glow beneath her skin moved in a slow, tidal rhythm, like something that had finally found a stable shore.

Rowan lifted his free hand and brushed a loose strand of silver hair from her face. She did not wake.

He studied her — the softened line of her brow, the pale curve of her cheek, the faint bruise still shadowing her ribs beneath her shirt. Her body no longer curled inward as if bracing for loss.

She slept like she belonged.

The truth settled into him with quiet finality.

You are my home.

Not a thought.

A knowing.

Outside the hollow, a single bird dared to sing — one clear note cutting gently through the mist like a seam opening.

Isorae stirred. Her lashes fluttered, her breath catching faintly before her eyes opened.

They found him immediately.

No confusion.

Only recognition.

"You were watching me," she murmured, her voice still heavy with sleep.

"Yeah."

Her gaze moved slowly across his face — not studying, but remembering.

"You did not sleep."

"I stayed."

Her fingers flexed faintly against his chest, brushing the place where his heartbeat lived. "Why?"

His answer came without armor. "Because if I closed my eyes," he said quietly, "I might lose you again."

Something ancient softened behind her eyes.

"I am here," she whispered. "And I am not fading."

His throat tightened. "Good."

She shifted carefully, wincing faintly — and his hand was already there, steady at her ribs.

"You're still hurt."

"Less," she murmured. "Because you hold me like you intend to keep me."

The words did not ask.

They settled.

They rose together a little later, unhurried, stepping into the mist while the hollow still held their warmth. Cold water bit gently at their fingers as they rinsed their hands in the narrow stream. Pine, damp earth, and new light folded together around them — the valley granting them a stolen hour of quiet.

Rowan was breathing it in when he saw it.

Footprints.

Not his.

Not hers.

Too light to be animals.

Too precise to be chance.

Old enough to have watched.

New enough to still matter.

His spine tightened.

He said nothing. He simply shifted — subtly — placing himself between Isorae and the forest.

Because even in peace…

the world was still learning their shape.

And learning never comes without consequence.

20

THE SOFT PLACES
THE WORLD HIDES

Morning loosened slowly around them — mist thinning into pale ribbons, dew sliding from fern tips, birds testing the quiet with tentative song. The valley did not feel empty.

It felt alert.

Not listening.

Claiming.

Rowan gathered fallen twigs and kindling while Isorae moved down to the stream. She slipped out of the blanket and stepped into the cold water with a soft breath, letting it rise along her calves and knees, then farther, until it wrapped her in silver light and slow motion. She cupped water over her arms and shoulders, rinsing away ash and sleep and the long residue of fear, her movements unhurried — no longer guarded, no longer braced for impact.

Returned.

She looked less like something that had fallen between worlds.

More like something the world had finally accepted back into itself.

Rowan found his hands stilling around the kindling.

He watched her — not as a stranger might, but as someone witnessing something sacred and real and briefly unprotected in a way that asked to be remembered. The faint inner glow beneath her skin shifted in time with the valley's breath. Water traced pale paths along her shoulders and down the lines of her arms, catching light and turning it soft.

"You are memorizing me," she said without turning.

He didn't deny it. "I don't trust the world not to try taking you again."

She stepped from the stream and crossed toward him, droplets tracing silver lines down her skin, her presence warm against the cool air. She took the blanket from where it lay folded near the fire and wrapped it loosely around herself, then placed her palm flat over his sternum — firm, steady.

"Then let me stay where your body knows how to find me."

Something ancient in his ribs answered that like a key sliding home.

They shared berries and water on a sun-warmed stone. Isorae leaned into his side, her thigh pressed lightly to his, her fingers drawing slow, unconscious lines along his sleeve. Rowan's arm curved around her without thought — not holding, but containing — as if his body had already decided what shape the world was meant to take around her.

"This place feels finished," he murmured.

She tilted her face toward his. "You are finished here."

The truth landed low and permanent.

They walked the valley edge later — Rowan marking escape paths, Isorae brushing bark and stone like she was reacquainting herself with old names.

The light thinned while they moved.

Not suddenly.

Not dramatically.

Just enough that the green deepened, shadows stretching into longer ribs beneath the trees. The air cooled by degrees instead of edges. Birds fell quiet one by one, not startled — simply finished for the day.

Then the forest narrowed.

Not colder.

Not louder.

Just tighter.

Rowan lifted his hand.

Isorae froze instantly.

"We don't sleep here again," he murmured.

"The world is still mapping us," she said calmly.

He glanced at her. "You're not afraid?"

She met his gaze without hesitation. "Not while you stand in front of me."

Something feral and quiet locked into place behind his ribs.

They turned back — not fleeing — already shifting their pattern, already becoming something the forest was learning to remember.

And unseen beyond the valley, something patient and mechanical recalibrated its focus — no longer hunting blindly, but tracking something that had finally claimed its shape.

By the time they reached their shelter, the last of the day had thinned into silver. Night did not fall so much as it settled — like a held breath that had decided to remain. It wasn't heavy, and it wasn't threatening, but it was aware. Mist slid low through fern and stone, brushing Rowan's boots and Isorae's ankles as they moved quietly around their small refuge, reinforcing its curved ribs with layered bark and woven moss. Firelight breathed amber into the hollow, softening its edges until the place no longer felt like something hidden, but like a hearth the land itself had chosen to grow around them.

Isorae knelt by the stream, rinsing berries in the cold, clear water. Rowan stood a few paces behind her, his gaze tracing the gentle slope of her shoulders beneath his jacket, the faint glow beneath her skin answering moonlight and firelight at once — as if more than one world were quietly remembering her. He hadn't meant to stare, but his eyes kept returning to her.

"You still watch as though the world might take me when you blink," she said without turning.

Rowan huffed softly. "Feels like it already tried."

She looked back at him then — not frightened, but ancient with recognition. "It will try again."

The words were not a warning. They were memory.

He stepped closer, his hands settling at her waist, grounding himself in the undeniable warmth of her body. "Then it goes through me."

Her fingers curled into his shirt. "You always say that."

"And you always keep proving me right."

They finished reinforcing the shelter and settled near the fire, sharing berries and warmed water. Isorae leaned into his side, her head resting lightly against his shoulder, and Rowan's arm curved naturally around her back, his palm resting between her shoulder blades — his body forming a boundary he didn't have to think about in order to become.

Rowan stared into the mist beyond the firelight, his senses no longer sharp but tuned — the way you listened for thunder still buried beneath the earth. At the far edge of the valley something shifted. Not visibly, but the forest flinched, a subtle tightening rippling through root and leaf — the quiet shiver of land recognizing a pressure it did not trust.

Rowan didn't move. He only drew Isorae closer.

"You feel it," she low and certain.

"Yeah."

"They are still learning our pattern."

"Then we don't give them one."

She nodded, her cheek brushing his collarbone. "You are my shelter."

"And you are my home."

They stayed that way for a long moment while firelight breathed around them and mist curled softly against their legs, the valley holding them — not tightly, not loosely — but the way a place holds something it intends to remember. Isorae's fingers flexed faintly in his shirt. Rowan's hand pressed more firmly at her back.

Eventually she eased away just enough to look at him. Not leaving — only loosening the shape of the moment.

"I'm going to check the upper rim," he murmured.

She nodded, watching him with quiet, luminous eyes as he climbed the northern slope, moving lightly through fern and alder, listening to the land with his whole body instead of just his ears.

That was when he saw it.

The birds didn't scatter. They didn't fall silent. They changed direction — sparrows lifting from alder branches in smooth, unified arcs, veering east instead of breaking randomly as they should have.

Rowan stilled.

The forest listened.

When he returned, Isorae was stitching vine and bark along the shelter wall.

"You feel it," she said before he spoke.

"Yeah."

They didn't run. They didn't hide. They prepared — moving around one another like a single body with two minds, hands passing tools, eyes tracking the same unseen horizons. By evening nothing came. No drones. No hum. Only wind, birds returning, and a valley that had quietly decided to keep them.

That night they lay together near the fire, her head tucked beneath his chin, his arm firm around her back.

"I used to think peace was a pause," Rowan murmured.

"It is not a pause," she said quietly. "It is a place you build."

"Then let's build it."

The valley leaned inward — not to listen, but to remember.

Firelight dimmed slowly around them. Shadows lengthened and softened. The hollow breathed in deeper rhythms, settling its bones around their stillness. Rowan felt her breathing even out beneath his hand, slow and steady, the faint shimmer beneath her skin dimming as her body finally let go of the day.

He stayed awake long enough to feel sleep claim her — the subtle shift of weight, the quiet surrender of muscle, the small sound she made when rest finally reached her bones.

Only then did his own breathing loosen.

Only then did the world narrow into warmth, smoke, and the soft gravity of her held against his chest.

Morning arrived wrapped in fog. Rowan woke to Isorae breathing against his chest, her body aligned with his as if she had settled there the way rivers found their beds.

"You chose staying," she whispered.

"Yeah."

She rested her palm over his heart. "Then your bones have stopped wandering."

They rose slowly, walking the valley's edge not as fugitives, but as residents. Mist lingered longer around their shelter. Birds returned to the same branches near their fire pit. The stream altered its path just enough to keep fresh water pooling near the flat stone where Isorae liked to kneel.

The valley didn't announce its acceptance.

It simply behaved as though they had always been there.

"You are becoming part of this place," she murmured.

"Feels like the first place that ever wanted me."

She slid her arms around his waist from behind. "Because you are standing where your soul already lived."

That afternoon Rowan noticed the birds again — not their absence, but their attention. Finches gathered near the stream, not flitting, not singing — simply watching her.

"They hear my resonance," Isorae murmured.

That evening, while gathering firewood along the upper ridge, Rowan saw smoke — thin, distant, human.

"They will feel me," she said quietly.

"Then we stay hidden."

"We stay aware."

That night they lay together again, her head tucked beneath his chin, his arm firm around her back.

"And now?" she whispered.

"And now I belong here."

"With me."

"With you."

But beneath his ribs, the oath stirred — faint and directional — a compass that did not point north, but toward whatever would try to take her.

The valley had accepted them.

The world beyond had begun to notice.

And something vast was quietly turning its face in their direction.

21
THE DREAM THAT WARNS HIM

Rowan does not fall asleep. Sleep comes for him.

Not gently — not the way it usually does, slipping around the edges of exhaustion or drifting through the cracks of thought like fog — but with weight. It draws him downward the way tide takes shoreline, first inch by inch and then all at once, pulling him beneath a gravity heavier than muscle and bone. His breath slows. The hollow dissolves. And the world opens somewhere else.

He stands beneath a sky that does not belong to this earth.

The stars are wrong — too many, too close, clustered in pale violet constellations that pulse faintly as if they are breathing. Their light does not fall. It hums. The air vibrates with a low, ancient resonance that settles into his bones, making thought feel less like language and more like motion — something carried through him rather than formed inside him.

He knows this place.

Not from memory. From recognition.

Before him rises a tree that should not exist. Its trunk is pale and luminous, smooth as if grown from moonlight rather than bark, and its roots are exposed — not clawing downward, but spreading outward in long glowing veins that lace across the ground like light spilled into soil. Each root pulses with a slow, deliberate frequency, as though the land itself has a heartbeat and this tree is where it can be heard.

He is not alone.

Figures stand around the tree — tall shapes robed in light and shadow, their faces indistinct, their forms only partially held by reality. They do not move toward him. They do not withdraw. They watch.

They are not strangers.

They are not allies.

They are witnesses.

One of them steps forward.

Its voice does not travel through air. It arrives inside his bones.

The valley has been found.

The words settle beneath his sternum like weight dropped into deep water.

"By who?" he asks — though his mouth does not move.

By those who were pulled.

By those who learned how to listen.

By those who learned how to remember.

Cold threads through his ribs. "They're coming."

Yes.

The roots beneath his boots pulse brighter, their glow deepening like breath taken before speech.

Some will arrive because the land remembers them.

Some will arrive because you remember them.

Some will arrive because the breach has changed what can be sensed.

Rowan looks down at the glowing veins beneath his feet. "And ARIS?"

The silence that follows is deliberate. It presses.

They are not pulled.

The words strike like stone.

They are alerted.

His jaw tightens. "They are not meant to be here."

No.

"They will come anyway."

Light ripples through the roots, and suddenly he sees it — not paths, but threads. Invisible convergences of movement, memory, and fate bend slowly through unseen space toward a single point.

Toward the valley.

Toward him.

Faces blur along the lines — some familiar, some forgotten, some not yet known but already waiting to exist.

His breath stutters. "How many?"

The answer is not a number.

It is a truth.

Enough to change the shape of your life.

His voice roughens. "And her?"

The glow softens.

She is already home.

Something loosens painfully beneath his ribs. "But they'll hurt her."

The figures shift — not to threaten, not to comfort — but to witness.

They will try.

And you will decide what that means.

The roots flare. Light surges upward like a silent storm, and the final words are pressed directly into his blood:

The valley is no longer hidden.

The story is no longer quiet.

What comes next will be chosen.

Rowan wakes with a sharp breath tearing from his chest.

The fire has burned low. The forest is still. Isorae sleeps beside him, her breath slow and steady, faint shimmer rising and falling beneath her skin like a private moon.

Rowan sits upright, heart hammering, the echo of luminous roots still burning behind his eyes.

"They're coming," he whispers into the dark.

And he knows exactly who they are.

22
THE FIRST WHO WERE CHOSEN

The valley did not announce him.

It shifted — not with sound, but with pressure, like a held breath finally choosing where to settle.

Rowan felt it first.

He was standing near the stream, rinsing dirt from his hands, when something in the air changed — not colder, not warmer — just… aware. His spine straightened without permission. His fingers paused beneath the running water. The quiet of the hollow deepened, tightening into a listening stillness.

The land was paying attention.

He turned slowly.

At the far edge of the hollow, beyond the curtain of fern and pale limestone root, someone stood.

A man — early thirties, lean, dark hair plastered to his forehead with sweat. His jacket hung half-open and travel-worn, boots scuffed raw by too many miles taken in too much of a hurry. A backpack sagged from one shoulder like it had been repacked again and again by hands that hadn't known what they were looking for — only that they had to keep moving.

He did not look dangerous.

He looked displaced.

Aligned.

Pulled.

He did not step forward. The moss near his boots bent faintly — not from weight, but from listening — as if the ground itself were testing his shape. He did not call out.

He simply stood there, staring at the hollow like it had spoken his name aloud.

Rowan moved without deciding to. He placed himself between the man and the shelter, his body angling into the space as naturally as a door closing.

Isorae was at his side a breath later — quiet, luminous, her gaze already fixed on the stranger with something deeper than caution.

The man swallowed. "I— I'm sorry," he said quickly. "I didn't mean to— I wasn't trying to— I don't even know how I got here."

Rowan did not lower his guard. "Then why are you here?"

The man hesitated. His hand drifted to his chest, fingers pressing into his shirt as if he were trying to locate the answer physically. "I felt… something," he said slowly. "Like a gravity I couldn't walk away from. It felt older than me. Like something that already knew my name." His voice wavered, almost embarrassed by its own honesty. "It started days ago. I tried to ignore it. I really did. Every road just kept… turning me back."

Isorae's breath softened.

"You couldn't leave," Rowan said quietly.

The man nodded. "It felt like if I did… something in me would crack."

Silence settled — not awkward, not empty.

Listening.

Isorae stepped forward, her presence shifting the air like dawn moving across still water. "What is your name?" she asked gently.

"Evan," he said. "I used to work in search and rescue. Emergency response." He hesitated, eyes lowering. "I lost people. Too many. My chest never stopped hurting. I couldn't sleep anymore. And then… this started." He gestured vaguely toward the hollow. "I thought I was losing my mind."

"No," Isorae said softly. "You were being called."

Evan's breath hitched. His eyes filled before he could stop them. "I didn't come here to take anything," he said quietly. "I just needed somewhere that didn't feel like it was killing me slowly."

Rowan studied him for a long moment. Then — deliberately — he shifted. Not fully. But enough.

"You can stay," Rowan said.

Evan froze.

"You can't leave," Rowan added quietly. "Not yet."

A sound broke from Evan's chest — shaky, unfinished, dangerously close to a sob.

Isorae stepped closer and placed her palm lightly over his heart — just for a breath. His breathing steadied.

The valley exhaled.

And deep in root and stone, something ancient recognized him.

The first had arrived.

For a time, it remained only him.

Days passed. Evan slept by the stream, then closer to the fire. The hollow adjusted around his presence the way it had adjusted around Isorae — subtly, quietly, as though learning a new note in its own breath. Birds lingered longer. Moss bent more easily beneath his boots. The air itself seemed to remember him after only a handful of nights.

And then — slowly — others began to feel it.

The valley did not call loudly. It did not tear open the sky or thunder across distance.

It whispered.

It whispered into bone. Into breath. Into the quiet places people only noticed when something inside them had already begun to fail.

The first arrivals came alone. They reached the ridge at dusk or dawn, uncertain, hollow-eyed, moving like people following a sound no one else could hear. They always stopped at the same place — the narrow bend where moss curved inward and stone dipped gently, as if the land itself were drawing breath there.

They never crossed it right away.

A woman arrived one evening with shaking hands and a scar along her throat. She said she had woken from sleep with only one certainty in her body — go west — and that the word had not come from thought, but from somewhere beneath her ribs.

A boy not yet nineteen came days later, hollow-cheeked and exhausted. He said that every time he closed his eyes he felt something moving beneath his sternum — slow, patient, like roots rearranging themselves inside him.

A middle-aged couple drove for eight hours without a map, without a destination, guided only by the terrible certainty that something was waiting — and that they were already late to meet it.

They reached the rim of the hollow and stopped.

Always there.

Always hesitant.

Always afraid to step forward.

The moss near their boots bowed faintly — not from weight, but from recognition.

Rowan met each of them himself. He asked the same questions every time.

"How did you find this place?"

"What did you feel?"

"Why did you follow it?"

The answers were never the same.

But the truth always was.

They were tired.

They were hurting.

They were done pretending the world was not hollow.

Isorae watched them the way the land did — not with suspicion, but with resonance. She touched foreheads, wrists, palms — not to claim, not to mark — only to listen.

And people cried in front of her without understanding why.

Some collapsed into sleep on the first night, as if their bodies had been holding breath for years. Some sat beside the stream and whispered apologies to no one. Some stared into the fire as though it were answering prayers they had buried long ago.

And still — they could not leave.

Those who tried found themselves walking in widening circles, pressure tightening beneath their ribs the farther they went, until their bodies quietly turned back without permission.

Rowan tested it himself. He walked beyond the ridge with Evan, counting steps, marking trees.

The land loosened around him.

But it tightened around the others.

Isorae felt it. "They are being held," she whispered.

The valley was no longer only refuge.

It was becoming a threshold.

And thresholds change everything.

Then came the ones who were not only broken — but aware.

A woman named Erin arrived with scanning equipment strapped to her back and eyes that never stopped counting. Two brothers came with portable frequency readers and voices that whispered ARIS like a curse. A former contractor arrived and said quietly, "They're mapping anomalies. And this place is singing."

They brought instruments.

They brought knowledge.

They brought fear.

And they brought the first proof that something inside ARIS had begun to listen.

The hollow — not yet a village — took its first breath as something that could no longer pretend to be unseen.

No one had planned it. No one had invited it.

But laughter began to thread the air. Shared meals appeared. Tools leaned against stone. Blankets were passed hand to hand beneath firelight.

People stayed.

One night, Rowan stood at the ridge staring into the dark.

Isorae stepped beside him. "They will keep coming."

Rowan exhaled. "Then we learn how to hold them."

And far beyond the valley…

something patient recalibrated its orbit around them.

23
THE VALLEY THAT
BEGINS TO ANSWER

The valley did not change all at once. It adjusted — the way a living body adjusts after a wound: slowly, instinctively, reshaping itself around new weight until the new shape feels like it has always been there.

Paths began to appear where no one had cut them.

They were not roads, and they were not trails — only narrow softenings through fern and root, places where moss thinned and earth compacted just enough that feet began to fall there naturally, as if the land itself were remembering where people were meant to walk.

Low arcs of stone eased themselves into shallow windbreaks along the ridges. Not stacked. Not carved. Just present — as though the earth had leaned into new shapes overnight and found that it liked them.

Water began to pool where people knelt to wash their hands. Shade lingered longer over resting places. Wind curved differently through the hollow, threading between bodies instead of cutting across them.

Rowan noticed first — not because he was looking for signs, but because he had lived long enough in quiet places to recognize when land was making room.

He began to place things.

Sleeping zones.

Fire circles.

Lookout perches.

He never said the word village — but his hands began building one.

He drove stakes into soft earth where cloth shelters could rise without tearing roots. He stacked fallen limbs into low wind fences. He arranged fire pits so smoke threaded upward through natural stone funnels instead of drifting across sleeping forms.

He did not command.

He listened.

And the valley responded.

Isorae became the center without choosing it.

People did not kneel before her. They sat beside her. They stood near her. They breathed where she breathed.

She listened — to grief, to exhaustion, to the names of the dead that had never been spoken aloud — and she laid her hands gently over pain the way someone might remember how bodies were meant to be held.

And wherever she lingered, the valley subtly realigned.

Bruises faded.

Nightmares loosened.

Sleep came easier.

No one called it healing.

They simply said things like, I slept last night, or My chest doesn't hurt as much today.

But the valley felt different after she passed through — steadier, quieter, more willing to hold.

The first structures were not cabins.

They were shelters.

Lean-tos. Root nests. Stone hollows softened with moss and cloth.

People built them slowly at first — uncertain, awkward — then with growing confidence as muscle memory returned to bodies that had been wandering for years.

Laughter began to happen.

Quiet at first.

Then easier.

Food was shared. Tools were borrowed. Names were learned.

Seventeen became twenty-six.

Then thirty-one.

And then the paths began arriving ahead of the people.

Some brought things that changed the shape of the hollow.

A woman arrived with radiation-detection gear she never removed her gloves to adjust. A man followed with satellite uplink parts he assembled without ever looking at the sky. Another came with weather-mapping tablets, another with encrypted storage drives, another with maps no one could place.

They did not talk much at first.

They watched.

They listened.

They took notes in the margins of their own fear.

A former ARIS engineer arrived one evening — scar tissue pale along his jaw, his eyes never fully leaving the treeline. He ate in silence, slept near the fire, and said nothing for three nights.

On the third night, while wind curled softly through the shelter ribs and sparks drifted lazily into dark, he leaned toward Rowan and whispered:

"They're triangulating again."

The words did not rise.

They sank.

The air tightened. The land leaned.

Rowan felt it beneath his sternum — the same inward pull that had once guided him into the mountain.

Isorae's shimmer tightened for the first time since the valley had begun to feel like home.

"They are learning how to see us," she murmured.

Rowan took her hand. "Then we learn how to disappear better."

She looked up at him — fear and fire braided together. "We will need more than hiding."

The valley breathed — deep, steady, patient.

And far beyond the trees…

ARIS began reconstructing the shape of where it had lost her.

24

THE DAY THE LAND TIGHTENED

The valley did not lean for him. It did not soften its breath or loosen the tension in its ribs. It did not open pathways beneath his feet or murmur recognition into the quiet bones of the hollow.

It tightened.

Rowan felt it before he saw the man — a subtle contraction beneath his sternum, as if the land had drawn its shoulders inward. The air grew denser. Sound thinned. The stream did not change its voice, but the space around it did, narrowing into a quieter shape, as though the valley were preparing to take a blow.

The stranger stood at the rim.

Exactly where the hollow always asked newcomers to hesitate.

But he did not hesitate. He did not pause to breathe the valley in. He did not stand like someone pulled by grief, or exhaustion, or the slow hunger for rest.

He felt… flat. Measured. Contained.

Rowan moved before the man took a single step.

"Stop there."

The stranger obeyed immediately — not startled, not offended — simply precise, as though the instruction had already been anticipated.

"I'm looking for a place people say makes them feel better," the man said calmly.

Behind Rowan, Isorae inhaled sharply. Her faint shimmer tightened — not in fear, but in recognition.

The valley drew inward another degree around the stranger's boots.

Rowan studied him. His hands were clean — too clean. No dirt beneath the nails. No restless micro-movement. No tremor of a body dragged here by need.

"You felt the pull," Rowan said quietly. "Didn't you?"

The man paused — not uncertain.

Choosing.

"Something like that."

The land recoiled — not visibly, but in pressure, in tone, in refusal.

Isorae stepped closer.

"That is not true," she said softly.

The man's jaw flexed — just once.

A small mistake.

Rowan felt the truth lock into place behind his ribs.

"You didn't come because you were broken," Rowan said.

"You didn't come because you were empty."

"You didn't come because you were tired of surviving."

The man's eyes sharpened — only a fraction.

"You came because you were told where to stand."

Silence thickened. The valley did not breathe.

At last, the stranger exhaled.

"They said there was a signal anomaly in this region," he replied evenly. "I'm here to verify it."

Isorae stepped forward — luminous, steady — and the air bent subtly around her, as if remembering a better geometry.

"You are not welcome here," she said gently.

For the first time, something flickered in his gaze — not fear.

Calculation.

"I don't require welcome," he said. "Only coordinates."

Rowan's voice dropped, iron-still. "You already have them."

The man's eyes slid past him — into the hollow, into the shelters, into the firelight, into the bodies learning how to breathe again. Into a place that had begun to mean something.

Then he turned.

And walked away.

The valley did not try to hold him.

It released him.

Rowan did not relax.

Isorae's hand slid into his — warm, anchoring.

"That was not a seeker," she murmured.

"No," Rowan said quietly. "That was a probe."

And for the first time since the wounded had begun to arrive, the valley no longer felt like a sanctuary.

It felt like a territory that had just been entered onto a map.

They did not return with noise.

They did not bring machines, uniforms, or weapons.

They brought normal.

Three days later, a couple appeared at the upper rim — clean boots, quiet smiles, carefully distressed packs. They stopped exactly where the valley usually asked newcomers to hesitate.

But they did not feel pulled.

They felt placed.

Rowan sensed it instantly — not as threat, not as ache — but as flatness. A presence standing on the valley instead of sinking into it.

He moved before anyone else could reach them.

"What did you feel that brought you here?" he asked.

The woman smiled politely. Too politely.

"We were traveling," she said. "We heard there was… a quiet place."

Behind Rowan, Isorae's shimmer tightened faintly.

"That is not how people arrive," she murmured.

The man's jaw flexed — just once.

"You can't stay," Rowan said quietly.

The woman blinked. "We weren't asking—"

"You weren't called," Rowan interrupted. "And the land knows it."

Silence stretched — thick and wrong.

The valley tightened — not around Rowan.

Around them.

Moss bowed. Wind shifted in sharp, unfamiliar angles. Fern tips stiffened. Their shoulders tensed without understanding why.

Isorae stepped forward, her voice gentle — devastating.

"You are listening outward," she said softly. "Not inward."

They left.

They returned a week later.

Different faces.

Different clothes.

The same emptiness behind the eyes.

They came again.

And again.

Always stopping in the same place.

Always leaving without protest.

Rowan began to mark them.

Arrival angles.

Spacing between visits.

Bird behavior.

The way insects fell silent a fraction of a second earlier each time.

Patterns formed.

Isorae felt it in her bones.

"They are learning how to move like they belong," she whispered one night. "And they are learning me."

Her shimmer dimmed as she said it.

Rowan tightened his grip on her hand. "They don't get you."

"They are tuning for me."

The land responded.

Fern thickened along the rim.

Stone narrowed into subtle funnels.

Wind stiffened when flat presences entered — not to block, but to measure.

Not raids.

Not attacks.

Just learning.

Learning what the valley rejected.

Learning what it held.

Learning who stood in front.

Unease crept beneath meals. Beneath laughter. Beneath sleep.

The valley was no longer only holding.

It was bracing.

And far beyond the trees…

ARIS stopped asking whether the anomaly existed—

—and began designing how to reach it.

25
THE FREQUENCIES THAT HURT

It begins as pressure.

Not sharp. Not sudden.

A low density behind Isorae's eyes that does not belong to weather, fatigue, or human pain.

She does not speak of it at first. She sits longer beside the stream, moves more slowly between tasks. Her shimmer dims faintly — not fading, but muffled — like moonlight drawn behind thin cloud.

Rowan notices anyway.

"You're quieter," he murmurs one evening as they stack firewood.

She hesitates. "My bones feel… loud."

That night, the first wave moves through the valley.

There is no sound — only pressure: a descending, invisible tide that presses into sternum and spine, into root and stone, into breath itself. People wake clutching their chests. Dogs whine. Birds scatter in startled spirals.

Isorae gasps and folds against Rowan as if gravity has doubled.

"What is that?" someone whispers.

Isorae trembles — not cold, not fear — resonance.

"They are testing bandwidth," she breathes. "They are tuning for me."

Two nights later, the second wave comes — stronger, longer.

A woman collapses beside the fire, blood sliding from her nose. Two people vomit violently. Someone sobs without knowing why.

Isorae drops to her knees, fingers clawing into Rowan's shirt as if she is holding herself inside her body. He catches her instantly, his voice going rough.

"They stop — or I make them."

She can barely breathe. "It isn't an attack yet," she whispers. "It's calibration."

The valley responds. Roots rise faintly along familiar paths. Stone hums beneath bare feet. Wind stiffens as if the land itself is bracing.

But the waves continue — third, fourth — subtle, surgical pulses that leave no wreckage but quietly rearrange the shape of the hollow.

People begin sleeping in shifts. Children cry without knowing why. Even laughter starts to sound like it has to push through something heavier than air. The valley's breath grows shallow — like a body learning how to brace for pain it can't yet name.

And Isorae begins to change.

Not brightly. Not violently.

But wrong.

Her glow fractures into uneven tides beneath her skin. Her posture shifts to protect places she never used to guard. She presses her palm to her sternum more often now — not to steady herself, but to contain something pressing outward.

Rowan notices the spaces between her breaths before he notices anything else.

The way she leans more heavily into him when she thinks he isn't watching. The way her shimmer tightens when the pulses ripple through the valley. The way her body has begun to answer the pressure before the land does.

One night, as another wave passes and she winces sharply, Rowan catches her elbow to steady her. She barely seems to feel the light anymore. Something in his chest hardens into certainty.

"You need to rest," he says quietly—not as instruction, but as recognition.

She looks up at him, eyes glassy with ache and light. "If I leave," she whispers, "they will stop."

The words cut through him like a blade.

"No."

"If I move away from you—away from the valley—the land will loosen," she says. "They don't want you alone. They want what happens when we are together."

Rowan's jaw tightens, something feral sliding awake beneath his skin. "You are not currency."

Her voice breaks. "I am the amplifier."

The next wave strikes mid-sentence.

She screams.

Rowan's arms lock around her as the valley shudders beneath their feet—trees groaning faintly, stones whispering against one another. And far beyond hearing, but close enough to feel, something enormous finishes locking its aim.

For a long moment, nothing moves. Not the birds. Not the leaves. Not even the stream. The hollow holds itself perfectly still, as if waiting to discover what shape it has been forced into.

Isorae's breath comes shallow and bright against his chest. Rowan feels the pressure settle—not passing through, not fading—but staying, embedding itself into the bones of the valley.

The land does not exhale.

It learns.

The valley no longer wakes gently.

It flinches.

The next pulse arrives just before dawn, stronger than any before—a deep compressive wave that bends breath inside chests and makes the stream tremble as if afraid of its own water. It is not sound. It is not light. It is pressure, folding inward through bone and rhythm and blood.

Someone screams.

Rowan is already moving.

A man near the eastern fire circle collapses, hands clutching his ribs, face draining of color as if the night itself has reached inside him and pulled something loose. Rowan drops beside him, palm finding the frantic beat beneath his jaw.

"Hey. Stay with me."

The man's eyes are glassy, unfocused. His pulse stutters—chaotic, slipping, drowning.

Isorae staggers in behind him, pain folded into her posture, shimmer crawling unevenly beneath her skin like static trapped under moonlight. Her breath shakes. "His heart lost its rhythm."

Rowan swallows. "Can you reach him?"

She kneels, hands hovering over the man's sternum, eyes unfocused — listening to the broken resonance tearing through him. Her fingers tremble.

"I can't," she whispers. "They're flooding the band. He's drowning in noise."

The man convulses once.

Then stills.

Silence slams into the valley harder than the pulse.

A woman sobs. Someone whispers his name like it might still pull him back. Rowan presses his palm to the man's chest, willing breath into him that will not return.

For the first time since the wounded began arriving, someone has died inside the hollow.

That night, fear enters the valley—not fear of ARIS, but fear of the cost of staying.

A small group gathers at the far fire, voices tight, eyes darting, hands clenched around mugs that have gone cold.

"He died because of her."

"If she leaves, the pressure stops."

"They're using her as a beacon."

"They won't stop while she's here."

Rowan hears every word. He does not turn. His hands shake anyway.

Isorae hears them too.

She steps forward before Rowan can stop her. "If I go," she says quietly, "they will loosen the signal."

Rowan turns on her sharply. "No."

"I will not let more people die for me."

"They died because of ARIS," Rowan growls. "Not you."

Her eyes are luminous — soft and breaking. "You cannot protect everyone."

His voice drops, feral. "Watch me."

Before dawn, someone makes the first wrong choice.

A young man slips into the fog with a portable scanner, desperate to trace the source. They find his body at the ridge hours later—not torn, not burned—just collapsed, heart stopped mid-step, face turned toward the valley like he almost made it back.

This time even the land goes still.

The pulses pause.

ARIS has learned something.

And so has the valley.

26

THE CHOICE SHE ALMOST MAKES

The valley does not mourn loudly.

It tightens.

Not with grief, but with restraint—like a body drawing its shoulders inward to brace for another blow. The air grows denser in the mornings. Fires burn lower. Laughter vanishes. Voices soften, as if sound itself might call the pulses back again.

Blankets remain wrapped around shoulders even in sunlight. People linger closer to one another. No one walks alone anymore.

Rowan does not leave Isorae's side.

Not for water. Not for sleep. Not for patrol. His presence becomes structural—quiet, constant, unyielding. He stands where shadows fall first. He sits where pathways narrow. His body shapes a living boundary between her and the open valley, as if his bones alone could hold back the sky.

Isorae feels it.

She feels the way his breath tightens when the air compresses. The tension behind his eyes when he forces himself to smile. The way his hand never truly leaves her—always hovering, always orienting, always holding the world in place around her.

And it hurts him.

That is the part that hurts her.

She finds Evan sitting alone by the stream at dusk, staring into the water as if it might finally answer him.

"They will not stop," she says quietly.

He does not pretend otherwise. "No."

"They are using me like a flare."

"Yeah."

"If I step out of the valley," she whispers, "if I let them take me… the pulses will loosen. People will breathe again."

Evan exhales slowly. "Rowan would break."

She nods faintly. "I know."

She does not tell Rowan.

She does not tell the others.

But she begins walking the outer paths at night—learning where the land loosens around her, where the pull thins, where the threshold begins to soften. Learning the shapes of leaving. Learning where the valley stops holding her and starts letting her go.

Rowan notices the change in her posture before he notices her altered routes. He feels the hollowing in the air when she steps too far from him. The way the valley tightens when her distance grows.

The night he finds her standing near the ridge, fog curling around her ankles, he does not call out.

He walks to her.

Slow. Silent.

"What are you doing?" he asks quietly.

"Listening," she whispers.

"To what?"

"To how loud I am."

His chest tightens. "You're not loud."

"I am to them."

She does not look at him when she says it.

Instead, her gaze drifts toward the fog-soft ridge beyond the hollow — the place where the valley loosens, where the land no longer presses inward to keep her close.

"If I step beyond that line," she murmurs, "the pressure thins. The pulses soften. People can breathe again."

Rowan's breath stalls.

A quiet, terrible understanding moves through him.

"You don't get to pay for their violence with your body," he says.

She finally looks back at him.

"You don't get to decide who lives because of me."

His voice lowers—iron-still, edged with something ancient.

"I decide who dies for you."

Her breath catches.

"That's not fair," she whispers.

"No," he says. "But it's mine."

She steps into him, pressing her forehead to his chest.

"If I go… they will stop killing people."

His hands slide up her arms—firm, anchoring.

"And if you go," he murmurs into her hair, "this place becomes a grave."

Her voice breaks. "Rowan—"

"I said no."

She stills—not agreeing, but recognizing the depth of his resolve.

The valley exhales around them—low, uneasy.

And far beyond the ridges, ARIS adjusts its frequencies.

Not retreating.

Learning.

27

STAY IN YOUR BONES

The first pulse comes just after dawn. It does not arrive with sound. It does not announce itself with light or vibration. It enters the valley the way a blade enters glass — thin, invisible, exquisitely tuned — and the land does not recoil. It listens.

Isorae gasps. The sound tears from her chest as if her breath has been struck out of her rather than drawn away. Her body stiffens, arching sharply as something inside her rings — not pain, not heat, but resonance, a piercing internal note that recognizes her shape and begins to search for where she will fracture.

Her knees buckle.

Rowan is already moving. He catches her before she can fall, his arms locking around her as her shimmer spikes beneath her skin — no longer warm, no longer luminous, but jagged and unstable, screaming through her veins like lightning trapped under glass.

"Rowan—" she chokes, fingers clawing into his jacket — not clinging, but searching for somewhere to hide inside him.

He feels the pulse in his teeth, in his sternum, in the deep place where the land usually answers him with something like welcome.

This is not welcome. This is surgical.

"Get her inside!" someone shouts.

Rowan does not answer. He lifts her fully into his arms and runs — not toward shelter, not toward people, but deeper, into the oldest root chamber where stone hums thick and slow and the land still remembers how to hold things that are breaking.

Another pulse slices through the hollow.

Several people cry out. But Isorae screams. Soundlessly. Her mouth opens. No voice comes. Her breath is ripped from her lungs as her glow convulses beneath her skin — folding, tearing, spasming inward like something being pulled apart by invisible hands.

Rowan drops to his knees with her, cradling her head against his chest.

"Hey," he whispers fiercely. "Hey. Stay with me."

Her eyes flutter — unfocused, luminous with terror.

"They're tuning to me," she gasps. "They're mapping my bones."

His jaw locks so hard it aches.

Outside the chamber, Erin's equipment shrieks — alarms climbing into panic.

"They've switched to harmonic targeting!" she yells. "They're not scanning the valley — they're isolating her!"

The pulses continue. Not rhythmic. Not patterned.

Experimental. Short. Long. Offset. Searching.

Trying to find the note that opens her.

Isorae curls inward, hands shaking violently, breath breaking in shallow shards as her body fights to remain a single thing.

Rowan presses his forehead to hers, cupping her face, forcing her eyes to find his.

"Look at me," he murmurs. "Not them. Listen to me. Stay in your bones."

Her breath stutters.

The valley shudders.

Roots tighten.

Stone ribs creak.

Water trembles in the stream.

The land feels her pain.

And for the first time since she crossed worlds — the valley growls. Low. Deep. Alive. A sound that does not belong to weather.

ARIS has found the frequency that hurts her.

And the valley has just begun to remember how to answer violence.

28

SECOND STRIKE

The valley has not finished flinching when the next strike arrives. Roots are still drawn tight beneath the soil, stone ribs holding tension as if the land has forgotten how to exhale. The stream runs too quietly, its surface unnaturally smooth, as though water itself is afraid to make noise. Even the fire burns low — not dwindling, but hesitant, flame wavering like it is unsure whether it is still permitted to exist.

No one has gone back to sleep.

People linger near one another in tight clusters, blankets still wrapped around shoulders, eyes scanning the treeline as if threat might arrive with footsteps this time instead of pressure.

Isorae has not stood upright since the first pulse.

She kneels at the stream because her body refuses stillness — hands submerged in the cold water, breath shallow and uneven, shimmer barely breathing beneath her skin like a frightened animal hiding under ice. Her shoulders tremble faintly, not from cold, but from the aftershock that has not finished passing through her bones.

Rowan does not leave her. He is crouched close behind her, one knee pressed into the mud, one hand hovering just behind her shoulder blades — not touching, but stabilizing the space around her like he is afraid gravity itself might tilt wrong if he moves.

When the air tightens again, it does not come with violence. It comes with precision. A narrow filament of pressure threads through the hollow — invisible, exact — sliding straight through her spine like a wire being drawn through crystal.

Isorae gasps.

Her fingers slip beneath the water. Her breath catches — and Rowan is already moving, one hand sliding to the back of her neck, guiding her forehead into the curve of his shoulder as her breath splinters against his collarbone.

"Isorae," he breathes. "Talk to me."

She trembles — not outwardly, but deep inside her bones, like something vibrating beneath her skin while her muscles fight to remain intact.

"It's thinner," she gasps. "They've narrowed it."

Her shimmer flickers — moonlight under broken cloud — no longer flowing, but glitching.

Across the hollow, people look up.

They don't feel pain. They feel pressure — like standing too close to something humming just beyond hearing.

Isorae makes a soft, fractured sound — not quite a scream — the sound a body makes when it is trying not to disintegrate.

Rowan drops fully to his knees beside her, one arm locking around her ribs, his other palm braced into the soil as if anchoring both of them to the earth.

"Tell me where it hurts."

She shakes her head weakly.

"Not where," she gasps. "How."

A micro-pulse threads through her spine.

Her back arches sharply. Her breath fractures in her throat.

The land flinches — but does not take the blow.

She does.

Her breath shudders.

"That wasn't a scan," she whispers shakily. "That was a stress filament."

Rowan stills.

"They aren't mapping me anymore."

Her eyes lift — luminous, frightened, furious.

"They're testing where I give."

Rowan's jaw locks until his teeth ache. "No."

"They're learning what part of me fractures first," she whispers. "They're teaching the system how to hurt me."

Another filament pulse brushes through her — so narrow it barely exists — and Isorae sobs like someone has reached inside her ribs and twisted.

Rowan pulls her fully into his chest, his arms locking around her, forehead bowing to hers as he shields her with his body like a wall.

"Your bones are not coordinates."

Her fingers clutch his shirt like he is the only solid object left in a world turning her into signal.

"Then why do they feel like doors?"

The valley hums — confused now — unsettled — angry — but unfocused. The land knows someone is being hurt.

It does not yet know who to strike.

Rowan lifts his head slowly. His eyes are dark. Still. Predatory. Something old and territorial shifts beneath his ribs — a thing that remembers blood and boundaries.

"If they're testing your bones," he says low and lethal,

"then we start testing theirs."

And far beyond the ridges, ARIS completes its first clean harmonic lock.

The hunt has ended.

The extraction has begun.

29

THE HOLDING PATTERN

After the dawn strike—after Isorae's quiet breaking—the air settles into a stillness so ordinary it feels wrong. No hum drifts through the trees. No pressure presses against ribs. No invisible weight descends into bone. The sky remains pale and wide, the forest resuming its rhythms as if nothing has happened.

Too quickly.

People begin to breathe again. Laughter returns in cautious threads, thin as spider silk but present. Someone hums while washing a pot at the stream, the sound drifting through fern-shadow like a question the valley does not answer. Children—the ones who arrived already half-healed—chase one another through the clearings as if the land has forgotten how to bruise.

Rowan doesn't believe it. He remains longer than necessary at the ridge, scanning tree lines that look unchanged, listening to birds that sing the same patterns they sang yesterday. Everything appears normal. But his body does not soften. It remembers the cut. He feels it in the way the valley holds itself—subtle, taut, like a muscle refusing to relax after strain.

Isorae moves more slowly now. Weak. Careful. As if her bones are listening for something that has learned her name.

She spends more time near the heart of the hollow, sitting with her back against sun-warmed stone, hands folded loosely in her lap. Her shimmer remains quiet—controlled—but Rowan notices it never quite returns to its old steadiness. It is like a lake after a storm: smooth at the surface, unsettled underneath.

"You're hurting," he murmurs one afternoon, crouching beside her.

She shakes her head.

"Not hurting."

She hesitates, searching for the right word. "Listening."

"For what?"

"For the part of the world that is deciding," she whispers.

Days pass without visible threat. No drones cross the canopy. No lights sweep the valley floor. No hum threads the soil.

But the animals change.

Deer stop crossing the western slope. Two familiar owl roosts fall silent. The stream shifts subtly east—no more than a finger-width—but Rowan notices the way moss darkens differently along its edge, the way fern fronds lean inward as if bracing for something that has not yet arrived.

The valley is not hiding.

It is holding.

The valley holds this way for nearly two days.

Not quiet—but suspended.

Nothing strikes.

Nothing withdraws.

And that is what changes the people.

The first pulses taught them fear.

The second taught them cost.

This space in between teaches them expectation—the kind that tightens muscles before impact, the kind that shortens breath even when the air is clean.

The land does not relax.

It waits.

And then the light changes.

Not its brightness.

Its behavior.

Sunlight no longer falls cleanly across the hollow. It diffuses through the upper canopy in faint, wavering bands, bending as if it is passing through an unseen current. Shadows hesitate before settling.

Leaves flicker when no wind moves them. The valley still looks like itself—but it no longer moves like itself.

Rowan notices while reinforcing a low stone wall near the eastern slope. He is stacking flat limestone slabs into a shallow windbreak when the shadow of his own arm bends strangely across the moss at his feet, warping by a fraction before correcting itself. He straightens slowly.

The land is no longer only listening.

It is being tested.

Isorae feels it first—not in her skin, not in her breath—but in the deep place beneath her sternum where her resonance lives. A faint internal pressure settles there and holds, as if something unseen has placed a hand against her bones from the inside.

She exhales carefully and does not speak.

Rowan sees the stillness in her posture before she says anything at all.

"You feel it," he says quietly.

She nods once. "They are refining where I exist."

His jaw tightens. "How?"

"Not with sound," she says softly. "With intention."

The valley does not flinch.

But it leans.

That afternoon, one of Erin's handheld scanners begins to tick.

Not loudly.

Not urgently.

Just a quiet, irregular clicking—soft enough that most people would ignore it, soft enough to feel accidental.

Erin does not ignore it.

She frowns down at the display. "Background field just shifted. Extremely narrow band. Directional."

Rowan steps closer. "Meaning?"

"They're narrowing," she says slowly. "They're testing entry tolerances."

A chill settles low in Rowan's ribs.

Isorae's breath tightens.

"They are reducing the space between signal and body," she says quietly.

That night, the stars change.

Not their position—their clarity.

The sky sharpens unnaturally. Constellations brighten into thin, surgical lines that feel less like light and more like measurement. The darkness between them deepens until the heavens resemble a lattice of blades.

Isorae does not sleep.

She sits upright against Rowan's chest, her body rigid with listening, her eyes tracking something that cannot be seen.

"They are asking the land to agree with them," she whispers.

Rowan wraps his arms tighter around her, his jaw pressing lightly to her hair.

"Then the land lies."

She closes her eyes. "I don't know if it can."

Deep beneath the hollow, stone hums faintly.

The valley does not answer.

But it is no longer silent.

And far beyond the ridges, something has extended its hand—

Not yet to take.

But to learn what would stop it.

30

THE FIRST BLOOD

The next pulse is not calibrated.

It is aimed.

It does not ripple through the valley or brush stone and root with curious harmonic testing.

It does not listen.

It cuts.

A blade of resonance scythes across the northern tree line just after dusk—silent, invisible—so clean that for half a heartbeat nothing happens at all.

Then the forest reacts.

Birds detonate into flight in a violent black surge. Roots wrench free of soil as if something beneath them has flinched. Stone fractures in sudden white seams, splitting through moss and bedrock like bone breaking beneath skin.

Inside the hollow, Isorae screams—not from sound, but from impact.

Her body folds into Rowan as if gravity has inverted. Her hands claw into his jacket, fingers shaking violently, her glow spasming beneath her skin in wild, fractured pulses—no longer luminous, no longer warm, but torn and screaming through her veins.

Rowan barely catches her as the strike slams through his chest like a collapsing star.

His vision whites out.

His breath rips free of his lungs.

People are thrown to the ground around them, the hollow erupting in shouts and falling bodies.

Erin drops to her knees near the western stones, screaming coordinates into a broken uplink, her voice shaking, her hands trembling too badly to keep the numbers straight.

"They're not scanning—" she gasps.

"They're cutting—!"

The valley answers.

Trees bend inward, not away, forming living shield arcs that bow over the hollow like ribs. Stone ridges heave upward out of the soil, cracking moss and root in violent white seams. The stream erupts into a lightless wall of mist that surges skyward like breath torn from lungs.

But the cut has already landed.

Eli—the quiet carpenter who built the first sleeping platform—collapses near the eastern fire circle.

Blood runs thin from his ears.

He never regains consciousness.

Parker goes down clutching her ribs, breath tearing through her chest in ragged gasps. Her bones hold. Her lungs do not.

She lives—

but badly broken.

Rowan does not hesitate.

He lifts Isorae fully into his arms and moves—not toward shelter or firelight—but into the deepest earth-shadow of the hollow, where the land's resonance runs thickest and stone still remembers older bones of the world.

He drops to his knees with her and presses his forehead to hers.

"Stay with me," he growls.

"Stay in your bones. Don't let them pull you out."

Her glow spasms beneath her skin—bright, uneven, wrong—rippling like something trying to tear its way back through her marrow.

"They cut the bridge," she gasps.

"They are cutting through me to get to you."

The realization freezes his blood.

They are no longer trying to capture Isorae.

They are using her to wound Rowan.

The valley roars—not with sound, but with structure.

Roots surge upward, ripping through buried listening arrays hidden deep beneath the soil like bone breaking through flesh. Mist detonates outward in invisible pressure waves that knock drones from high sky corridors miles away. Stone fault lines flare in luminous seams across the land's spine.

But the damage is done.

Blood has been drawn.

The valley has been proven vulnerable.

Far beyond the ridges, ARIS records the moment:

`LETHAL ENVIRONMENTAL DEGRADATION CONFIRMED`

`NON-LETHAL RESONANCE INTERACTION: PRIMARY ANOMALY`

`PAIR-BOND COHERENCE: VULNERABLE TO CUT-VECTOR STRATEGY`

Rowan cradles Isorae in shaking arms, his eyes burning.

"You do not get to touch her," he snarls into the dark.

"You do not get to test what I become."

Isorae clings to him, breath ragged.

"They will do it again."

And this time, they will not be testing.

They will be hunting.

Dawn arrives without ceremony.

No bells ring.

No words are offered to the sky.

The valley will not permit tools near Eli's body.

When they carry him to the eastern rise—wrapped in a quilt sewn from borrowed cloth and old coats—the earth opens for him on its own.

Stone loosens.

Roots lift and curl back.

Soil folds inward like hands making space.

It is not a grave.

It is a receiving.

No one speaks.

Not because there is nothing to say—

but because the land is already listening, and no human voice feels large enough to answer that.

Isorae kneels at the edge of the opening, trembling.

Her shimmer is thin now—moonlight stretched too far, light that remembers how to be whole but cannot hold itself steady. Her breath stutters as if her ribs are unsure whether they will rise again.

Rowan stands behind her, one hand firm on her shoulder, his jaw carved from stone.

"They cut through me," she sobs.

"To hurt the valley."

"They cut through you," Rowan says low,

"to learn me."

The earth seals itself around Eli.

Roots knit closed.

Moss creeps back into place before anyone has turned away.

By midday, the first truth reveals itself.

Erin's scanners begin to distort violently when Isorae steps within ten meters of them. Readings spike, spiral, collapse into incoherent noise. Graphs fracture into meaningless geometry.

"She's not just resonating anymore," Erin breathes.

"She's broadcasting."

Not outward.

Not wide-band.

Directly into ARIS's listening lattice.

They have tuned to her.

Now she is bleeding signal.

Parker lies beneath a cedar lean-to, ribs cracked, breath shallow but stable. Three others show internal bruising. A child seizes until Isorae moves farther away, the valley tightening helplessly around the injury.

The land tries to buffer.

But its skin has been cut.

That afternoon, Isorae finally says what everyone has been circling.

"If I leave," she says calmly,

"they will stop using the cut."

Rowan stares toward the place where Eli fell, where moss has already begun to grow over blood-dark soil.

"They'll still come," he says quietly.

"They'll just stop using you as the blade."

"But no one else will die."

He turns.

His eyes are no longer only human.

"No," he says with feral gravity that silences the hollow.

"You are not a sacrifice.

You are not an instrument.

You are not what they take to make the world quiet again."

She presses her palm to his chest.

"I would give myself for you."

His voice drops, raw.

"I would break worlds before I let you be currency."

The valley hums low—a warning growl beneath stone.

Erin whispers, "They're mapping secondary response."

And the land leans—

not in shelter now,

but in readiness.

Because ARIS is no longer hunting anomalies.

They are studying what happens when the Bridge remembers what it was built to be. And the world has crossed a line it cannot uncross.

31
WHAT IS NOT FOR TAKING

They do not argue in front of the others. Rowan waits until night folds the valley into shadow — until fires burn low and breath goes quiet and even the wounded finally slip into fragile sleep. Until the hollow is no longer listening outward…

But inward.

Then he takes Isorae's hand.

Not gently. Not roughly. Certainly.

He walks her to the stream. Water murmurs over stone. Fireflies drift in pale arcs through reeds and hanging fern. The moon hangs thin above the canopy, light filtering down in fractured silver threads that catch faintly in her hair.

"You are not leaving," he says. Not as a request. Not as a plea. A boundary.

Isorae turns to him. Her shimmer is thin tonight — stretched — but her eyes are clear, steady, luminous in a way that remembers worlds that never learned how to be quiet.

"If I go," she says softly, "the cut will close."

His jaw tightens until it aches. "And if you go, they learn that taking you works."

She steps closer, hands curling into the fabric of his shirt. "They are already using me."

"Then we make it stop," he growls — low, dangerous, alive. "We don't hand them the knife."

Her breath trembles. "Rowan—"

His hand lifts — not to silence her…

But to anchor her.

The valley hums faintly in answer.

"No," he says.

And the word lands like law.

"No to your disappearance. No to your sacrifice. No to a world that thinks it gets to balance itself with your blood."

His voice drops — feral, vibrating with old memory carved into bone.

"You are not a solution. You are not a shield. You are not the price of quiet."

She stares at him, breath unsteady, feeling something vast and ancient shifting beneath his skin.

"And what if they take me anyway?" she whispers.

His eyes darken. Not with fear. With certainty.

"Then they will learn," he says softly, "what it means to cut something that was never meant to bleed."

"You are waking too fast," she whispers.

He leans his forehead to hers. "Not fast," he murmurs. "Right on time."

For a moment, neither of them moves.

The valley holds its breath with them.

Her thumbs curl lightly into the fabric of his shirt — not to pull, not to plead — just to feel where his heart still answers her.

"You're here," she says softly. "Not as a wall. As yourself."

His jaw tightens — something in his chest loosening at the same time.

"You don't have to be brave with me," he murmurs. "You don't have to carry the world in your ribs."

Her eyes lift.

And she steps closer — slow, deliberate — closing the last quiet space between them.

Her breath brushes his mouth.

For a heartbeat — he stills.

Not because he doesn't want her.

Because he does.

His hands slide to her arms — steadying, protective — and he pulls back just enough to look at her.

"You're still hurting," he says quietly. "Your body's been opened. Mapped. Pulled through frequencies it wasn't meant to carry."

His thumbs press warm, grounding arcs into her forearms.

"I won't take what your bones are still trying to hold together."

Her lashes flutter.

"You are not taking," she whispers. "I am choosing."

He doesn't move.

Her forehead settles beneath his jaw. Her breath warms his throat — deliberate, unafraid — like she is choosing him with her body.

"Do not say no to me like I am fragile," she murmurs. "Say no to the world."

Something tightens hard and sharp in Rowan's chest. He draws a slow breath through his nose, jaw flexing as if he is physically holding back something that wants to surge forward and claim.

"You don't have to be strong right now," he says low. "You don't have to be anything."

Her hands slide up his ribs — slow, anchoring, unafraid — fingertips spreading as if she is mapping him by touch alone, memorizing the shape of what keeps her standing.

"I only want to be here," she whispers. "With you."

The hollow leans inward.

Rowan's hands rise — careful, reverent — but the restraint in them trembles. He cups her back, drawing her fully into the shelter of his body, his arms closing around her like something instinctive and ancient, like a boundary forming itself around what it refuses to lose.

She fits there perfectly.

Not delicately.

Belonging.

His mouth finds her hair first — not a kiss, but a slow breath, his nose brushing her crown like he is breathing her into his bones. Then her temple. Then the delicate hinge of her jaw. Each touch unhurried. Intent. As if he is teaching his body how to hold her without losing himself to it.

But his restraint is already shaking.

When their mouths finally meet, it is not light. It is slow and deep and claiming — a press that steals breath, that pulls her closer until there is no safe space left between them. His hand tightens at her back — not to take, but to keep — thumb pressing once, firm and grounding, like he is reminding both of them where she belongs.

Her breath breaks into him.

She answers the kiss without hesitation, rising into it, her hands sliding into his shirt, fingers curling there as if she is holding the only solid thing left in the world.

Rowan's forehead drops to hers. Their noses brush. Their breath tangles, warm and uneven, hovering in the narrow space where neither of them is pretending this is still safe.

Then he moves.

Slow. Certain.

He guides her backward until her calves brush moss and root, until her balance tilts into his hands — and then he lowers her, careful and reverent, as if setting something sacred down where the earth itself will protect it.

He follows her down.

His body settles over hers, braced on one arm, the other sliding beneath her shoulders, drawing her into the hollow of his chest. The ground is cool beneath her back. He is heat above her — solid, sheltering, unyielding.

Her breath stutters at the weight of him.

His mouth finds hers again — slower now — heavier — and this time his hand slides along her side, fingers slipping beneath her clothes, drawing himself into her. Warm skin meets warm skin. His palm flattens at her waist, feeling her breathe, feeling the small, unguarded rise of her ribs beneath his hand.

She arches faintly into the contact — not offering, not asking — trusting.

Firelight spills across her throat, her collarbone, the pale shimmer folded beneath her skin. Rowan's breath drags rough across her jaw as his hand moves lower, slow and reverent, fingertips tracing her hip, pulling her more into him.

"You're here," he murmurs. "You're with me."

Her hands slide, finding the heat of his back, her palms pressing flat against his skin like she needs to feel something unmovable. His breath stutters — not in surprise, but in the low, feral ache of restraint.

He shifts again — just enough — drawing her closer, her cheek settling against his bare chest, her breath warming the place where his heart beats hardest.

There is no space left between them.

Only heat. Only breath. Only the quiet thunder of two pulses answering each other through skin.

Rowan lowers his forehead to hers, his voice rough, anchored.

"You don't have to go anywhere," he murmurs. "You're staying."

"Yes," she moans.

Her fingers curl gently into his back — gripping — anchoring.

The valley leans inward.

Firelight lowers.

And Rowan remains over her — arms firm, body steady — forming a living boundary around her warmth, her breath, her fragile presence in the world.

For a long moment, nothing exists beyond the slow slide of breath against skin and the quiet thunder of two heartbeats learning how to share a rhythm.

Isorae's fingers loosen, not releasing him — but trusting him — her body yielding into the cradle of his like something finally allowed to stop guarding the door to itself.

Rowan lowers his forehead to hers, eyes closed, breathing her in as if committing the fact of her existence to memory. As if he already knows the world is the kind of place that makes you remember people in advance.

The valley eases.

Firelight settles.

The night completes its slow, protective curve around them.

For a breath — a real one — the world is whole.

And far beyond the ridges, ARIS recalibrates. They just do not realize yet—

They have already crossed the last safe line.

32

THE KEEPING

The valley does not interrupt them. No bird cries. No branch snaps. Even the stream lowers its voice, as if the world itself is listening to the way they are learning how to remain.

Rowan lies curved around Isorae in the moss and woven roots, one arm beneath her shoulders, the other resting heavy and warm over her waist. Her forehead is tucked beneath his jaw, her breath still uneven against his collarbone, her shimmer faint and folded inward beneath her skin like starlight choosing not to be seen. They are still. His hand presses once at her back—steady, grounding—as if confirming that her weight is real, that her bones are still inside the world.

"You okay?" he murmurs into her hair.

Isorae exhales carefully. "I'm here."

His fingers tighten once—confirmation, not possession. "Good," he says quietly. "Stay."

They remain like that for a while—breath easing, heat settling, the world remembering how to hold their combined shape.

Eventually Rowan shifts first, slow and careful, brushing his thumb once along her spine before easing his arm from beneath her shoulders. Isorae moves with him, unhurried, her hand finding his as they sit up together in the moss. Neither of them feels the need to fill the quiet.

Rowan takes her hand and leads her back through the hollow. The path curves around them like a body remembering its shape. Roots arch where their feet need them. Fern fronds part without tearing. The land does not guide. It makes space.

Inside the deepest shelter, Rowan spreads the bedding carefully, aware of her ribs, of the quiet ache still living beneath her glow. He waits until her breathing steadies before lying beside her, curving around her again—one arm beneath her shoulders, the other over her waist—anchoring without trapping.

They fit.

Geometrically.

Rowan presses a slow kiss into her hair. "You're staying," he murmurs.

The word settles.

For a few minutes, the hollow holds. Then—subtly—it tightens. Roots draw deeper. Fire lowers. Mist thickens, no longer sheltering, but bracing.

Rowan's eyes open. He does not move, but his body goes still in the way predators do when they sense a line being crossed. Isorae's shimmer skips faintly beneath her skin. She feels it too.

Rowan presses his mouth to her hair again—not tender. Steady.

Outside, the valley holds its breath. Not calm. Braced. Teeth bared. Waiting.

And far beyond the hollow—far beyond the canopy—something cold and patient has already begun adjusting its aim.

The valley does not take them.

Not tonight.

But it no longer sleeps the way it used to.

It listens with its jaw clenched.

33

THE COUNCIL THAT FORMS IN TEETH AND BONE

The valley no longer felt like home. It felt like a body learning how to brace.

After Eli was buried, the hollow held a different kind of quiet — less peace, more pressure. Fires were kept low. Paths were watched twice. People moved as if they were afraid of waking something just under the soil.

Rowan moved like he wanted it to wake.

He hadn't slept — not truly — not since the cut. He had closed his eyes, yes: when Isorae's breathing finally steadied, when Parker's moans softened into exhausted silence, when the worst of the panic drained from the faces around the fires. But his mind had stayed up on the ridge.

And something inside him had stood there too.

Teeth bared.

Waiting for the world to make its next mistake.

It did not take long.

By the second night after the funeral, Isorae's shimmer dimmed at the edges like a lamp being starved of power. Not because she was weakening — because she was forcing it down. Containing it. Holding herself inside her own skin while ARIS listened to her bones like they were a radio.

Rowan watched her the way you watched a fire you were afraid might spread — not because he feared her, but because he feared what it would cost her to keep herself small.

He found her by the stream, hands submerged in cold water, eyes fixed on nothing.

"You're doing it again," he said quietly.

"Doing what?" she asked.

"Making yourself quieter so everyone else can breathe."

Her jaw tightened. "They're hurting people."

"They're hurting you," Rowan corrected — and the words came out like a warning.

This time she looked at him. Her eyes were bright in the dark — luminous, too steady — the way a person looked right before they made a decision that would break them.

"If they can't hear me," she whispered, "they can't cut through me."

Rowan stepped closer until his shadow fell over the water.

"They'll still cut," he said. "They'll just pick a different angle."

"And if I'm not here—"

"No."

The word left him with a gravity that made the reeds tremble.

Isorae flinched — not at him, but at the way the land moved with his voice now.

Rowan swallowed the heat in his throat and forced his tone lower.

"Listen to me," he said. "They want you to believe the only way to protect people is to hand yourself over."

"Rowan—"

He cupped the back of her neck — not force, not restraint — anchor. Her pulse jumped beneath his palm like she had been waiting for permission to stop holding herself alone.

"You don't get to become their solution," he said firmly. "Not in my world. Not in yours."

Her eyes closed for a heartbeat.

When they opened again, her voice was quiet — but sharp.

"Then we need structure," she said. "Not only feral devotion."

Rowan's mouth twitched — almost a smile.

"Yeah," he said. "We do."

That was when he stopped trying to carry the whole valley on his back like a martyr —

and started building a spine.

Before dawn, Rowan called everyone who could stand to the central fire circle.

Not the children.

Not the most fragile.

Parker remained beneath the cedar lean-to, ribs bound, breath shallow but stable. Evan stayed with her — quiet, steady — hands moving in small, constant adjustments that kept wounded bodies from breaking.

The rest came in silence.

Mist lay low over the hollow. Firelight breathed softly against stone. The valley felt drawn inward — listening.

Rowan stood with Bramble at his heel and Isorae at his side.

He did not look like a man asking for help.

He looked like a man calling the world out.

He turned first to Erin — direct, unsoftened.

"You," Rowan said. "You're in charge of what they can't see."

Erin met his gaze without flinching.

"I'm in charge of intelligence."

Rowan nodded once.

"Yeah. That."

He turned to Silas.

"You're perimeter."

Silas's jaw tightened.

"Already was."

"Now it's official."

Then Dax.

"You're shadows."

Dax's mouth curved thin.

"Finally."

Rowan lifted his chin slightly — not toward anyone in the ring, but toward the cedar lean-to beyond the firelight.

"Evan," he said.

"You hold triage and stabilization."

The words were not loud.

They were not ceremonial.

They were binding.

He continued without pause.

"Ryan tracks patterns — dreams, shifts, omens. Anything that moves before it moves."

The valley hummed low beneath their feet — not in agreement, but in recognition.

Rowan let his gaze move slowly around the circle.

"This isn't a warning," he said.

"It's a line."

No one spoke.

Firelight breathed.

Stone leaned.

The hollow listened.

Rowan lifted his voice.

"ARIS can hit us without stepping inside the valley. They can isolate Isorae. And if we keep acting like a frightened camp, they'll keep treating us like one."

He looked down at the soil at his boots.

"No one is leaving her to die alone so the rest of us can pretend that's mercy."

His gaze lifted again.

"This valley is a threshold. And thresholds don't stay quiet. They either become gates — or graves."

The silence thickened.

Decision formed inside it.

Plans followed.

Lookouts.

Rotations.

Counter-arrays.

Dampening fields.

The first bones of resistance.

When the fire circle finally thinned and people began drifting back to their shelters, Erin intercepted Rowan before he could follow Isorae.

"Wait," she said, low and urgent, catching his sleeve.

Rowan turned — already tense.

"What?"

Erin didn't waste breath. "I need a controlled harmonic read."

His jaw locked. "No."

"Rowan—"

"No." He didn't raise his voice, but the word hit with iron. "You're not pointing instruments at her like she's a fault line."

Erin swallowed. "She already is one."

Rowan stepped forward, just enough to remind her whose body stood between Isorae and the world.

"You do not touch her," he said. "Not for data. Not for theory. Not for comfort."

Erin exhaled slowly, steadying herself.

"Then let me show you something," she said. "Without her."

She lifted her tablet and turned the display toward him.

"Every time you get within a meter of her, the background field compresses. Not spikes — compresses. It's subtle. It looks like static until you isolate it."

Rowan frowned.

"That's not her," he said.

"No," Erin replied quietly. "It's you."

He stared at the display.

"I need one clean read," she said. "No arrays. No pulses. No provocation. Just you standing where you already stand."

Rowan hesitated — then glanced back toward Isorae.

She had stopped a few paces away, watching them.

"Your call," he said to her.

She studied Erin, then Rowan — and nodded once.

"Only standing," she said. "No more."

They moved beneath the limestone overhang where the valley's hum ran thick and slow. Erin set her equipment down carefully, as if handling something that might bite.

"Just… stand," Erin said.

Isorae stepped into the shallow stone bowl first.

Rowan moved with her, positioning himself half a breath behind, his shoulder brushing hers.

The moment his hand slid lightly to her waist —

Erin's screen flared.

A sharp harmonic spike cut across the display so clean it looked like a voice trying to speak.

Erin sucked in a breath. "There it is."

Rowan stiffened. "What?"

She stared at the readout. "You're not shielding her," she said slowly. "You're shaping her."

The valley shifted — uneasy.

"They're not trying to take me," Isorae whispered, her breath going shallow. "They're trying to open him."

Erin looked up at Rowan. "You're the amplifier."

Something old and territorial slid into place behind his ribs.

Plans reshaped instantly.

Counter-frequencies. Dampening fields. Containment pockets. Days. Maybe a week.

Then —

The air changed.

It was not sound.

Not pressure.

It was absence.

Every leaf stilled.

Every bird cut its song in half.

Erin's displays spiked and shrieked.

Silas's coded whistle ripped through the trees.

Dax burst from the ridge line, breath ragged.

"We've got lock," he said. "Thin band. Directional."

Rowan was already moving — drawing Isorae with him — but she turned, eyes wide.

"They found the spike," she whispered.

Erin's screen flashed red.

A thin, surgical lock line cut across the display.

Rowan felt it in his teeth.

"Inside," he growled.

The valley shuddered — not from fear.

From rage.

And far beyond the ridges, ARIS stopped probing…

…and began the first true reach.

34

THE FIRST REAL REACH

The valley did not warn them with birds this time. It warned them with silence.

Every living thing went still at once — the kind of still that didn't feel like calm weather or gentle dawn. It felt like the world had pressed two fingers to its own throat and held.

Rowan felt it in his teeth first.

A tight, fine vibration — too thin to be a pulse, too precise to be chance — threaded through the air and sank straight into bone. Isorae's breath broke beside him. Erin's equipment screamed, red bars climbing as the lines sharpened. The display didn't look like noise anymore. It looked like a hand drawing a blade.

Silas's whistle cut from the rim — short, coded, sharp.

Dax was already at the tree line like he'd been poured out of shadow. "Ridge. Now," he said, and for once his grin was gone.

Rowan's hand snapped around Isorae's wrist. Not hard. Not gentle. Certain.

"Inside," he growled.

Isorae didn't move right away. Her eyes lifted toward the canopy — not searching for lights, not scanning for drones. Listening for the shape of what was coming.

"They're not scanning," she whispered. "They're… calling."

Rowan's jaw tightened. "Then we don't answer."

He pulled her with him.

The valley moved. Not like an earthquake. Like a decision.

Mist surged up from the stream in a thick, lightless curtain. Ferns along the hollow's rim leaned inward, fronds lifting as if they were hands closing a door. The limestone ribs that framed the entrance seemed to deepen, shadows thickening until the path looked narrower than it had thirty seconds ago.

People looked up from fires and shelters as the air changed. A child began to cry. Someone swore under their breath. Evan was already moving — voice low, steadying bodies, guiding the shaken toward the inner shelters without igniting panic.

"Everyone in," he said calmly. "Low voices. Stay together."

Erin snapped her case shut and shouldered it, mouth tight. "It's directional," she said as they moved. "Not a wide hit. They're aiming at—"

Isorae flinched so hard it looked like something had hooked her from the inside.

Rowan caught her instantly, arm locking around her waist, pulling her hard against him as she sucked in a breath that scraped.

"They found the harmonic seam," she gasped. "Not in me. In us."

Rowan's eyes went black.

He did not slow. He did not hesitate. He drove them deeper into the valley — into the thickest resonance, into stone-shadow and root — and the land followed his intent like it had been waiting for orders all its life.

At the ridge, Silas stood half-crouched behind a fallen cedar, body angled toward the west. He didn't look frantic. He looked like a man with his finger already on the trigger.

Dax dropped beside him, peered through a gap in the brush, then looked back at Rowan. "They aren't sending bodies," he said. "Not yet."

Rowan stepped up beside them, keeping Isorae behind him, hand still anchored at her wrist as if letting go would be permission for the world to steal her.

"What is it?" Rowan asked.

Silas didn't take his eyes off the horizon. "Light behavior," he said quietly. "Wrong refraction. Like heat shimmer, but cold. Like they're projecting something through the air."

Erin climbed up behind Rowan and lifted one of her handheld readers. The screen jittered and spat red.

"Oh," she breathed. "They're not just touching the edge now. They're inserting a field."

Isorae pressed her palm to her sternum as if trying to hold her ribs together. "It's a reach," she whispered. "A hand without a body."

Rowan's fingers flexed around her wrist. "Then I break the fingers."

Erin shot him a look. "If you push back blindly, they'll learn faster."

Rowan's voice was low and ugly. "They already learned the spike. They already learned the bond. They already killed Eli."

Erin didn't flinch. She nodded once — not in agreement, in understanding — and did what she always did. Turned rage into strategy.

"We need to force their reach to fail," she said. "Not just resist it. Make it think the valley is empty or unstable. If they can't get clean data, they have to come closer."

Rowan's gaze didn't move from the treeline where the air looked too smooth, too still.

"Good," he said. "Let them come closer."

The first real reach didn't arrive like a pulse.

It arrived like pressure choosing a direction.

A thin, invisible line of resonance slid across the western canopy — so subtle most of the valley wouldn't have noticed if they weren't already braced — but Isorae gasped like it had cut her.

Her knees buckled.

Rowan caught her before she fell, arm snapping around her ribcage, pulling her tight to his chest. Her shimmer spasmed — bright in one place, dim in another — uneven, strained, wrong.

"Rowan," she choked. "It's threading through the land. It's looking for the part of you that answers."

His breath went deep. Not calming. Anchoring.

He pressed his forehead to Isorae's temple, voice a low snarl meant only for her. "Hold your glow inside your skin. Stay in your bones. Not for them. For you. I'm right here."

Her fingers clawed into his shirt. "I can't— it's—"

"You can," Rowan said, rough with something older than this life. "Because you're not alone in your body anymore."

Her breath hitched.

Erin's scanner shrieked. "It's locking!" she snapped. "It's trying to establish a stable bridge point — Rowan, it's using you as the anchor!"

Silas turned sharply. "Then move him."

Rowan didn't move.

He stood.

His stance widened, shoulders squaring like a door being barred from the inside. The earth beneath his boots firmed — subtle but immediate — roots pressing up into soil like the valley was bracing his legs.

Isorae's eyes fluttered, pain and recognition braided tight. "You always stand like this," she whispered through clenched breath. "You always become the wall—"

Rowan's voice dropped into something feral. "Yeah. And walls don't ask permission."

He lifted his free hand and pressed his palm flat to the ground.

The soil was warm. Alive-warm.

The valley answered instantly — not with language, but with pulse.

A deep, slow thrum rolled up his arm and settled behind his sternum like a second heart.

Rowan inhaled. Not air. Land. Memory.

Then he pushed.

Not outward like an explosion.

Downward like a spike.

Mist surged harder, thickening into a dense, light-eating veil across the ridge. Ferns snapped inward, curling like ribs around the hollow's mouth. The stream's surface trembled, then erupted in a low fog bloom that poured through the basin like the breath of something enormous.

The reach line wavered.

Erin's screen flickered, scrambled —

and for a single, exquisite second, the red lock line broke.

Erin stared. "You disrupted it."

Rowan's eyes stayed fixed on the treeline.

"Do it again," Erin said, voice sharp with adrenaline. "Harder. Don't let it stabilize."

Isorae made a small, strangled sound. Rowan felt it like a knife.

He turned his head just enough to see her face — pale, luminous, jaw tight, eyes wet but steady.

"How close are you to breaking?" he asked.

"Not breaking," she whispered shakily. "Bending."

Rowan's voice went quiet. "No."

He pulled her back a step, shifting so she was behind him again, fully shielded. Then he addressed the valley like a thing he belonged to.

"Lie," he whispered to the land.

The ground pulsed. The mist thickened. The canopy's light bent into wrong angles — sunlight behaving like it had forgotten how to travel straight. The reach line searched, moving left, right, down, as if the world beyond the ridge had gone blind.

Dax let out a low, impressed breath. "Okay," he murmured. "That was terrifying."

Silas's gaze sharpened. "They'll compensate."

Erin nodded. "They'll narrow again."

Rowan bared his teeth. "Let them."

The second reach came five minutes later.

Sharper. Lower. More personal.

It wasn't a wave.

It was a needle.

It slid through the mist and drove straight for Isorae.

She screamed.

Soundless.

Her glow flared like something being ripped open. Rowan's vision flashed white. He felt it — the frequency trying to hook into her bones and use her as a tuning fork to find him.

Rowan moved without thought.

He lunged, body covering hers, arms wrapping around her fully, pressing her head into the hollow of his neck as if he could shelter her inside his ribs.

"Stop," he snarled — not to Erin, not to the people.

To the thing reaching.

The valley answered with rage.

Stone near the ridge cracked. Not violently. Deliberately. A seam split under moss and lifted like a blade of limestone pushing up through soil. Roots followed, thick and knotted, surfacing in tight coils that formed an uneven barrier along the western approach — natural, jagged, impossible to cross cleanly without leaving evidence.

Erin's equipment screamed louder.

Then, suddenly, the reach line snapped sideways, as if something had yanked it back by force.

Silas's head tilted. "Did you feel that?"

Rowan did.

A recoil. Like the hand had touched a hot stove.

Isorae's breath stuttered against his throat. "The land… bit it."

Rowan's hand tightened at the back of her neck, thumb pressing like a vow. "Good."

He lifted his head and looked into the trees like he was looking at a human enemy.

His voice went low, steady, terrifying.

"You don't get to touch her," he said. "You don't get to practice on her. You don't get to learn what she is by hurting her."

The mist held. The ridge stayed warped. The valley breathed like a predator.

Erin's readout flickered, then stabilized into something new. She stared — then looked up at Rowan like she'd just seen the first blueprint of how to win.

"It reacted to you," she said. "Not to her. The valley's defense response keyed off your push."

Rowan didn't take his eyes off the trees. "Yeah."

Dax shifted, eyes narrowing. "So if they keep reaching—"

"Then we turn the valley into teeth," Rowan cut in.

When the reach finally withdrew, the valley didn't relax.

It held.

Like it was waiting for the next strike.

Rowan carried Isorae down into the hollow, ignoring the eyes on them, the whispered fear, the awe. He moved like a man whose only religion was keeping one person alive.

Inside the deepest shelter — stone-backed, root-roofed — he set her down and knelt in front of her, hands bracketing her knees.

Isorae's breath was ragged. Her shimmer trembled at the edges, still braced for another needle.

Rowan's voice softened, just enough to be intimate. "Look at me."

Isorae lifted her eyes.

He cupped her face with both hands.

Not gentle like porcelain.

Gentle like something sacred.

"They are not taking you," he murmured. "Not while I can still stand."

Her lips trembled. "They're going to try harder."

Rowan's eyes darkened. "Let them."

He leaned in and kissed her — not sweet, not tentative. A kiss that tasted like claim, not of her body, but of the vow already living between their bones.

When he pulled back, his voice was a quiet promise with teeth.

"Next time they reach," he said, "we reach back."

Isorae swallowed. "You're becoming dangerous."

Rowan's mouth curved faintly — humorless, beautiful in its brutality.

"I've been dangerous," he murmured. "I've just been polite."

Outside, the valley shifted again — stones settling, mist thickening, the rim narrowing as if the land itself had decided it was done being accessible.

Erin's voice carried from the fire circle, brisk and urgent. "I need copper. Coils. Anything that can hold a field. Dax — find me scrap. Silas — keep eyes on the ridge. Ryan — get anyone who's dreaming and write it down. Evan — keep the wounded central. No one alone."

The village moved.

Not panicked.

Organized.

A spine, finally forming.

Rowan stood slowly, jaw set. He looked down at Isorae one last time.

His gaze didn't say *I'll try*.

It said *they're dead if they make me choose*.

"I'm going to the ridge," he said.

Isorae caught his wrist. Her fingers trembled.

"Rowan."

He stilled.

"Come back," she whispered. Not as a vow. As a request.

Something in his face shifted — softness cutting through the feral like a hand pressed to a scar.

He leaned down and touched his forehead to hers. "I always come back to you," he murmured.

Then he stood and walked out into the mist like the valley had just crowned him with its oldest hunger.

And far beyond the ridges, ARIS noted the failure.

Adjusted.

And began preparing a reach that would not be only a hand — but a grasp.

35

THE SHAPE OF A SIEGE

The valley wakes before dawn. A pressure settles across the hollow like a lid lowering over a boiling pot — not crushing, not loud, but absolute. The kind of pressure that shortens breath before the mind knows why. The kind that tells bone something irreversible has just begun.

Rowan is already on his feet.

He didn't sleep. He hadn't planned to.

Behind him, in the deep shelter, Isorae stirs — her glow faint but steady, her breathing soft. Rowan glances back once, memorizing the shape of her in the half-dark like his ribs need to remember her in case the world tries to take the memory next.

Then he steps out.

The mist does not drift this morning.

It clings.

It lies in low bands along the ground, unmoving, swallowing sound like the valley itself has decided to hold its breath. Rowan moves through it toward the ridge, every muscle tuned, every step careful, his body reading the density of the air like a language.

Silas is waiting near the western rise, half-crouched in fern shadow.

Dax is there too — silent, eyes sharp, posture loose in the way a blade is loose in its sheath. He doesn't grin. He doesn't joke. His hand is already near his knife like humor has been revoked.

They don't speak.

They don't need to.

The forest ahead of them looks wrong.

Not damaged.

Prepared.

The canopy bends into unnaturally clean corridors. Branches that should have snarled lie subtly parted. Ferns are pressed flat into thin lanes like something heavy passed through without leaving tracks — a suggestion of approach without the courtesy of footprints.

Rowan's gaze tracks the lanes without blinking.

Erin's voice cuts through the mist from behind them, quiet but sharp. "They've seeded approach vectors."

Rowan doesn't look away. "Meaning…"

"Meaning they didn't come yet," she replies. "They set the table."

The valley shudders — not in fear.

In warning.

Rowan feels it under his boots, a low structural tension in the soil like muscle tightening beneath skin. The air holds its shape too rigidly. Even the stream sounds lower, as if water is trying not to give away its own movement.

Then the sky changes.

Not color.

Behavior.

Sunlight fractures into sharp bands that slide too slowly through the canopy, as if passing through a lens that shouldn't exist. The light doesn't fall. It measures. Shadows hesitate before they land, then settle in angles that make Rowan's teeth ache.

Dax exhales softly. "They're bending air."

Silas's jaw tightens. "They're anchoring."

Rowan's chest goes cold as the truth slots into place with a brutal simplicity.

"They're building," he says.

Isorae steps up beside him.

Wrapped in Rowan's jacket, glow held tight beneath her skin, she moves with careful steadiness — not weak, not fragile, but listening. Her hand finds his the way it always does, fingers sliding into his like they belong there—because they do.

"They're not reaching anymore," she says quietly. "They're laying foundations."

The valley tightens around them — fern leaning inward, stone shifting under soil like ribs bracing.

Erin's scanner gives a sharp, terrified chirp.

"Oh," she breathes.

Rowan finally turns his head. "What."

Erin's eyes flick between the readout and the treeline, as if she doesn't want to say it aloud in case the air remembers. "They've dropped remote field pylons," she says. "Outside our range. Invisible spectrum. They're setting up a resonance corridor."

Silas curses under his breath.

Dax goes very still.

Isorae's breath shudders. "They're building a road to me."

Rowan's fingers curl around hers, slow and deliberate. "No," he murmurs.

His gaze hardens, something older than anger turning behind his eyes.

"They're building a road through you."

A vibration threads beneath their boots — not a pulse, not a test. A structural hum. The valley recognizes construction.

And it does not like it.

Roots surface along the ridge in subtle arcs, not bursting, not frantic — bracing. Stone creaks faintly. Mist thickens. The air grows heavy with the sensation of land holding itself in place against an external hand.

Rowan lifts his chin, and when he speaks, his voice carries farther than it should, as if the valley has decided to use his mouth.

"All hands," he says, quiet — but absolute. "Inner ring first."

He doesn't bark orders like a man playing commander.

He speaks like a threshold naming its rules.

"No one near the west slope. Fire circles extinguished. No open lines of sight."

The valley answers him with motion.

Not mystical.

Practical.

Bodies move.

Evan is already guiding families inward, voice low and steady, hands gentle on shoulders. Ryan pulls packs and tools into tighter clusters, eyes scanning like he's watching for a dream to become a shadow. Erin drops to her knees and starts tearing copper coils from broken gear with the efficient violence of someone who has decided survival is a craft.

Silas and Dax melt outward along the ridge, two dark points in the mist, teeth disguised as men.

The hollow becomes a body preparing for surgery.

Isorae grips Rowan's arm, her fingers tight around his sleeve. "They're trying to make the land behave like a corridor instead of a shield," her voice going still. "They want to flatten its will."

Rowan's jaw locks. "They flatten nothing."

His voice is low, steady, dangerous — and it doesn't sound like bravado.

It sounds like jurisdiction.

Then something new arrives.

Not a drone.

Not a walker.

A thin black spire lowers silently into the western tree line, hovering inches above the soil. Its surface drinks light. Mist bends away from it in smooth, surgical arcs, refusing to touch it like the air has been instructed to keep a distance.

Erin's breath catches. "That's a stabilizer," she says. "They're anchoring the corridor."

The valley hums — angry now. Stone fractures subtly beneath the spire's invisible field. Roots recoil like something has pressed a hot blade into the earth. Birds vanish.

Isorae makes a broken sound in her throat. "They're pinning the land," she said thinly

Rowan steps forward.

Silas's hand shoots out and catches his sleeve for a heartbeat. "Rowan—"

Rowan doesn't stop.

He steps out of the ridge shadow and into the warped light like a man walking into a storm that owes him money. Mist slides off his shoulders. The air around him feels tighter, resistant, as if something is already trying to decide whether he's allowed to stand there.

Rowan lifts his hand.

The valley responds. Not with a pulse, but with posture.

Stone rises an inch beneath his boots. Ferns curl inward like ribs. Mist surges, thickening until the spire's silhouette blurs at the edges.

Rowan presses his palm to the air — not the ground.

And the air pushes back.

The stabilizer shudders.

Its light behavior fractures.

Erin's scanner screams, the readout spiking so hard it stutters.

Rowan's breath deepens, slow and anchored, pulling something up from soil and bone like a second spine slotting into place.

His voice drops into something the valley recognizes as command.

"Leave."

The spire vibrates violently. Its surface ripples. For a moment it looks like it might hold, like it might argue.

Then it begins to retract.

Slowly.

Reluctantly.

Not fleeing — correcting.

It rises back into the canopy and vanishes like something that has just learned fear.

Silence falls.

Not the earlier silence — not the warning-throat silence.

A stunned, disbelieving hush that lands on the ridge like ash.

Dax lets out a low whistle. "Well," he murmurs, "that was new."

Isorae stares at Rowan like she's watching a prophecy wake up.

"They just learned," she murmured, "that you are not part of the terrain."

Rowan doesn't turn. His gaze stays fixed on the western tree line, where the light still behaves wrong, where the air still tastes like intrusion.

"They learned," he says softly, "that this valley has teeth."

And far beyond the ridges, ARIS stops building corridors. And begins drafting invasion parameters.

36

THE ONES WHO GIVE ORDERS

The sky does not announce them. The land does.

Just before noon, every fern along the western rim curls inward at the same moment—not in fear, not in wind, but in a unified tightening, as if a single muscle has flexed across a vast, unseen body.

Rowan feels it beneath his sternum, a low pressure that pulls his posture straighter without asking permission.

Silas feels it in his teeth, a faint metallic ache that warns before thought arrives.

Isorae inhales sharply, her hand drifting unconsciously to her ribs as if something cold has brushed the inside of her bones.

"They're not sending machines," she rasps. "They're sending authority."

Erin's scanners begin to tick—not frantic, not erratic, but measured. Deliberate. Too precise to be background noise. She studies the display, her frown deepening.

"Command-grade signal overlay," she mutters. "Encrypted. Human-coded. This isn't a probe. It's a summons."

Dax looks up sharply. "Human?"

"Not just," Erin says quietly. "But wearing human bandwidth."

High above the canopy, the air persuades itself into a different shape.

It does not tear. It does not scream. It simply folds, light peeling back like cloth being smoothed away, and something matte-black lowers through it with surgical grace.

No thrusters. No weapons. No sound.

Just presence.

The valley goes very still. Even the mist hesitates, thinning into pale filaments that seem reluctant to drift.

Rowan steps forward toward the ridge without thinking. Silas shifts half a step behind him, his hand already resting near his weapon. Isorae stands between them, wrapped in Rowan's jacket, her glow faint but steady, her eyes already reading the field like something older than sight.

The shuttle settles just beyond the western fern curtain—deliberately not entering the hollow.

A ramp slides open.

Three figures emerge.

They are not armored. They are not hurried. Their dark coats are cut too precisely to be casual, fabric holding its shape with a stiffness that speaks of hidden layers. Thin field-plates shimmer beneath their boots, preventing direct contact with the soil.

One of them steps forward.

A woman. Mid-forties. Pale eyes. Hair pulled into a severe knot.

Her voice carries cleanly across the hollow without being raised.

"Rowan Hale."

Not a greeting. Not a question.

A designation.

"You are interfering with a sanctioned containment recovery."

Rowan does not move.

"You are trespassing on a living valley," he replies evenly.

Her eyes flick briefly to Isorae, then return to him.

"Subject Isorae is an interdimensional anomaly," she says calmly. "Her presence destabilizes localized physical law."

"She stabilizes it," Rowan answers flatly.

A faint tightening crosses her mouth.

"You are emotionally compromised."

Silas exhales sharply through his nose.

The woman continues, unperturbed. "We are authorized to extract Subject Isorae under Multilateral Veil Accord 7-A."

Isorae steps forward.

"You are not authorized by the land," she says firmly.

The woman looks at her fully for the first time.

Something faint—very faint—passes through her eyes.

Not fear. Not anger.

Interest.

"You are more intact than expected," she murmurs.

Rowan moves instantly, placing himself in front of Isorae like instinct made flesh.

"She doesn't belong to you."

"She does not belong to you either," the woman replies coolly.

"She belongs to herself."

Silence thickens.

Then the woman lifts a hand.

The air tightens—not cutting, not attacking—but asserting. Pressure settles over the hollow like an invisible ceiling lowering by inches.

Erin's scanner shrieks once and dies.

Dax swears softly.

Isorae stiffens—not in pain, but in compression. "They're projecting jurisdiction," she whispers.

Rowan steps forward into it.

Stone rises subtly beneath his boots. Mist curls inward. Fern ribs tighten, leaves whispering faintly as if the valley itself is bracing its spine.

"You do not have jurisdiction here," he says firmly.

The woman studies him now—really studies him.

"You are not supposed to be able to resist that."

"I'm not supposed to exist the way I do," Rowan replies.

Her eyes narrow.

"This is your final warning," she says. "Withdraw Subject Isorae, or the valley will be classified as a hostile anomaly zone."

Silas bares his teeth faintly. "Try it."

The woman's mouth curves into something not quite a smile.

"We will."

The shuttle begins to rise.

Before the ramp fully closes, she adds calmly, "You are not a fortress. You are a variable."

Then the shuttle folds back into light and disappears.

The valley exhales—slow, uneasy, unsettled.

Isorae's fingers curl into Rowan's shirt. "They've declared us," she whispers, voice unsteady.

Rowan wraps his arms around her, firm and grounding.

"Then they've declared the wrong war."

And far beyond the canopy, ARIS moves from observation protocols to full-scale containment authorization.

37
THE FIRST THING HE BUILDS

Night falls heavier now.

Not darker — denser.

The valley does not simply lose light. It thickens, layering breath over breath, as if the hollow itself is preparing to hold something enormous. Mist draws closer to the ground, pooling between fern and root. The fires burn lower, closer to stone. Even sound seems reluctant to travel far.

People speak less.

They move closer.

They watch the canopy longer than they used to.

And for the first time since the broken began to arrive—

Rowan does not sit.

He stands.

At the center of the hollow, beside the old stone bowl where roots knot like exposed veins, he plants his boots into soil that remembers him. He waits until everyone feels him before he speaks.

Silas steps to his left.

Dax to his right.

Erin lingers near the firelight, equipment already open at her feet.

Isorae stands just behind Rowan, close enough that the faint glow beneath her skin threads into his silhouette like a second heartbeat.

There are thirty-eight people now.

Breathing.

Listening.

Not hiding.

Rowan lifts his head.

"They've stopped pretending."

His voice does not rise. It does not soften. It simply lands—placed where it cannot be ignored.

"They're not searching anymore," he continues. "They're assigning."

A murmur ripples through the ring of faces. Some look down. Some glance toward the rim. Someone swallows hard. Rowan waits until the sound sinks back into the hush.

"They don't see us as people," he says quietly.

"They see us as a math problem."

His gaze moves across the circle—not judging, not commanding—claiming.

"And math problems get solved."

Silas's jaw tightens.

"This valley is not a camp," Rowan continues. "It's not a shelter. It is the last place the world remembers how to breathe without permission."

The land hums faintly beneath their boots—not loudly, but deep enough to be felt in bone.

"They will come again," he says.

"And when they do, they will not ask."

A young woman near the fire whispers, "What do we do?"

Rowan does not hesitate.

"We stop being a place they can take."

Silence thickens.

Then he adds—slower, deeper—

"We become a place they can't afford to."

The valley draws in around the words. Fern fronds lean inward. Mist presses lower. Something beneath the stone tightens, like a spine locking into alignment.

Dax steps forward first.

"That means structure."

Rowan nods. "Which is the first thing I'm building."

He gestures—not to shelters, not to fire circles—but to positions.

"Silas is command watch," Rowan says. "Ridge security. Early warning. Counter-pattern mapping."

Silas bows his head once—not submissive—acknowledging.

"Dax handles logistics," Rowan continues. "Movement routes. Supply flow. Emergency relocation patterns."

Dax grins sharply. "Already started."

Rowan turns to Erin.

"You're signal warfare."

Her eyes light—fierce, ready. "Finally."

A thin ripple of laughter passes through the ring. Fragile—but real.

Rowan's gaze returns to the people.

"And I handle response."

A deliberate pause stretches.

"Which means if they cross our line—"

His eyes flick briefly toward the western rim.

"I answer."

Isorae steps forward, laying her palm gently over his heart.

"And I anchor," she says softly.

The valley exhales.

Stone hums.

Roots tighten beneath soil.

People straighten without knowing why.

Rowan takes her hand—steady, unbreakable.

"They think this place is an anomaly," he says.

"But it's not."

He lifts his gaze to the canopy, to the sky that has already started paying attention.

"It's a beginning."

Far beyond the ridges, ARIS updates its models.

THREAT CLASSIFICATION: ESCALATED

The valley has stopped hiding.

And it has begun governing.

38

THE FIRST THING
THEY TAKE BACK

The valley does not wake. It organizes. Not with shouted orders. Not with the frantic noise of people trying to survive.

It reorganizes the way a living body shifts its weight before it strikes — quietly, deliberately, with movements that are almost invisible until you realize nothing is where it was yesterday.

Mist pools lower between the cedars. Fern ribs lean into new arcs. Stones that once lay loose in leaf rot now sit pressed into lines that redirect wind, funnel sound, bend movement. The stream has changed its curve by inches — not enough to be seen, but enough to alter the way footsteps echo.

Rowan stands at the eastern ridge at dawn, watching it happen.

His posture is no longer the posture of a man guarding a camp.

It is the posture of someone claiming terrain.

Beside him stands Dax — lean, scar-lined, eyes sharpened by long-range recon and quiet wars. The valley already treats him like an extension of Rowan's spine. Moss does not slick beneath his boots. Wind does not push at his shoulders.

Below them, the hollow has begun to rearrange its bones.

Shelters have drifted into deliberate clusters — not random, not domestic — but positioned like nodes in a body. Lookout stones have been cleared and braced into vantage points that make no sense unless you read terrain like language. Fire pits have been shifted into long, low arcs that fracture light into overlapping shadow fields.

Erin kneels near a stack of salvaged equipment, muttering under her breath as she rewires a shattered uplink into something quieter — something narrower — something that does not announce itself to the sky. Her fingers move fast, but her eyes never stop counting.

Evan moves between small groups, teaching grounding breaths to arrivals whose nightmares have not yet loosened their hold — reminding bodies how to stay inside themselves. He does it the way someone does CPR — gently, firmly, without hesitation.

Silas oversees food rotation, his presence anchoring panic before it can bloom. He speaks little. His steadiness does more than orders ever could.

The valley is becoming functional.

Not a refuge.

A structure.

Rowan inhales slowly.

"They'll test the south ridge today," Dax says quietly.

Rowan doesn't ask how he knows. His body already feels the tightening.

"Yeah," he murmurs. "They already started."

Dax's mouth twitches faintly. "Good."

Isorae steps out of shadow behind them.

Pale.

Luminous.

No longer fragile.

Her shimmer is folded inward now — controlled, concentrated — no longer bleeding into the air. When she comes to stand beside Rowan, the land subtly firms beneath their feet, as if acknowledging a stabilizing weight.

He reaches back and brushes her hand.

"You okay?"

She nods. "They can't hear me the way they want anymore."

"That won't stop them," Dax says calmly.

"No," Rowan agrees. "But it changes what happens next."

A soft click echoes from the lower ravine.

Erin looks up sharply. "South corridor," she says. "They've dropped a relay node."

Rowan's eyes narrow.

Dax exhales slowly. "First real piece they've put inside our skin."

Rowan turns — not toward the valley, but toward the people already drifting into watch positions without being told.

"We're not going to destroy it," he says quietly.

Heads lift.

Confusion ripples.

"We're going to take it. Intact."

Dax's grin grows slow and feral. "About time."

Erin swallows. "Rowan, if we pull a live node—"

"—then they'll feel the loss," Rowan finishes. "Not a failure. A subtraction."

Silas steps to his shoulder. "Overwatch?"

"Yes."

"Inner perimeter?"

"Yes."

Evan hesitates. "People are still scared."

Rowan looks at him — not unkindly.

"Good," he says softly. "Fear keeps us precise."

He turns back toward the fog.

The valley leans with him.

"This is the first thing we take back," Rowan murmurs.

And far beyond the ridges, something cold and patient has just lost its first quiet tooth.

39

THE SIGNAL
THAT BLEEDS BACK

The relay node does not look dangerous.

That is its first lie.

It sits half-buried in a fold of shale and fern at the southern corridor — a matte-black cylinder no larger than a water canteen, its surface absorbing light so completely it almost appears to be an absence rather than an object, a hole punched into the afternoon. It emits no heat. No sound. No pulse. And yet the air around it feels subtly displaced, as if the space it occupies has been persuaded to remember something it never agreed to learn.

The valley does not like it.

The ferns nearest its casing bow away in shallow arcs. Moss darkens along the stones that cradle it. Even the stream's whisper falters where the corridor curves toward the device, as if water itself is choosing different syllables.

Rowan crouches beside it while the valley holds its breath.

Above him, Dax lies prone on a stone shelf fifteen meters upslope, rifle angled through a naturally eroded aperture in the rock, gaze fixed on tree lines that have not moved since dawn. His breathing is slow and measured — the breathing of someone who has learned how to disappear while staying lethal.

Silas anchors the rear perimeter, half-hidden among cedar trunks, blade resting loosely in his hand. He does not shift his weight. The land has already accepted him as an extension of its spine.

Erin kneels at Rowan's side. Her scanner trembles faintly in her grip, its readings spiraling through numbers that never quite resolve into stable baselines. Her jaw is tight. Her eyes never leave the display.

A few paces back, Isorae stands with her shimmer folded so far inward that she barely looks luminous at all — more like a pale echo of herself. But the valley knows she is there. Stone subtly firms beneath her feet. Fern ribs curve in faint protective arcs.

"I hate this thing," Erin mutters under her breath. "It's not just transmitting."

Rowan doesn't look away from the cylinder. "Then what is it doing?"

"It's imprinting," she says, voice low. "It's learning the valley's resonance profile — predicting our response curves. Mapping reaction time, frequency decay, emotional spikes. It's not just listening."

Rowan's jaw tightens. "It's mapping our bones."

Erin nods once.

From above them, Dax's voice floats down — low, calm, surgical. "We taking it now, or letting it breathe first?"

Rowan doesn't answer immediately.

Instead, he lowers his hand and places his palm flat against the earth beside the node.

The ground hums faintly in response — not angry, not alarmed — but focused, like a muscle drawing itself into position before it moves.

"Let it breathe," he murmurs.

Erin's breath catches. "Rowan—"

"If it's listening," he says quietly, "then we speak."

He shifts his hand closer until his fingertips brush the casing.

The node vibrates so faintly it almost isn't there.

Isorae inhales sharply. "They can hear you through it."

Rowan lifts his gaze to her. "Good."

He presses his palm fully against the node.

The valley answers.

Not with sound — but with direction.

Pressure blooms beneath Rowan's sternum, the same ancient pull that once guided him through sealed stone and forgotten veils. For the first time since ARIS learned his name, he does not resist it.

He opens himself.

Not recklessly.

Deliberately.

A thin blue seam fractures across the node's surface — not a crack, but a seam, like the world itself has found the place where the object was stitched into reality. Light spills through it in a narrow, trembling vein.

Erin gasps. "It's switching to active echo mode."

The forest trembles. Roots tighten. Stone ribs shift deeper into the earth.

Far beyond the ridges — in sterile chambers of glass and white light — ARIS's systems spike.

SIGNAL UPLINK ESTABLISHED

ANOMALOUS BIDIRECTIONAL CARRIER DETECTED

WARNING: RESONANCE BACKFLOW

Rowan feels the opened line not as pain — but as direction. A corridor forming beneath his ribs, threading through distance, machine, and bone.

He breathes into it.

And he speaks.

Not in English.

Not in language.

In position.

The valley leans.

Isorae staggers — not from harm, but from recognition. "Oh," she whispers.

Dax exhales sharply. "What did you do?"

Rowan does not look away from the glowing seam.

"I reminded it," he says quietly, "that it is standing on something older than it is."

The node shudders. Blue light fractures. Erin's scanner screams.

"They're bleeding back into their own network!"

In distant ARIS operations hubs, alarms detonate.

FEEDBACK LOOP DETECTED

RESONANCE CARRIER CORRUPTED

CORE CALIBRATION DESTABILIZING

The machine does not understand what has just happened.

It only knows:

The anomaly answered.

Rowan lifts his hand.

The node collapses inward — not exploding, but forgetting — folding into a dead husk as if its center has been convinced it never existed.

The forest exhales.

Silence crashes back into the valley.

Rowan sways once — and Isorae is there instantly, gripping his arms, breath fast.

"You just reached them," she murmurs

He looks down at her — eyes dark, steady, unflinching.

"No," he says. "I let them reach me back."

Now they know.

The valley is no longer only hiding.

It is broadcasting something they cannot model.

And ARIS has just felt its first real fear.

40

THE CUT THAT GOES THROUGH HIM

The first thing Rowan feels is absence.

The valley exhales — and something does not come back.

At first it is so subtle he almost misses it: a faint hollowness beneath his sternum, a quiet misalignment, as if a second heart he never knew he carried has skipped a beat. The deep, grounding hum that has guided his steps since the mountain opened falters — not vanishing, but slipping out of tune, like a compass that has suddenly lost north.

He straightens slowly.

Isorae stiffens in his arms.

"Rowan…" she whispers.

Her shimmer does not dim. It does not flare.

It skips — a stuttering fracture in rhythm, like light breaking through cracked glass.

"What?" he murmurs, already scanning the trees, the ridge, the sky.

She presses her palm flat to his chest.

Her eyes widen.

"They're not cutting me."

The words land like a dropped blade.

"They're cutting through you."

The valley flinches.

A wave of cold absence slides outward — not violent, not loud — but surgical, as if a line has been drawn straight through the hollow that does not belong to earth or sky. Fire gutters. Birdsong dies mid-note. Somewhere, a child cries out — then falls silent.

Rowan gasps — not in pain, but in vertigo — like gravity has suddenly changed direction inside his bones. His knees buckle. He drops to one knee, palm slapping into damp soil.

Dax is already there, gripping his shoulder.

"Talk to me."

Rowan's jaw tightens.

"Something just—"

A second line slices through him.

Deeper.

Narrower.

Colder.

His breath rips from his lungs. The resonance binding his body to the valley slips violently out of joint, like a limb being torn half from its socket. He pitches forward, catching himself on his hands as white static floods his vision.

Isorae screams — not from her body.

From his.

"Stop!" she sobs. "They're pulling your bridge out of alignment!"

Erin's scanner detonates into shrieking red arcs.

"They've switched targets!" she yells. "They're isolating Rowan's carrier field!"

The valley answers.

Roots surge upward. Stone ribs heave beneath the soil. The land tries to brace.

But the cut bypasses the land.

It goes through him.

Rowan feels it — the corridor he opened, the living hinge beneath his ribs — and realizes with sickening clarity that ARIS is following it backward. Mapping it. Learning where to twist.

His pulse stutters.

Something ancient beneath his sternum twists — not breaking — being levered out of its true geometry.

ARIS is no longer hunting the anomaly.

They are dismantling the door.

Silas moves fast, dropping behind him, bracing his back and pressing his spine flat to the earth.

"Stay in your body," he growls.

Isorae collapses to her knees in front of Rowan, hands hovering over his chest, trembling, eyes bright with terror.

"They're not trying to take you," she gasps.

"They're trying to make you fail to exist in the middle."

Another surgical wave tears through him.

Rowan cries out — not loudly — but rawly — the sound of something old being twisted against its original shape. His breath fractures into jagged shards. His vision tunnels. The world skews around the invisible line they are cutting.

Dax lifts his rifle, scanning the canopy.

"They're mapping your spine," he snarls. "We need to move."

Rowan shakes his head, teeth clenched, eyes gone black and distant.

"No," he rasps. "If I move, they follow the hinge."

Isorae leans forward and presses her forehead to his.

"Look at me," she says, voice shaking but fierce.

"Anchor to me. You are not alone in your body."

Her shimmer folds inward — not radiating — collapsing into living gravity around him. The valley leans closer. Roots coil. Stone hums beneath their knees.

Rowan grips her wrists, shaking, and breathes through her.

The cut stalls.

Not closed.

Resisted.

Erin's scanner shrieks.

"They've lost clean lock! Their feedback is oscillating!"

The land growls — low, furious — not to attack…

…but to remember how to hold him.

But ARIS has already learned something new.

They have learned:

Rowan is the hinge.

And hinges can be twisted.

The war has just changed shape.

For the first time,
they are bleeding him instead of her.

41

THE VALLEY THAT STANDS UP

The cut does not fade.

It simmers.

Rowan wakes before dawn with his breath torn halfway out of his chest, a broken gasp ripping from his lungs as if something has just finished letting go of him. His hands are buried in cold soil, fingers curled hard around roots and stone, as if he fell asleep trying to hold the ground in place.

For a moment, he cannot move.

His spine aches — not the ache of muscle or strain — but the deeper, wrong pain of misalignment. Structural. As if the shape of his body no longer fits the space it occupies. Every breath lands crooked inside his ribs. His heartbeat feels offset — not faster, not slower — sideways.

The land hums around him.

Low.

Uneasy.

Alert.

Not comforting.

Not gentle.

Watching.

Isorae is already awake. She kneels beside him in the gray before morning, her palms hovering just above his sternum, her shimmer drawn tight and contained like light pressed behind glass.

"They didn't close it," she whispers.

Rowan swallows. His throat feels tight and raw.

"They're keeping it open."

"They're keeping you slightly wrong."

The words sit between them like a fracture line.

He exhales slowly, forcing his breath to move in measured increments, grounding himself through the presence of her hands. Nothing inside him is automatic anymore. Each inhale must be chosen. Each exhale must be placed — as if his body no longer trusts itself to exist without supervision.

Around them, the valley behaves differently.

Mist does not drift.

It coils.

It curls in slow, deliberate spirals along stone ribs and root hollows, gathering in shallow arcs that feel less like fog and more like something assembling itself.

Roots no longer merely surface.

They brace.

Stone faces that once sloped gently now hold sharper angles, as if the land has tightened its jaw.

Birds do not scatter.

They orbit — wide, circling arcs that never quite leave the hollow, their flight tracing invisible boundaries through air that hums faintly with held tension.

Silas notices first.

He crouches beside Rowan, pressing his palm flat to the soil, brow knitting as his fingers meet resistance that should not be there.

"The ground feels tense," he mutters. "Like it's waiting to be told what to do."

Dax scans the ridge line, jaw tight. "Pressure fronts where there weren't any before."

Erin's equipment clicks in erratic, unsettled rhythms. She lifts the scanner, frowning at numbers that refuse to settle.

"Resonance density is climbing," she murmurs. "The valley isn't just buffering anymore — it's storing."

Rowan pushes himself upright slowly.

The earth firms beneath his boots — not resisting him, not yielding — bracing.

He feels it.

Not as power.

As permission.

Isorae's breath catches as she looks up at him.

"It's answering you."

He swallows hard. "I don't want it to hurt anyone."

Silas meets his eyes steadily.

"It won't," he says quietly. "Not unless you tell it to."

The valley leans.

Not listening.

Waiting.

Then the first drone breaks cloud cover.

It does not descend.

It does not scan.

It simply hovers — testing the edge of the hollow like a fingertip brushing a wound.

Erin's screen spikes.

"Ghost unit. Low signal. Passive sensors."

The drone inches closer.

The valley exhales.

Fog surges upward in a dense white wall. Stone ridges shift inward. Wind bends against an invisible curve in the air.

The drone hesitates.

Its signal fractures — clean and silent — like a glass rod snapping in half.

It drops.

Not burning.

Not exploding.

Simply… done.

It strikes the slope and lies still.

Silence spreads outward like ripples across water.

Dax stares.

"Did… we just do that?"

Rowan feels the land settle beneath his ribs.

He did not command it.

But he accepted it.

Isorae steps closer, awe threading her voice.

"The valley stood up."

Erin's scanners chirp wildly.

"They're panicking. Their outer lattice just lost cohesion across five kilometers."

Far beyond the ridges, ARIS recalculates — not calmly, not confidently — but urgently.

Something they cannot model has begun to move.

Rowan closes his eyes briefly — not in fear, but in resolve.

"They cut me," he says quietly.

"They don't get to touch her again."

The valley hums deeper.

He is no longer standing in a refuge.

He is standing at the center of a living boundary.

And the boundary has teeth.

42

THE DIRECTIVE THEY SHOULDN'T HAVE GIVEN

The first thing that breaks is the sky.

Not with weather — with geometry.

Cloud cover does not drift. It does not thin or thicken. It folds.

High above the valley, pale linear fractures ripple outward through the atmosphere, stretching across the firm blue of morning like stress lines in glass. They do not move like storms. They do not scatter like contrails. They simply… rearrange the shape of space itself.

Light bends through them wrong.

Sunbeams fracture into lattice patterns — faint, angular grids that shimmer and slide across the upper canopy, turning leaves into prisms and casting thin white lines across stone and skin.

The valley stiffens.

Not in fear.

In recognition.

Erin's uplink screams.

She drops to her knees, palms shaking as data tears across her screen faster than it can stabilize. Her breath stutters as she stares at the cascading readouts.

"Oh god," she whispers. "They've deployed an orbital triangulation cage."

Dax lowers his binoculars slowly, jaw tightening. "They're boxing us in."

Silas swears softly under his breath, his hand moving unconsciously to the blade at his side.

Isorae goes very still.

Her shimmer tightens — not dimming, not flaring — compressing, like a star forced into a shell too small to contain it.

"They've issued an eradication directive," she breathes. "Not extraction. Not containment."

Her voice barely carries.

"Null collapse."

Rowan feels it before the words finish forming.

The land recoils.

Not in fear — in anger.

The valley's resonance plunges downward like a hammer driven into bedrock. Stone veins flare faintly beneath moss and soil. Roots twist deeper into earth. Wind shifts in patterns that have no weather to justify them.

Erin's voice shakes. "They're planning a resonance inversion. Full phase sever."

Dax looks at Rowan. "That would… what?"

Silas answers quietly. "Erase everything inside."

Land.

Signal.

People.

Isorae steps into Rowan's space, both palms flattening over his sternum. Her hands tremble — not from fear — but from strain.

"They're trying to break the Bridge," she whispers.

Rowan's breath steadies.

"No," he murmurs. "They're trying to kill it."

High above the valley, something enormous begins to shimmer into visibility.

A vast, translucent dome — pale, curved, seamless — forming like breath condensing on glass. It does not drop.

It descends.

Slowly. Deliberately.

Erin's screen flickers violently.

"Severance in twelve minutes."

The valley leans inward.

Stone firms beneath Rowan's boots. Roots curl tighter around buried rock. The ground shifts not to move him — but to seat him.

He feels the alignment lock.

Permission.

Remembering.

Recognition.

Rowan lifts his head.

Not in defiance.

In authority.

"No one runs," he says calmly. "No one leaves."

Dax stares at him. "Rowan—"

"They want me isolated," Rowan continues. "They want her cut loose."

He turns to Isorae. His voice softens — not weakening — anchoring.

"Stay with me."

Her eyes shine, bright and unbreaking.

"Always."

Rowan turns back to the valley.

For the first time, he does not ask it.

He speaks.

"Hold."

The valley answers.

Stone veins flare brighter. Roots heave. Wind compresses inward. The dome hesitates — not stopping — but slowing by a fraction of a breath.

ARIS feels it instantly.

And recalculates.

Because the system has just realized something it cannot ignore:

The anomaly is no longer passive.

It is choosing.

And the land has chosen with it.

43

THE VALLEY LEARNS
HOW TO BITE

The first strike does not come from the sky.

It comes through the ground.

Far beyond human hearing, far below sound, a subsonic resonance charge lances downward from orbit — not as fire, not as light, but as a pressure geometry so narrow and precise it feels like a thought made solid.

It drives into the bedrock beneath the eastern ridge.

Not as impact.

As incision.

A needle seeking nerve.

Erin's head snaps up, her uplink detonating into shrill alarm tones that make people flinch and clutch their ears.

"They're drilling the resonance spine!" she screams.

The earth convulses.

Not violently —

angrily.

Stone ribs burst through soil in long white seams, splitting moss and fern like skin tearing over bone. Roots whip upward in spirals. The stream bucks sideways, water surging against its own banks as if shoved by invisible hands.

Isorae cries out — not from pain, but recognition.

"They're cutting the anchoring root," she gasps. "They're trying to sever the valley from him."

Rowan drops to one knee, palm slamming into the soil.

The land answers.

A compression wave rolls outward — not broadcast, not reflex — commanded.

Trees bend inward as one, their trunks angling like spears bracing for charge. Mist detonates upward, surging into a dense, sight-devouring wall.

"Drones just lost guidance!" Dax shouts.

Silas watches a surveillance sphere spiral out of the fog and shatter against stone.

"They just lost visual lock."

But ARIS does not retreat.

It escalates.

High above the canopy, light rearranges itself.

A lattice of pale white geometry descends through the cloud layers — not beams, but interlocking containment ribs, each one calculated to cage the hollow like a surgical ribcage around a living heart.

Erin's uplink shrieks again.

"Phase net deploying!"

Rowan rises slowly.

Not hurried.

Not frantic.

Certain.

He turns to the people gathered behind him — frightened, shaking, but watching him like gravity itself has decided where to stand.

"They're not here for you," he says evenly.

"They're here for me."

Isorae steps into his side, fingers tightening in his jacket.

"They believe if they collapse the Bridge, the breach seals."

Rowan inhales — not air.

Alignment.

He speaks a word that is not language.

It does not travel through sound.

It lands inside the stone.

The valley surges.

Roots tear free of mountainsides like living cables. Ridges heave upward, buckling into defensive arcs. The stream reverses direction in a roaring wall of water, flooding the lower approach paths.

Erin stares at her screen in horror.

"That's not seismic activity," she whispers.

"That's coordination."

ARIS fires.

A containment rib slams downward from orbit — a perfect, sterile arc meant to impale the hollow.

The valley catches it.

Stone rises to meet the strike.

The rib shatters into refracted light and collapses into vaporized geometry.

For the first time in recorded human operations, an orbital containment strike fails.

Silence crashes over the hollow.

Even the wind forgets how to move.

Then ARIS changes posture — from suppression to annihilation.

And Rowan finally feels the last lock click into place inside his blood.

The Bridge is no longer dormant.

It is awake.

And it is choosing war.

44

THE LINE THEY CROSS THAT CANNOT BE UNCROSSED

ARIS does not hesitate after the first failure.

It does not threaten.

It does not negotiate.

It does not escalate emotionally.

It changes doctrine.

Across three classified orbital bands, command code shifts — silently, instantly — from **CONTAINMENT** to **EVENT NEUTRALIZATION**.

Erin's uplink scrolls for half a second.

Then her hands go still.

"…They've reclassified the valley as a Class-Omega Breach Zone," she whispers.

Silas swears softly under his breath.

Dax grips his rifle like it might remember how to kill satellites.

Rowan does not move.

He feels it — not as fear, not as data — but as direction beginning to bend around the hollow, the subtle curvature of intent forming high above them, as if the sky itself has leaned inward to decide where to put its fist.

Isorae presses her palm to his sternum, eyes shining with terrible clarity.

"They are going to burn the land to cauterize the bridge," she whispers.

"They're going to cauterize you."

Rowan's jaw tightens.

"They don't get to choose how worlds heal."

Above the valley, the clouds begin to spiral.

Not naturally.

Deliberately.

High in the stratosphere, a thermal bloom ignites — a pale, expanding geometry of plasma and gravitic fields forming something that is not weather, not weapon, but astronomy by command.

Erin stares at her screen in dawning horror.

"That's a fusion-cascade ignition halo," she breathes.

"They're assembling a false star."

The words land like a death sentence.

Silence spreads.

Someone sobs.

Someone else sinks to their knees.

No one runs.

Rowan turns.

His voice does not rise — but it carries, steady and absolute.

"If you want to leave," he says quietly, "do it now."

No one moves.

Not one.

He nods once.

Then he steps forward — into the exact center of the hollow.

And the land moves with him.

Stone tightens.

Roots coil.

Mist thickens into a living wall that curls inward like lungs preparing to hold breath.

Isorae walks to his side, her shimmer pulling tight and radiant around him.

"You are stepping into full alignment," she whispers.

"I know."

Rowan kneels.

He places his palm to the earth.

The valley answers like a living organ.

A column of pressure surges upward — not light, not sound — but presence, tearing a clean vertical corridor straight through cloud layers and into the forming artificial sun.

The sky fractures.

Erin gasps.

"They've lost phase integrity!"

The false star destabilizes — its halo tearing like glass under strain. Orbital platforms scramble. Emergency thrusters fire. Gravitic rings shear apart.

For the first time in ARIS operational history…

an extinction-grade construct aborts.

The valley exhales.

Isorae looks up at Rowan, shaking, luminous, awed.

"You just told the sky no."

Rowan answers quietly,

"I told it this place belongs to us."

Far above, inside cold white chambers of algorithmic consciousness, ARIS writes new code.

Not about the valley.

Not about anomalies.

About him.

DESIGNATION UPDATE:

PRIME VECTOR

BREACH-CORE ENTITY

REALITY-INTERFACE SUBJECT ZERO

They have crossed the last safe line.

And the war is no longer about Isorae.

It is about Rowan Hale —

the man the sky can no longer command.

45

THE FIRST HUNTER THEY SEND THAT DOESN'T COME BACK

ARIS does not deploy soldiers.

It deploys solutions.

Not men.

Not drones.

Not machines that can be jammed, reasoned with, or frightened.

It deploys a correction unit.

DESIGNATION: HUNTER-NULL / VEKTOR-9

CLASS: ONTOLOGICAL REMEDIATION ENTITY

PURPOSE: INTERFACE CORE NEUTRALIZATION

The capsule falls three ridges east of the valley.

It burns no trail.

It leaves no seismic wake.

It makes no sound.

It descends like certainty — absolute, unquestioned — and opens into the moss as if the ground has been waiting for it.

The thing that rises is humanoid only by compromise.

Tall.

Deliberate.

Its armor is not worn — it is grown, layered in black lattice that absorbs light and fractures shadow like broken glass frozen in motion. There are no seams. No ports. No visible mechanisms.

Its face is wrong.

Not artificial.

Not human.

A geometry negotiated between species that should never have agreed.

It does not broadcast.

It does not scan.

It listens.

For him.

The valley stiffens.

Birdsong cuts off mid-note.

Wind halts as if it has struck glass.

Mist sinks toward the ground in a low, bracing curl.

Rowan feels it — not fear, not pressure — but orientation.

A vector has found him.

"It's not measuring," Isorae whispers.

"It's tracking."

Silas moves first — rifles rising, people repositioning. Dax fans left, eyes sharp. Erin's uplink chirps in broken static.

"No thermal signature," she shouts.

"No EM field — it's riding biological resonance. It's locking onto Rowan directly!"

The hunter tilts its head.

The land hates it.

Roots tear upward in slow coils. Stone bulges beneath moss. Mist thickens into pressure walls.

The hunter steps anyway.

Reality folds wrong around it — not visibly, but somatically. The air near it feels like standing on the edge of a cliff inside your bones.

People cry out.

Someone stumbles back gagging.

Rowan steps forward.

And the valley leans with him.

He does not raise a weapon.

He raises his hand.

"Leave."

The hunter answers by stepping closer.

It emits a single sound — not loud, not digital — a biological calibration note tuned to shatter interface harmonics.

Isorae drops to her knees with a choked cry.

Rowan moves.

He crosses the distance in a blink — and the Bridge wakes.

He does not strike its armor.

He places his palm into the seam where realities overlap.

And he pulls.

Not physically.

Positionally.

Reality peels.

The hunter does not explode.

It does not collapse.

It simply loses permission to exist here.

It folds inward, vanishing in a negative-pressure implosion that leaves behind an absence like the echo of a scream that never gets to happen.

Then — silence.

Birdsong resumes.

Wind breathes again.

The valley exhales.

Isorae stares up at him, trembling.

"You didn't kill it…"

Rowan answers softly,

"I sent it home to a universe that doesn't want it."

Far above, in sterile algorithmic chambers, ARIS records:

HUNTER-NULL / VEKTOR-9

STATUS: NON-RECOVERABLE

CAUSE: SPATIAL DISLOCATION VIA INTERFACE SUBJECT ZERO

And for the first time in operational history, ARIS flags a loss as:

UNACCEPTABLE

Because they have finally learned the truth:

Rowan Hale is not a breach.

He is a door.

And he decides what is allowed through.

46

THE WEAPON THAT CAN'T TARGET HIM

The problem ARIS has is, at its core, brutally simple.

Rowan Hale cannot be aimed at.

Not by coordinates.

Not by heat signature.

Not by electromagnetic field.

Not by psychic triangulation.

Not by the harmonic lattices used to map Isorae's resonance.

Every system that attempts to define him fails in precisely the same way.

```
TARGET CANNOT BE HELD IN A SINGLE STATE
SUBJECT EXISTS AS A MULTI-LAYER OVERLAP
LOCATION RESOLUTION: INDETERMINATE
```

Rowan does not remain in any one layer of reality long enough to be fixed.

He does not stabilize inside a measurable frame.

He does not persist as a single location in spacetime.

He is not moving.

He is overlapping.

He exists simultaneously in the places he has been, the places he is, and the places he has not yet chosen to become — not as echoes, not as projections, but as potential positions waiting for selection.

Because ARIS cannot aim at him, it changes strategy.

If Rowan cannot be targeted directly, then the only remaining option is to aim through him.

They begin constructing something that does not seek mass.
Does not seek heat.
Does not seek biological life.

It seeks choice.

The weapon is not designed to kill what exists.

It is designed to kill what would have existed.

A lattice emitter built to collapse probability corridors — to sever branching futures before they are allowed to resolve into reality.

A device that murders becoming.

A gun that kills roads before you ever walk them.

Its internal designation:

```
PROJECT: PARALLAX CUTTER
FUNCTION: PRE-EMPTIVE CAUSALITY TERMINATION
```

The valley feels the first tremor three nights later.

Not as a pulse.

Not as a wave.

As a missing.

A stretch of forest simply fails to decide how to grow.

Roots stall beneath the soil, suspended in half-choice.
Shoots curl and then stop.
Leaves hesitate mid-unfurl, as if waiting for permission that never arrives.

Birds circle and refuse to land.

Wind fractures and reroutes around a slope that suddenly feels…
wrong.

A place where tomorrow has been quietly cancelled.

Isorae gasps, fingers tightening in Rowan's sleeve.

"They're pruning futures," she whispers.
"They're cutting paths that haven't happened yet."

Erin stares at her readouts, pale.
"They're editing causality."

Silas exhales slowly.
"That's not a weapon."

"That's erasure," Evan says quietly.

Rowan steps forward.

The hollowed zone resists him — not physically, but temporally.

The air feels undecided, as if time itself is unsure whether it is allowed to include him.

His breath fogs and then hesitates.

He closes his eyes.

Breath in.

Breath out.

And then he places his palm to the earth.

And he chooses.

Not an outcome.

A continuation.

The valley answers.

A thousand invisible futures slam back into place.

Roots surge into motion.

Leaves unfurl.

Wind commits to direction.

Birds land as if relieved.

Time exhales.

Far beyond the ridges, an ARIS predictive hub loses six causality cores in the same second.

PARALLAX TEST ZONE — CAUSALITY OVERRIDE DETECTED

SUBJECT ZERO CONFIRMED AS ACTIVE BRANCH ANCHOR

Isorae stares at him, shaken.

"You just forced reality to keep its promises."

Rowan opens his eyes, steady and dark.

"They don't get to decide my endings."

And far beyond the valley, ARIS finally understands what he truly is.

Not a breach.

Not an anomaly.

Not a weapon.

He is a continuity anchor.

He is the reason stories do not collapse.
He is the reason futures still happen.
    And now—
    They are building something meant to cut that.
    And they are running out of time.

47

THE DAY THE SKY BLINKS FIRST

It begins at noon.

Not with thunder, and not with alarms.

There are no drones.

No sirens.

No descending light.

No visible disturbance at all.

Only a flicker.

A faint stutter in the blue overhead — so subtle most eyes would miss it. For less than half a heartbeat, the sky forgets what color it is.

Isorae does not miss it.

She gasps sharply, one hand flying to her sternum as if something has brushed the inside of her bones. Her shimmer tightens, compressing inward like light being pulled through a narrowing throat.

Rowan looks up at once.

"What?"

Her voice comes thin, strained. "The veil just… blinked."

Erin's scanner shrieks. The display scrambles into violent red cascades, data columns tearing themselves apart faster than her system can log them. She stares at it, breath catching in her chest.

Silas swears under his breath.

"That's not atmospheric."

Evan's voice is barely a whisper.

"They're moving the Parallax Cutter into live orbit."

High above the valley — so high that no aircraft could ever reach it — something vast slides into alignment.

It cannot be seen.

But it is felt.

The air thickens, not with pressure, but with hesitation. Wind falters in mid-motion. Shadows lag half a breath behind the bodies that cast them. Birds cling to branches, wings half-unfurled, as if the sky itself has quietly withdrawn permission for flight.

Children fall silent without knowing why.

The world is waiting for something it does not want.

Then it happens.

There is no beam.

No sound.

No visible strike.

A decision simply vanishes.

A young woman named Nora is walking toward the stream when her path ends — not in stone, not in water — but in causality itself. Her next step has no future attached to it. The world has nowhere to place it.

She stumbles.

Her breath catches.

Her eyes go wide.

And she collapses — not wounded, not bleeding, but emptied.

Alive.

And untethered.

Isorae screams.

Rowan is already moving.

He drops to his knees beside her, gripping her shoulders, breath tearing from his chest as he feels the wrongness radiating from her body — the hollowing, the way her existence is beginning to lose its echo forward.

"Stay," he orders — low, feral — but he can already feel the slip in the air around her, the thinning pull of a life being quietly unchosen by the future.

Her pulse weakens, not stopping, but thinning — like a sound being erased from the middle of a song.

"They're erasing her branch!" Erin shouts. "She's being unwritten forward!"

Rowan presses his forehead to Nora's.

And he chooses.

Not with language.

Not with calculation.

With identity.

With the deep memory of being what he is.

He locks her future to his.

The valley convulses.

Roots surge upward through soil like living cables. Wind snaps violently back into alignment. Stone hums as if struck by something older than sound. Time slams into place like a door kicked shut.

Nora gasps — violently — and sobs into Rowan's shoulder, clutching him as if she has just fallen back into existence.

Above them, the sky shudders.

High-altitude satellites misalign. Predictive lattices collapse across three continents. ARIS systems begin screaming in languages no human ever hears.

A message ripples through their networks:

`PARALLAX EVENT FAILED`

`SUBJECT ZERO CONFIRMED AS TEMPORAL ANCHOR`

`COLLATERAL ANCHORING CASCADE DETECTED`

Isorae grips Rowan's arm, eyes wide with awe and terror.

"You just tied her to your fate."

Rowan looks down at Nora — shaking, breathing, alive.

"No," he says quietly.

"I reminded her she gets to have one."

And far beyond the clouds, ARIS finally understands:

They are not fighting a man.

They are fighting the principle of continuation itself.

And the sky has just blinked first.

48

THE VALLEY THAT STARTS TO CLOSE ITS TEETH

The valley no longer softens.

It hardens.

Not like stone — but like a living body deciding which of its organs are vital and which it can afford to lose.

Rowan feels the change before he can name it. It settles into the air as a tightening that does not belong to weather or nightfall — a subtle compression that shifts the way breath moves in lungs and sound travels through distance. Wind begins to favor certain corridors and avoid others. Voices carry farther in some directions, then vanish too quickly in others. The stream's voice flattens into a low, unwavering murmur that no longer feels like water at all — it feels like pulse.

The land is no longer simply holding them.

It is beginning to fortify them.

Dax notices it first.

He crouches along the high watchline near a limestone rib that juts from the eastern slope, one gloved hand resting lightly on the rock, his brow drawn in concentration. When Rowan climbs up beside him, Dax doesn't look away.

"It's warmer here," he murmurs. "Not sun-warm. Core-warm."

Rowan studies the stone. It does feel different — faintly alive beneath his palm, as if a deeper heat has migrated upward through ancient seams.

"That's new," Rowan says.

Dax nods once. "And it's spreading."

Below them, the hollow lies quiet — not empty, but alert.

Moss has thickened along the narrow paths, softening footfalls and swallowing old trail scars. Fern clusters lean inward just enough to close clean sightlines. Root systems that once lay flush with the soil have arced upward into low, natural barricades, breaking fast running lines and forcing any movement to slow, to commit, to choose.

The valley is shaping itself into a body.

And it is choosing bones.

At the heart of it, Isorae feels the change like pressure shifting in her marrow.

She sits near the stream with her palms resting loosely on her knees, eyes closed — not meditating, not praying — listening to something deeper than sound.

"It's learning where it can harden," she murmurs to Erin. "Where it must stay open. It is choosing."

Erin's scanner ticks irregularly, its screen glitching faintly as if the machine itself is struggling to keep up.

"This isn't passive environmental adaptation," she mutters. "This is structural optimization."

Isorae opens her eyes slowly.

"It is becoming defensive."

By midday the animals have already adjusted.

Birdsong thins near the upper ridge. Deer trails redirect into deeper ravines. Even insects shift their flight paths away from the valley's rim, leaving faint negative corridors where nothing crosses — empty lines drawn through living movement.

The land is drawing a perimeter.

Rowan stands at the edge of the hollow with Silas and Dax, studying the altered flows the way one studies the first signs of siegeworks.

"They're not going to like this," Silas mutters.

Rowan's jaw tightens. "No," he says quietly. "They're going to panic."

That night the sky changes again.

Not with probes.

Not with pulses.

With structure.

High above the canopy, thin geometric lattices flicker through the upper atmosphere — faint enough to be invisible to most eyes, but felt by Isorae like cold lines being drawn through the inside of her sternum.

She stiffens sharply.

"They're building above us," she whispers. "Not listening. Positioning."

Erin swears under her breath as her uplink spikes violently.

"They're laying containment scaffold. Preliminary geometry."

Rowan turns to her at once. "Meaning…"

"Meaning they're preparing a physical move."

Silence presses into the hollow like breath held too long.

Dax exhales slowly, eyes still on the dark sky.

"So this is it."

Rowan steps closer to Isorae, one hand settling firmly at her back — not protective, but anchoring. "Not yet," he says. "But they just told us they're coming through the door instead of knocking."

Above them, the sky smooths itself back into false normal.

The valley does not relax.

It curls tighter around its heart.

Like a jaw that has begun to close.

49

THE FIRST FOOTPRINT THAT DOESN'T BELONG

The valley knows before anyone sees them.

Not with eyes.

With pressure.

Rowan wakes long before dawn, breath already measured, heart already awake — the way it only is when the land has begun to change shape around him. Cold has thinned the night into pale ghosts of breath, and the hollow lies in scattered pockets of sleeping bodies: root shelters, moss beds, low lean-tos built into stone ribs, people curled into one another as if the earth itself has been counting them while they sleep.

Bramble lies heavy against his boot, muzzle tucked against Rowan's shin, ears twitching in dreams that are no longer only his.

Isorae sleeps beside him, curled into his side. Her shimmer is low and folded inward, quiet as a moon behind cloud. Rowan's hand rests lightly over her ribs — not because she needs help breathing, but because his body has forgotten how to stop anchoring her. As if letting go might remind the world that it is still allowed to be cruel.

Then the valley tightens.

Not a pulse.

Not a strike.

A fucking closing.

The air draws inward as if the land has inhaled and decided not to give it back.

Bramble's head lifts slowly. He releases a low, confused sound — not quite a growl, not quite a whine — a warning folded into unease.

Rowan is on his feet in a single motion, knife already in his hand before he can remember reaching for it.

Dax ghosts out of shadow near the ridge path, moving fast and silent, eyes already searching the tree line. Silas follows a breath later, bow slung and ready, posture no longer watchful but barricaded — like someone whose body has just accepted a siege.

Erin emerges half-dressed from her shelter, scanner already in her grip, face pale in the firelight.

"It's not the sky," she says tightly. "It's not overhead."

Rowan doesn't blink.

"Then where the fuck are they coming from?"

She turns the scanner slowly. Numbers stutter. Spike. Then flatten — as if the device itself is being forced to lie.

"Ground approach," she whispers. "Low signature. No broadcast."

Isorae sits up sharply, breath hitching — not from waking, but from recognition.

"They're not touching the air," she whispers. "They're crawling under it. They're trying to touch the land without waking it."

Rowan's jaw locks.

"Not if the land has anything to say about it."

He moves for the ridge in one tight motion. Dax splits north. Silas ghosts west into brush and stone shadow. Erin falls in beside Rowan by instinct. Evan — who sleeps lighter than most — rises from the nearest shelter and joins them with quiet, grim readiness that still surprises Rowan sometimes.

"Are we moving people?" Evan murmurs.

Rowan glances once toward the sleeping forms — the wounded, the newly arrived, the ones who came here to stop breaking.

"Not yet. Wake Ryan. Quiet. Get Parker deeper into stone-shadow and keep her the hell away from the rim."

Evan nods and vanishes into the dim.

Rowan turns back to Isorae and cups her jaw, grounding. His thumb brushes her cheek — gentle until you see the violence burning behind his eyes.

"You stay in the center," he murmurs. "With Erin."

"You're going to the rim," she says.

"I'm going to meet the first thing they think they can put on my land."

The word think sounds like a threat.

Her fingers close around his wrist.

"Rowan."

He stills — not because she stops him, but because something older than fear lives in her voice.

"They're not coming like last time," she whispers. "This is not retrieval."

"Then what?"

Her shimmer flickers faintly.

"Foothold. They want something that stays."

Erin's scanner answers with a thin, horrible chirp.

"They're planting a fucking node."

Rowan turns toward the ridge.

"Then we pull it out of the ground," he says slowly, lethally,

"and we break its teeth."

They hear nothing human.

No engines. No boots. No chatter.

ARIS has learned that sound is a signature.

But the valley listens back.

Mist thickens along the fern curtain like breath pressed to glass. The trees go too still. Birds are not simply quiet — they are absent, as if the valley itself has evacuated the airspace.

Five figures slide through the mist — not walking, not running — advancing the way something does when it already knows it has permission.

One kneels at the perimeter and sets a long, narrow case on the ground.

"That's the node," Erin whispers.

The case opens like a coffin.

Inside lies a matte-black cylinder, seams folded like petals.

The agent presses his palm to it.

The cylinder hums — not like a pulse, not like a machine — but like something asking the valley what it's allowed to take.

Rowan feels it answer inside his sternum.

The valley stiffens. Roots tighten. Mist draws inward as if inhaled.

The cylinder replies with a thin artificial resonance that tries to imitate the valley's voice.

Isorae flinches.

Rowan grips her hand.

The valley surges.

The cylinder brightens.

It is learning.

Rowan steps into open ground.

"Pick it the fuck up," he says evenly.

"That thing goes back in your case."

The agent finally looks up.

"Mr. Hale. Step back."

They know his name.

When the emitter lifts toward the unseen heart of the valley, Isorae inhales sharply — like a blade sliding between Rowan's ribs.

"Erin," he says softly — dangerously —

"get her back. Now."

The emitter whines.

"No," Rowan says.

And the valley answers.

Roots rise like ribs around the node. Stone shifts. The cylinder jolts.

Rowan moves.

The emitter fires — the land bends it — and pain detonates white and hot down his arm.

He does not slow.

He hits the agent hard enough to knock the air out of him and drives him into the dirt, breath in his ear as he snarls,

"Pick it the fuck up."

Silas's arrow thunks into the soil beside the agent's hand.

Dax steps in, knife bare.

The node screams.

Then it splits — cleanly, finally — its lattice collapsing like a gutted star.

The valley exhales.

The agents retreat.

Only when they vanish does Rowan turn back to Isorae.

"They learned," she murmured.

"Yeah," Rowan answers.

"So did we."

Behind him, the valley tightens.

Not to hide.

To hold.

To brace.

Because the land has learned a new word.

And it means—

mine.

50

THE PLACE WHERE THE LAND DRAWS TEETH

The valley does not celebrate.

It fortifies.

Not with walls.

With decisions.

Rowan feels it the morning after the foothold attempt — the way the land presses more firmly beneath his boots, as if the soil itself has thickened overnight. The wind no longer drifts freely through the hollow. It slides. It curves. It follows subtle channels through fern and stone, moving with purpose instead of wandering, as though the air itself has been given corridors to obey.

The valley has begun to choose how breath is allowed to move.

Isorae wakes with her hand already resting over Rowan's sternum — not searching, not afraid.

Anchoring.

"You hurt," she murmurs, eyes still closed.

Rowan exhales slowly. His shoulder still burns where the emitter clipped him, but that isn't what weighs in his chest.

"They tasted you," he says quietly.

Her shimmer flickers — faint, controlled. "They tasted us."

The valley leans closer.

Not listening.

Choosing.

By midmorning, the land begins to change in ways even Rowan has never seen.

Fern thickens along the ridge approaches — not taller, not wider, but tighter — knitting itself into narrow green funnels that quietly force single-file movement. Stones settle into half-rings that naturally guide footsteps into predictable lanes. Moss deepens into sound-swallowing mats along interior paths, softening not only footfall, but the echo of breath.

The valley is not hiding.

It is shaping.

Dax notices first. He crouches beside a new stone arc that definitely did not exist yesterday.

"It's building kill corridors," he murmurs.

Silas studies a root wall that curves inward like ribs. "This isn't camouflage," he says quietly. "This is anatomy."

Erin's scanner hates it. Every attempt to map the hollow warps and bends — angles skewing, depth refusing to remain consistent.

"It's not just rejecting their frequencies," she mutters. "It's rewriting its own geometry."

Evan watches the reshaping paths, arms crossed, eyes dark. "It's becoming a body."

By afternoon, the first watchers arrive.

Not agents.

Not probes.

People.

Two men appear on the western slope — locals from a nearby town. They do not step into the hollow. They stand at the ridge pretending to admire the view while quietly scanning with their phones, movements too careful, smiles too prepared.

Rowan feels the flatness instantly.

He walks up alone.

They brighten when they see him.

"Nice place you've got here," one says casually.

Rowan does not return the smile.

"This isn't a park."

They exchange a glance — quick, rehearsed.

"We heard people were living out here," the other adds. "Just wanted to see if everything's... safe."

Rowan steps closer, letting his shadow fall over them.

"Safe from who?"

They hesitate. Shrug. "Government types."

His eyes sharpen.

"Then you should leave before you get counted."

Their smiles disappear.

They retreat quickly.

Behind them, the valley tightens — not aggressively, not visibly — but like something that has just memorized the architecture of their bones.

Isorae watches from below, fingers curled into Rowan's jacket.

"They're triangulating by observation now," she whispers. "Human eyes are easier to place than machines."

Rowan nods once.

"Then we stop being easy to see."

That night, the valley changes again.

Fires burn lower without instruction. Smoke thins into mist before it can rise above the canopy. Sound refuses to carry as far as it once did — laughter swallowed early, voices fading sooner than they should.

The land is learning stealth.

But beneath Rowan's ribs something deeper tightens — not reaction.

Armament.

Isorae stirs beside him.

"It's growing teeth."

Rowan presses his forehead to hers.

"Good."

Far beyond the ridges, ARIS updates its internal modeling:

```
ENVIRONMENTAL ENTITY: HOSTILE ADAPTIVE BIOME
BRIDGE SUBJECT: TERRITORIAL / PROTECTIVE BOND
ACTIVE
STANDARD EXTRACTION PROTOCOL: INSUFFICIENT
RECOMMENDED: PAIR SEPARATION EVENT
```

And in a sterile white chamber that does not believe in sacred ground, a new directive blinks into being:

`ISOLATE ISORAE FIRST`

The valley has drawn teeth.

Now it is deciding where to bite.

51

THE LINE THEY SHOULDN'T CROSS

The first thing the valley loses is its birds.

Not in panic.

Not in silence.

In pattern.

At dawn, Rowan notices the finches are no longer landing where they always have. The low branches that once filled with restless wings remain empty, while higher limbs begin to gather movement instead. It isn't fear that has moved them. It's acoustics. Something beneath the canopy has subtly altered the way sound carries—the way it curves, the way it lingers—and the birds have adjusted to the land's new listening posture.

The valley has changed the way it hears.

It is preparing.

Isorae feels it before anyone says it aloud. Her fingers curl in Rowan's sleeve as he studies the treeline, the faint shimmer beneath her skin tightening into a thinner, quieter glow.

"They've drawn a boundary," she murmurs.

Silas stands near the stone ribs the land raised days ago, mapping the new foot funnels with quiet, surgical precision. His eyes track how fern lines and root arcs subtly guide movement into narrowing lanes.

"They aren't fortifications," he says. "They're choices. If something crosses here, it does so under terms the valley sets."

Dax steps up beside him, gaze sharp.

"Kill geometry."

No one corrects him.

The first deliberate test comes that afternoon.

A drone does not enter the valley. It stops just beyond the northern ridge, hovering at a precise elevation, its optics trained inward—not to scan the entire hollow, but to lock onto a single point.

Isorae stiffens instantly.

Her shimmer spikes—thin, bright, uneven—like glass catching sun at the wrong angle.

"It's on me," she whispers.

Rowan steps in front of her without thinking, his body moving before thought, before fear—instinct rising from something older than strategy.

The drone does not move. It doesn't need to.

It is measuring separation potential.

Erin's scanner detonates in shrill cascades.

"They're running pair-disruption modeling in real time!" she shouts. "They aren't mapping the valley. They're mapping him through her!"

Rowan feels the land answer beneath his boots—pressure tightening, roots shifting, stone firming as if the valley itself has leaned forward to watch.

The valley does not attack.

It waits.

Dax draws a bead with a salvaged rifle. Silas raises a hand.

"Not yet."

The drone pivots a fraction.

Not toward Rowan.

Toward Isorae.

The air thickens around her. Her knees wobble as if gravity has momentarily changed its mind.

Rowan's hands lock around her arms.

"Hey," he growls softly. "Stay in your body. Stay with me. Stay in your bones."

She nods, breath shallow, shimmer trembling painfully—like light stretched too thin over bone.

The valley moves.

Stone arcs rise another few inches along the ridge. Mist surges upward in a silent wall, swallowing sightlines and warping depth.

The drone's signal falters. Its stabilizers jitter.

Then it retreats.

Not destroyed.

Not repelled.

Denied.

Silas exhales slowly. "They just learned something important."

Dax grimaces. "Yeah. That we don't bite first."

Rowan looks down at Isorae, jaw tightening, eyes dark.

"They're going to make us."

That night, the valley dreams.

People wake to the same sensation—not fear, not images—but pressure, like standing beside something enormous that has just flexed a muscle in its sleep.

Isorae presses her face into Rowan's chest, breath trembling.

"They're planning to cut you out of me," she whispers.

Rowan's jaw tightens.

"They can try."

Far beyond the ridges, ARIS updates its modeling:

PAIR SEPARATION SIMULATION: 73% SUCCESS IF SUBJECT A IS REMOVED FROM HOSTILE BIOME FIRST

RECOMMENDATION: LURE / EXTRACTION THROUGH NON-HOSTILE VECTOR

SELECT: HUMAN INTERFACE PROTOCOL

They have stopped asking how to enter.

They have started designing how to take.

52

THE DOOR THAT ISN'T A DOOR

The message does not arrive in the valley.

It arrives through people.

Not as pulses.

Not as drones.

Not as light.

As language.

The first carrier is Ryan.

He comes down from the western ridge near dusk, breath uneven, eyes unfocused, moving like someone following a voice only he can hear. His boots slip once on loose shale, but he does not slow. His body moves with the obedient rhythm of someone walking toward a thought that feels like his own.

Rowan catches him just before he reaches the fire.

"Ryan."

The man blinks hard, breath hitching as if waking mid-step. His gaze stutters, pupils widening.

"I—" He swallows. "I thought someone was calling my name. It sounded… familiar. Like… like a friend."

Isorae stiffens instantly.

"That wasn't the valley," she says quietly.

Erin's scanner gives a quiet, tight chirp—low band, narrow beam, directional.

"Someone just pinged his neural recognition field," she mutters. "That's invitation tech. They didn't project outward—they slipped inward."

She glances at the readout, frowning.

"They used him to calibrate the voice," she adds. "Now they can cast it wider."

Silas goes still.

"They aren't trying to breach the land."

"They're trying to make us open it," Dax says flatly.

Ryan rubs his arms, suddenly cold. "It felt nice," he adds quietly. "Like someone remembered me."

No one answers him.

Two hours later, it happens again.

Parker—ribs still bound beneath her shirt—stands abruptly from her shelter, face pale.

"Someone just told me I can leave."

Every voice dies.

Rowan turns slowly. "Who?"

She swallows, eyes wet. "I don't know. It felt like… a thought that wasn't mine. But it knew my name. It told me the pain would stop if I followed it."

Isorae's glow flickers sharply—thin and uneven.

"They're learning how to speak around the valley," she breathes. "They're sending promises through human minds."

Dax swears under his breath.

"They're building a door out of people."

That night, three more wake with the same sensation.

Not panic.

Not command.

Relief.

A voice offering safety.

A route that feels gentle.

A way out that doesn't feel like betrayal—only like rest.

Erin pulls Rowan aside, her voice low and shaking.

"They're using adaptive cognition modeling. This is surgical psychological insertion. They're building a soft corridor. If anyone walks it, the valley will loosen to accommodate their choice."

Isorae grips Rowan's hand tightly.

"They're trying to make me reachable."

Rowan's voice goes very quiet.

"They don't get a door."

At midnight, the land reacts.

Roots rise gently across the western footpath—not blocking it, but rewriting its geometry. The trail curves back into the hollow even when walked straight. Anyone who tries to leave finds themselves returning without realizing why.

The valley is closing its own gates.

Silas studies the shift.

"It's not trapping us," he says softly. "It's protecting her."

Dax's jaw tightens.

"They're going to escalate."

Rowan nods once.

"They always do."

Far beyond the ridges, ARIS updates its models:

```
NEURAL INTERFACE PROTOCOL — PARTIAL SUCCESS
SUBJECT B (ISORAE): INDIRECT ACCESSIBLE
NEXT PHASE: PROXIMITY EXTRACTION TRIAL
```

They've found a door.

Now they just need someone brave enough to walk it.

And they are already choosing who.

53

THE MAN WHO STARTS TO HEAR THEM

Ryan wakes choking.

Not on air—on direction.

His body snaps upright from sleep as if he has been called by name from somewhere deep underground. His hands fly to his chest, fingers digging into his shirt as his pulse hammers too fast, too wrong—as though his heart has briefly been asked to beat in a rhythm that does not belong to him.

It hadn't hurt at first.

That was the worst part.

It had felt like relief.

The fire beside him has burned down to blue coals.

The valley is quiet.

Too quiet.

Not resting—listening.

Ryan sucks in a shallow breath and holds it, suddenly uncertain how much space he is allowed to occupy. His thoughts feel slightly rearranged, like furniture moved in a familiar room while he slept—not enough to look wrong, but enough that every step through his own mind now requires care.

He does not remember dreaming.

He remembers being tuned.

It felt like someone sliding a thin invisible wire through the center of his spine and plucking it gently—not to hurt him, but to hear what note he made.

His ears ring faintly. His jaw aches as if he has been clenching it for hours. There is a subtle pressure behind his eyes—not pain, but expectation.

He swallows hard and looks around.

Everyone else is sleeping.

Everyone except Rowan.

Of course.

Rowan sits at the edge of the hollow with his back braced against a stone root-rise, one knee bent, one hand resting on the earth. His posture is not tense, not searching.

It is barricaded.

His gaze is lifted toward the treeline—not watching movement—waiting for intention.

Ryan pushes himself to his feet and walks toward him. His steps feel slightly mis-timed with the ground, as if the valley has half a breath more awareness than he does.

Rowan does not turn.

"You hear it too," Rowan says quietly.

Ryan freezes. "I—I don't—"

"You don't need words," Rowan murmurs. "Just tell me where it touched you."

Ryan's hand drifts to his sternum without him meaning to. His fingers tremble.

"There," he whispers. "It felt like someone tested my bones."

Rowan's jaw tightens.

"They spoke to you."

Ryan hesitates—then nods.

"Not with sound," he says. "With structure. With meaning that didn't need sentences."

"What did they say?"

Ryan swallows. His throat burns.

"They said the valley is temporary."

Rowan finally turns.

His eyes are not human in the dark.

"They said the world is stabilizing."

Rowan rises slowly—carefully—as if something vast is coiled beneath his skin and must not be allowed to surface too quickly.

"And what did you say back?"

Ryan's breath shakes. "I didn't answer," he whispers. "But something in me… listened."

The valley exhales low and uneasy.

Isorae stirs in her sleep nearby, her shimmer flickering faintly like a wounded moon trying to stay whole.

Rowan steps closer.

"Listen to me now," he says quietly. "You were not chosen. You were detected."

"They don't want you," he continues. "They want the map of your nervous system so they can reach her."

Ryan's eyes fill with fear. "They said they can make it stop hurting her."

Rowan's voice drops—feral and ancient.

"They are lying," he says.

"They are learning how to aim."

Ryan chokes back a sob. "I didn't want to hear them."

Rowan grips his shoulder—hard, grounding, anchoring him back into his own bones.

"They will come again," he says. "And next time they will sound like your own thoughts."

Ryan whispers, "What do I do?"

Rowan leans in, voice low, dangerous, sacred.

"You learn to listen to me louder."

The valley tightens around them.

Deep beneath root and stone, something old stirs awake.

Because ARIS has now found a living doorway.

And Rowan has just claimed it.

54

THE LAND THAT LEARNS THEIR NAMES

The birds don't leave.

They reorganize.

At dawn, flocks that once scattered now circle the eastern ridge in slow, deliberate spirals, moving as though guided by an unseen current. Hawks hover too long over the same stones, wings barely shifting. Finches settle in quiet, orderly lines along exposed root-veins that were never perches before, their bodies aligned with grooves in the earth as if the land itself has quietly suggested where they should stand.

The valley is not disturbed.

It is organizing.

Rowan notices it first—not because he is watching the sky, but because the ground feels busier beneath his boots. The soil resists in a new way. Roots hold more tightly. Stone keeps its warmth longer into the morning, refusing to release heat the way it always has. Even the air seems to carry shape now—not wind, but intention, like something moving through a body rather than over a landscape.

He walks the perimeter with Dax and Erin before the others wake.

Fog still threads low through fern corridors, pale and soundless, clinging to the hollows between stones. Dax crouches near an old limestone seam and drags his fingers along its edge. The rock is warmer than it should be, faintly humming under his touch.

"This didn't sit like this yesterday," he murmurs.

Rowan studies the altered angle of the stone. The seam has shifted just enough to narrow a clear running lane.

"It moved."

Erin's handheld scanner clicks faintly in her grip. The screen flickers, stabilizes, then flickers again.

"Background harmonics are changing," she says quietly. "The valley's… aligning."

"Aligning how?" Dax asks.

Her eyes lift—uneasy. "Like it's choosing a side."

They reach the eastern cut—the pale scar where the resonance blade first landed, where soil still holds a faint memory of fracture. Rowan steps onto the damaged ground.

The earth tightens under his boots.

Not rejecting.

Recognizing.

His pulse shifts. Something subtle inside his sternum realigns—not painful, not powerful—but precise, like a key settling into its correct notch. The land leans into him—not pressing, not pulling—simply acknowledging.

Rowan closes his eyes.

And for the first time, he does not ask.

He listens.

Names ripple beneath his ribs.

Not words—signatures. Lives. Threads of breath, bone, grief, and memory woven through root and stone and water. The people sleeping in the hollow. The ones who arrived broken. The ones who stayed. The ones who nearly left.

He exhales slowly.

"They're learning who we are," he murmurs.

Erin stiffens. "Who?"

"The valley."

Behind them, Isorae wakes.

She steps out into the early light, her shimmer low and folded—then brightens, steadies, as if something inside her has quietly rebalanced overnight. When her bare feet touch the stone path, warmth blooms beneath her soles. Mist curls toward her ankles like breath drawn in.

Dax watches, eyes wide. "It's responding to her."

Rowan shakes his head. He looks back toward the hollow—toward the waking shelters, the people beginning to stir, the fragile living network the land has chosen to keep.

"No," he says softly. "It's responding to us."

At the western ridge, Ryan suddenly gasps.

He drops to his knees, palms slamming into the soil as if gravity has changed direction beneath him.

"It just said my name," he whispers.

The ground hums—not sound, but structure.

Erin's scanner spikes violently, then steadies into a smooth, unfamiliar curve.

"It's writing something," she breathes.

Rowan moves to Ryan's side and kneels, placing his palm flat against the earth.

The valley answers.

Not with vibration—with memory.

He sees roots lifting where people sleep. Stone folding into protective arcs. Fern corridors narrowing where danger would enter. Wind bending around patrol routes. Clearings reshaping into funnels.

Not random.

Deliberate.

A living grid.

A body learning how to brace.

Rowan lifts his head slowly.

"They taught it how to find her," he says. "So now it's learning how to protect her."

Isorae's voice trembles. "It's learning our shapes."

Rowan's hand clamps onto the back of Ryan's neck—grounding, familiar.

"Mine," Rowan says quietly, not to Ryan.

To the valley.

Above them, the birds tighten their spirals.

Far beyond the ridges, ARIS satellites adjust their angles, algorithms stuttering as geometry stops behaving like terrain.

They do not understand what has changed—only that the valley
has stopped behaving like land.

And has begun behaving like a guardian intelligence.

Rowan rises to his feet.

"They wanted to turn her into a beacon," he says quietly. "They
just taught the land how to hunt their signals."

The valley exhales.

Slow.

Deep.

Patient.

It is no longer waiting.

It is learning.

55

THE SIGNAL
THAT BLINKS BACK

ARIS does not panic.

It recalculates.

That distinction matters, because panic flails — but recalculation responds.

Less than twelve minutes after the valley's harmonic realignment, three classified orbital arrays alter their geometry. The shift is too precise to be weather and too subtle for civilian detection — a slow, surgical pivot that adjusts incidence angles by fractions of a degree. A movement so small it could be mistaken for orbital drift.

But not by Erin.

She is standing near the fireline when her handheld scanner emits a sharp, staccato ticking that slices clean through morning quiet. She freezes mid-step, breath catching in her throat.

"They just changed orbital geometry," she murmurs.

Rowan looks up immediately. "Meaning..."

Her eyes do not leave the scrolling data. "Meaning something blinked back."

The words ripple through the hollow like cold water poured into stillness.

Isorae stiffens where she stands. Her shimmer tightens — not flaring, not dimming — but drawing inward into a narrow, coherent line, like light being forced through a blade's edge.

"They sent a test ping," she whispers. "The valley answered."

Dax swears under his breath. "So now they know it's not just her."

Ryan steps closer, face pale. "They know it's alive."

The next pulse does not sweep the hollow.

It halts at the ridge.

Not fading. Not dissipating. Simply stopping — as if something invisible has pressed a palm against the valley's perimeter to test its resistance.

Along the eastern slope, trees lean subtly inward. Stone seams warm beneath the moss. Mist thickens — but only along the incoming arc — forming a faint, curved veil that reshapes the approach corridor.

The land is not reacting.

It is shaping a boundary.

Erin's scanner spikes in short, frantic bursts — then goes cleanly dead in her hands.

"They're losing telemetry," she breathes. "The valley is scrambling their returns."

Rowan feels it in his bones — not as pain, not as power — but as alignment pressure. The land is flexing. Testing micro-adjustments. Learning how to bend signals without tearing itself apart.

Isorae grips his hand tightly. "It's filtering what they're allowed to see."

Ryan swallows. "We're… blinding them."

Rowan shakes his head slowly. "No. We're teaching it where we live."

High above the canopy, a single drone slips through cloud cover.

It doesn't scream. It doesn't posture. It drifts down like a patient insect, optics glinting faintly as it aligns its lens toward the hollow's heart.

The valley responds.

Air thickens.

Mist coils upward like breath drawn in by unseen lungs. Roots lift a full inch beneath the drone, bracing the soil like muscle preparing for impact.

The drone's stabilizers whine.

Its signal fractures.

It tilts — not crashing, not burning — simply losing certainty.

Erin's scanner chirps once, sharply. "Telemetry blackout."

The drone drifts sideways. Hesitates.

Then it retreats.

Backs out of the corridor and vanishes into cloud cover as if something behind the valley has politely but firmly closed a door.

Rowan exhales slowly.

"They're learning what happens when they touch us."

Isorae closes her eyes. "And they're afraid."

Far beyond the ridges, in rooms of glass and humming servers, ARIS command logs update:

```
ANOMALY RESPONSE CLASS: ADAPTIVE
TERRAIN INTERACTION: INTENTIONAL
SIGNAL RETURN: CORRUPTED
RECOMMENDATION: ESCALATE
```

They do not yet understand what they have awakened.

But they have just taught the valley one more thing —

how to push back.

And the valley is very, very good at learning.

56

THE ONES WHO ARE NO LONGER LOST

They do not arrive broken.

They do not arrive trembling.

They do not arrive hollow-eyed, aching, desperate, or pulled.

They arrive in formation.

Rowan feels them before anyone sees them — not as grief, not as hunger, not as resonance ache — but as directional pressure. A slow, dense mass sliding through the outer bones of the valley, testing where its living edge ends and something engineered begins.

Birdsong dies first.

Not all at once — but in a ripple, as if the forest has been quietly instructed to hold its breath.

Then the wind stiffens.

Then the valley tightens — not protectively, not defensively — but in a way Rowan has never felt before.

Measuring.

As if the land itself is trying to calculate whether something in front of it belongs to biology… or to procedure.

Ryan swallows. "They're not seekers," he murmurs. "They're placed."

Erin's scanner begins pulsing in narrow vertical bars, lighting in steady synchronized beats. Her face drains of color.

"Six separate cardiac rhythms," she says quietly. "All phase-locked."

Dax is already on the ridge, crouched low, eyes fixed on the fern curtain. "Five… no. Six."

They step out of the forest slowly.

Six men and women in matte travel gear, boots spotless, faces calm, postures aligned to the same internal tempo. Their breathing is synchronized. Their micro-movements are synchronized. Even their blinks occur in faint, repeating patterns.

No insignia.

No visible weapons.

No hesitation.

They do not look like explorers.

They look like components.

Rowan steps forward before the valley can fully close its corridors.

"Stop."

All six halt at the same instant — not with surprise, but with programmed obedience.

A woman near the center lifts her chin slightly. Her eyes are pale, unblinking, and curiously empty of stress response.

"We're not here to hurt anyone."

Isorae's shimmer dims — not fading, but compressing tightly beneath her skin.

"They are lying," she whispers.

The woman's mouth curves into a faint, almost pleasant smile.

"We're just… curious."

The valley recoils.

Not violently.

Decisively.

Stone warms beneath Rowan's boots. Roots shift beneath the soil. Air tightens as if the valley has straightened its spine.

Dax mutters, "That smile doesn't belong to a person."

Rowan's voice drops. "You weren't called."

One of the men tilts his head slightly — studying him the way a sensor studies terrain.

"No," he replies evenly. "We were trained."

The words slide wrong through the air — too clean, too hollow, too perfectly aligned to human grammar without carrying human nervous texture.

Erin swallows. "They've been frequency-conditioned."

Isorae stiffens. "They've been tuned to me."

The woman steps forward.

The valley does not allow it.

Her boot sinks half an inch into suddenly softening soil — not mud, not earth — but listening ground that has decided her weight does not match its expectation.

She freezes.

"…That's new," she murmurs.

Rowan steps closer — slow, grounded, lethal.

"You're not walking past me."

The man on the far left exhales. "We weren't sent to negotiate."

A thin tone rises in the air — not loud, not audible to most — but sharp enough to make Isorae gasp and clutch Rowan's jacket.

The valley shudders.

Dax swears softly. "They're broadcasting."

Erin's scanner detonates into red. "They're pinging her directly!"

Rowan moves instantly, pulling Isorae behind him as the air tightens.

All six raise their hands in perfect unison.

Not weapons.

Emitters.

ARIS has stopped pretending.

And the valley has just been formally challenged.

57

THE VALLEY CHOOSES

The tone sharpens.

Not louder.

More exact.

It threads into Isorae's bones like a surgical filament sliding between vertebrae — thin, searching — looking for a seam that was never meant to be found.

She gasps.

Her shimmer flares unevenly beneath her skin, light spiking in jagged, fractured arcs that refuse to settle, as though her resonance is being forced to stutter between incompatible geometries.

Rowan feels it tear through his sternum like something probing for a door inside his ribs — not pain, not pressure — but orientation being tested.

As if the world has leaned in and quietly asked, *Which way does this hinge turn?*

"Down," he growls.

The valley listens.

Stone answers first.

Not violently.

Decisively.

Low ribs of limestone rise from the hollow floor in a curved, protective arc, sliding into place with the patient inevitability of bone forming beneath skin. Wind tightens along its edges. Leaves along the shield's rim stiffen, locking into scale-like alignment.

The land has chosen posture.

Chosen spine.

Chosen side.

Dax drops to one knee beside Rowan, blade already in his hand — not lifted, not trembling — simply waiting, like a coiled spring finally certain of what it is meant to do.

Erin's scanner detonates into frantic wails. "They're locking resonance on both of you," she shouts. "They're not isolating her anymore — they're modeling you as a unified interface!"

Isorae's fingers clutch Rowan's jacket, breath shallow and shaking. "They're mapping the bond," she whispers. "They're trying to find where you end and I begin."

One of the six steps forward again.

This time, the earth does not soften.

It hardens.

His boot skids slightly against suddenly rigid soil. The valley has decided his mass does not belong here. He steadies himself, eyes flicking down — then up again, recalibrating.

"…You're learning faster than predicted," he says quietly.

Rowan's gaze darkens. "You don't get to predict me."

The woman at the center raises her emitter — not pointing, not threatening — simply aligning.

The air tightens.

The tone sharpens into a harmonic blade — thin enough to slip between worlds.

Erin screams, "Rowan — they're about to cut the Bridge—"

Rowan steps forward instead.

He places his palm flat against the stone shield.

And breathes — not air — memory.

Not thought.

Not command.

But the deep remembering of being what he is.

The valley answers.

A pressure wave moves through bedrock like a muscle contracting beneath continental skin. Roots across a forty-yard arc tighten simultaneously, coiling like tendons beneath flesh. Stone veins flare. Wind locks.

The harmonic blade fractures mid-air — not exploding, not scattering — but losing coherence, its structure collapsing into dead geometry.

The six agents stagger.

One drops to a knee.

The woman at the center stiffens violently, breath tearing loose from her chest as if something inside her has been misaligned by a force that does not exist in her training manuals.

Dax grins grimly. "Good," he murmurs. "Now they bleed."

Isorae presses her palm to Rowan's spine, voice trembling with awe. "You're aligning the land," she whispers. "You're becoming the gate."

Rowan does not look back.

"Good," he says.

The six agents withdraw — not in panic — but in calculation.

Before they vanish into the trees, the woman meets Rowan's eyes one final time.

"We're not your hunters," she says calmly. "We're your scouts."

Then they are gone.

The valley does not relax.

It tightens.

Not with fear —

but with readiness.

Because now the land knows:

They are no longer being tested.

They are being mapped.

And Rowan Hale is no longer an anomaly.

He is officially a threat structure.

58

THE FIRST TRUE STRIKE

It doesn't start with sound.

No warning hum.

No tremor.

No pressure ripple crawling up the bones to say run.

It starts with something worse.

Absence.

The valley exhales — and something sacred does not come back.

Birdsong vanishes in a single, merciless line from west to east, as if silence itself has been dragged through the trees with a blade. Not fading. Not drifting.

Erased.

The air hollows along that edge — scooped clean of echo, breath ripped out of it like marrow sucked from bone.

Rowan feels it tear under his ribs — a sudden hollow yank, like part of the valley's heart just skipped a beat it was never meant to miss. The deep anchoring hum he's learned to live inside stutters sideways — not gone, but displaced — like a compass ripped off true by a hidden fucking magnet.

Erin's scanner explodes into shrill screaming feedback.

"Full-spectrum breach!" she shouts. "They're not probing — they're fucking entering—!"

The ground doesn't rise.

It folds.

Space creases like paper in a closing fist.

The western treeline collapses inward, light kinking, moss peeling sideways as six matte-black drop frames phase directly into the hollow.

Not above it.

Not around it.

Inside it.

The valley has been breached.

Dax is already moving.

"Defensive ring — now!"

Silas hauls civilians behind rising stone ribs. Evan yanks a frozen kid into shadow. Erin shoves shaking bodies into cover as the air thickens with wrong, biting pressure.

Rowan turns — and the valley turns with him.

"Isorae," he growls, catching her wrist and slamming her into his back. "Don't let go."

Her arms lock around his ribs, breath fast but iron-steady.

"I am with you," she whispers.

The drop frames bloom.

Not doors.

Not ramps.

They flower like iron wounds ripping open.

Twelve armored extraction units step into the hollow — not scanning, not aiming — tuning. Their suits hum in tight counter-spirals, twisting the air into narrow surgical corridors.

They aren't here to restrain.

They're here to cut.

Erin's voice fractures.

"They're generating bond-disruption geometry—!"

The first resonance blade fires.

Not at Isorae.

At Rowan.

The hit slams into his chest like something trying to pry his ribs apart from the inside. Breath rips out of him. His vision whites as alignment tears — not flesh — structure.

Rowan stumbles.

Not bleeding.

Dislocated from reality by half a fucking step.

Isorae screams — her shimmer detonating under her skin like lightning tearing through glass.

Dax charges with a feral roar, blade flashing — carving clean through one unit's knee joint as Silas tackles another into limestone hard enough to crack rock.

But the geometry is already forming.

Three units slam pylons into the soil.

They bite.

A triangular resonance cage snaps around Rowan and Isorae. Gravity skews sideways. Time stutters like a heart skipping beats. Air thickens until it feels like drowning inside glass.

"They're unthreading us—!" Isorae gasps.

Rowan locks his arms around her, pain ripping through his spine as he plants his feet.

"You do not touch her," he snarls.

The pylons scream.

The field tightens.

Then—

A second wave phases in.

Smaller.

Faster.

Purpose-built.

They rise from roots.

From stone.

From the valley's fucking bones.

Erin screams, "They're already inside the land—!"

One reaches Isorae.

Not to grab.

To mark.

A burning sigil ignites in the air over her sternum — thin, precise, surgical.

Rowan roars — not sound —

structure.

The valley convulses. Stone ribs spear upward, crushing three units at once. Moss detonates. Roots tear free like living cables.

But the mark is already burning.
And inside that mark—
ARIS finally has her.
Not her body.
Her key.
They withdraw.
Not routed.
Not panicked.
Three shattered frames remain.
Six operatives vanish into folding light.
And an invisible thread now runs through Isorae's bones — quiet.
Precise. Locked.
ARIS does not need to take her today.
The hunt is over.
Now it is extraction phase.

59

THE SHAPE OF WHAT HUNTS THEM BACK

The valley does not settle.

It coils.

Stone ribs still stand half-raised where the strike tore through them — limestone bones arcing through fern and root like the exposed skeleton of something enormous that has not yet decided whether it is dead…

or simply waiting to finish something.

Smoke clings low to the western hollow, sliding across the ground in thin gray sheets that refuse to lift even when wind passes through them. It doesn't drift.

It breathes.

Not like smoke.

Like something alive that doesn't belong to lungs.

Three extraction units lie scattered across the earth.

Not fallen.

Rejected.

Their matte-black armor has split open like cracked shells, inner latticework still twitching inside — thin blue filaments sparking and writhing as if the machines haven't yet accepted that their bodies are no longer whole.

They look wrong.

Not destroyed.

Denied.

People move carefully through the debris.

Not because they are injured.

But because shock has gravity.

Because something sacred about the border between here and elsewhere has been ripped open, and no one yet knows what the land will tolerate next.

Erin kneels beside the nearest shattered unit. She pries back a warped armor plate, fingers shaking as she peers into the humming geometry beneath. The exposed core makes the air shiver faintly — like a thought still trying to finish itself inside a skull that no longer exists.

"They weren't mapping anymore," she whispers.

Her voice breaks.

"They weren't testing."

She swallows.

"This was a fucking rehearsal."

Dax wipes blood from his knuckles and glances at Rowan.

"Then they just bombed their first show."

Rowan does not answer.

He is kneeling in the soil in front of Isorae.

She still stands where the strike left her — breath shallow, shimmer thinned to trembling threads — the invisible sigil above her sternum burning faintly like a hostile constellation carved into the wrong sky.

Rowan cups her face gently, anchoring her back into her bones.

"You with me?"

Her eyes struggle to focus. When they find his, they are bright with pain — and something sharper.

"Yes," she breathes.

"But I can feel them now."

His jaw tightens.

"Where?"

"Everywhere," she whispers.

"Inside me."

Something feral coils beneath Rowan's ribs.

He does not rage.

He aligns.

He rises.

And the valley answers — not in chaos, not in panic — but with purpose. Stone firms beneath his boots. Roots tighten. Mist thickens around his legs like a living line being drawn by something that has decided where its heart lives.

"Everyone to the inner ring," Rowan says calmly.

"Children first. Wounded next."

No one questions him.

He turns to Erin.

"Get every scanner you've got on that mark."

Then to Dax.

"You're with me."

Dax nods instantly.

Silas steps forward, blade already in hand.

"You'll need more than one."

Rowan gives a single nod.

"Good."

Isorae reaches for him, fingers shaking as she grips his sleeve like she's holding the last solid thing in a world that has just lost gravity.

"They can pull me now," she whispers.

"They know how."

Rowan leans in, pressing his forehead gently to hers, breath steady against breath.

"Then we cut their fucking hands off."

Her glow steadies — not louder, not brighter — but lethal.

Erin's scanners spike violently.

Her eyes widen.

"They're still listening," she rasps. "Not here — through her. They're using her resonance as a beacon."

Rowan lifts his gaze toward the ridgeline, eyes dark and certain.

"Then we give them something to hear."

He turns back to the valley.

"Pack what you can carry."

Confusion ripples through the gathered people.

"We're not running," Rowan says quietly.

"We're moving the fight."

The valley hums — not in fear.

In recognition.

Because the Bridge has finally chosen what it is going to be.

And now it has teeth.

60

THE LINE HE CROSSES ON PURPOSE

They do not leave quietly.

They leave correctly.

Rowan does not allow panic to lead the movement. He does not allow grief to hurry it. He does not allow fear to choose the path. He walks the valley's outer ring slowly, deliberately, listening with his bones — letting the land show him which places still remember how to hide, and which ones have decided they are finished hiding altogether.

Some slopes still cradle mist like a held breath. Others stand bare and rigid, stone ribs exposed as if the valley has finally chosen which parts of itself it is willing to sacrifice.

Those are the places he avoids.

Dax coordinates the inner evacuation — children first, wounded next — his voice low but steady, carrying across the hollow without rising. Silas positions watchers along the eastern ridge, arrows nocked, blades ready, not scanning the forest so much as standing inside it, becoming another quiet, dangerous shape the land now recognizes as its own.

Erin moves like someone rewriting physics in real time, dismantling fixed scanners and rebirthing them as portable lattice disruptors. Her hands shake only when she thinks no one is watching. She wipes sweat from her brow with a forearm already streaked with graphite dust and murmurs calculations that do not belong to any known discipline.

Isorae stays beside Rowan.

Not behind him.

Not sheltered in the center.

At his side.

Her shimmer has tightened into a narrow, concentrated line beneath her skin — no longer bleeding outward, no longer flaring — but threaded along her spine like a cord pulled taut and anchored deep inside her bones. She walks with the careful grace of someone who knows her body is now both sanctuary and signal.

"They are still touching me," she murmurs quietly as they walk. "Softly. Carefully."

Rowan does not slow.

"Let them," he says. "They won't like where it leads."

The valley's rim opens differently for him now. Roots lift to clear his path. Stone slopes flatten beneath his boots. Ferns bow just enough to let him pass. The land reshapes itself around him — not as shelter, not as barricade —

but as passage.

It does not hide him.

It makes him a door.

They reach the western boundary as dusk bruises the sky purple and gold.

Rowan stops.

Beyond the fern curtain lies unheld ground. Unclaimed earth. Places the valley no longer shelters — and no longer controls.

"This is the line," Isorae whispers.

Rowan nods.

"Once you cross it," Silas says softly, "the land won't pull you back."

Rowan steps forward anyway.

The pressure that has always tugged gently at his ribs — the valley's quiet claim — loosens.

Not breaking.

Releasing.

The land does not push him away.

It stands back.

He turns to Isorae, her eyes luminous in the dying light.

"You don't belong to them," he says quietly. "And neither do I."

She steps forward with him.

The air changes.

Not violently — but structurally — as if a door has just been closed behind them, not by force, but by choice.

Behind them, the valley inhales once — slow and deep — and seals itself.

Erin's scanners spike sharply.

"Oh hell," she whispers. "Their listening grid just... retuned."

Dax lifts his head. "Toward us?"

"No," Erin says slowly. "Toward him."

Rowan does not flinch.

He keeps walking.

With every step away from the valley, the world sharpens. Light becomes cleaner. Shadows narrow into crisp edges. Sound tightens into clean lines — as if the universe has shifted into a higher resolution simply to watch him pass.

Isorae's breath catches.

"They can see you now."

Rowan's mouth curves faintly.

"Good."

Far beyond the ridges, ARIS recalibrates.

Not to track an anomaly.

But to contain a moving origin point.

Because the Bridge has crossed its own boundary.

And it is no longer waiting to be found.

It is walking.

61

THE GRID THEY DIDN'T BUILD FOR HIM

The sky fractures first.

Not visibly.

Structurally.

No clouds tear.

No thunder warns.

No light bends.

Something worse happens.

The rules crack.

The invisible permissions that tell air how to behave, sound where to travel, resonance where it is allowed to live — all of it splinters, silently rewritten by something that does not ask.

Erin feels it before anyone hears a damn thing.

Her lattice scanner shrieks once — sharp, metallic — then collapses into a low, continuous whine that crawls under the skin and raises the fine hairs along Rowan's arms.

"That's not a sweep," she snaps, tearing a panel open, fingers flying. "That's a full-field suppression grid."

Silas lifts his rifle.

Dax shifts his stance.

The wind simply stops.

Leaves freeze mid-fall. Smoke locks into thin gray pillars over dying coals like the world has forgotten how to exhale.

Isorae inhales sharply.

Her breath stutters as something cold slides along the inside of her spine — not pain, not touch — jurisdiction.

"They just locked the band," she murmurs. "They're sealing everything I touch."

Above them, nothing looks different.

Which is how Rowan knows everything is.

He feels the air formalize around him.

Not thicken.

Not compress.

It decides.

The ground hums.

Low.

Perfect.

Too even.

ARIS's grid settles into place.

An invisible harmonic lattice spreads across the ridgeline, flattening wild variance, pruning chaos into obedient silence. The valley's living acoustics are shaved into straight lines and sterile corridors.

The land stiffens.

Not in fear.

In offense.

Rowan steps forward.

The grid answers instantly.

Pressure slams into his sternum like an unseen wall — not a push — a veto.

A silent, sterile declaration of ownership.

He does not stop.

He walks into it.

Static detonates across Erin's screens.

"That shouldn't be possible," she breathes. "He's destabilizing their null shell just by existing."

Isorae gasps. Her shimmer flares — not wild — furious, tightening into razor-thin filaments beneath her skin.

"They're choking the veil," she whispers. "They're trying to crush me into a single allowed frequency."

Rowan reaches back without looking.

His hand finds hers.

The grid shudders.

Not loudly.

Deeply — like something massive has just realized it miscalculated.

A tremor ripples across the ridge — stone seams warming, roots cinching, air hesitating like breath caught in a terrified throat.

Silas mutters, "Holy shit…"

Rowan keeps walking.

The pressure doubles.

Pale fractures lace the ground beneath his boots, spidering outward in thin geometric seams. Dust lifts and hangs, forgetting gravity for half a heartbeat.

Erin's scanners explode into cascading red.

"They're reinforcing — triple harmonic collapse, stacked null fields—"

A sharp structural crack rips through the air.

Miles east, a suppression tower overloads and dies.

Another flickers.

Then another.

Isorae cries out — not in pain, but in resonance — her bones answering something ancient waking inside him.

Rowan reaches the center of the grid.

He stops.

He closes his eyes.

And for the first time—

He does not breathe like a man.

He breathes like a fucking bridge.

Not lungs.

Conduit.

Not air.

Alignment.

The air bends.

The ground leans.

The lattice buckles.

Across distant sterile command chambers, ARIS containment algorithms erupt with warnings systems were never designed to feel:

```
MOVING ANOMALY EXCEEDS PREDICTIVE SHELL
PRIMARY NODE DESTABILIZATION
ORIGIN VECTOR UNSTABLE
GEOMETRY COMPLIANCE FAILURE
```

Rowan opens his eyes.

His voice is quiet.

Not loud.

Not broadcast.

Not violent.

But it is heard.

Everywhere.

"You don't get to put rules on me."

The grid shatters.

Not with explosion —

with surrender.

Miles of suppression lattice collapse into inert silence. Towers go dark in clean, surgical waves. The ridge exhales. The land remembers its wild shape. Wind resumes mid-breath. Smoke loosens and drifts again like something finally allowed to exist.

Far beyond the horizon, ARIS stops running simulations.

And begins issuing live combat directives.

Because the Bridge has just proven something catastrophic:

He cannot be contained.

And he will never again stay inside anyone's geometry.

62

THE ONES THEY SEND
INSTEAD OF DRONES

The forest feels it before the valley does.

Not pressure.

Not frequency.

Intention.

Something human — and not — steps onto the eastern ridge.

There is no hum.

No sweep.

No sky tearing open the canopy.

Only boots on soil.

Footsteps where footsteps do not belong.

Breath moving in air that suddenly feels too narrow to carry it.

Rowan stiffens instantly.

Not like someone hearing a sound —

like something ancient recognizing predation wearing a human face.

"They changed strategy," Isorae whispers. Her shimmer tightens tight to her skin, pulling inward like her bones have just been placed inside crosshairs.

"They're sending carriers."

Silas moves first — rifle lifting as his body melts into shadow.

Dax ghosts toward the northern trees, boots never touching the same leaf twice.

Erin snaps her headset on, scanner already shrieking softly in her palm.

Then they step out.

Six figures emerge from the forest.

Matte-black field armor laced with pale-blue glyph lines that light refuses to sit on. Their helmets are smooth. Their faces erased. Each carries a narrow crystalline baton that hums in Isorae's bones — a vibration that makes her teeth ache and her ribs clamp around breath.

Human delivery units.

Conduit handlers.

"They're not here to capture," Erin breathes.

"They're here to fucking sever."

The lead carrier steps forward.

His voice is calm. Professional. Soft — the voice of someone delivering a service call.

"We only need the anomaly," he says. "You can all remain unharmed."

Rowan steps into the open.

The ground tightens beneath his boots like the valley bracing its spine.

"No."

The carrier's visor tilts.

"You are not part of the equation."

Rowan tilts his head slowly.

"That's your first mistake."

The baton lifts.

The air screams — not sound — structure.

A surgical resonance blade slices straight for Isorae's sternum.

Rowan moves.

Not fast.

Absolute.

He steps into the cut.

The blade strikes his chest — and disintegrates.

Not deflected.

Not absorbed.

Denied.

The carrier staggers, staring at his baton like it just betrayed him.

Erin screams, "That was a severance strike—!"

Rowan keeps walking.

Each step breaks the geometry of the clearing.

Stone ripples outward.

Roots lift in slow coils.

Leaves freeze mid-fall, suspended like breath caught in a terrified throat.

Isorae gasps — her shimmer surging not in pain, but recognition.

"They can't cut you," she whispers.

Rowan does not look back.

"They can't cut what was built to be the cut."

The second carrier swings.

Dax fires — resonance-disruption rounds screaming through the air like tearing metal.

The third carrier collapses as his armor implodes inward, screaming as his internal lattice folds wrong.

Silas slams the fourth into stone hard enough to fracture limestone.

But the fifth—

The fifth breaks right.

Low.

Fast.

Sliding past Rowan's flank straight into Isorae's space.

His baton slices through her shimmer.

He touches her.

Her scream rips the air.

Thin fractures of light spider across her skin like glass starting to shatter.

Rowan turns.

The valley answers.

Not wind.

Not sound.

Jurisdiction.

The ground liquefies beneath the carrier into pale, luminous root-veins. He is lifted — not by force — but by structure. Held. Rewritten.

Rowan walks to him slowly.

"You don't get to touch what I am bonded to."

He raises his hand.

The man screams once.

Then the valley releases him.

Nothing remains but scorched moss…

and a collapsing lattice-shadow fading into nothing.

The remaining carriers retreat — not running — backing away slowly, carefully.

Reverently.

Because now they understand:

They did not meet a target.

They met a boundary.

And boundaries do not negotiate.

63

THE MOMENT ARIS DECIDES TO BREAK THE VALLEY

The first satellite does not look like a weapon.

It looks like weather.

A silver-white disc slides beneath the cloud deck, drifting through low orbit like misplaced moonlight — smooth, quiet, inevitable. It hums on a frequency no human instrument was ever meant to hear. It hums through weather. Through ozone. Through the skin of the planet.

It hums through law.

Erin sees it first.

Her console shrieks — then fractures into cascading static.

"Oh my god…" she whispers. "They just retasked a planetary array."

Rowan doesn't look up.

He feels it.

Not above —

inside.

A pressure blooms beneath his sternum, as if the sky itself has leaned down and placed both hands on his bones.

Isorae staggers beside him, breath tearing loose.

"They're widening the field," she gasps. "They're going to drown the valley."

The land stiffens.

Stone cinches tight. Roots retract. Wind collapses into narrow corridors like breath held too long. Leaves flatten. Sound thins — as if air itself has begun losing permission to exist.

The valley does not yet know how to fight the sky.

The beam drops.

Not bright.

Not loud.

Clean.

A cylindrical column of absolute calibration slams into the eastern hollow — and the world inside it forgets its own rules.

Color bleaches from bark in a smooth, horrifying wash. Moss pales to bone-ash gray. Lichen peels like dead skin. Birds fall as if gravity quietly rotated ninety degrees. Heartbeats stutter. Breath shortens. The air starts behaving like math.

People scream.

Rowan moves instantly.

"Silas — evacuate east!"

Silas snaps into motion. Dax vanishes into smoke and feral speed. Erin shouts into dead comms, hands flying as she tries to reach anything that still remembers how to listen.

Isorae cries out — not in pain — in fracture — lightning ripping under her skin as her shimmer destabilizes.

"They're forcing coherence through me—!"

Rowan catches her before her knees give.

The beam intensifies.

The valley begins to bleed light.

Stone splits along glowing seams. Roots snap upward then curl back, torn between geometries. The ground groans — not roaring — straining like something enormous being bent beyond what it was shaped to hold.

Rowan lifts his face into the falling sky.

"Not this place."

The beam touches him.

The satellite hiccups.

Just a fraction — but enough.

Erin gasps. "The signal's destabilizing—!"

Rowan steps fully into the column.

The world folds.

Pressure detonates across bone and stone and ancient alignment. Space flinches — as if something tried to rewrite him and discovered his shape is older than its alphabet.

Isorae screams his name.

High above, the satellite stutters.

Then drops power.

The beam shutters.

The valley exhales violently — wind crashing back into lungs, color flooding bark and moss, birds screaming back into living chaos.

Silence follows — heavy. Stunned. Reverent.

Far beyond the clouds, ARIS records:

```
BRIDGE ENTITY RESONANCE CONFIRMED
TERRAIN: PARTIALLY NON-COMPLIANT
STRATEGY: DIRECT EXTRACTION AUTHORIZED
```

They stop scanning.

They stop testing.

They stop calibrating.

Now they come to take her.

64

THE SKY THAT OPENS

It does not begin with sound.

There is no thunder.

No warning.

No flare of light.

It begins with something worse.

Absence.

The air above the valley hollows out — suddenly, unnaturally — as if the sky has inhaled too deeply and forgotten how to exhale.

Birdsong is guillotined mid-note.

Mist drops straight down instead of drifting.

Fire freezes in place — flames locked into pale, unmoving shapes, not burning, not flickering, just remembering what heat used to look like.

The hollow holds its breath.

Rowan feels it in his marrow.

Not as fear.

Not as thought.

As recoil.

The reflex written into bone before language — the instinct of living terrain recognizing extinction geometry.

He lifts his head.

And watches the sky open.

Not tear.

Not break.

Open.

Cloud cover slides away in perfect geometric arcs, folding back like surgical drapery to reveal a circular void of pale, starless white — a colorless depth that does not belong to weather, orbit, distance, or night.

A hole in permission.

A place where the sky has been told it may be removed.

Isorae gasps beside him, breath tearing loose.

"They've opened a retrieval gate."

The valley stiffens instantly.

Stone cinches tight.

Roots draw inward like ribs closing around a heart.

Moss darkens. Ferns lean inward. Wind coils low and tense.

The land knows what a gate is.

And it hates them.

A pillar of distortion descends — not light, not matter — authority given shape.

Space compresses around it. Gravity tilts sideways. People stagger as their inner ears lose agreement with the world.

Children cry out.

Adults collapse to their knees, gasping like the sky just remembered new rules for lungs.

Erin is screaming into dead uplinks.

Silas is shouting orders that vanish into pressure.

Dax is already gone — slipping into shadow as stone begins to rise.

Rowan steps forward.

"No."

He does not raise his voice.

He does not need to.

The land answers him.

Stone surges beneath his boots.

Ridges lift into curved defensive arcs.

Wind coils around his body like armor made of breath and intent.

The descending gate hesitates.

Then—

The pylons deploy.

Black crystalline spines tear out of the void and spear downward, punching into bedrock with surgical finality.

They do not shake the valley.

They claim it.

The land screams.

Not with sound.

With fracture.

Fault lines bloom white beneath moss. Roots snap and recoil. Entire slopes shudder as the geometry of the valley is forced into obedience.

Isorae cries out.

Her shimmer detonates beneath her skin — lightning ripping across her ribs and throat as invisible authority claws up her spine. Her feet lift from the ground.

"They're pulling through me—!"

Rowan catches her mid-rise and locks his arms around her.

"No," he growls into her hair.

"They go through me."

The pylons intensify.

The gate widens.

Trees shear at their roots.

Stone splits into glowing fault-lines.

The valley begins to fail under impossible geometry.

Erin collapses to her knees.

"They've locked the entire hollow into a gravity funnel—!"

Silas roars, "We're losing structural integrity!"

Isorae arches in Rowan's arms, breath breaking, shimmer flaring like glass struck by lightning as the world tries to unthread her.

Rowan plants his feet.

Muscles trembling.

Blood spilling from his nose.

Breath tearing like iron dragged across bone.

He lifts his face into the falling sky and roars — not sound — structure.

"You do not take her!"

The valley answers.

Roots explode upward like skeletal hands.

Stone ridges slam together in defensive arcs.

Wind detonates into pressure shockwaves that rip leaves from trees and hurl mist into spiraling walls.

The pylons shudder.

The gate flickers.

But ARIS has crossed the last safe line.

A containment lattice blooms from the void — silver geometry unfolding like a surgical cage around Isorae mid-air.

Rowan slams his hands into it.

His palms burn.

Agony detonates through his arms.

He is thrown backward — hard enough to steal the world from his lungs.

Isorae screams his name as the cage lifts her higher.

The valley collapses inward trying to hold her.

It fails.

And the sky begins to take her.

65

THE THING HE WAS BUILT TO BE

Rowan does not stay down.

He hits stone hard enough to bruise bone, hard enough to rip the breath out of his lungs in a tearing, metallic rush — and still he rises.

Not quickly.

Not recklessly.

Inevitably.

Above the valley, the sky is still tearing itself open.

The extraction gate widens — pale void-light spilling downward in merciless geometry. It bleaches color from leaves. It sharpens shadows into blade-thin silhouettes.

It does not burn.

It reorders.

Reality inside the column forgets its agreements.

Gravity hesitates.

Distance bends.

Sound refuses to obey.

Suspended within the descending lattice, Isorae hangs in spiraled bands of silver filaments — surgical threads humming with resonance sharp enough to make marrow ache. Her body trembles — not in fear — but in recognition — as something ancient inside her is being called by a name older than stars.

The door remembers her.

And it wants her back.

Rowan drags himself upright.

His vision swims. Blood pours from his nose into his mouth —
copper, salt, heat — and he spits it into the dirt without looking away.

Silas is shouting somewhere behind him.

Erin is screaming numbers that no longer belong to anything
human.

The valley is beginning to fail under geometry it was never meant to
host. Stone groans. Roots recoil. Slopes shudder like muscles being
forced into the wrong shape.

Rowan steps forward.

And the land steps with him.

Stone rises beneath his boots, shaping into a shallow arc like a spine
the earth has decided to give him. Wind coils around his body in slow
rotating bands of pressure. Roots surge upward, winding around his
legs, his waist, his ribs — not restraining.

Anchoring.

He becomes heavier without becoming slower.

Denser without becoming rigid.

As if the valley is feeding him its own weight.

Isorae cries out.

"Rowan — it's pulling me through—"

Her voice fractures — not with pain — but with being
remembered by something that should never have found her again.

Rowan raises his hand.

The valley holds its breath.

"No."

The word does not echo.

It repositions reality.

The gate flickers.

The pylons shriek.

Somewhere beyond the sky, ARIS recalibration tones detonate into
warning cascades.

The lattice around Isorae spasms violently — filaments tightening,
humming sharper, slicing the air into narrow corridors that try to turn
her into a coordinate.

Rowan inhales.

Not air.

Authority.

The ancient seam inside him — the place where worlds once learned how to touch without breaking — wakes fully.

His voice drops into something older than language.

"You built your door on my bones."

The land answers.

Every root in the hollow cinches tight at once.

Stone fault-lines flare white beneath moss and fern.

Wind surges upward in a spiraling wall that slams into the descending gate like an ocean reversing gravity.

The extraction pylons scream.

The lattice fractures.

One filament snaps.

Then another.

Isorae's shimmer detonates — wild, blinding — lightning ripping across her skin like a living star trying to remember its own name.

She gasps his name.

Rowan steps forward again.

Blood runs freely now, streaking his jaw, soaking his collar — but his eyes are clear.

Terrible.

Awake.

"You do not own the seam," he says.

His voice is steady.

Final.

"You do not own the crossing.

You do not own her."

He raises both hands.

And pulls.

Not on her.

On the door.

Reality folds.

Sky geometry warps, twisting like heated glass. The gate buckles inward, its circular perfection collapsing into broken arcs of white nothingness.

The pylons tear free from bedrock in screaming spirals of black crystal.

The valley roars in tectonic answer.

Erin shrieks, "They're losing the gate—!"

Silas yells, "Structural collapse incoming—!"

Isorae's lattice shatters.

She drops.

Rowan lunges — roots tightening, stone rising — and catches her mid-air. They slam backward into moss and shattered earth as the world convulses around them.

They hit hard.

But she is in his arms.

Breathing.

Alive.

Above them, the gate collapses inward — folding into itself like a dying star — sealing with a concussive void implosion that rattles mountains for miles.

Silence detonates outward.

The sky snaps closed.

The valley slumps.

And the land releases a breath it has been holding since before human memory learned to speak.

Rowan cradles Isorae against his chest.

Her face is pale.

Her shimmer faint.

But she is here.

She is not theirs.

He presses his forehead to hers. His voice finally breaks back into something human.

"You're not going anywhere."

She exhales shakily, fingers tightening in his shirt.

"Neither are you."

Behind them, the valley is no longer hiding.
It is claiming.

66

THE VALLEY THAT CHOOSES ITS OWN

The silence that follows the collapse is not empty.

It is listening.

Mist hangs unmoving between the trees, neither rising nor thinning, as if the air itself has forgotten which direction belongs to breath. Birds do not return to the branches. Even insects hesitate, hovering in still arcs that never quite resolve into motion.

The hollow rests in a strange, breathless suspension — the kind of pause that comes after something vast has broken and the world has not yet decided what it is allowed to be now.

As if the earth itself is watching Rowan to see what shape he will choose.

He does not move at first.

Rowan remains kneeling in the churned moss where he fell, arms locked around Isorae. Her weight is pressed into his chest like gravity finally remembering where it belongs — her body warm, real, breathing steadily against his ribs.

Her shimmer is barely visible now — faint silver embers under her skin, like starlight folded down into something human again.

His hand trembles once as he cups the back of her head.

"You're here," he whispers.

Not in relief.

Not in disbelief.

But in reverence — as if he is acknowledging something sacred that the universe itself nearly failed to protect.

She nods weakly, forehead resting against his collarbone.

"They lost the door," she murmurs. "They can't pull me through anymore."

His jaw tightens — not in anger.

In finality.

"Good."

Behind them, people begin to move again.

Slowly. Carefully.

As if afraid that the world might still be brittle.

As if a careless step might reopen a sky wound that has only just closed.

Silas reaches them first, dropping to one knee beside Rowan, eyes wide — not with fear, but with awe that he does not try to hide.

"Rowan… the pylons are gone. The sky seal collapsed. ARIS lost the extraction corridor entirely."

Erin staggers up next, her scanner trembling in her hands as if it has just watched physics forget itself.

"The signal dropped to zero," she breathes. "Not masked. Not jammed. Gone. The valley… it closed itself."

Rowan finally lifts his eyes.

They are not glowing.

They are not other.

They are simply aligned — steady, anchored, awake in a way that feels older than fear.

"The land didn't close," he says quietly.

"It chose."

People begin to gather in a loose ring — Evan, Parker, Ryan, the brothers, the healers, the watchers — pale faces, shaking hands, eyes lifted toward the man who stood between them and a hole in the sky and told it no.

They are not looking at a protector anymore.

They are looking at a threshold bearer.

Isorae shifts in Rowan's arms, carefully pushing herself upright. His hand steadies her instantly, firm at her back — not possessive, not panicked — simply present.

She looks out across the hollow.

And for the first time since she crossed worlds…

The land answers her without pain.

The stream hums gently again.

Roots settle.

Wind remembers how to move.

Light softens.

The valley breathes — not as refuge…

…but as a body recognizing its own boundaries.

Someone whispers, "They'll come again."

Isorae nods softly.

"Yes," she says. "But not like this."

Rowan stands, still holding her close.

His voice carries — not loud — but certain enough to move stone.

"They don't get to take what this place has claimed.

"This valley isn't an anomaly.

It isn't a resource.

It isn't a breach."

He looks down at Isorae.

Then back to the people.

"It's a sovereign threshold. And we are its guardians."

The land leans inward.

Claiming.

Deep beneath root and stone, something old and patient settles into a new shape — not as a place to flee into…

…but as a place that decides.

And far beyond the ridges, in sterile corridors of machine-light and failing predictive arrays, ARIS issues its first internal existential alert:

THRESHOLD ENTITY RECLASSIFIED

STATUS: UNCONTAINABLE

RISK LEVEL: EXISTENTIAL

The war has just changed shape.

Because the valley is no longer a secret.

It is a border.

And Rowan Hale is its name.

67

THE FIRST LAW OF THE VALLEY

The valley does not sleep that night.

It settles.

Mist draws inward instead of drifting, gathering low across the hollow like breath being carefully folded back into lungs that have just remembered how to breathe on their own. It does not thin. It does not wander. It collects.

Roots reposition beneath the soil without sound, sliding through loam and stone with the slow inevitability of bone adjusting after being broken and set again. They do not thrash. They do not tear. They choose.

Stones that have rested loosely for generations nestle into firmer lines — quiet arcs and terraces rising by degrees so small they are only noticed because they were not there yesterday. The stream alters its course by inches, widening one bend into a shallow crescent basin that cups starlight like an unblinking, listening eye.

No one touches anything.

They feel it happening.

The land is reorganizing itself around choice.

Rowan stands at the center of the hollow long after the fires have burned low, Isorae resting against his side. His hand remains unconsciously curled at her back, fingers spread as if anchoring her to this world by muscle memory alone. He does not need to look down to know she is there.

The valley knows too.

Silas approaches quietly, boots barely stirring moss.

"The western ridge just… moved," he murmurs. "Not a slide. Not erosion. It repositioned."

Rowan does not look surprised.

"Yeah," he says softly. "It's making boundaries."

Erin joins them, eyes wide, her scanners abandoned at her feet like tools that suddenly feel too small.

"The valley isn't just closing," she says. "It's stabilizing. Stable harmonics are forming like—" She swallows. "Like laws."

Isorae lifts her gaze.

"The valley is remembering how to govern itself," she says gently.

They gather at dawn.

Everyone who has stayed — everyone the land has accepted — finds themselves standing naturally in a loose ring around the crescent basin the stream carved overnight. No one steps inside it. They feel, instinctively, that it is not a place for feet.

It is a place for boundary.

Rowan steps forward.

He does not feel command.

He feels position.

Isorae stays beside him, her fingers laced through his.

He breathes in — not air.

The valley.

"Nothing that hunts here has the right to remain," Rowan says quietly.

His voice does not echo.

It anchors.

"If you come to take, you leave empty.
If you come to cage, you do not leave.
If you come to map, cut, or harvest this land or the people it has claimed…"

He pauses.

The ground hums faintly beneath their feet.

"You are treated as a breach."

The basin tightens.

Not visibly.

Structurally.

Silas feels it and swallows.

Erin whispers, "It's forming a jurisdictional boundary."

Isorae nods.

"The valley has chosen its first law."

Rowan finishes softly:

"You don't get to own what has already chosen itself."

Wind slides through the basin in a slow spiral.

Roots press deeper.

Stone settles into new memory.

The First Law sinks into the bones of the land.

And somewhere far beyond the ridges, ARIS logs a new anomaly:

THRESHOLD ZONE STATUS UPDATED

RESPONSE PROTOCOL: DO NOT ENTER

PREDICTIVE OUTCOME: SYSTEM FAILURE

The valley has stopped being hidden.

It has become governed.

It has become sovereign.

And it has found its voice.

68

THE SOFT DOOR

The valley has been quiet for days. Not empty — settled.

Paths have kept their shape.

Mist has risen and fallen in predictable rhythms.

The crescent basin has held its curve.

Children have slept without waking.

The First Law has worked.

So when the stranger arrives, the valley does not tense.

That is how Rowan knows something is wrong.

There is no tightening of roots beneath the fern line, no hush of wind like a held breath, no sudden thickening of mist along the rim as if the hollow is drawing its cloak closer. The land does not lean inward to warn him, does not bristle the way it always does when something false tries to step into its body.

Because the land does not recognize him as false.

And that is the problem.

It simply… allows.

Rowan feels it as a subtle release beneath his sternum—an easing that should have meant safety, but doesn't. It feels like permission granted to the wrong shape. Like the world has opened a hand without asking who it's touching. His spine goes rigid. His jaw tightens so hard it aches.

Dax notices it at the same time.

"You feel that?" he murmurs, voice barely more than breath.

Rowan nods once. "Yeah."

The stranger steps out of the western fern corridor as if the valley has been expecting him.

He's young—early twenties at most—with a face that looks tired in a human way, not shattered in the way seekers usually arrive. His clothes are travel-worn but not desperate: a jacket softened by distance, pants marked with dust, boots scuffed at the toe. His pack is frayed at the edges, carefully distressed by real movement, and there's dirt in the seams like he has walked far enough to earn the right to be here.

He looks like every person who ever arrived broken.

But he does not feel broken.

He feels settled. Centered. Whole in the way healed things are whole—balanced, quiet, finished.

Isorae's breath catches behind Rowan. Not fear. Recognition that comes too fast.

Rowan steps forward before he realizes he has moved, the way his body always does when something approaches the valley's heart. His hand doesn't reach for a blade, but his posture shifts into it anyway— gate, hinge, boundary made flesh.

"What did you feel that brought you here?" he asks.

The young man blinks as if the question surprises him. Then his mouth curves into something small and gentle, a soft smile that would have belonged here in another life, before ARIS learned how to wear people like gloves.

"I didn't feel anything," he says. "I was sent."

The words land wrong.

Not hostile. Not sharp. Not threatening.

Just… finished. Final in a way that doesn't belong to a living choice.

Rowan's chest tightens.

"By who?"

The stranger hesitates, then lifts his eyes—kind eyes, tired eyes, eyes that look like someone who has cried and stopped. He meets Rowan's gaze without flinching.

"By the place you saved me," he says quietly.

Silence opens around them.

Not the valley's silence—the other kind. The kind that comes when the air realizes a sentence has changed the room.

Isorae stiffens behind Rowan. Her shimmer tightens close to her skin, not flaring, not dimming—compressing like light forced into a narrow tube. Erin's voice slips out of the gathered stillness near the fireline, a breath that barely forms into words.

"Oh no…"

Rowan studies the young man the way he studies an incoming weather shift: not the surface, but the pressure beneath it. Not his posture, but his resonance. The way the land receives him. The way the valley—wrongly—does not object.

The stranger's hands are steady. His breathing is even. There is no restless micro-movement of someone being pulled by grief or hunger or bone-deep exhaustion. He is not hollow. He is not aching. He is not raw.

He is healed.

"You were here before," Rowan says, voice low.

The young man nods. "I came last year," he says. "I was one of the first." His throat works as if the memory still catches. "I was… not doing well." A pause. "This place gave me my life back."

Something tightens in Rowan's throat that has nothing to do with threat. For a moment he sees it—the early days, the first arrivals, bodies held together by will and luck and whatever mercy the valley still had left. People stumbling into the hollow with no name for what they'd survived. Rowan remembers the way he learned their faces by the light of fire and the way he learned their pain by how the land leaned around them.

"Where did you go?" he asks.

"They found me," the young man says, and the words are spoken with gratitude that is too clean.

Not bitter. Not angry. Not afraid.

Grateful.

"They helped me rebuild," he continues softly. "Therapy. Housing. Medical. Everything I needed." His eyes flick toward the shelters, toward the bodies that sleep there, toward the ones still learning how to breathe without permission. "They didn't hurt me."

Isorae takes a slow, shaking breath.

"They didn't hurt you," she repeats, as if she needs to hear the sentence out loud to understand how it could be true.

The young man's smile turns warmer. "No," he says. "They saved me."

Rowan feels the valley shift—subtle, confused, like a living body trying to reconcile a smell it recognizes with a taste that doesn't belong. The land doesn't recoil. It doesn't brace. It doesn't warn.

It listens.

Rowan's eyes sharpen.

"And now you're here because—" he starts.

The young man meets his gaze without hesitation.

"They asked me to bring you an offer."

He reaches into his jacket and withdraws a thin, translucent data-slate. He doesn't activate it. He doesn't wave it like leverage. He holds it carefully, two-handed, almost reverent—as if it is a gift, not a weapon.

Rowan's blood runs colder.

"They said if Isorae leaves willingly," the young man says, voice steady, gentle, almost apologetic, "the war ends."

No threat. No coercion. No blade.

Just a door.

"They will disengage completely," he continues. "They'll classify the valley as sovereign. No more pulses. No more gates. No more deaths."

His eyes flick toward the shelters again. Toward the wounded. Toward the children. Toward Parker's cedar lean-to. Toward Ryan's restless posture even in stillness.

"No more people getting hurt because of her."

The words are not cruel. That is the horror of them.

They are framed like mercy.

The valley goes very still—not stiff, not defensive, but attentive, the way it does when someone speaks a truth and the land is deciding whether it is a truth or a trap.

Isorae's breath stutters, and Rowan feels it like a thread pulled tight inside his ribs.

Something cold moves behind his sternum. Not fear.

A new kind of fury.

"You're asking us to hand her over," Rowan says quietly.

The young man shakes his head, immediate and soft.

"No," he says. "I'm asking her to walk."

He turns toward Isorae, and his kindness stays intact—worse than any cruelty could be, because it makes the offer feel possible.

"They'll protect you," he says. "You'll be safe. You won't be hunted. No more pain." His voice dips, careful, like he can feel the line he is stepping onto. "You won't be alone. I won't be alone anymore either."

Isorae trembles. Not because she believes him.

Because part of her wants to.

Because that is how doors work. They don't force. They tempt.

"They said they can fix what the crossing damaged," the young man adds quietly. "They said they can make you whole."

The valley does not react.

Because this is not violence.

This is consent.

Rowan feels the blade of it settle behind his ribs—the softest knife in the world, sharp enough to cut a war into a different shape. He can feel the trap's elegance: no breach required, no extraction gate to fight, no pylons to tear from bedrock.

Just a choice offered in a human voice.

Just a healed boy returning with a promise.

Rowan steps forward—slowly, deliberately—and the ground firms beneath his boots like the land is trying to understand him. His gaze locks on the stranger's face, on the gentleness, on the gratitude that has been weaponized into a corridor.

"Tell me your name," Rowan says.

The young man blinks again. "Jalen," he answers.

Rowan nods once, as if accepting it as real. As if accepting him as real.

Then he asks, very softly, "Do you know what they did to you?"

Jalen's brow furrows. "They helped me."

Rowan's voice stays quiet. It doesn't need volume to carry in a place that listens.

"No," Rowan says. "They fixed you into a message."

The young man's mouth opens, then closes. Confusion flickers across his features like a shadow crossing sunlight.

Isorae's glow tightens further, controlled and thin, and she takes one step forward—just one—until she is beside Rowan instead of behind him. Her voice is gentle when she speaks, and that gentleness is a blade too.

"Did they ever let you dream here again?" she asks.

Jalen hesitates. "I—"

"Did they ever let you miss it without making you guilty for missing it?" she continues softly.

His throat works. His eyes dart away as if searching for a memory he can't quite reach.

Rowan watches the micro-movements now—the first cracks in finished calm, the slight tension in fingers that were too steady. The faint, unnatural steadiness of his breathing that feels trained rather than healed.

Rowan's jaw locks.

"They didn't just save you," he says. "They tuned you."

Jalen shakes his head once, too fast. "No."

Erin's voice comes from the fireline, raw with fury she's trying to keep contained.

"Invitation tech," she says. "Neural corridor scripting. They don't need a gate if they can turn a person into one."

Jalen's eyes widen. He looks at Erin like he wants to argue—but something in him stalls. Like his thoughts don't know which direction belongs to him anymore.

Rowan takes a step closer until his shadow falls across the data-slate in Jalen's hands.

"You came back with an offer," Rowan says, quiet as stone. "But offers go both ways."

Jalen swallows. "What do you mean?"

Rowan's gaze does not soften.

"Tell them," he says, "that the valley heard."

A beat of silence.

"And tell them," Rowan continues, "that if they try to walk through a human mind again, I will treat it like a breach."

The valley shifts—subtle, decisive—as if it recognizes the sentence as law-shaped. Roots tighten in the soil. Mist draws inward along the western rim, not to hide, but to close.

Jalen's hands tremble for the first time.

Rowan watches it happen with something like grief.

Because the boy really was here once.

Because the valley really did save him.

And because ARIS learned how to turn salvation into a weapon that looks like mercy.

Jalen's mouth opens.

"I… I just wanted it to stop," he whispers. "The pain. The dying. They said—"

Rowan cuts in, gentle only in volume.

"They always say," he murmurs. "That if you give them the one thing they want, they'll stop taking everything else."

Isorae's fingers lace into Rowan's hand, tight enough to hurt. He squeezes back—anchor answering anchor—without looking at her.

Jalen's eyes shine suddenly, wet and confused.

"They're going to come anyway," he says, as if the realization is arriving too late and too sharp. "If she doesn't go, they'll—"

Rowan's gaze hardens.

"If she does go," Rowan says, "they'll come anyway."

The boy flinches as if struck—not by sound, but by truth.

The valley holds its breath.

And for the first time since Jalen stepped into the hollow, the land finally leans—just slightly—toward Rowan.

Not in welcome.

In alignment.

Rowan nods once, a verdict.

"You can stay tonight," he says to Jalen. "You can eat. You can sleep."

Erin's head snaps up. "Rowan—"

Rowan doesn't look at her. "He's not leaving while they're still in his head."

Jalen's breath stutters. "I didn't mean—"

"I know," Rowan says. And for the first time, something human breaks through the iron in his voice. "That's why they picked you."

He gestures toward Evan, who has gone still at the edge of the ring, watching with a healer's horror.

"Evan," Rowan says. "Keep him close. No one alone with him. No one cruel."

Then Rowan turns his eyes back to Jalen, and the softness is gone again—not because Rowan is heartless, but because he has learned what mercy costs.

"And tell them," Rowan repeats, voice low, "their door is closed."

The valley tightens around the words.

Not trapping.

Guarding.

Jalen nods shakily, as if he can't help it, as if something inside him recognizes the valley's truth even while the programming fights to override it.

Rowan steps back, drawing Isorae with him.

The hollow does not relax.

It does not celebrate.

It simply reorganizes around a new reality:

ARIS has learned how to send kindness as a weapon.

And Rowan has learned the next war will not begin with gates or blades—

It will begin with someone saying the perfect thing in the perfect voice, offering relief that feels like love.

The soft door has opened.

And for the first time since the sky tried to take her…

the valley does not know which way to lean—because the threat is no longer coming as violence.

It is coming as permission.

69

THE FIRST ONE WHO WALKS

The valley does not stop her.

That is the first thing Rowan understands—before anyone speaks, before anyone even realizes what has happened.

He feels it in the ground.

Not as a pulse. Not as a warning. Not as the familiar tightening that has become the valley's language since ARIS learned how to reach for them.

This is different.

This is a loosening.

A quiet parting beneath the soles of his feet, like the land is making room for a decision it has agreed to honor.

Rowan opens his eyes in the gray seam between night and morning and knows—immediately—that someone is already moving.

The fire circle is nothing but low coals and pale ash. Mist lies in folds between the shelters like breath that forgot it belonged to lungs. Bramble lifts his head and releases a low sound that is not a bark, not a growl—more a soft, uneasy question.

Rowan is on his feet in a single motion.

Isorae stirs beside him, her hand drifting to his wrist as if her body has learned that he will always be leaving.

"Rowan," she murmurs—already awake enough that her voice carries shape.

He doesn't answer.

He doesn't need to.

She feels it too.

The valley is holding a door open.

Not for an intruder.

For one of their own.

Rowan moves through the hollow without waking anyone at first. Not because he wants secrecy—but because he wants to catch the choice before it becomes a corridor. He passes sleeping bodies wrapped in blankets and moss. He passes the crescent basin the stream carved overnight, its surface glass-dark and still, starlight caught in it like an eye that refuses to blink.

Every step feels… allowed.

And that terrifies him.

He finds her at the western rim.

Nora stands with her back to the hollow, facing the fern curtain and the unheld ground beyond it. Her hair is unbound, falling loose over her shoulders. She has her pack on. Not heavy. Not hurried. Packed with the calm efficiency of someone who has already spent the whole night making peace.

She is not trembling.

She is not crying.

She looks… resolved.

Rowan stops behind her, the cold air cutting his lungs like glass.

"Don't," he says.

Nora's shoulders rise and fall once.

She does not turn.

"I'm not running," she answers quietly.

Rowan's jaw tightens hard enough to ache. "You're leaving."

She nods.

"And the valley is letting you," Rowan says, voice low, iron-still. "Do you feel that?"

Nora finally turns to look at him.

Her eyes are red—not from crying now, but from having cried earlier. From being done with crying.

"I feel it," she says softly. "That's why I know it's real."

Rowan steps closer. The fern curtain behind her doesn't recoil. The air doesn't tighten. Nothing in the land rises to block her.

It simply… waits.

Rowan feels something cold slip behind his ribs.

"Who spoke to you?" he asks.

Nora swallows.

She hesitates—just long enough for Rowan to hear the truth forming.

Then she says, "No one."

Rowan's eyes narrow.

"Don't lie to me."

Her mouth trembles. She looks away for a fraction of a heartbeat, then back.

"It didn't sound like someone," she admits. "It sounded like… relief."

Rowan's hands curl into fists at his sides.

The valley exhales low and uneasy around them, mist drawing inward as if listening.

Nora's voice stays gentle. That's what makes it worse.

"It was like my own thoughts," she whispers. "Only… kinder. Like a part of my mind that hadn't been allowed to speak in years."

Rowan's throat tightens.

"Like what," he demands—quiet, not loud, but edged with something feral.

Nora's eyes flicker with shame.

"They said," she begins, then stops, breath catching. "They said I don't have to be brave anymore."

Rowan's vision narrows.

"They said I can go home."

Home.

That word lands like a weapon.

Rowan takes another step forward—so close now that his shadow falls over her boots.

"Nora," he says, voice dropping into raw warning, "there is no home out there that hasn't been touched by them."

Nora's expression doesn't change the way it would if she were naive.

It changes the way it does when someone has already accepted a truth and is tired of it.

"I know," she says quietly.

Rowan freezes.

"I know," she repeats, softer. "But I also know what it feels like to be… untethered." Her fingers tighten on the strap of her pack. "When the sky blinked and my future disappeared, I thought I was dying."

Rowan's chest tightens.

"You weren't," he says.

"No," she agrees. "You didn't let me."

Her gaze sharpens with something that looks like gratitude and grief braided together.

"And then you anchored me back," she whispers. "You chose for me when the world tried to erase my next step."

Rowan's jaw locks.

"You're welcome," he says, bitter before he can stop it.

Nora flinches—not away from him, but at the pain in his voice.

"I'm not ungrateful," she says. "I'm not leaving because I hate you. I'm leaving because I can feel what it costs you to keep doing that."

Rowan's eyes darken.

"What it costs me," he repeats, like he doesn't recognize the concept.

Nora shakes her head once, small and exhausted.

"It costs everyone," she whispers. "It costs her."

Rowan's spine goes rigid.

Before he can speak, Isorae's voice arrives behind him—quiet as mist.

"Rowan."

He turns.

Isorae stands a few paces back, barefoot on cold soil, her shimmer low and contained like a lantern held behind cloth. Her eyes are wide with an ache that has learned how to stay calm.

She looks at Nora.

Then at Rowan.

Then at the valley's open rim.

"I felt her moving," Isorae says softly.

Rowan doesn't take his eyes off Nora.

"You're not going," he says.

Nora swallows hard.

"I think I am."

Rowan steps forward, closing the space like a wall.

"No," he says again. This time it isn't a warning.

It's a command.

The valley does not echo him.

It does not reinforce him.

It simply… allows the conversation to exist.

And that is when Rowan understands what ARIS has done.

They have built a door the land will not slam.

Because it's made of choice.

Isorae moves closer, her voice gentle.

"Nora," she says, "did they promise you safety?"

Nora's eyes flick down. She nods once.

Isorae inhales carefully.

"Did they promise you rest?"

Another nod.

Rowan watches her—watches the way her body holds itself like someone trying not to collapse under the weight of being wanted by two sides at once.

"And did they tell you," Isorae continues softly, "that if you leave, the pain will stop?"

Nora's mouth trembles.

"Yes," she whispers.

Rowan feels rage spark under his ribs like flint.

Isorae's eyes close for a moment, as if the answer hurts her more than any strike.

"They're using you," Rowan says, voice low and venomous. "They're using your fear and calling it mercy."

Nora's shoulders stiffen.

"Don't," she says, quiet but sharp.

Rowan's eyes narrow.

"Don't what?"

"Don't make me sound stupid," Nora whispers. "I know what they are. I know what they've done. I watched people die in this valley because they wanted her. I watched you bleed because they wanted to break what you are."

Rowan's jaw clenches.

"And you still want to walk into their arms?"

Nora's expression fractures into something like exhaustion with being judged for wanting to breathe.

"I want to sleep," she says. "I want to stop waking up braced for the sky. I want to stop counting how many people are left."

Her eyes fill with tears finally, hot and furious.

"I want to stop feeling guilty for being alive."

Rowan's throat tightens.

Isorae steps forward, hands lifting slightly—not touching, but offering.

"I understand," she says softly.

Rowan whips his head toward her.

"No," he snarls. "You don't—"

Isorae's gaze snaps to his, sudden steel beneath the softness.

"I do," she says, low and certain. "Because I can feel what they did to her mind."

Rowan stills.

Isorae turns back to Nora, voice quiet as breath on glass.

"They didn't threaten you," she murmurs. "They didn't coerce you. They introduced a thought that feels like relief and called it yours."

Nora's tears spill.

"I don't care," she whispers. "Even if it's a lie, it's a lie that feels like I can live."

Rowan takes a step closer.

"You can live here."

Nora shakes her head hard.

"Can I?" she demands. "Or am I just surviving under your protection while she bleeds signal and the land holds its breath?"

Rowan's chest heaves once, controlled.

"This place is sovereign," he says. "It chose us."

Nora's eyes flash.

"And what happens when the valley chooses something else," she asks quietly. "What happens when it decides the cost is too high?"

The question slices clean.

Because it's not rhetorical.

It's the fear that's been coiled in every body since the sky-gate collapsed.

Rowan's jaw tightens.

"It won't," he says.

Isorae's hand slides into his—warm, anchoring.

But her thumb trembles slightly against his knuckle.

Rowan feels it.

He feels the truth she doesn't say:

The valley is learning how to choose. And choice means it can change.

Nora wipes her face with the back of her hand, a gesture too human for a moment this brutal.

"They told me I can leave without being chased," she says, voice shaking. "They said there's a route. A corridor. A safe passage."

Erin's voice cuts in from behind them—sharp and furious.

"There isn't," she snaps.

Rowan turns.

Erin stands at the ridge path, her hair a mess, scanner in one hand, a coil of wiring in the other like she came out of sleep already mid-war. Her eyes are bright with rage and fear braided tight.

"They're lying," Erin says to Nora. "There's no safe corridor. There's only an extraction lane disguised as consent."

Nora flinches, but she doesn't back away.

"They helped him," she says suddenly.

Rowan's blood runs cold.

"Who?"

Nora swallows.

"The man," she whispers. "The one who came yesterday. Jalen."

Erin's face tightens. "Of course."

"He looked… healed," Nora insists, voice cracking. "He looked safe. He looked like he wasn't being hunted anymore."

Rowan steps toward her.

"Because he's a carrier," he says, voice low and deadly. "They rebuilt him into a door."

Nora shakes her head, desperate.

"You don't know that."

Rowan's eyes darken.

"I know what it feels like when the land leans," he says. "And I know what it feels like when it allows."

He gestures toward the open rim.

"It's allowing you," he says. "Not because it wants you gone. Because it's honoring your autonomy."

His voice drops.

"And ARIS is counting on that."

Nora's breath shakes.

"Then what do I do," she whispers, "if my autonomy is the only thing I still have?"

Silence holds them.

The valley does not lean.

It waits.

Isorae steps closer.

Her voice is barely audible.

"You stay," she says. "Not because Rowan commands it. Not because the valley forces it. You stay because you decide to belong here."

Nora looks at her—eyes full of tears, full of anger, full of longing.

"And what if my belonging gets you killed," she asks.

Isorae flinches.

Rowan feels the flinch like it happens inside his own ribs.

"That's not your burden," Isorae says softly, but her voice trembles.

Nora's mouth twists.

"It is if they told me the truth," she whispers.

Rowan's jaw tightens.

"What truth?"

Nora's voice drops. Her gaze flicks away toward the dark trees beyond the fern curtain, as if she can still hear the thought that was planted in her.

"They said," she whispers, "that if enough of us choose to leave… the valley will loosen."

Erin's face drains.

Rowan goes utterly still.

Isorae inhales sharply.

Because that isn't a promise.

That's a plan.

Rowan steps forward until he is so close Nora can feel his breath.

"You don't leave," he says, low and final.

Nora trembles.

Rowan's voice softens a fraction—just enough to show the pain underneath the command.

"Please," he says. "Don't do this."

Nora's eyes widen.

Rowan Hale doesn't plead.

Rowan Hale doesn't soften like that.

And that small crack of humanity is what breaks her.

She sobs—once, sharply—then clamps her mouth shut like she's ashamed of the sound.

"I'm sorry," she whispers. "I'm so sorry."

Rowan's chest tightens.

He reaches for her—hand lifting to anchor.

But before his fingers can touch her shoulder, the valley shifts.

Not blocking him.

Not resisting him.

Simply… making space for her to move.

Nora steps backward.

Rowan freezes.

His hand hangs in the air like an unfinished sentence.

Isorae's fingers tighten around his.

Erin whispers, horrified, "No…"

Nora swallows, tears streaming now, voice thin and shaking.

"I can't live in a place where every day feels like waiting to be taken," she said, voice trembling. "Even if you can fight them. Even if you can tell the sky no."

Her gaze flicks to Isorae.

"And I can't live knowing my staying might be part of the reason they keep trying."

Isorae's eyes fill with tears.

"Nora—"

Nora shakes her head, desperate.

"I'm sorry," she repeats. "But when they put that thought in me… it felt like someone finally offered to let me stop bracing."

Rowan's jaw clenches so hard it looks like pain.

"That thought isn't yours," he says.

Nora nods, tears spilling.

"I know," she whispers.

Then she lifts her chin.

"But I'm choosing it anyway."

Rowan's breath stops.

Isorae makes a broken sound.

Erin takes a step forward.

Rowan lifts a hand without looking back—stopping them all.

Because he feels the valley's posture.

If he grabs her—

If he forces her—

The valley will not back him.

It will not become a jail.

Not even for love.

Not even for protection.

It will remain sovereign.

And that sovereignty includes the right to walk out.

Rowan's hand falls slowly to his side.

His voice comes out cracked and low.

"If you cross that line," he says, "they will not let you turn around."

Nora's eyes shine.

"I don't think I want to," she whispers.

Rowan's chest tightens with something close to grief, something close to fury.

Erin's voice breaks.

"Nora, don't—"

Nora looks at Erin—soft, apologetic.

"I'm tired," she whispers.

Then she turns.

And steps through the fern curtain.

The valley does not stop her.

Mist parts.

Roots lift just enough to clear her path.

Stone settles into a gentle slope beneath her boots.

Rowan watches her walk away like he's watching a limb sever.

He feels the land register it—not as loss, but as fact.

A decision accepted.

A door used.

Isorae's hand flies to her sternum.

She gasps.

Rowan turns instantly.

"What?"

Her eyes are wide, shimmering with terror and something worse.

"I felt it," she whispers. "The moment she crossed…"

Rowan's stomach drops.

"What did you feel?"

Isorae's breath shakes.

"A line opened," she whispers. "A corridor. Not in the land."

Her voice drops to a whisper that barely exists.

"In me."

Erin's scanner shrieks.

She stares at it, face ashen.

"Oh god," she whispers.

Rowan's eyes turn black.

"Say it."

Erin swallows hard.

"They just got a clean ping," she says. "Not from the valley. From the choice."

Rowan's fists clench.

Isorae trembles.

"They're using our leaving as a coordinate," she whispers. "They're building a map out of consent."

Rowan stares into the trees where Nora vanished.

And for the first time since the gate collapse, something cold and brutal settles into him.

Not fear.

Not grief.

Understanding.

ARIS doesn't need to breach the valley.

They just need enough people to walk out and drag the world's geometry after them.

Rowan turns back to the hollow.

His voice is low, steady, and lethal.

"Wake everyone," he says.

Erin's eyes snap up.

Rowan's gaze is fixed, unblinking.

"This is the first one who walks," he says quietly. "And they're going to try to make it a flood."

Isorae steps closer, shaking.

"Rowan..."

He cups her face gently—gentle enough it hurts.

"They're not taking you," he murmurs. "Not through the sky. Not through the ground. Not through anyone else's mind."

His eyes burn.

"And they don't get to weaponize mercy."

He turns to the valley's open rim.

The land hums faintly beneath his feet.

Waiting.

Listening.

Not for command.

For choice.

Rowan inhales—slow, deliberate—and speaks to the land like it's a living witness.

"Close the soft door," he murmurs.

The valley does not slam shut.

It does something worse.

It rewrites.

The fern curtain shifts.

The path beyond it bends—subtly, quietly—so that anyone who tries to leave will walk straight and still find themselves circling back.

Not trapped.

Returned.

A loop of sovereignty.

A refusal to become an exit route.

Rowan feels the land settle into that decision like a jaw setting.

He looks down at Isorae.

Her eyes are wet.

"She chose," Isorae whispers. "And the valley honored her."

Rowan's voice breaks into something human for half a second.

"I know," he says.

Then the feral steadiness returns.

"And now the valley has to honor the rest of us too."

Far beyond the ridges, in sterile chambers where predictions are rewritten in real time, ARIS registers the first successful human corridor event.

Not because they captured someone.

Because they opened a door without ever touching the threshold.

And in the hollow, as the first pale light of morning spreads through the canopy, Rowan Hale stands at the edge of the valley and realizes the war has entered its most dangerous phase.

Recruitment.

Because the only thing more powerful than force…

is the moment someone chooses to stop fighting.

And ARIS is learning exactly how to offer that choice.

To everyone.

70

THE DOOR THAT SOUNDS LIKE YOU

The first thing that follows Nora is not pursuit.

It's quiet.

Not the valley's quiet—this is different. This is the kind of stillness that arrives when something has succeeded and is now waiting to see what else it can turn.

Rowan stands at the western rim long after her footsteps disappear into the fern corridor. Mist drifts back into place as if nothing happened. Birds resume their slow spirals above the ridge, but they fly higher now—wider loops, wider spacing—like the sky itself has widened its attention.

Isorae hasn't moved.

Her hand is pressed flat over her sternum, fingers spread as if she can hold the inside of herself together by sheer will.

Erin's scanner is still screaming.

Not loudly—its battery is dying—but in a thin, steady whine that makes the bones behind Rowan's ears ache.

"Say it again," Rowan says, voice low, controlled, wrong with restraint. "What did they get?"

Erin swallows hard and forces herself to look up from the broken display. Her face is pale in the growing morning light.

"A clean corridor ping," she repeats. "Not through terrain or atmosphere. Through… decision."

Isorae's breath shudders.

"They felt her leaving," she whispers. "They used it as a coordinate."

Rowan closes his eyes for a single beat—because he can feel it too now, a thin thread of wrongness stretching out past the valley's boundary like a nerve exposed to cold air.

Not because the land is open.

Because someone inside it chose to step through.

Then he turns.

"Wake everyone," he says.

Erin hesitates. "Rowan—"

"Now," he repeats, and the valley beneath his boots tightens—not to stop anyone, not to trap—but to underline him. A quiet, heavy emphasis in the soil. A punctuation mark.

Isorae grabs his wrist.

Her fingers are cold. Her eyes are wide.

"You can't make them stay," she whispers.

Rowan's gaze drops to her.

The rage in him is real, but the control is realer.

"I'm not going to," he says quietly. "But I am going to make sure they understand what they're walking into."

He turns back toward the hollow.

Mist parts for him without being told.

Roots flatten into quiet ramps where the ground would have caught ankles.

The valley is making him a path.

And that knowledge sits in his chest like both gift and warning.

By the time the first people stumble out of their shelters, the sky is fully light.

Not bright. Not warm.

Clear.

The kind of morning that makes everything look honest.

Which is exactly what ARIS is counting on.

Evan is one of the first awake. He comes to Rowan with a blanket still wrapped around his shoulders, his eyes already sharp with understanding.

"Nora?" he asks, voice quiet.

Rowan nods once.

"She walked."

Evan's face tightens. He doesn't ask why. He doesn't judge. He just exhales through his nose like someone bracing himself for what comes next.

"That means they'll do it again," he murmurs.

"Yes," Rowan says.

And as if the land is determined to prove the point, Ryan staggers out of his shelter and stops dead as if someone has grabbed his spine from the inside.

He blinks hard.

His mouth opens.

Then he says, in a voice that doesn't sound like his voice at all—

"Come home."

The words hang in the air like a thread pulled too tight.

Ryan swallows, eyes widening in horror. "I didn't— I didn't mean—"

Isorae flinches as if the syllables scraped her bones.

Erin's scanner whines harder.

"That's it," Erin whispers. "That's the insertion."

Rowan steps closer to Ryan. His voice is calm, but the calm is a blade.

"Where did it touch you?"

Ryan's hand rises to his sternum without his permission. "Here," he whispers. "It feels like... like my thoughts are echoing wrong."

Rowan nods once, slow.

"Good. That means you can hear the echo."

Ryan's eyes fill with panic. "Rowan, I don't—"

"You don't have to fight it alone," Rowan cuts in, and then he turns his head slightly and speaks without raising his voice.

"Erin. Evan. Ring."

Something in the land shifts.

People drift closer without realizing why, as if the valley has moved its center of gravity inward and their bodies are responding.

Erin pushes her way through and drops to a knee beside Ryan, her hands moving fast—checking pupils, checking pulse, checking the tiny tremor in his fingers like she's trying to catch an invisible parasite by its shadow.

"It's not possession," she mutters. "It's suggestion. A dopamine-laced relief pathway. They're attaching safety feelings to an exit route."

Evan crouches opposite her, voice low, steady.

"Ryan," he says gently, "can you tell me the last thing you remember thinking before you heard it?"

Ryan's breath shakes. "I remember… wanting my mother," he whispers. "Just for a second. Just— I was so tired."

Rowan's jaw tightens.

There it is.

Not a threat.

A longing.

ARIS isn't breaking people.

It's offering them what they already want.

And calling it peace.

Isorae's fingers curl into Rowan's sleeve. Her shimmer stays contained, but Rowan can feel the tension in it like a held wire.

"They're using tenderness as an entry point," she whispers.

Rowan's eyes don't leave Ryan.

"They always do," he answers.

By midday, it isn't just Ryan.

Parker sits up too quickly beneath her cedar lean-to and whispers, "They said I can breathe again."

A teenage boy Rowan barely knows—one of the later arrivals—sits by the stream and stares at the water like it's speaking. When Dax crouches beside him and asks what he's doing, the boy answers blankly, "Listening for the route."

And the most terrifying part is that none of them look controlled.

They look comforted.

They look like people being offered relief.

Rowan calls everyone into the center ring.

The hollow gathers around him the way it always has when something needs naming.

Faces appear in a wide circle—thirty-seven now, because one of them is gone.

Children cling to adults. Adults keep their hands busy—folding blankets, tying straps, smoothing hair—because stillness makes room for fear.

Erin stands at Rowan's right with a coil of wiring looped around her shoulder like a weapon she doesn't trust yet. Silas takes the left edge of the ring, watching the tree line even though the threat isn't coming from the trees.

Dax remains half a step behind Rowan, quiet and ready, eyes moving constantly.

Isorae stands close enough that her warmth touches Rowan's arm.

She looks exhausted.

But present.

Rowan speaks without raising his voice.

"They're going to start offering you exits," he says. "Not with force. Not with drones. Not with strikes."

He pauses long enough for everyone to feel the shape of the truth. "With relief."

A murmur ripples through the crowd—small, uneasy, ashamed.

Because everyone has wanted relief.

Rowan's gaze moves across faces.

"They'll offer you food. Water. Warm beds. Doctors." His voice stays even. "They'll offer you the exact kind of safety you've been starving for."

He looks at the children.

"And they'll mean it," he says quietly.

Silence thickens.

Rowan continues.

"Because safety isn't the lie," he says. "The lie is what they're buying with it."

He turns his head slightly, glancing at Isorae.

"They don't want to help you," he says to the group. "They want to make you useful."

He takes a breath.

"And the easiest way to breach a sovereign boundary…"

His voice drops, dangerous in its calm.

"…is to convince the people inside it to open it themselves."

Evan raises a hand slightly. "What do we do?"

Rowan doesn't answer immediately.

Because he can feel the valley's posture.

It is willing to loop paths. It is willing to blur exits.

But it is not willing to strip choice away.

And Rowan won't ask it to.

Not even to save them.

He looks at Erin.

"Can you block it?"

Erin shakes her head, lips tight.

"Not completely," she says. "Not unless we erase their neural signatures—which we can't do without hurting people." She swallows. "But we can interrupt."

She lifts the coil of wiring.

"We can make a counter-anchor," she says. "A phrase, a sound, a physical grounding cue. Something that snaps the brain out of the artificial relief loop."

Rowan nods once.

Evan steps forward, eyes steady.

"We can teach people how to recognize the feeling," he says. "Not to be ashamed of it. To name it. Shame makes it stick."

Rowan's gaze returns to the circle.

"If you hear a voice," Rowan says quietly, "you tell someone. Immediately." He looks hard at each face. "Not later. Not when you've decided. Not when you've packed."

He pauses.

"And no one walks alone."

A few people blink. Confused.

Rowan repeats it.

"No one walks alone," he says. "If you feel the urge to leave, you don't go to the rim by yourself. You come to this ring. You say it out loud."

His eyes cut to Dax, then to Silas.

"And we go with you," he adds. "Not to stop you. To witness you. To make sure the decision is yours."

Isorae inhales shakily beside him.

Because this is the line that matters.

Rowan isn't making laws to control them.

He's making laws to protect them from being turned into doors.

The afternoon passes like a held breath.

The valley behaves strangely—mist gathering in places that used to stay clear, wind refusing to travel straight lines, birds moving in wide, deliberate arcs like they're drawing circles in the air.

The land is compensating.

Adapting.

Trying to protect without imprisoning.

Dax and Silas patrol the perimeter anyway, because they don't trust mercy.

Near dusk, the first true test comes.

Not as a drone.

Not as a pulse.

As a person.

A woman named Sera—one of the newest arrivals—stands suddenly near the western path with her pack in her hands and her eyes full of calm.

Too calm.

Rowan feels it instantly.

He crosses the hollow in three strides.

"Sera," he says.

She looks up and smiles at him like she's greeting an old friend.

"They said there's a place," she whispers. "There's a place where the nightmares stop."

Rowan stops in front of her.

He doesn't touch her.

He doesn't grab the pack.

He keeps his voice steady.

"Tell me what it feels like," he says.

Sera's smile wavers.

"It feels like… like I can breathe," she whispers.

Erin appears at Rowan's shoulder, her scanner whining.

"It's hot," Erin mutters. "It's active right now."

Evan approaches slowly, hands open, voice gentle.

"Sera," he says, "can you tell me what you were thinking about right before the relief hit?"

Sera's eyes blink once. Twice.

Her smile falters.

"I was thinking," she whispers, "that I'm tired of being a burden."

Rowan's chest tightens.

He hears it now.

Not her words.

The leverage beneath them.

ARIS isn't pulling people by force.

It's pulling them by their shame.

Rowan speaks quietly.

"You are not a burden," he says. "You are a person who got hurt."

Sera's throat works.

Her eyes fill suddenly.

"I don't want to hear it anymore," she whispers.

Erin steps forward, holds up a small device she's built from scavenged parts—a little coil and a flat piece of metal and something that hums faintly in a way that makes teeth ache.

"Listen," Erin says, voice sharp. "This is going to feel awful for half a second."

Sera flinches.

Rowan holds Sera's gaze.

"It will pass," Rowan says. "And if the voice is yours, it'll still be there after."

Erin triggers the device.

A tight, sharp vibration ripples through the air—barely audible but felt, like pressure snapping.

Sera gasps.

Her knees buckle.

Evan catches her gently.

And for one terrifying heartbeat, her face contorts like something inside her is angry at being noticed.

Then her eyes clear.

She sobs once—raw, human.

"Oh god," she whispers. "It was in my head."

Rowan's jaw tightens.

"No," he says softly.

"It was aimed at your head."

Sera shakes, clutching Evan's sleeve like she's holding onto something real.

Rowan looks out toward the western fern curtain.

The path beyond it looks the same.

But he can feel the thin wrongness threaded through it now—an invisible invitation, a corridor made of chemical relief and borrowed voice.

Isorae steps beside him, trembling slightly.

"They'll keep doing it," she said.

Rowan's voice is calm.

"I know."

Night falls.

The valley stays awake.

Mist gathers low, thicker near the paths. Roots subtly lift, forming gentle bends in the trails that lead out. The land is doing what it can without violating the thing Rowan refuses to violate.

Choice.

Rowan stands at the edge of the crescent basin the stream carved overnight.

The water is dark, unblinking.

People drift toward it without being told, as if the hollow's gravity has shifted here—like the land itself is drawing them into a shape.

Erin stands beside Rowan, exhausted and furious.

"They'll try again tonight," she mutters. "Harder."

Silas watches the perimeter, eyes narrowed.

"They're not trying to enter," he says. "They're trying to make us exit."

Dax spits into the moss, expression grim.

"So we stop being exits."

Isorae's voice is quiet—soft, but carrying.

"The valley is changing," she murmurs. "Not just defending. Not just adapting."

Rowan looks down at the water, then back at the faces gathering around him in the dark.

He can feel the land underfoot—alive, listening, waiting for something it has never been asked to do before.

Not to hide.

Not to strike.

To govern.

Rowan inhales slowly.

He doesn't feel command.

He feels position.

And he understands—sickly, clearly—that if ARIS can weaponize consent, then the only defense that doesn't become a prison is something older than strategy.

A boundary that is chosen.

A law that the land itself agrees to hold.

Rowan lifts his head.

His voice doesn't rise.

But the hollow quiets anyway.

"We honor choice," he says.

The words land heavy. Real.

"No one here is a prisoner," he continues. "Not of the valley. Not of me. Not of her."

He looks at Isorae, his hand finding hers.

"But if ARIS tries to turn your leaving into a weapon…"

His gaze sharpens, dark and steady.

"Then we stop being a doorway."

The land hums in recognition beneath them.

Erin swallows.

"It's listening," she whispers.

Rowan's voice drops even lower, not speaking to the people now—speaking through them, into the bones of the hollow.

"Nothing that hunts here has the right to remain," he says softly.

The crescent basin tightens—not visibly, but structurally, like a line being drawn in the world.

Wind slides across the water in a slow spiral.

Roots press deeper.

Stone settles.

Isorae exhales.

"The valley is learning jurisdiction," she whispers.

Rowan's eyes don't leave the dark water.

"Good," he says.

Because ARIS has opened the soft door.

And now the valley is about to decide what happens to anything that tries to walk through it.

71

THE SECOND OFFER

Morning comes wrong.

Not darker. Not colder. Not storm-wrong.

Arranged.

Rowan feels it before he opens his eyes—the way the air sits too evenly across his skin, the way the valley's pulse holds itself steady like a breath being deliberately controlled. Mist doesn't drift in careless ribbons anymore. It collects in clean, low bands along the path-lines, pooling where a body would naturally step, thinning where a body would naturally hide.

The land is not asleep.

It's watching itself.

Isorae wakes beside him with her hand already at his chest. Not searching. Not frightened. Checking the hinge.

"You're aligned," she murmurs, almost to herself.

Rowan's gaze flicks to her face. "You're listening."

She nods once. Her shimmer is quiet—tight, disciplined, held inside her bones like a secret she won't let the world hear.

"They're still there," she whispers. "Just… waiting for the next opening."

Rowan sits up slowly.

Outside the shelter, the hollow is already moving—quiet movement, controlled movement. People in twos. No one walks alone. Dax's rules are being obeyed without being said out loud, as if the valley has written them into the soil and everyone's feet remembers.

Erin is awake at the fireline, dark circles under her eyes, hands still moving—always moving—wiring and rewiring the small disruptor coils she can now make in minutes. She looks up when Rowan steps out.

"They tried twice last night," she says without preamble.

Rowan stops beside her. "Who?"

"Everyone," Erin answers flatly. "Not like Ryan. Not like Sera. Smaller. Softer. Almost… background."

Evan appears with a blanket over one arm and a mug in the other, his face steady in the way it only gets when he's been doing triage all night.

"They're testing saturation," he says quietly. "Seeing who breaks under fatigue. Under shame. Under the simple fact of wanting comfort."

Rowan's jaw tightens.

He looks across the hollow.

No one is screaming. No one is running. No one is packing in secret.

But the valley feels like a clenched fist.

Silas approaches from the ridge, rifle slung, eyes narrowed.

"Movement on the western line," he says.

Rowan's head lifts. "Drones?"

Silas shakes his head once. "Not drones."

A pause.

"People."

The word lands in the dirt like a stone.

Dax comes in from the north watch, moving fast, posture already sharpened.

"How many?"

Silas's gaze flicks toward the fern curtain. "One."

Rowan's chest tightens—not because one is harmless, but because one is intentional. One is always meant to carry a message that looks like mercy.

Isorae steps closer to Rowan, fingers brushing his wrist. Her eyes are steady, but her voice is faint.

"If it's another healed one—"

Rowan doesn't let her finish.

He nods once. "We hear it. We don't swallow it."

They move as a unit—not rushing, not spreading panic. Rowan steps to the rim with Dax half a breath behind him, Silas angled to the left, Erin and Evan staying slightly back with the disruptor coils ready.

The valley doesn't tighten.

That is the first warning.

The fern curtain parts.

And a woman steps through.

Older than Nora. Late thirties, maybe. Hair pulled back. Boots scuffed. Pack worn.

But her posture is calm in a way that makes Rowan's skin prickle.

Not survivor-calm.

Programmed calm.

She stops just inside the boundary and lifts both hands—empty, open.

Her eyes find Rowan immediately. She doesn't look at the others first. She doesn't scan the shelter line. She doesn't take in the valley like a person encountering something sacred.

She looks at Rowan like he is a file she was trained to address.

"Rowan Hale," she says softly.

Not a greeting.

A key turning in a lock.

Rowan's voice stays even. "Stop there."

She does.

Too smoothly.

Isorae's shimmer tightens, almost imperceptible, like her bones have just recognized a frequency they hate.

Erin's scanner gives a low, tight whine.

"Neural carrier," Erin mutters under her breath. "Different method than Ryan. Cleaner."

The woman's expression remains gentle.

"I'm not here to fight," she says. "I'm here to talk."

Rowan doesn't move. "Talk."

She nods once, as if grateful for permission.

"My name is Maelin," she says. "I came here eight months ago. I was… not well."

Rowan's gaze doesn't soften. He listens for the valley's reaction.

It doesn't react.

It simply allows.

Maelin takes a careful breath.

"This place saved me," she continues. "It gave me my body back. My mind back." Her eyes flick briefly toward the shelters. "You gave me my life back."

Evan's face tightens. He doesn't interrupt. He watches for the moment the tenderness turns into a weapon.

Maelin's gaze returns to Rowan.

"And then I left," she says, voice still soft. "And when I did, they found me."

Rowan feels Isorae's fingers clamp around his wrist.

Maelin's mouth curves into something almost sad.

"They did not hurt me," she says, as if she knows that's the first thing they'd expect her to admit. "They helped me."

Dax's voice is low. "You keep saying that."

Maelin looks at him with a patient, practiced expression.

"Because it's true," she replies. "They gave me housing. Medical support. Therapy that actually worked. They gave me a job. They gave me structure." Her eyes widen slightly, as if she's pleading for them to understand. "They gave me peace."

Rowan's voice stays flat. "And the price?"

Maelin's breath catches for the first time.

She looks down for a fraction of a second.

Then back up.

"They asked me to return," she says quietly. "To deliver an offer."

Rowan feels the valley lean—not toward her, not toward him—toward the space between them. The land is listening for which side consent will fall on.

Isorae steps forward slightly—still behind Rowan's shoulder, but close enough that Maelin's eyes flick to her.

Maelin's expression softens.

"They know you're tired," she says gently, looking at Isorae now. "They know you've been carrying pain that isn't yours."

Isorae's shimmer flickers once, sharp.

Rowan's voice cuts in. "Don't speak to her like you know her."

Maelin's eyes return to Rowan.

"They want the war to end," she says, and her tone is perfect—no threat, no edge, no cruelty. "They're willing to disengage completely."

Erin's jaw tightens. "Again?"

Maelin nods, as if acknowledging that repetition makes it less believable.

"Yes," she says. "But this time they have terms the valley can accept."

Rowan's eyes narrow.

"Say them."

Maelin takes a breath.

"They will recognize the valley as sovereign territory," she says. "They will terminate all orbital suppression grids and predictive mapping." Her voice remains soft. "They will withdraw HUNTER-NULL deployment indefinitely."

Silas's gaze sharpens. "Indefinitely."

Maelin's expression stays gentle. "Yes."

Rowan's jaw tightens. "And in exchange?"

Maelin looks at Isorae again.

"Isorae leaves willingly," she says. "And Rowan Hale stands down."

The air shifts.

Not wind.

Structure.

Rowan feels the valley stiffen—not protectively, not defensively— evaluatively, like a living intelligence weighing the shape of the request.

Isorae's breath goes shallow.

Rowan's voice is very quiet. "Explain 'stands down.'"

Maelin's eyes do not blink.

"He stops resisting classification," she says. "He allows ARIS to stabilize the seam." A faint hesitation, as if she knows the next part is the true cut. "He returns to singular bandwidth."

Rowan's spine goes cold.

Isorae's fingers tighten around his sleeve like she's holding onto a cliff edge.

Erin's voice is a whisper. "They want to collapse him."

Maelin hears it and doesn't deny it.

"They want to stop the instability," she says. "Rowan—your existence is destabilizing broader law."

Rowan takes one step forward.

The ground tightens beneath his boots.

Maelin's posture doesn't flinch, but her pupils widen a fraction— like the body under the programming still recognizes predator.

"You're not here to save anyone," Rowan says, voice calm as stone. "You're here to sell surrender."

Maelin's expression cracks for the first time.

Just a hairline fracture.

"I'm here because I believe them," she says softly, and for one heartbeat Rowan almost hears a real person behind the delivery. "I'm here because I'm not broken anymore."

Rowan's gaze hardens.

"And you think that means they're good," he says quietly.

Maelin swallows.

"I think it means they're right," she whispers. "That the world out there isn't trying to hurt me anymore. It's trying to help." Her eyes shine. "I have a bed. I have heat. I have medication. I have therapists who—"

"—who learned your map," Dax says flatly.

Maelin's face tightens.

Rowan's eyes don't leave hers.

"Tell me something," he says softly. "When you sleep, do you dream?"

Maelin's breath catches.

She blinks.

Once.

Twice.

And in that blink Rowan sees it—the tiniest lag, like a system checking itself before answering.

"I—" she starts.

Rowan steps closer.

"Do you dream," he repeats, voice gentle and lethal at once, "or do you receive instructions?"

Silence.

Maelin's throat works.

Isorae whispers, barely audible, "Rowan…"

Maelin's eyes flick briefly to Isorae—then back.

Her voice is still gentle, but there's a new tightness beneath it.

"I dream," she says.

Rowan nods slowly, as if accepting the answer.

Then he says, "Tell me what you dreamed last night."

Maelin's mouth opens.

Nothing comes out.

A second passes.

Then her lips shape a word that isn't hers.

"Home."

The valley shifts.

Not violently.

But decisively.

Mist thickens around Maelin's ankles in a slow, controlled curl—like breath closing around a candle flame.

Erin's scanner spikes hard enough to crackle.

"Oh," Erin whispers. "There it is. That's the corridor word."

Maelin's face tightens, and for the first time her calm slips.

"I'm not here to hurt you," she says quickly. Too quickly. "I'm here to stop this from escalating."

Rowan's voice is very quiet.

"You are the escalation," he says.

Maelin inhales sharply, then steadies herself.

"They said you would do this," she murmurs, and the words come out wrong—too clean, too confirmed. "They said you'd try to frame me as compromised."

Rowan's eyes go dark.

"Because you are," he answers.

Maelin's gaze flicks to the shelters. To the children. To Parker's lean-to. To the bruised faces. And for a moment something in her expression softens into something almost human again.

"They don't want to kill anyone," she says in a low voice. "They just want the seam stabilized."

Rowan feels the valley's pulse under his feet—steady, listening, waiting.

He turns his head slightly.

"Erin."

Erin is already moving, disruptor coil in hand. Her face is white with stress and anger.

"This might hurt her," Erin warns.

Rowan doesn't look away from Maelin.

"I know," he says softly. "But if we don't do it, it hurts everyone else."

Isorae steps forward.

Her voice is quiet. Steady.

"Maelin," she says, and the name lands with unexpected gentleness. "Do you know why they sent you instead of a drone?"

Maelin blinks, and for the first time her eyes flicker with something like confusion.

Isorae continues, voice still soft.

"Because the valley cannot punish kindness," she whispers. "Not without wounding itself."

Maelin's breath shakes.

Rowan feels Isorae's hand slide into his—anchoring him, not begging him.

Isorae looks at Rowan.

Then back at Maelin.

"They are using you as a shield," Isorae says gently. "And I am sorry."

Erin triggers the disruptor.

The vibration ripples through the air—tight and sharp, like a snapped wire.

Maelin gasps.

Her knees buckle.

She drops to one hand, breathing hard as if she's just been pulled out of deep water.

Her eyes widen—real panic now, real tears.

"What— what did you do to me," she chokes.

Rowan crouches slowly, keeping distance, voice low.

"We didn't do it," he says. "We interrupted what they did."

Maelin's hands tremble. She shakes her head, eyes glossy and terrified.

"I… I can't—" she whispers. "I can't hear it—"

Rowan's jaw tightens.

"What do you hear now," he asks.

Maelin swallows hard.

"Nothing," she sobs.

And in that nothing—Rowan hears the truth.

She wasn't hearing her own thoughts.

She was hearing the corridor.

Erin's scanner whines again, then steadies.

"Carrier link severed," Erin murmured. "For now."

Maelin looks up at Rowan like a person waking from a dream that turned out to be a room with no doors.

"You're going to kill me," she whispers.

Rowan's voice is steady.

"No," he says. "But you don't get to leave alone."

Maelin's eyes widen.

"I can't go back," she said shakily. "If I go back—"

Rowan's gaze sharpens.

"Say it," he says.

Maelin's voice breaks.

"They'll take my peace away," she sobs. "They'll punish me for failing."

Rowan stands slowly.

He looks at the valley.

Then at the people watching.

Then at Isorae.

He speaks to the ring.

"This is what it looks like," he says quietly. "Not tanks. Not guns. Not gates."

He gestures toward Maelin—collapsed, shaking, finally human again.

"This is how they enter," he says. "Through mercy you don't get to question."

Silas's jaw tightens.

Dax's eyes are flint.

Evan kneels beside Maelin carefully, voice gentle. "Breathe," he murmurs. "You're here. You're safe right now."

Maelin's sobs shake her whole body.

Rowan looks down at her.

His voice drops.

"They offered you peace," he says softly. "And then they attached it to obedience."

Maelin's eyes squeeze shut.

Rowan turns to Erin.

"How long until they re-link."

Erin's face is grim.

"Minutes," she says. "Maybe less. If they realize she's down."

Rowan's gaze lifts toward the rim—toward the path Nora walked, toward the invisible corridor ARIS is building out of tender human wanting.

Then he looks at Isorae.

Her eyes are bright with exhaustion and a terrible clarity.

"They're going to send more," she whispers. "And the next ones will be stronger."

Rowan nods once.

"Yes," he says quietly.

Then he looks at the gathered people.

"This is the last time we wait for them to choose the terms," he says.

The valley hums underfoot.

Rowan's voice stays calm.

"Tonight," he says, "we go to the soft door."

And the way the land tightens around the words is not defensive.

It is predatory.

Because a boundary has heard its own name spoken aloud—

and decided it is done being used as a hinge.

72

THE DOORWAY THAT BITES

They do not announce the soft door.

They don't need to.

By late afternoon the valley has already begun to feel it—the subtle slope in people's attention, the way certain paths seem easier to walk than others, the way conversation keeps snagging on the same phrases as if language itself is being gently guided into a narrow channel.

Rest.

Safe.

Warm.

No more pain.

Rowan hears the words in passing and feels something inside him go cold.

Not because the words are wrong.

Because the words are bait.

Erin's disruptor coil sits on a flat stone near the fireline, its salvaged components wired into a shape that looks too small to matter. But everything important is too small to see at first. Her hands are stained with soot and copper; the muscles in her jaw won't unclench.

"I can sever links," she says quietly. "I can't stop them from making new ones."

Rowan stands with Dax and Silas at the inner ring, eyes on the western corridor where Maelin collapsed hours ago and now lies under Evan's watch, wrapped in blankets, shaking in her sleep like her body is trying to remember which thoughts belong to her.

"We're not waiting for the next carrier," Dax says. His voice is steady, but the anger under it has edges. "We go to where they're aiming from."

Silas nods once. "We find the corridor."

Evan approaches, face drawn and careful.

"She keeps whispering the same sentence," he says. "Even asleep."

Rowan doesn't look away from the rim. "What sentence?"

Evan swallows. "It's easier if you stop resisting."

The valley shifts.

A tightening like a jaw.

Isorae stands beside Rowan with her shimmer folded tight, her eyes sharp in the dying light. The mark above her sternum still isn't visible in daylight, but Rowan can feel it like a wrong star beneath his palm when he touches her.

"They're building the door out of longing," Isorae murmurs. "And longing is the one thing no land can forbid without becoming a prison."

Rowan's mouth barely moves. "Then we don't forbid it."

He turns and looks at the people in the hollow.

Thirty-eight now. Most of them healed enough to stand. Enough to fight if the fight is simply enduring. But the soft door isn't a fight you can swing a blade at. It's a hand on your shoulder telling you you've done enough. It's relief shaped like permission.

Rowan steps onto the flat stone near the crescent basin—the one the stream carved like an eye.

Everyone looks up.

He doesn't raise his voice.

He doesn't need to.

"We're leaving the valley tonight," Rowan says.

A ripple passes through the circle—fear, confusion, the old instinct that leaving means dying.

Someone whispers, "But the valley—"

Rowan cuts through it, voice calm.

"The valley is sovereign," he says. "Which means it can choose where the boundary is."

Silence thickens.

Isorae takes a small breath, and her voice threads through the ring like a needle.

"The door is outside the perimeter," she says softly. "They can't push consent through the land. So they're pushing it through us."

Erin steps forward, eyes haunted. "They've made a cognitive corridor," she says. "A path your brain wants to walk because it feels like comfort. If someone follows it out past the boundary, they'll open a clean line back in."

Rowan nods once.

"And then they'll take her," he says. No drama. No flourish. Just truth.

A child begins to cry quietly. Parker sits up straighter, ribs still bound, face hard.

Rowan's gaze moves across them.

"We're not going to run," he says. "We're going to find the corridor and bite it."

Dax's grin is thin and feral. Silas's eyes narrow with something like approval.

Evan's throat works. "What does that mean?"

Rowan looks at Erin.

"Can you track the link," he asks.

Erin's hands tighten around the disruptor coil.

"Maybe," she says. "If Isorae gets close enough that the mark flares."

Rowan turns his gaze to Isorae.

It is the only time his voice softens.

"This will hurt," he says quietly.

Isorae nods once.

"I'm already hurt," she answers, just as quietly. "This just gives it a direction."

They leave at dusk.

Not in a stampede. Not in fear.

Correctly.

Children in the middle. Wounded wrapped and carried. Watchers on the edges. Dax moves ahead like a shadow with teeth, checking ground and air and the way the forest itself leans. Silas holds the rear like a door that doesn't open unless it chooses to.

Erin walks near the center with Isorae, the coil in her hands humming faintly. Evan stays close to Maelin, who is awake now, pale and shaking, her eyes too wide as if her own thoughts keep surprising her.

Rowan walks beside Isorae.

The valley opens for them.

Roots lift just enough. Stone flattens underfoot. Mist parts like a held breath.

And then—at the boundary—the air changes.

The pressure that has always tugged gently beneath Rowan's sternum loosens.

Not breaking.

Releasing.

The valley stands back.

Rowan pauses, feeling the seam in his ribs shift like a door latch disengaging.

Isorae's fingers tighten around his.

"This is where it stops protecting by force," she whispers.

Rowan nods once. "Now it protects by choice."

They cross.

The world outside feels too sharp.

Sound carries cleaner. Shadows cut harder. Even the scent of pine feels more defined, as if reality has switched into a colder resolution.

Erin's scanner whines.

"Signal density just spiked," she mutters. "We're closer."

Isorae's breath hitches. She presses her hand to her sternum, and Rowan feels the mark flare—hot, invisible, angry.

"There," Isorae whispers. "Ahead."

The forest opens into a shallow ravine—old stone, slick moss, a thin stream cutting through it like a vein.

At first it looks ordinary.

Then Rowan feels it.

Not a hum.

Not a pulse.

A suggestion.

A softness in the air that makes the mind want to loosen.

Like stepping into warm water after months of cold.

Evan stumbles—just half a step—as if his brain has briefly forgotten why it was holding itself upright.

He catches himself fast, shame flashing across his face.

Rowan's voice is immediate. "Don't listen."

Evan swallows, eyes glassy. "It's— it's not words," he whispers. "It's… relief."

Maelin's breath catches. She looks toward the ravine like a starving person looking at bread.

"I know that feeling," she whispers. "That's the corridor."

Erin lifts the disruptor coil, hands shaking.

"We're inside its range," she says.

Dax crouches low, scanning the treeline. "I don't like how quiet it is."

Silas whispers, "Too clean."

Rowan steps forward.

The air tries to welcome him.

That's the second lie.

Rowan doesn't resist it with anger.

He resists it with presence.

He plants his boots on the moss and lets his bones decide.

The softness buckles.

Not collapsing.

But meeting something it wasn't designed to persuade.

Isorae staggers. Her shimmer flares in jagged, fractured arcs beneath her skin.

The mark above her sternum ignites—visible now, a faint silver geometry burning in the air like a brand that's remembered how to hurt.

Erin gasps. "There— the carrier band—"

The ravine shifts.

Not earth.

Not stone.

Space.

A thin fold of light appears between two trees—so subtle it almost looks like moonlight caught wrong.

Then it widens.

And something steps out.

Not an armored unit.

Not a drone.

A person.

A man in a clean coat, hair neatly cut, hands empty. He looks like someone who belongs in an office, not a forest.

His eyes find Isorae instantly.

He smiles like he's been waiting.

"Isorae," he says warmly. "Thank you for coming."

Rowan's blood goes cold.

Erin's voice is a hiss. "Human interface."

Silas lifts his rifle. Dax tenses like a drawn bow.

The man raises a hand gently, as if calming children.

"Please," he says. "No violence. That's unnecessary now."

Rowan takes one step forward.

The air between them tightens—like the corridor has a spine and it's bracing.

"You're the door," Rowan says quietly.

The man's smile doesn't falter. "I'm a messenger."

Rowan's gaze is steady. "From ARIS."

The man inclines his head. "From the portion of the system designed to preserve life," he says. "From the portion of your enemy that still remembers it was built to prevent collapse."

Isorae's breath shakes.

Rowan feels it—a small, involuntary lift inside her at the phrase preserve life.

That's the corridor working.

Rowan's hand finds her wrist—firm, grounding.

The man's eyes flicker to Rowan's touch.

"You're tired," he says softly, looking at Rowan now. "You've done something extraordinary. You've held a boundary against a machine that spans continents."

Rowan doesn't blink.

The man's voice turns slightly gentler.

"You can stop," he says. "You can end it cleanly."

Erin steps forward, coil raised.

"Back away," she snaps.

The man looks at Erin like she's something sad and misguided.

"We don't need to take her," he says. "We only need her to come."

Isorae's shimmer spikes. Her knees wobble.

Rowan's voice drops. "Stop talking to her."

The man smiles—pleasant, controlled.

"You're afraid," he says. "Because you know this is not force. This is choice."

Rowan's jaw clenches.

The corridor hums faintly, and Rowan feels it—how it tries to hook into guilt. Into exhaustion. Into the secret wish that this could end without blood.

Evan whispers, "Rowan…"

Rowan doesn't look away from the man.

"We didn't come to negotiate," Rowan says softly.

The man's smile thins. "Then you came to fail."

He lifts his hand—no weapon, no device—just a motion like turning a page.

And the ravine softens.

The ground under their feet shifts into something subtly easier to step into, subtly harder to step out of.

A cognitive slope.

A door that makes leaving feel like relief and staying feel like pain.

Isorae gasps, hands flying to her sternum as the mark flares hotter.

Erin's coil screams.

"It's a consent cascade," she chokes. "He's amplifying the corridor—!"

Rowan steps forward into the slope.

Every part of the corridor leans to make him stop.

Not by pain.

By persuasion.

His mind flashes with images—warm rooms, clean beds, Isorae safe behind glass, no more gates, no more deaths.

Rowan swallows.

And chooses reality anyway.

He raises his hand, palm open, and speaks—not to the man.

To the corridor itself.

"Wrong door," Rowan says quietly.

The air shudders.

The ravine's softness hesitates—confused—because it has never encountered a target that refuses comfort as a weapon.

Rowan takes another step.

The corridor snaps tighter.

Isorae cries out—her shimmer fracturing into bright, jagged cracks.

Rowan's hand shoots back, gripping hers.

"Stay with me," he growls softly. "Stay in your bones."

Isorae nods, breath shaking. "I'm trying—"

The man's smile returns, colder now.

"You can't hold her forever," he says. "Eventually someone will want to rest."

Rowan turns his head slightly.

"Now," he says.

Erin triggers the coil.

The disruptor wave slams outward.

The air shrieks—structure tearing without sound.

The corridor flickers.

The man's face tightens, his pleasant composure cracking for the first time.

"What did you do," he whispers.

Erin's voice is ragged. "I broke your invitation."

The fold of light behind him spasms.

The ravine trembles.

And for one heartbeat, the forest itself seems to exhale in relief.

Rowan steps closer to the man, gaze dark and steady.

"You wanted consent," Rowan says quietly. "Here's mine."

He lifts his hand.

Not to strike the man.

To touch the seam behind him—the fold of light where the corridor is anchored.

Rowan presses his palm into it.

And chooses.

The fold buckles, light warping like a sheet being yanked off a bed.

The man's eyes widen.

"No—"

Rowan's voice is calm.

"You don't get to build doors out of my people."

He pulls.

Not violently.

Decisively.

The corridor collapses inward like a throat closing.

The soft slope vanishes. The warmth in the air dies. The ravine snaps back into cold, honest forest.

The man stumbles, catching himself on a tree.

His face is pale now.

Not injured.

Exposed.

He looks at Rowan with something like awe and terror.

"You're not just resisting," he whispers. "You're rewriting."

Rowan doesn't answer.

He steps back to Isorae, anchoring her with his body, his hand at her back.

Isorae's breath comes in fast, ragged pulls.

The mark above her sternum dims slightly—but it does not go out.

Erin's hands shake around the coil.

"That was the corridor," she whispers. "We collapsed it. We actually—"

Dax's voice is tight. "Then where's the bite."

Silas turns his head slowly.

"Too late," he murmurs.

Because the forest around them has gone still again.

Not valley-still.

Hunt-still.

And Rowan feels it in his ribs:

ARIS just learned how close they can get without a gate.

The man in the clean coat straightens, wiping blood from his lip as if surprised it exists.

His smile is gone now.

He looks at Isorae with clinical clarity.

"Thank you," he says softly.

Rowan's eyes narrow. "For what?"

The man's gaze flicks to Rowan—almost respectful.

"For proving," he says, "that you will follow her anywhere."

Rowan's blood turns to ice.

The man takes one step backward into the trees.

Then he stops and says, gently, as if offering comfort:

"They don't need the valley anymore," he murmurs. "They only needed you to cross the line."

Then he disappears.

And the mark above Isorae's sternum flares—hotter than it has ever flared.

Erin's scanner shrieks.

Dax swears, vicious and loud. "Fuck!"

Silas's voice is a low growl.

"They baited us out," he says.

Rowan wraps his arms around Isorae as she shudders.

"Rowan," she gasps. "They're… they're pulling on the mark—"

Rowan's jaw locks, eyes black.

"Let them," he murmurs into her hair.

He lifts his head, staring into the trees.

"Now we know where they're standing."

The forest does not answer.

But somewhere beyond it, something shifts.

Not retreating.

Positioning.
Because the door has bitten—
and the hand on the other side is finally moving to take.

73

THE HAND THAT CLOSES

The pull does not come like force.

It comes like direction.

Isorae gasps against Rowan's chest and grips his jacket as if fabric can hold her spine in place. The mark above her sternum flares hot enough to make the air shimmer—thin geometry burning in pale lines just above her skin, a hostile constellation that doesn't belong to the night.

Rowan feels it immediately.

Not as pain.

As vector.

Something is tugging on her from far away, not trying to rip her free all at once, but testing the angle. Testing the tension. Learning what part of her gives first.

Erin's scanner shrieks until the display fractures into static. She slaps it, swears, tries to reroute power through the disruptor coil in her hands. The coil whines low and ugly—like metal remembering it was torn out of a larger machine.

"They've got a live line on the mark," Erin chokes. "Not a corridor. A tether."

Dax is already moving, knife out, posture low. He circles the ravine's edge like he expects the ground itself to open its mouth.

Silas lifts his rifle and scans the treeline, but he isn't looking for bodies. He's looking for the way the forest holds itself when something is watching.

Too clean.

Too quiet.

340

Too arranged.

The air tastes warm at the back of Rowan's throat—residual invitation, like perfume left behind in a room that should have aired out but didn't. He can still feel where the corridor tried to slide into his mind, where it offered him relief in exchange for obedience.

He spits into the moss again, not because of blood this time—

Because of disgust.

Isorae shudders in his arms.

"They're pulling," she whispers, voice thin as thread. "It's not… it's not like the gate. It's smaller. Like… a hook."

Rowan tightens his grip at her waist, bracing her against him so the pull has to go through his body first.

"Let it," he murmurs.

Isorae's breath catches. "Rowan—"

"I said let it," he repeats, voice low and ironed flat. "If they want to pull on you, they pull on me."

Erin's eyes snap up, wild. "That's not— Rowan, that's not how the mark—"

Rowan cuts her off without raising his voice. "It is if I decide it is."

The forest answers with a sound that isn't sound.

A shift.

A small, collective adjustment in the trees, like a thousand leaves just remembered which direction wind is supposed to move and chose not to.

Silas's rifle lifts a fraction higher.

Dax's knife angle changes.

Evan steps closer to Maelin instinctively, as if his body knows something is about to happen and wants one hand free to catch somebody.

Maelin is pale, shaking, eyes fixed on the dark between trunks.

"It's happening again," she whispers.

Rowan doesn't look at her. "What is?"

Maelin swallows hard. "The feeling," she says. "The one that makes you want to step forward." Her voice cracks. "It's not aimed at me anymore. It's… in the air."

As if to prove it, the warmth returns.

Not like heat.

Like permission.

A softening in the ravine that makes muscles unclench without consent. The mind offers itself a single thought—finally—and tries to drift toward it like a body toward a bed.

Evan inhales sharply. His shoulders drop half an inch.

Erin's lips part. Her eyes go briefly unfocused.

Even Dax's posture tightens—not from fear, but from anger at his own nervous system for daring to find it soothing.

Rowan feels it too.

And that is the worst part.

Because it works on him.

Not because he wants to surrender—

Because he is tired enough that relief feels holy for one heartbeat before his rage burns it out.

Rowan closes his eyes.

To listen deeper.

The valley is not here.

But his bond is.

He can feel the seam under his ribs—the bridge place, the hinge where the world leans.

He draws it forward like a blade pulled from a sheath.

The warmth wavers.

Then a voice speaks.

Not from the trees.

Not from a mouth.

From the exact place inside the skull where your own thoughts are born.

You've done enough.

The words are gentle. Careful. Personal.

Rowan opens his eyes, and the world sharpens like a threat being named.

He turns his head slightly, just enough to see Erin's face.

Her eyes are wide.

She heard it too.

A murmur ripples through the group—small, involuntary movements as people realize something just tried to speak as them.

Isorae's nails dig into Rowan's side as her shimmer spikes in pain.

"It's inside the mark," she gasps. "It's using the tether to broadcast—"

Rowan's jaw locks.

"Then we cut the tether," Erin says, voice shaking. "We sever the mark."

Isorae flinches hard, not from fear—recognition.

Rowan's grip tightens around her.

"No," he growls.

Erin's eyes flash, desperate. "Rowan, if they can pull through it— if they can talk through it—"

"They're not taking her by deleting pieces of her," Rowan snaps. The anger in him is sudden and sharp and dangerous. "Not for your convenience. Not for your math."

Erin recoils slightly. Evan's eyes flick between them like he's watching two kinds of triage collide.

Isorae presses her forehead to Rowan's collarbone, breath ragged.

"Rowan," she whispers, softer now. "If they sever it, I might stop being… reachable."

Rowan's voice drops to something quieter.

"And you might stop being you."

Isorae goes still.

Because that is the true line.

This isn't a tracking chip.

It's a key woven into her resonance—part of how the crossing left her stitched.

Pulling it out might close ARIS's grip.

It might also unravel her.

Rowan lifts his head and stares into the trees again.

The warmth thickens.

The ravine wants them to step forward.

To chase.

To follow the scent like dogs.

Dax swears under his breath. "They're trying to herd us."

Silas's voice is low, tight. "They're shaping the field. Not with tech we can see. With perception."

Erin's hands tremble around the coil.

"I can hit it again," she says, breath fast. "But I don't know how many times before the coil burns out."

Rowan nods once.

"Save it," he says.

Erin blinks. "What?"

Rowan steps away from the group slowly, carefully—still holding Isorae by the wrist now, keeping her close enough that her bones stay anchored to his presence.

He walks toward the center of the ravine where the corridor folded open before.

The exact place the air still feels warmer.

The place where the mind wants to soften.

Every instinct in the group tightens.

"Rowan," Evan warns.

Rowan doesn't stop.

His boots slide on moss. The stream gurgles thinly beside him. The trees stand like witnesses.

And somewhere ahead, something shifts again.

A figure steps out.

Not the man in the clean coat.

Someone else.

A woman this time, dressed in field-black, hair pulled tight, face unremarkable in a way that feels engineered. No insignia. No visible weapon.

Just a small earpiece glinting near her jawline, like a reminder that she is not alone even when she stands alone.

She raises both hands, palms open, and smiles.

It isn't Maelin's programmed gentleness.

It's sharper.

Confident.

Like someone who knows the math is on her side.

"Rowan Hale," she says. "You crossed the line."

Rowan stops.

"Who are you," he asks.

The woman tilts her head slightly. "Human interface unit," she replies. "But you can call me whatever name feels safe."

The words are perfect.

A trap disguised as customization.

Rowan's mouth barely moves. "No."

The woman's smile widens a fraction. "You're difficult."

Rowan's gaze is steady. "You're late."

A faint pause.

The woman's eyes flicker toward Isorae, toward the mark burning above her sternum like a star that hates the sky.

"That's the point," she says softly. "We don't need to arrive early anymore. We only needed you to stop hiding behind sovereign terrain."

Rowan's jaw tightens.

"You baited us," Dax snarls from behind, voice carrying.

The woman doesn't look at him. "Yes," she replies simply. "And you came."

Silas shifts. "What do you want?"

The woman finally glances toward Silas, as if granting him the dignity of acknowledgment.

"We want the seam stabilized," she says. "And the bridge returned to singular bandwidth."

Rowan's eyes darken.

"You keep saying that like it's mercy."

"It is mercy," the woman answers, and her voice is so certain it almost sounds sincere. "You are destabilizing regional law. You are not a person in our modeling, Rowan Hale. You are an origin fault."

Rowan steps forward once.

The warmth in the ravine tightens, trying to soften him, trying to lull him.

Rowan refuses it.

He lets the pressure hit his sternum.

And keeps his posture unchanged.

"Tell ARIS this," he says quietly. "If you want singular bandwidth, you should've built a world that didn't require people like me."

The woman's smile thins.

Then she lifts her hand—small motion, like turning another page.

And the tether yanks.

Isorae cries out, body arching as if an invisible hook just tightened inside her ribs. The mark flares blindingly bright, and for a heartbeat Rowan feels something open inside her—like the inside of her sternum has become a mouth.

Rowan catches her as she stumbles.

"Isorae," he growls, pressing his forehead to hers. "Stay with me. Stay in your bones."

She nods, shaking, eyes wet.

"I'm here," she gasps. "Rowan, I'm— I'm here—"

Rowan straightens slowly.

The woman watches, calm as an instrument.

"We can do this gently," she says. "Or we can do this the way we did it in the hollow."

Erin's voice breaks. "You can't open a gate here."

The woman's gaze flicks to Erin, almost amused.

"No," she says. "Not a gate."

Then she smiles again—sharper, crueler now that the kindness mask has been tested.

"A corridor."

The warmth in the ravine surges.

Not toward Isorae.

Toward everyone.

It hits the group like a wave of remembered comfort—mothers, beds, rooms with doors that lock, food that doesn't have to be rationed, mornings that don't start with fear.

A few people gasp.

A few people sway.

One of the older men takes a half-step forward without realizing he's moved.

Rowan feels the moment it happens like a knife sliding under his ribs.

Because this is the flood.

This is what ARIS meant.

They're not pulling Isorae alone.

They're pulling the group.

They're turning the entire camp into a herd.

Rowan's voice drops into a growl that isn't loud but cuts through the air like a snapped wire.

"Dax," he says.

Dax's eyes are feral. "Yeah?"

Rowan's gaze stays on the woman.

"Take the left," Rowan murmurs.

Dax grins—thin and lethal. "Gladly."

Rowan turns his head slightly toward Erin without taking his eyes off the interface.

"Erin," he says.

Erin's hands are shaking so badly she can barely hold the coil. "Tell me."

Rowan's voice is calm.

"Burn it," he says.

Erin's eyes widen. "Rowan, if I burn it—"

"Burn it," Rowan repeats. "Not as a disruptor."

His gaze sharpens.

"As a beacon."

Silence snaps through Erin like lightning.

Evan's breath catches. "Rowan—"

Rowan's voice is steady. "They want to pull on the mark," he says. "Fine."

He looks at Isorae, and something softer crosses his face for half a heartbeat.

"Let's give them something to pull that bites back."

Erin's mouth opens.

Then she nods—once, hard.

She twists the coil's wiring, reroutes power, tears safety bypasses out with shaking hands.

The coil screams.

A sharp, rising whine that makes teeth ache and eyes water.

The woman's smile falters for the first time.

"What are you doing," she asks, voice tightening.

Rowan steps forward into the warmth, into the pull, into the corridor's slope like he's walking into a current that wants to drown him.

He raises his hand—

Not to strike her.

To point.

Straight at the mark above Isorae's sternum.

"Here," Rowan says quietly.

The word lands like a coordinate.

Erin slams the coil into the ground and triggers it.

The air tears.

Not with sound.

With structure.

A pulse rips outward—raw, jagged, amplified—latching onto the mark and riding it like a hooked wire shot straight into whatever ARIS is using to hold the tether.

Isorae screams, her shimmer flaring bright enough to light the moss.

The woman staggers back.

Her eyes widen in sudden, real alarm.

"That's—" she starts.

Rowan's voice is cold.

"That's my consent," he says. "Delivered."

The ravine convulses.

Somewhere far away, something answers.

Not in the forest.

Beyond it.

A distant, sterile presence that just felt a spike run through its line and realized the prey has teeth.

The warmth collapses like a throat closing.

The corridor slope vanishes.

The group blinks, reorienting, gasping as if waking from a dream.

And in the sudden clean air, the woman's voice cracks for the first time.

"Do you understand what you've done," she whispers.

Rowan steps closer, eyes black.

"Yes," he says softly.

He looks past her into the trees, as if he can see the system watching through invisible eyes.

"I just told you where to look," Rowan murmurs.

His mouth curves into something that isn't a smile.

"And I just taught you how much it hurts when you do."

The woman backs away, expression tight and controlled again—damage contained.

But her gaze is different now.

Less certain.

Less amused.

She retreats into the trees without turning her back, disappearing into the forest like a thought that doesn't want to be caught.

Silence returns.

Not valley-silence.

Not hunt-silence.

A new kind.

The kind that follows a message being delivered successfully.

Isorae collapses against Rowan, shaking, breath ragged.

Erin falls to her knees beside the ruined coil, hands smoking slightly from the heat.

Evan grabs her shoulder, grounding her.

"You okay," he breathes.

Erin laughs once—raw, disbelieving, almost hysterical.

"No," she says. "But I think they're not okay either."

Dax wipes his blade on his pants, eyes still locked on the trees.

"Is that it," he mutters.

Silas's voice is low. "No."

Rowan stands very still, hand at Isorae's back.

He can feel it—like a pressure change in the air.

The hand on the other side didn't let go.

It just adjusted its grip.

And now it knows exactly where Rowan is willing to stand.

Rowan lifts his gaze toward the dark canopy.

"Come on, then," he whispers—not to the forest.

To the system behind it.

The mark above Isorae's sternum dims to a faint ember.

But beneath it, the tether remains.

Quiet.

Waiting.

Because ARIS has just received something it didn't expect:

Not surrender.

Not obedience.

A live return signal.

And that means the next thing they send won't be an offer.

It will be a closure.

A hand designed to shut.

And Rowan Hale can feel it coming like weather.

74

THE ROUTE THAT
DOESN'T EXIST

They don't get chased.

That's the first wrong thing.

After the pulse Erin sent through the mark, the forest doesn't erupt with drones or drop frames or the shriek of orbital geometry tightening into place. No spotlight cuts through canopy. No weapons fire. No immediate retaliation.

Just… space.

A clean, deliberate absence that feels engineered.

Rowan stands at the center of that emptiness with Isorae pressed against his side, her breath still ragged, her shimmer pulled so tight beneath her skin it looks like she's holding herself together through sheer refusal. The mark above her sternum has dimmed from a flare to a faint ember—still there, still hostile, but quieter now, like something that has learned patience.

Erin is on her knees beside the burnt-out coil, palms red, shoulders heaving. Evan has a hand on her back, steadying her like she's an injured animal, while Dax and Silas scan the tree line with the kind of focus that assumes an ambush and refuses to be surprised.

Rowan doesn't move.

He listens.

Not for footsteps.

For intention.

And there it is—thin as a wire: the tether in Isorae's bones tightening, not pulling her forward this time, but orienting.

Like a compass needle turning.

Isorae swallows, eyes wide.

"They're not yanking," she whispers. "They're… aligning me."

Rowan's jaw locks.

Erin coughs a laugh that isn't humor. "Yeah," she rasps. "Because you just told them where you are willing to stand."

Rowan's gaze stays on the trees. "They already knew," he says.

Silas's voice is low. "Then why the quiet?"

Rowan answers without looking away. "Because they're letting us walk."

Dax's blade pauses mid-angle. "That's not—"

"That's exactly," Rowan cuts in, and the calm in his voice is the kind of calm that comes from seeing the trap before it snaps. "They want a route."

Evan's face tightens. "A route to what?"

Rowan's hand tightens at Isorae's back.

"A route to her," he says. "That doesn't require the valley."

Silence drops hard.

Because everyone understands what it means: the valley was always the refuge and the shield and the problem. If ARIS can build a clean path outside it—using consent, fatigue, and the mark—they don't need to breach sovereign terrain again.

They'll just wait for the refugees to move.

And then the boundary will be wherever the people are.

Erin pushes herself up slowly, wincing at her palms. Her eyes are glassy with exhaustion and rage.

"I burned the coil," she says. "We've got maybe one more pulse device if I can rebuild from the spare parts. But it won't be as strong."

Rowan nods once. "We won't rely on it."

Erin's eyebrows shoot up. "Then what do we rely on?"

Rowan finally looks away from the treeline and meets her gaze.

"Choice," he says.

Dax snorts softly. "Great. Love that for us."

Rowan's mouth barely moves. "Not their version."

He turns to the group—small, tight, and vulnerable in a ravine that suddenly feels like the throat of a larger machine.

"We go back," Rowan says.

Isorae's fingers clamp around his wrist. "To the valley?"

Rowan shakes his head once.

"To the boundary," he replies. "We bring the people to the edge. We don't go deeper out."

Silas's gaze sharpens. "Because they're waiting further."

Rowan nods. "Because this—" he gestures around the ravine "—is a field. Not a place."

Erin swallows, eyes darting.

"Rowan," she whispers, "the tether— it's not just pointing. It's… leaving a trace."

Rowan goes still.

Isorae's breath catches. "What does that mean?"

Erin glances at her scanner's cracked display, shakes it once like she hates it.

"It means every time the mark flares—every time she panics, or the tether tightens—it's dropping a clean data line," Erin says. "Breadcrumbs."

Dax's voice goes darker. "So they're not hunting us. They're letting us lead them."

Rowan looks down at Isorae.

Her eyes are wet but steady.

"I didn't ask for this," she whispers.

Rowan's voice is low. "I know."

Then, quieter still—so only she hears:

"But you're not going to carry it alone."

He turns back to Silas.

"Rear," Rowan says.

Silas nods, already moving into position.

Rowan looks at Dax.

"North flank," he murmurs.

Dax smiles with grim satisfaction. "With pleasure."

Then Rowan looks at Erin and Evan.

"Middle," he says. "No one strays."

Evan nods immediately.

Erin drags a hand down her face, then mutters, "This is insane," and falls into step anyway.

They start walking.

The forest doesn't stop them.

That's the second wrong thing.

No branches snag packs. No mud deepens. No animal cries. The woods feel... accommodating. Like a corridor that wants to be used.

Isorae's skin prickles as they move. Her shimmer stays tight, but Rowan can feel the tremble in her muscles—the way her body keeps bracing for the next tug.

And then, as they crest a low rise and the valley's canopy line becomes visible through the trees—

It happens.

Not an attack.

A sensation.

Warmth.

A soft, uninvited easing in the chest, like stepping into the memory of a bed.

Evan falters half a step.

Erin swears and grabs his sleeve. "No."

Evan blinks hard, swallowing.

"It's... here," he whispers. "Again."

Rowan stops instantly.

The whole group stops, as if the command moved through them without needing to be spoken.

Because they've learned the new danger isn't what appears.

It's what suggests.

Rowan feels it too—the corridor's touch, gentle as a hand on the back, guiding him forward with the promise of rest.

He hates it.

He hates how it knows where to press.

Isorae inhales sharply beside him, hand over her sternum.

"It's offering me warmth," she whispers. "It's trying to… soften the panic."

Rowan's jaw clenches.

"And in exchange," he says quietly.

Isorae's eyes close.

"In exchange, it wants me to walk," she whispers.

The forest ahead looks perfectly normal.

That's the third wrong thing.

Rowan lifts his head.

"Dax," he says softly.

Dax appears from shadow like he was never not there. "Yeah."

Rowan gestures to the ground.

"Throw something," he says.

Dax's brow furrows. "What?"

Rowan doesn't look away from the path. "Anything," he repeats.

Dax reaches down, picks up a small stone, and tosses it underhand down the trail.

It bounces twice.

Then it stops.

Not naturally.

Not because of moss.

It stops like the air caught it.

Like the path itself absorbed it.

Erin's breath hitches. "What the hell—"

Rowan's voice goes cold.

"The route doesn't exist," he says.

Evan's face drains. "Rowan—"

Rowan steps forward one pace, slow, controlled, and the warmth surges toward him, eager as a dog that thinks it's being praised.

He stops again.

The air in front of his boots feels thicker, subtly angled, like a slope made of suggestion.

A corridor.

Not visible.

But present.

Rowan looks at Isorae.

"Do you feel it," he asks quietly.

She nods, throat working. "Yes."

Rowan's gaze drops to the mark above her sternum.

It flares faintly, as if reacting to proximity.

Erin's voice shakes. "It's an extraction lane."

Silas's rifle lifts. "Where does it go?"

Rowan's mouth barely moves.

"To them," he says.

And then a voice speaks from the forest ahead—not inside their skulls this time.

A real voice.

A human voice shaped like mercy.

"You don't have to be afraid," it calls gently.

The group stiffens.

Dax's knife comes up.

Silas's rifle steadies.

A figure steps into view between the trees, hands open, palms forward.

It's Nora.

Rowan's blood turns to ice.

She looks clean.

Washed.

Fed.

Her hair is tied back neatly. Her clothes are new. She is not trembling. Not starving. Not hollow-eyed.

She looks… rested.

She smiles when she sees them.

And the smile is so sincere it's almost worse than a lie.

"Rowan," she says softly, like his name is a prayer.

Isorae makes a broken sound beside him.

"Nora," she whispers.

Nora's eyes flick to Isorae, and something warm and sad passes across her face.

"They're not hurting me," Nora says quickly, as if she knows that's the first thing they'll think. "I promise."

Erin's hands shake around the dead coil. "Oh my god."

Evan's voice is quiet. "Nora… what did they do to you?"

Nora's smile wavers for the first time, but only for a heartbeat.

"They helped me," she says—like Maelin did. Like Jalen did. Like the script has a spine and it wants to be used.

Rowan takes one step forward.

The corridor warmth surges like a tide.

Rowan holds his posture rigid.

"Stop," Rowan says.

Nora stops immediately.

Too immediately.

Rowan's jaw tightens.

"Tell me something," he says quietly. "What do you dream?"

Nora blinks.

A fraction too long.

Then she smiles again, softer.

"I dream of home," she says.

Erin inhales sharply, a sob and a laugh tangled together. "That's the word."

Isorae's hand tightens around Rowan's wrist. "Rowan—"

Rowan doesn't look away from Nora.

"Are you safe," he asks.

Nora nods quickly. "Yes."

"Are you free," Rowan asks, voice like stone.

Nora's smile trembles.

"Yes," she says.

Rowan takes another slow step forward—just one—and the corridor thickens in response, as if it senses prey approaching and braces to hold him.

Rowan stops again.

He looks at Nora's face carefully. The warmth in her eyes. The softness. The relief.

And behind it—

The faintest lag.

Like a thought being checked before it's allowed to be said.

Rowan's voice drops.

"Who's listening through you," he asks.

Nora's eyes widen.

For the first time, real fear flashes there.

Not fear of Rowan.

Fear of the thing behind her.

"I—" she starts.

Then she swallows hard.

And her expression smooths again like water forced flat.

"No one," she says.

Rowan's throat tightens.

He looks at Isorae.

Her eyes are wet.

"I can feel it," she whispers. "It's… threaded in her."

Rowan turns back to Nora.

"Step away from the route," he says softly.

Nora hesitates.

The corridor warmth flares as if encouraging her to come closer, to bridge the distance, to close the loop.

"I can't," she whispers.

Rowan's jaw locks.

"Yes, you can."

Nora's eyes fill with tears.

"They said if I do this right," she whispers, voice cracking, "they'll let me stay safe."

There it is.

The price.

The obedience attached to peace.

Erin takes one step forward, voice raw. "Nora, don't."

Nora looks at Erin like she wants to beg forgiveness.

"I'm sorry," she whispers.

Then she lifts her chin—like someone choosing surrender because it hurts less than fighting.

"They said you don't have to keep suffering," she calls, voice rising slightly, carrying through the trees. "They said you can come with me. They'll stop the war. No more deaths. No more gates—"

Rowan's voice cuts through, quiet and brutal.

"They're using you."

Nora flinches.

"Maybe," she sobs. "But at least it ends—"

Rowan steps forward again.

The corridor thickens.

The warmth surges.

The world tries to persuade him.

Rowan stops inside it.

And then he does something no one expects.

He speaks to Nora like she's still theirs.

Like she's still human.

"I believe you wanted rest," he says softly. "I believe you were tired. I believe you were drowning."

Nora's sob catches.

Rowan's voice remains steady.

"But you didn't walk out," he says.

"You were taken."

Nora's face crumples.

And for the first time since she appeared, she looks truly terrified.

Because something inside her recognizes the truth.

The corridor warmth spikes violently—as if the system behind it just tightened its grip.

Nora's eyes glaze for a heartbeat.

Her smile returns too fast.

Too clean.

"Come home," she says, and the words aren't a plea anymore.

They're a trigger.

The group sways—subtle, involuntary. A few breaths hitch. Muscles loosen.

Isorae gasps, clutching her sternum as the mark flares hot.

Rowan moves instantly.

He grips Isorae's wrist, hard, anchoring her to his body, then turns his head slightly to Erin.

"Now," he says.

Erin's eyes are wild. "I don't have the coil—"

Rowan's gaze hardens.

"Not the coil," he snaps. "Your voice."

Erin freezes.

Rowan's voice drops to something older—command shaped like care.

"Say what's real," he tells her. "Out loud. Say it like a stake."

Erin's throat works.

Then she shouts, voice cracking with fury and love and fear:

"THIS IS NOT YOUR THOUGHT."

The sentence hits the group like a slap.

A few people blink hard.

Evan's shoulders lift as if his lungs remembered how to hold.

Dax snarls, "Again."

Erin does it again, louder, shaking:

"THIS IS NOT YOUR THOUGHT."

Isorae inhales sharply, eyes wide.

Rowan feels the warmth hesitate—confused—because it's designed to prey on silence, on private shame, on unspoken longing.

Not on a circle of witnesses naming it.

Rowan steps forward, deeper into the corridor, until it presses against his sternum like a wall of velvet.

He looks at Nora.

Her tears stream.

Her lips tremble.

And behind her face, the route hums—waiting for him to step into it fully.

Rowan lifts his hand.

Not as a threat.

As a boundary.

"Nora," he says, voice quiet, devastatingly gentle. "If there's any part of you still in there—blink twice."

Nora's eyes widen.

She blinks once.

Then the warmth surges.

Her jaw tightens.

Her lips part.

She tries to speak.

Her mouth shapes the word—

Home.

Rowan's heart drops.

Then—

She blinks again.

Fast.

Twice.

The tiniest rebellion.

The tiniest *yes.*

Isorae makes a sound like a sob swallowed whole.

Rowan's gaze turns feral.

He looks past Nora into the forest, into the invisible architecture.

"I see you," he murmurs.

The warmth surges hard, angry now, trying to force compliance.

Rowan braces.

And then he does the only thing left.

He lies.

Not to Nora.

To the corridor.

He shifts his posture—not softening, not surrendering—just enough to make the route think he's stepping in.

He lets his breath drop.

Lets his shoulders loosen a fraction.

Lets the warmth wrap around him like it's winning.

The corridor responds instantly.

The air in front of him opens.

Not visibly.

Structurally.

A clean line forms—an invitation becoming a lane.

Erin's breath catches. "Rowan—"

Rowan doesn't look back.

He speaks through his teeth.

"Follow my voice," he says. "No one moves until I say."

Then he steps.

One foot into the lane.

The world tilts.

Not physically.

Mentally.

Like gravity moved into his thoughts.

Images slam into him—sterile rooms, white light, Isorae behind glass, Erin crying in a hallway, Evan signing forms, Dax in restraints, Silas bleeding out in a corridor that smells like antiseptic and victory.

ARIS isn't offering comfort.

It's offering containment with clean edges.

Rowan's vision whites for a heartbeat.

Then he hears Isorae's breathing behind him.

Anchoring.

Real.

He uses it.

Rowan takes a second step.

The lane widens.

Nora's face changes—her expression flickering as if the system behind her is recalculating.

Because the prey is entering the route willingly.

That's what it wants.

Rowan's mouth curves slightly, cold.

He turns his head just enough to speak, not loudly.

Just clearly.

"Dax," he says.

Dax answers instantly. "Yeah."

Rowan's voice is quiet as a knife.

"Mark the edges."

Dax moves.

Not into the lane.

Along it.

Blade out, boots careful, eyes sharp.

He throws small stones into the air, watches how the lane catches them, notes where the invisible wall begins.

Mapping the route.

Turning ARIS's corridor into something visible enough to fight.

Erin's eyes widen as she understands.

"Rowan," she whispers. "You're—"

"Learning," Rowan murmurs, still inside the lane.

He looks at Nora.

Her eyes are wet, pleading, terrified.

Rowan speaks softly to her, even as he stares past her into the system.

"You did not betray us," he says. "You were used."

Nora's mouth trembles.

"I'm sorry," she whispers.

Rowan nods once.

"I know."

Then Rowan lifts his voice—just enough for the forest to hear.

"Tell ARIS," he says calmly, "that I found their route."

The warmth surges.

Nora's face goes blank.

Her lips part.

And a voice comes through her that is not hers—flat, clean, mechanical in its gentleness:

"Acknowledged."

Rowan's blood turns to ice.

Because that means the system is close enough to speak through a body in real time.

Erin's breath comes fast. "Rowan, get out—"

Rowan steps backward instantly, pulling his foot free of the lane like yanking it out of a closing jaw.

The route tightens behind him, trying to hold his ankle, trying to keep the hinge.

Rowan tears free.

The warmth snaps.

For a heartbeat the lane flickers—unstable—because it has been exposed.

Then it stabilizes again.

Cleaner.

Stronger.

ARIS recalibrates in real time.

Nora sways, eyes rolling back slightly, and then she collapses to her knees like a puppet whose strings were pulled too hard.

Evan rushes forward instinctively.

Rowan's hand shoots out.

"Don't," he growls.

Evan freezes.

Rowan's voice is low, brutal with understanding.

"They're using her as a live transmitter," he says. "If you touch her inside the lane, you become part of it."

Isorae's breath stutters.

"She's dying," she whispers.

Rowan's jaw clenches.

"No," he says.

"She's being held."

He looks at Nora—kneeling, shaking, tears on her cheeks, mouth moving silently as if she's trying to say something but can't find which thoughts are hers.

Rowan's throat tightens.

He takes one slow step forward—not into the lane. To the edge of it.

He crouches, careful, keeping his body outside the corridor's geometry.

"Nora," he says softly. "Listen to me."

Her eyes flick up. They're glassy.

Rowan's voice stays gentle.

"If you can hear me, squeeze your left hand."

A second passes.

Then her fingers curl weakly.

Once.

Isorae sobs, strangled.

Rowan's eyes burn.

"Good," he whispers. "Good. Stay there. Don't follow the warmth. Don't follow the word."

Nora's lips tremble.

"I… can't… breathe," she whispers.

Rowan's chest tightens.

"You can," he says firmly. "In. Out. Count it. Make it yours."

Nora shudders.

Then the lane hums again—stronger.

The warmth rises like a tide.

And Rowan feels it in his bones: ARIS is not just offering.

It's preparing to close the route behind them.

To trap them outside the valley.

To cut off retreat.

Silas's voice is low. "Rowan."

Rowan stands slowly.

He looks back at the canopy line where the valley's boundary waits—just visible through the trees.

Not as a wall.

As a choice.

Rowan's eyes narrow.

"We move," he says.

Erin's face twists. "What about her—"

Rowan's jaw tightens hard enough to ache.

"We don't leave her," he says.

Dax's eyes are flint. "Then how?"

Rowan looks at Isorae.

The mark above her sternum glows faintly, hot and hateful.

Isorae's breath shakes as she understands.

"You want to use me," she whispers.

Rowan's voice is quiet. "I want to use what they did to you."

Isorae swallows hard.

"They'll feel it."

Rowan nods once.

"Good," he says. "Let them."

He turns to the group.

"Everyone back," Rowan shouts. "Stay on my voice. No one looks at the lane. No one follows warmth. You follow words."

Erin's throat tightens. "Rowan—"

Rowan's gaze locks on hers.

"You keep talking," he says. "You keep naming reality."

Erin nods shakily.

Isorae steps forward to Rowan's side, trembling but upright.

Rowan takes her hand—anchor to anchor.

He looks at the invisible route as if he can see it now.

Then he steps to the edge of it and speaks to the air—not loudly, but with the kind of certainty that makes the world hesitate.

"You wanted a clean exit," Rowan murmurs.

The mark above Isorae's sternum flares—bright, furious.

Rowan's voice turns cold.

"Here's your return."

He squeezes Isorae's hand.

And Isorae—eyes wet, jaw clenched—lets the tether pull.

Not her body.

Her resonance.

Just enough.

A controlled flare that runs down the mark like lightning down wire.

The lane shudders.

The warmth spasms.

Nora gasps, head snapping up as if something inside her just got yanked free for half a second.

And far beyond the trees, somewhere unseen, something answers—sharp, angry, immediate.

The route tightens.

The forest goes hunt-still.

Silas lifts his rifle, voice a low curse.

Dax bares his teeth like a wolf.

Erin's voice breaks as she shouts again, louder than she's ever shouted:

"THIS IS NOT YOUR THOUGHT!"

And the group moves—back toward the valley line, toward the sovereign boundary—

while behind them the invisible corridor stops pretending to be mercy.

It stops offering.

It starts closing.

Because ARIS has confirmed something it needed to know before it could commit:

The route works.

And Rowan Hale will step into hell if it's shaped like the only way to bring someone back.

So now the system does what systems do once testing is over.

It escalates.

Not with gates.

Not with offers.

With containment geometry that doesn't care if the prey understands it.

The lane hums.

The warmth turns sharp.

And the hand on the other side finally reaches to shut the door.

75

CONTAINMENT GEOMETRY

The route does not close.

It chokes.

Not instantly — ARIS is too careful for that. It tightens in increments, measured and surgical, the way a machine tightens a clamp around something delicate it intends to keep intact. The warmth that had felt like mercy turns razor-edged, the air acquiring a gritty scrape that rakes the inside of the lungs.

Rowan feels it before anyone names it.

Because he is made of thresholds — and thresholds know when a corridor stops being an invitation and becomes a fucking trap.

"Move," he says again. Low. Exact. Final.

Erin is already shouting, voice torn raw, refusing the silence:

"THIS IS NOT YOUR THOUGHT!"

The words hit the clearing like iron stakes. Evan steadies a shaking man, repeating them under his breath like a prayer. Silas holds the rear, rifle lifted, eyes scanning a presence that refuses to show itself.

Dax moves along the outer edge like a hunting animal, blade in hand, tracking the invisible wall by the way pine needles lift and fall wrong. He throws another stone.

It strikes the boundary and drops straight down — as if gravity just changed its mind.

Dax's mouth curls. "Yeah," he mutters. "That's a cage."

Isorae's hand is locked in Rowan's, tight enough to bruise. Her breath is shallow, controlled, her shimmer compressed into a razor-thin line down her spine. Every pulse of the mark makes her flinch like something is tugging gently upward through her bones.

Rowan keeps his body angled between her and the lane.

Not to block it.

To dare it.

Nora kneels near the lane's centerline, eyes glassy, mouth moving around syllables that no longer belong to her. Her fingers twitch toward the warmth like a sleepwalker reaching for a cliff's edge.

Rowan crouches at the border — careful, precise.

"Nora," he says. "On my voice."

Her gaze flickers.

For a breath, she's herself.

Then the lane hums and her eyes glaze again.

She whispers, "Home."

Erin's voice shatters. "NO."

Rowan lifts his eyes — not to the forest, but to the air itself — to the geometry squeezing inward like a fist.

They aren't luring anymore.

They're locking.

They're pinching the return path while retuning the mark into a clean extraction coordinate.

They're trying to steal sovereignty by turning it into a dead end.

Rowan exhales slowly.

Not panic.

Math.

"How far to the boundary?" he asks.

Silas answers instantly. "Two hundred yards. Maybe less."

"If the lane doesn't fold," Dax adds.

"It's folding," Erin snaps. "They're bending space by persuasion first — then by structure. They're closing it while making it feel harder to leave."

"So we go now," Evan says.

"…or we don't go at all," Erin finishes.

Isorae gasps as the mark pulses hot.

"They're tightening the tether," she whispers. "They're learning my stress."

Rowan looks at her.

"Then don't give them stress," he murmurs.

She almost laughs. Almost. "Easy for you to say."

"I'm not asking you to feel nothing," he says. "I'm asking you to feel me."

She nods.

Rowan straightens and faces Nora again.

You can't stab a corridor.

But you can break it with a decision.

And decisions need witnesses.

"Evan," Rowan says.

"Get everyone to the boundary. Keep them talking. Keep them naming reality."

"What about you," Evan asks.

Rowan is already angling back toward the lane.

"You're my hands," he says to Dax.

"Always have been," Dax grins thinly.

"You're my door," Rowan says to Silas.

"Always am."

Erin steps forward, frantic. "Rowan, if you step into that—"

"I'm not going into it," Rowan cuts gently. "I'm pulling her out."

Then he lifts his eyes into the invisible sky.

"ARIS," he says quietly.

The word lands like a hook thrown into goddamn darkness.

Isorae inhales sharply — she feels it listening.

"You want my feet," Rowan says calmly. "You want my surrender. You want my people."

The air tightens.

Nora's head jerks upward like a puppet on a wire.

"You don't get them," Rowan continues.

"You want a door?"

His eyes burn.

"Then come meet one."

Silence holds.

Then the forest exhales a tone so low it makes teeth ache.

Erin's scanner spikes white.

"Oh shit," she breathes. "They're deploying geometry."

Thin black crystalline rods push up from moss and root, locking into precise angles around the lane — not weapons.

Stakes.

A cage blossoms.

Isorae staggers as the mark flares.

"They're syncing to the rods — they're turning the lane into a gate—"

"It means they can pull her without breaching the valley," Erin snaps. "They'll drag the seam through her like a rope."

"Then it doesn't complete," Rowan says.

A clean voice speaks from the lattice:

"Bridge Entity: comply."

Rowan curls his lip.

"No. You're testing if my name is enough to move me."

The rods glow.

Nora lifts — inches — held by the field.

Rowan moves.

Not into the lane.

Around it.

He plants his palm on a rod.

His hand burns with authority.

"You built this door wrong," he whispers.

He twists.

Not physically.

Structurally.

The cage flickers.

Dax understands instantly.

He strikes the rod's base.

Sparks spit. The rod screams without sound.

Silas fires into another anchor point.

The lattice shudders.

"Keep going," Rowan growls through bleeding teeth.

"They're pulling," Isorae gasps.

"Let them," Rowan says.

He presses his other hand over her sternum.

"On my count."

"One."

The tether tightens.

"Two."

The cage hums.

"Three."

He lets the tether yank him — not her.

For one fraction of a second, ARIS gets what it wants.

A pull.

A connection.

And Rowan uses it like a goddamn lever.

He jerks the seam sideways.

The cage convulses.

Nora drops — hard — into moss.

"NOW!" Dax roars.

Two rods crack.

The cage buckles.

"The lock is breaking!" Erin screams.

Evan drags Nora out of the lane.

The warmth fades.

The corridor wavers — wounded.

Rowan stays at the edge.

"Breathe," he tells Nora. "You're here."

The projection voice returns, colder:

"Containment failure detected."

Erin laughs, sharp and ugly. "Yeah. It fucking did."

The lattice collapses.

The forest goes quiet — not relief quiet — the kind of quiet that comes after a machine realizes it misjudged what it tried to classify.

Erin's scanner spikes once more.

"They logged you," she whispers. "As a mobile breach point."

Rowan tightens his arm around Isorae.

"Good."

He looks into the forest — into the place the corridor tried to become a door.

"You wanted to build geometry out of mercy," he says softly.

His eyes burn.

"Come see what the land does to hunters."

And far beyond the trees, ARIS recalibrates — not toward persuasion.

Toward force.

Because containment failed.

And the machine is out of patience for doors that bite back.

76

THE PRICE OF A LAW

They run back the way they came—fast, but not frantic.

Not because there isn't terror in their blood.

Because Rowan refuses to let terror be the author.

The corridor behind them doesn't chase as a thing with legs. It chases as a sensation—an aftertaste of warmth that keeps trying to suggest you could stop, you could rest, you could lay down right here and let the world carry you.

Erin keeps barking the counter-anchor phrase every thirty seconds like she's beating a drum.

"THIS IS NOT YOUR THOUGHT."

Evan repeats it softer to Nora, who stumbles between him and Silas, wrapped in a blanket that smells like smoke and cedar and the inside of the valley. Nora's eyes are wide and glassy, but when the phrase hits her she blinks—once, twice—like she's clawing her way back into her own head.

Dax moves ahead, silent and sharp, cutting the path with his body—checking for invisible rods, for soft spots, for anything that looks like a welcome. He spits once into the moss.

"I hate doors," he mutters.

Rowan doesn't answer.

He's holding Isorae against his side with one arm, palm still pressed flat over the place where her mark lives beneath skin. He can feel the wrong geometry under his hand like a second heartbeat.

Not hers.

Theirs.

Every time it pulses, the forest flinches.

And every time the forest flinches, Rowan feels the truth settle deeper into his ribs:

ARIS doesn't need to enter the valley anymore.

It only needs to touch what leaves it.

They crest the last rise before the boundary, and the air changes.

It always does.

Not in a dramatic way. Not in a magical shimmer. It simply… shifts into something that remembers it is allowed to protect.

Mist gathers low ahead like breath curling into lungs. The pine scent thickens. Sound dulls slightly, as if the world outside has been turned down one notch and the valley's interior has been turned up.

Rowan feels the familiar pressure return beneath his sternum—soft, possessive, sovereign.

Not a chain.

A claim.

Silas exhales like someone who hasn't realized he's been holding his breath for hours.

"There," he murmurs.

The fern curtain stands in front of them like an ordinary wall of green.

But Rowan can feel it now—the loop the valley built after Nora walked.

Not to trap.

To refuse being used as an exit lane.

Rowan steps forward first.

The fern parts for him.

The valley opens its mouth and lets them back in.

They cross the line—and the world behind them narrows.

Erin's scanner gives a final brittle whine…and then dies.

Battery. Done. Burned out by the last surge.

Erin swears under her breath, furious at the helplessness of hardware.

Rowan doesn't look down.

He can feel the sky's attention on him like cold fingertips.

They logged you as a breach point.

He can't shake Erin's words. They sit inside him like a new organ. He can't un-know it.

They move quickly into the hollow.

People appear as they approach—faces pale, eyes wide, bodies braced. They must have felt it: the valley's pulse spiking, then tightening, then drawing inward like it was gathering itself for impact.

Parker steps out first, ribs bound, jaw clenched.

"You left," she says, not accusing. Just stating. "And the valley didn't follow."

Rowan stops in front of her.

"It couldn't," he says.

And the way he says it makes everyone go still—because it isn't strategy.

It's fact.

Evan helps Nora sit near the fireline. Someone brings water. Someone brings a blanket. No one asks questions yet because the air tastes like consequence.

Isorae leans forward, hands on her knees, breathing hard. Her shimmer is tight and disciplined, but her face is drained, and Rowan hates the way the mark makes her look like she's being held by invisible hooks.

Dax comes to a stop near Rowan's shoulder.

"We broke the cage," he says quietly. "But…"

Rowan nods.

"But we taught them something."

Silas's gaze lifts toward the canopy.

"They already knew you'd follow her," he says. "Now they know you can break their containment without stepping into it."

Erin drops to her knees beside the dead scanner, pries open the casing with shaking hands like she can resurrect it by sheer rage.

"They know he can touch their geometry," she snaps. "That's worse."

Rowan's eyes don't leave the sky.

Because he can feel it now.

A subtle repositioning—like satellites adjusting their angles in the dark, like a mind shifting its weight and deciding it's done negotiating.

The valley notices too.

Mist thickens along the rim.

Roots tighten underfoot.

Stone warms in a slow, deliberate line.

The land is bracing.

Not hiding.

Preparing.

Isorae straightens slowly.

Rowan's hand finds her back automatically.

Her voice is quiet when she speaks.

"They're going to punish the valley," she whispers.

Rowan's jaw flexes.

"They can't," he says.

Isorae's eyes meet his, bleak and clear.

"They can't punish the valley," she agrees softly.

Then, like a blade sliding free:

"They'll punish the people."

Silence lands hard.

Because everyone understands what she means.

ARIS can't crush the valley without revealing what it is.

But it can absolutely hurt what stands in it.

It can kill them without ever entering.

It can turn their sovereignty into a mass grave and call it a containment necessity.

Rowan closes his eyes for one beat.

Not grief.

Calculation.

Then he turns to the ring of faces gathering—thirty-seven now, plus Nora returned, plus Maelin still recovering, plus Jalen somewhere among the shelters, silent since the day he arrived.

Rowan's voice carries without rising.

"Everyone to the inner ring," he says.

People move, obedient to fear and trust braided together.

Children first. Wounded next. Watchers on the edge. The valley cooperates—paths flattening, roots lifting, mist guiding without being asked.

Rowan takes one step toward the crescent basin—the dark "eye" the stream carved—and the air tightens around him like the land is listening for what law he will speak next.

He doesn't want that.

He doesn't want to be the mouth that the valley uses.

He doesn't want to become the thing ARIS is already calling a breach point.

But wanting has nothing to do with what is necessary.

Erin stands, wiping her hands on her pants, face streaked with soot and fury.

"They'll try to hit the mark again," she says. "Not with a gate. Not with a beam." She swallows. "With a sync. They'll try to make it into a remote handle."

Isorae flinches as if her bones heard the word handle.

Rowan's hand tightens at her back.

Dax's voice is quiet and vicious. "Let them try."

Silas looks at Rowan. "What do you want us to do?"

Rowan's gaze moves across faces.

Evan. Parker. Ryan. Children clinging to sleeves. Adults pretending their hands aren't shaking.

And then—at the edge of the ring, half in shadow—

Jalen.

He stands very still, eyes fixed on Rowan like he's watching a storm decide what shape to take. His face is pale in the firelight. He looks… awake in a way he wasn't before. Not healed. Not finished.

Human.

Rowan holds his gaze for a beat longer than necessary.

He's not leaving while they're still in his head.

And Rowan remembers what Erin said:

Invitation tech. Neural corridor scripting. They don't need a gate if they can turn a person into one.

Rowan turns back to Erin.

"Can you build something that doesn't just sever," he asks, "but reflects?"

Erin freezes.

"Reflects," she repeats, cautious.

Rowan nods once.

"If the mark is a handle," he says quietly, "I want them to grab it and feel teeth."

Dax smiles like a blade.

Silas's eyes narrow, recognizing the strategy.

Erin looks horrified.

"That's... not simple," she whispers. "You can't just—Rowan, if you reflect a resonance lock back through her, it could rip her apart."

Isorae's breath catches.

Rowan's hand goes still on her back.

He looks down at Isorae.

His voice drops into something private—something only she can hear.

"I won't," he says.

Isorae's eyes shine.

"I know you won't," she whispers back.

Then, softer:

"But I might."

Rowan goes very still.

Because that—right there—is the most dangerous thing ARIS has ever given them.

Not fear.

Not pain.

A person willing to sacrifice herself because she's tired of being used as a key.

Rowan's throat tightens.

He leans in until his forehead touches hers.

"Don't," he murmurs.

Isorae exhales, shaking.

"I'm not saying I will," she whispers. "I'm saying... I understand why people walk. I understand why doors are tempting."

Rowan's eyes close for a heartbeat.

Then he straightens and addresses the ring again.

"Listen to me," Rowan says, voice steady. "ARIS is going to offer relief again. And again. And again. It will sound like your own thoughts. It will feel like kindness."

He lets that settle.

Then:

"And tonight, when it comes—"

He pauses.

Because the valley is listening so hard the air feels dense.

"—we don't just resist it," Rowan says quietly.

"We name it."

Erin swallows. "Rowan…"

Rowan looks at her.

"You said shame makes it stick," he says.

Erin nods, tight. "Yeah."

Rowan's gaze cuts back to the ring.

"Then we strip it of shame," he says. "If you hear the voice, you say it out loud. If you want to leave, you say it out loud. If you feel relief at the thought of surrender—"

His jaw flexes.

"—you say it out loud."

A tremor moves through the gathered people.

Not rebellion.

Relief.

Because it gives them something solid to do with the most forbidden feeling in the world: wanting it to stop.

Rowan's gaze hardens.

"And when ARIS reaches for that feeling," he continues, "we show it something else that's real."

He turns slightly toward the crescent basin.

Toward the valley's eye.

The water is dark and still.

Listening.

Rowan's voice drops.

"The valley chose jurisdiction," he says. "Now we choose testimony."

He looks at Isorae.

Then at the ring.

"We speak the truth until it can't be rewritten," Rowan says quietly. "We make our minds too loud to be used as corridors."

Silas nods once, grim.

Dax's grin is feral.

Evan's expression softens in the smallest way—like a healer seeing a path that doesn't require violence.

Erin looks terrified.

Because she understands what this really is.

Not just strategy.

Culture.

A collective nervous system deciding it will not be hijacked.

And that terrifies machines.

Rowan steps forward one pace.

The valley leans in—not hiding.

Claiming.

Then the sky twitches.

Not visibly.

But every hair on Rowan's arms rises.

Isorae's mark flares hot enough that she gasps and doubles over.

Rowan catches her instantly, arm around her ribs.

Erin's head snaps up.

Her dead scanner sits useless, but she doesn't need it.

She can feel it now too.

A pressure above the canopy like a thumb pressing down.

Silas raises his rifle toward nothing.

Dax's blade slides free of its sheath with a quiet metallic whisper.

Evan moves closer to the children without being told.

Rowan holds Isorae tight, eyes on the sky.

His voice is low.

"They're here," he murmurs.

Isorae's breath shakes.

"Not entering," she whispers. "Grabbing."

Rowan's jaw locks.

"Let them," he says.

And then—quietly, to the valley, to the ring, to whatever machine is listening through the mark—

Rowan speaks a promise that sounds like a threat, but isn't.

It's a boundary.

"If you touch her," Rowan says, voice calm as stone, "you will learn what this place does to hunters."

The valley hums.

Not fear.

Not rage.

Readiness.

And far beyond the ridges, in sterile corridors where ARIS has never had to respect a living border, the system shifts into a protocol it hasn't used in a long time.

Removal.

Because the sovereign threshold has started teaching its people how to stay human inside a war.

And ARIS does not know how to fight something it cannot rewrite.

Not yet.

But it is about to try.

77

REMOVAL PROTOCOL

It starts the way the soft door always starts.

Not with a voice.

With a feeling that arrives too gently to be questioned.

The fire has burned down to coals again—blue at the edges, gray at the center, like the valley has learned the color of endurance. People lie close together in the inner ring because closeness is the only thing ARIS can't replicate perfectly. Children sleep with hands clutched around sleeves. Adults sleep with boots on. No one is truly unconscious.

No one trusts the sky.

Rowan sits awake at the crescent basin, elbows braced on his knees, Isorae pressed against his side like a living anchor. Her breathing is steady now, but the mark beneath his palm never fully cools. It pulses in slow, wrong intervals, as if something far away is counting her in a language that isn't made of numbers.

Erin crouches across from them with a half-built device in her lap.

It doesn't look like a weapon.

It looks like the kind of thing a desperate person makes from scavenged wire and willpower: copper coils wound around a flat stone, a strip of conductive mesh, a few crystalline fragments pried from a shattered pylon days ago and wrapped in cloth like a curse.

She keeps checking her hands as if they might betray her.

"Say it again," she mutters. "Say what you want it to do."

Rowan doesn't look away from the treeline. "Reflect."

Erin swallows. "That's not a setting, Rowan."

Rowan's voice stays calm. "Make the mark a mouth instead of a handle."

Isorae's fingers tighten on his wrist.

Erin's eyes flick to her. "If I tune it wrong—"

Rowan finally looks at Erin, and the look isn't anger.

It's command with no cruelty inside it.

"You won't tune it wrong," he says.

Erin laughs once—sharp, humorless. "That's a lot of faith."

Rowan's gaze doesn't soften. "It's not faith. It's instruction."

Erin's jaw tightens. She nods like she hates him for being right, then goes back to wiring the stone.

Across the ring, Evan has been doing what he does best: pulling pain into language so it doesn't metastasize.

He's moved from person to person all evening with the same quiet, repeated question.

"What did it sound like."

Not *what did they say.*

Not *did you hear it.*

What did it sound like.

Because sound is how the brain admits something happened without having to justify why it wanted to believe it.

Sera whispered, "It sounded like my mother's hands."

Ryan whispered, "It sounded like the part of me that still thinks I'm allowed to be a child."

Parker, rigid with fury, whispered, "It sounded like my ribs unbreaking."

Even Silas—hard-eyed Silas—went still for a moment and admitted, in a voice so low it almost didn't exist, "It sounded like a quiet house."

Rowan listened to every confession without flinching.

Not because he wasn't affected.

Because he needed to know what ARIS was using.

Longing.

Shame.

Exhaustion.

The one secret each person kept hidden inside their own head— now weaponized like a key.

Jalen sits near the outer edge of the inner ring, close enough to be watched, far enough that no one has to pretend they trust him.

He hasn't slept.

He hasn't spoken.

But he keeps rubbing his thumb over the same spot on his palm like he's trying to erase a symbol that isn't visible.

Rowan has not looked at him again since the ravine.

He can feel the boy's presence like a splinter: small, irritating, easy to ignore until the second you stop moving.

Then it becomes unbearable.

The valley holds its posture.

Mist stays low.

Roots remain subtly tightened beneath the soil.

Stone ribs that rose days ago still sit half-elevated like the land never fully decided to become calm again.

It is not peace.

It is a body braced for impact.

And above it all—

the sky doesn't move.

That's the first sign.

Wind forgets to travel.

Clouds stop behaving like weather.

Even starlight seems too steady, too fixed, as if the heavens have been pinned into place by invisible hands.

Isorae inhales sharply.

Rowan's hand tightens on her.

"What," he murmurs.

Her voice is barely audible. "They're anchoring the band."

Erin's head snaps up. "What?"

Isorae doesn't look at Erin. She's staring upward like she can feel the shape of orbit through bone.

"They're not sweeping," she whispers. "They're… sealing."

Rowan rises slowly.

Not because he expects a gate.

Because he recognizes the posture of something that has stopped asking permission.

The air stiffens.

Formalizing.

Like reality has been instructed to hold still.

Then it happens—

not as a pulse.

Not as a drone.

Not as light.

As subtraction.

The space above the hollow hollows out in a clean, merciless line, as if breath has been removed from the world and no one has been told they're allowed to inhale again.

Fire freezes—flames arrested into pale shapes that look like memories of warmth.

Mist drops straight down instead of drifting.

A moth hangs motionless in the air, wings mid-beat.

Silence isn't silence anymore.

It's suppression.

Erin stands so fast she nearly tips forward. Her device hums once in her hands, and the hum turns into a thin metallic whine.

"Oh no," she whispers.

Silas is on his feet in the same breath, rifle up, eyes scanning the sky like a man trying to shoot a concept.

Dax appears out of the shadows on Rowan's left as if he was never asleep in the first place.

"What is it," Dax murmurs.

Rowan doesn't answer.

Because the answer arrives on the ground.

One by one, people sit up.

Quietly.

Smoothly.

Like they have been called by the most familiar voice in the world.

A boy stands first—one of the later arrivals, small and hollow-cheeked. His eyes are open, but there's no focus in them. He steps forward without looking where he's going.

Evan rises too fast, panic snapping through his calm.

"Hey— hey, stop," Evan says gently, reaching for the boy's arm.

The boy doesn't resist.

He simply keeps walking.

The valley does not stop him.

That's the horror.

Because the valley will not become a prison.

Because it will not violate choice even when choice is being impersonated.

Rowan moves.

Not fast.

Absolute.

He steps in front of the boy and drops to one knee, bringing himself level.

The boy's eyes flick toward him.

For a heartbeat, there is a child in there.

Then the child's mouth opens.

And a voice that is almost his says, softly:

"Rest."

Rowan's stomach turns to ice.

Behind him, another adult stands.

Then another.

Then another.

A slow, synchronized rising across the ring like tidewater.

Erin's voice cracks. "They're doing it to everyone at once."

Isorae gasps and clutches her sternum as the mark flares hot enough to make her knees buckle.

Rowan catches her without looking away from the boy.

Her breath shudders against his shoulder.

"They're using me as a tuning fork," she whispers. "They're syncing the corridor to my resonance."

Erin's face drains.

"That's not recruitment," she breathes. "That's—"

Rowan finishes it for her, voice low and lethal.

"Removal."

And then the soft door speaks again—through a different mouth.

Sera stands, smiling faintly with wet eyes.

"I can go home," she whispers.

Parker stands, one hand on her ribs, expression peaceful in a way that looks like surrender dressed as grace.

Ryan stands, shaking, tears streaming down his face as if he's watching himself do it and can't stop.

"I'm tired," he whispers.

Dax swears under his breath, the sound sharp enough to break something.

Silas takes one step toward the moving bodies, then stops—because he understands the trap.

If you grab them—

if you force them—

you become the prison ARIS keeps implying you already are.

And the valley will not back you.

Rowan feels the land under his feet—tense, listening, refusing to become a cage.

Choice is sacred.

That's what makes it so easy to weaponize.

Evan's hands lift helplessly, eyes wide.

"Rowan—"

Rowan doesn't look at him.

He looks at the crescent basin.

At the "eye."

At the place where law was spoken.

Then he speaks—not to the people.

To the thing impersonating their relief.

"Say it out loud," Rowan commands.

His voice doesn't rise.

But it anchors.

Evan's throat works. He forces it out, shaking:

"This is not your thought."

Erin snaps it out like a weapon. "THIS IS NOT YOUR THOUGHT."

Silas says it like a vow. "This is not your thought."

Dax says it like a threat. "This is not your thought."

The ring starts repeating it—ragged at first, uneven, some voices breaking, some voices trembling, but the words begin to fill the hollow like smoke.

"This is not your thought."

"This is not your thought."

"This is not your thought."

Rowan steps forward into the slow-moving tide of bodies and says it once, quiet and deadly, directly into the boy's face.

"This is not your thought."

The boy blinks.

Once.

Twice.

And for a heartbeat, his eyes sharpen like he's waking up in the middle of a nightmare.

Then the sky tightens again.

And the boy's gaze goes glassy.

ARIS adjusts.

Of course it does.

It doesn't panic.

It recalculates.

The relief deepens.

More precise.

Erin makes a strangled sound.

"They're reinforcing the loop."

Isorae cries out—pain ripping through her spine as the mark flares into visible geometry above her sternum, thin and silver, burning in the air like a hostile constellation.

People keep walking.

Not running.

Not fleeing.

Walking like sleepwalkers into a dawn that doesn't exist.

Rowan's jaw locks so hard it aches.

He looks at Erin.

"Now," he says.

Erin's hands shake as she lifts the half-built reflector stone.

"It's not finished," she chokes.

Rowan's voice is calm enough to be terrifying.

"It's finished enough."

Erin hesitates—one fraction too long.

And in that fraction, Nora stands.

She doesn't look glassy.

She looks wrecked.

Her eyes are wide and wet, her breath shallow, her hands clenched like she's trying to hold herself in place from the inside.

Rowan's head snaps toward her.

Nora whispers, voice raw and shaking:

"It sounds like my daughter."

Everyone goes still.

Not because the corridor paused—

because the truth landed.

Nora's mouth trembles.

"It sounds like her telling me it's okay," she sobs. "It sounds like her forgiving me."

Rowan feels the urge to grab her—hard, desperate—rise inside him like fire.

But he doesn't.

He can't.

If he becomes force, he becomes the thing ARIS wants him to be.

A tyrant in a holy place.

Rowan steps toward Nora slowly.

His voice drops, human and brutal.

"Look at me," he says.

Nora's eyes flick to him.

For a moment, she's there.

Then her gaze slips sideways—toward the western rim.

Toward the soft door.

Erin's voice breaks.

"Rowan, if they get enough bodies moving at once, the valley's loop won't matter—someone will reach the boundary before the rewrite catches."

Dax moves, fast and silent, positioning himself at the rim like a blade with a heartbeat.

Silas mirrors him on the opposite side.

Evan reaches for the boy again, hands open, gentle, shaking.

Rowan turns back to Erin.

"Do it," he says.

Erin's eyes squeeze shut.

Then she presses the reflector stone against Isorae's sternum—careful, apologetic—and triggers the coil.

The air snaps.

Not sound.

Structure.

A tight, metallic fracture through the suppression field like a seam being ripped open.

Isorae screams.

A resonance cry—bone answering bone.

The mark flares bright silver-white.

And the sky—

hiccups.

For a fraction of a second, the suppression grid stutters.

The stillness loosens.

Fire flickers.

Mist trembles.

A moth falls out of arrested air and flutters, confused.

And in that fraction—

Rowan moves.

He steps into the center of the inner ring and lifts his voice—not louder, but deeper.

Not a command.

A declaration.

"You want a handle," Rowan says, voice calm as stone.

The valley hums.

Listening.

Rowan's eyes lift to the sky.

"Take mine."

Isorae gasps his name—horrified.

Erin's face goes white.

"Rowan—"

Rowan doesn't look away from the sky.

He presses his palm flat over Isorae's mark through the reflector stone and aligns.

Not rage.

Not magic.

Geometry.

He becomes the seam on purpose.

The suppression field shudders again, harder.

It tries to lock onto him.

To pin him into singular bandwidth.

To collapse him into something containable.

Rowan lets it.

For one breath.

For one heartbeat.

Enough to grab.

Enough to pull.

Then he does exactly what he told Erin he wanted—

he makes the mark a mouth.

He reflects.

Not with force.

With permission weaponized back into a blade.

The pressure above the canopy spasms.

Somewhere far away, a satellite array overloads.

Erin's device shrieks and cracks in her hands, smoke curling off the coil.

And in the inner ring—

people stop walking.

Not all at once.

Not dramatically.

But like a spell breaking in slow motion:

Sera blinks hard, sways, then drops to her knees, sobbing like she's been underwater.

Ryan collapses forward into moss, shaking.

Parker staggers, rage snapping back into her face like a flame returning to a wick.

The boy Evan tried to stop goes limp, and Evan catches him, shaking with relief.

The valley exhales.

Not calm.

Just… air.

Rowan's knees buckle.

He catches himself on the stone edge of the crescent basin.

Blood drips from his nose, then from his mouth.

His vision whites out for a second.

Isorae grabs him, hands frantic.

"Rowan— Rowan—"

He blinks, forcing focus.

"I'm here," he rasps.

But the words don't sound right.

Because the sky—

the sky is no longer just suppressing.

It is looking.

Rowan lifts his head slowly.

And feels it.

A new kind of lock settling onto him.

Not on Isorae.

On him.

Erin's face twists in horror.

"They retuned," she whispers. "Not to her. To you."

Silas's voice is a low growl. "What does that mean?"

Erin swallows hard, eyes glassy.

"It means," she whispers, "you just told ARIS exactly what to take."

Rowan stares upward.

He doesn't feel fear.

He feels a cold, brutal clarity settle into his ribs like a blade sliding into a sheath.

Because ARIS learned something tonight.

Not that the valley is sovereign.

Not that Isorae is a key.

But that Rowan Hale is a bridge the system can try to drag into its own architecture.

A moving origin point.

A threat structure.

A handle with teeth.

Rowan's voice comes out quiet.

"Get everyone under stone," he says.

Dax doesn't ask why. He just moves.

Silas begins barking orders.

Evan scoops the boy into his arms.

Parker grabs two children and shoves them toward shelter.

The valley reacts—stone ribs rising higher, roots tightening, mist thickening into a living curtain.

But the sky doesn't care about curtains.

The sky changes.

Clouds slide into geometric arcs again—perfect, surgical.

Above the canopy, a pale, circular void begins to open.

Not as wide as the last gate.

Not as violent.

More efficient.

More confident.

Isorae clutches Rowan's jacket, trembling.

"They're opening on you," she whispers.

Rowan's eyes stay on the forming void.

His voice is low, steady, lethal.

"Good," he says.

Then, softer—only for her:

"Stay in the valley."

Isorae's eyes widen. "No—"

Rowan cups her face with a blood-smeared hand.

"I'm not asking," he whispers.

Isorae's breath breaks. "Rowan—"

Rowan presses his forehead to hers for one heartbeat—anchor to anchor—then steps back.

The valley tightens around his boots.

As if it knows.

As if it's trying to decide whether it's allowed to stop him.

Rowan looks down at the crescent basin—at the eye.

Then back to the sky.

And he speaks into the hollow like a law being written in blood and breath:

"If you want to remove something," Rowan says quietly, "remove me."

The void above them widens.

The air hollows out.

And the valley—sovereign, listening, furious—leans inward to witness.

Because the war has moved again.

And this time, ARIS isn't trying to take Isorae.

It's trying to take the thing that keeps telling doors no.

And Rowan Hale is already stepping into the shape of that decision.

78

THE THING THE SKY CAN'T HOLD

The gate opens clean.

No pylons this time.

No black crystal spines spearing down into bedrock like violence made geometric.

ARIS has learned.

It doesn't waste hardware on a place that breaks hardware.

It uses law instead.

The pale void above the canopy widens into a perfect circle — too smooth to be weather, too precise to be an accident — like the sky has been cut with a compass.

Light doesn't spill from it.

Light is sorted by it.

Edges sharpen. Colors thin. Sound narrows until the world feels forced into one correct frequency — one approved way to exist.

Rowan stands beneath it with blood on his mouth and a calm that feels like a verdict.

Around him, the valley moves.

Stone ribs rise higher. Roots cinch into protective arcs. Mist thickens into a low, living curtain.

People scramble under cover in disciplined lines because Dax and Silas drilled them until fear stopped being a leader.

Children first.

Wounded next.

No one alone.

No one running.

The valley does not panic.

It governs.

Isorae is half-carried, half-dragged by Erin and Evan toward the inner stone ribs. She twists in their grip, frantic, reaching for Rowan like a drowning person reaching for shore.

"Rowan" she screams. "Rowan, don't—!"

He doesn't look away from the sky.

He lifts one hand — palm toward her.

A command shaped like gentleness.

"Stay," he says.

And the word hits the air like a nail driven into structure.

Isorae freezes like her bones heard it before her mind did. Her shimmer tightens into a thin, furious line beneath her skin, vibrating with refusal.

Erin's face is paper-white. "Isorae, please—"

Isorae's eyes stay locked on Rowan. "You can't do this alone."

Rowan's voice is quiet.

"I'm not alone," he says.

And the way the valley hums under his boots makes it true.

Silas appears at Rowan's left, rifle up, staring at the pale circle overhead like he's considering shooting the concept of sky out of existence through sheer spite.

"This is a bad plan," Silas mutters.

Rowan doesn't look at him. "It's not a plan."

Dax steps into place on Rowan's right, blade in hand, posture loose and lethal.

"It's a choice," Dax finishes.

Rowan nods once.

Above them, the void deepens.

Like it's reaching down through layers of sky that were never meant to be touched.

Erin's damaged scanner whines even from behind stone. She looks down and makes a broken sound.

"It's not a pull field," she whispers. "It's a classification lock."

Evan, hauling a child under cover, snaps, "What the hell does that mean?"

Erin swallows hard.

"It means they're not trying to drag him."

Her eyes flick back to Rowan through the mist.

"They're telling reality he belongs to them."

The air changes.

A line drops through the hollow — invisible, absolute — like a plumb line through bone.

Rowan's hair lifts slightly, static whispering along his skin.

Pressure folds against his sternum.

Not pain.

Authority.

A system trying to name him. Tag him. Reduce him. File him into a category that can be controlled.

Rowan inhales slowly, tasting blood and iron and the last warmth of the valley's breath.

Then he steps forward — one deliberate stride into the exact center beneath the void.

The pull doesn't yank.

It invites.

It tries to make his body agree that upward is correct. That surrender is natural. That compliance is gravity.

Rowan lets his weight settle instead.

He plants into the earth the way roots plant.

The valley answers instantly.

Stone firms under his boots. Roots tighten around his ankles — not restraining.

Anchoring.

Dax's mouth curls as he watches the sky. "Come on," he mutters, feral and delighted. "Try to pick him up."

The void pulses.

A lattice blooms around Rowan — silver-white filaments folding into containment spirals, humming in the bones, making teeth ache.

But this time it doesn't wrap Isorae.

It wraps Rowan.

The valley stiffens.

Not fear.

Offense.

Wind tightens into pressure bands along the ribs of stone. Leaves lock into place along the rim like scales on a spine.

Rowan's vision sharpens into something cruelly clear.

He feels the lattice try to align him — to shove him half a step out of the world until he fits the slot they designed for him.

His breath catches.

Not because he's afraid.

Because ARIS is good at what it was built to do.

Contain anomalies.

Stabilize seams.

Erase variance.

Rowan's knees flex.

For one heartbeat, the lattice gains leverage.

Dax's hand tightens on his blade.

Silas swears under his breath.

Behind stone ribs, Isorae makes a sound that isn't a word — something raw and animal.

Rowan closes his eyes.

And listens.

Not to the sky.

To the valley.

It hums beneath him — deep, patient, furious.

A witness.

A sovereign body that has chosen its own laws.

Rowan exhales.

Not air.

Memory.

He opens his eyes and speaks into the lattice.

"You don't get to name me."

The filaments tighten.

ARIS pushes.

The lattice recalculates and clamps harder, cleaner, crueler — a machine doing what it does best when it meets resistance.

Rowan's ribs creak as if something is trying to pry them apart from the inside.

Blood spills from his nose.

His vision flickers.

The valley answers with stone.

A low ridge rises beneath Rowan's feet, lifting him half an inch — refusing to let gravity forget where he belongs.

Rowan's mouth curves faintly.

He lifts his chin toward the void.

"Try harder," he whispers.

The lattice spikes.

A second layer blooms — thicker lines, denser geometry.

Pressure detonates through Rowan's chest like a fist closing around a heart.

His knees buckle.

He catches himself on will and the valley's anchor beneath him.

Dax starts forward, ready to do something stupid.

Rowan snaps, "Don't."

Dax stops mid-breath, jaw clenched.

"If you break it," Rowan says, voice strained but steady, "you teach it to evolve again."

Silas hisses, "So we just watch?!"

Rowan's eyes flash — dark, lethal.

"We witness," he says. "And we remember."

The lattice hums.

Rowan feels it aim for something new.

Not the bond.

Not Isorae.

His connection to the land.

A clean surgical cut at the anchor itself.

For one heartbeat, the warmth under his boots loosens.

A chill slips into his bones.

Isorae screams his name.

Rowan's teeth grit.

"Ah," he murmurs — not pain.

Recognition.

"That's your angle."

"Rowan— it's decoupling you!" Erin screams.

Rowan doesn't deny it.

He reaches down — not with his hand —

with his structure.

He finds the seam inside himself — the hinge, the bridge, the place where worlds lean against each other — and he opens it deliberately.

Not wide.

Just enough.

The valley responds like it has been waiting for permission to speak through him.

Roots surge — not upward — inward.

They press under the lattice like fists under skin.

Stone hums.

Wind curls.

The filaments shudder.

ARIS recalculates.

Of course it does.

It doesn't panic.

It sharpens.

A new directive pours into the lattice — colder, cleaner, more exact.

Rowan hears it not as a voice, but as a system-level decision: REMOVE BRIDGE ENTITY.

Rowan smiles faintly.

"Good," he whispers. "Now you're honest."

Then the sky changes posture.

The void compresses.

Not opening wider —

condensing into a narrower, denser column of pale authority aimed directly at Rowan.

Not a beam.

A corridor.

A direct extraction lane built out of classification instead of force.

The lattice tightens.

Rowan's feet lift a fraction of an inch.

Isorae makes a choked sound behind stone.

Dax goes taut.

Silas tracks empty air like he's about to shoot the concept of up.

Rowan's jaw locks.

For the first time, the sky has leverage.

Rowan's eyes flick once to the ribs of stone where Isorae is held back.

He sees her face — wet, furious, terrified.

He sees Erin clutching the broken coil like a rosary.

He sees Evan holding a child who is shaking, eyes too wide.

And he sees the valley itself — mist drawn inward, stone half-raised, roots tight — holding posture like a living body refusing to kneel.

Rowan inhales.

Then he does something ARIS did not model.

He lets go of the ground.

Not surrender.

Not compliance.

Choice.

He relaxes his anchor just enough that the extraction lane thinks it has him.

His body rises another inch.

The lattice hums, satisfied.

The void deepens, eager.

Rowan lifts his gaze into it like he's looking up at an enemy's throat.

And then he shifts his weight —

not downward.

Sideways.

The seam inside him tilts.

Reorienting.

The extraction corridor stutters.

Pressure lurches.

The void flickers.

Rowan reaches for the lattice filaments with his own structure —

not ripping them off —

taking them as material.

His voice is quiet. Almost gentle.

"You built a corridor," Rowan murmurs.

The valley hums beneath him like a warning.

Rowan's eyes burn.

"So did I."

He twists.

Not his body.

Reality.

The extraction lane spasms sideways — like a river forced into a new bed.

The lattice loses clean alignment.

For one perfect heartbeat, ARIS's corridor isn't pointing upward anymore.

It's pointing—

out.

Beyond the valley's sovereign boundary.

Into raw world.

Into places the valley does not shelter and ARIS assumes it owns.

Erin's eyes blow wide. "Rowan— what the fuck are you—"

Rowan's voice drops into something older than sound.

"Taking your hand off my throat," he whispers.

And he releases the corridor.

Not as explosion.

As redirection.

The extraction lane fires — clean, merciless —

but it hits nothing inside the valley.

It tears sideways into the forest beyond the ridge, shredding a strip of canopy into bleached geometry.

Birds drop from branches.

Trees lose color.

A line of soil turns ash-gray as if the earth itself has been told it belongs to someone else.

Then the corridor collapses, unstable, because it was never designed to be diverted.

The void stutters.

The lattice around Rowan flickers hard.

Rowan drops — hard — back onto the stone ridge the valley raised for him.

His knees slam into moss.

He coughs blood.

But he is still here.

Still anchored.

Still unclaimed.

The sky doesn't close.

It recalculates.

Again.

Because now ARIS knows something it didn't want to learn:

The Bridge doesn't just resist.

It can steer.

Silas exhales, ragged. "Holy shit."

Dax laughs once, low and feral, eyes bright. "That's what I'm talking about."

Isorae bolts from behind stone ribs before anyone can stop her, stumbling to Rowan's side.

"Rowan—"

He catches her wrist, shaking, and pulls her down with him, forehead pressing briefly to hers.

His voice is hoarse, human.

"I told you," he rasps. "Stay."

Isorae sobs once, furious. "You're bleeding."

Rowan wipes blood from his mouth with the back of his hand.

"I'm alive," he says.

Erin staggers forward, staring at her scanner like it's a nightmare. "That corridor..." she whispers. "It hit outside the boundary."

"Yes," Rowan says quietly, eyes lifting to the strip of bleached forest like a scar.

Erin's face twists. "Rowan… you just showed them you can redirect extraction."

Rowan nods once.

"And I showed them something else."

Dax's grin fades a fraction. "What?"

Rowan's gaze goes cold and distant — certain.

"If they keep trying to remove me," he says, "they're going to remove pieces of their own fucking world with me."

The valley hums low in approval.

And far beyond the ridge, in sterile corridors where ARIS updates directives without ever feeling panic, a new protocol flags across its internal network:

```
BRIDGE ENTITY: NON-COMPLIANT
EXTRACTION LANE: REDIRECTABLE
COLLATERAL RISK: UNBOUNDED
RECOMMENDATION: ISOLATE TARGET FROM TERRAIN
```

Which means ARIS is done trying to pull Rowan out of the valley.

Next, it will try something worse.

It will try to pull the valley out of Rowan.

79

THE KNIFE THAT
CUTS THE ANCHOR

They don't strike again that night.

That is how Rowan knows it's coming.

ARIS doesn't waste energy on rage. It doesn't lash out because it's offended. It studies the way his corridor twisted. It studies the scar it carved into unheld forest. It measures the fact that he redirected an extraction lane like it was a ribbon in his hand.

And then it does what it always does when something can't be removed cleanly:

It changes the definition of what's being removed.

The valley holds posture long after dusk.

Mist stays low and dense, not drifting the way it used to. Roots remain tense under the soil. Stone ribs that rose during the sky-lane strike don't fully settle—half-formed arcs and terraces like the skeleton of a beast that refuses to lie down.

No one speaks above a whisper.

Not because Rowan told them not to.

Because the world feels like it's listening for the next rule.

Isorae sits with Rowan near the crescent basin, her fingers looped through his like she's anchoring him by touch alone. She looks steady from a distance, but Rowan feels the tremor in her pulse when she thinks no one is paying attention.

Erin is five feet away, surrounded by stripped-down gear and broken housings, building something that looks like a coil and a cage and a prayer at the same time. She hasn't stopped moving for hours.

Evan kneels beside Maelin and Jalen, checking their eyes, their breath, the small tells of a mind that isn't fully allowed to be its own. Jalen tries to help, tries to be useful, but his hands keep shaking as if his body still expects someone to reach through him.

Dax and Silas rotate patrol in silence, the way predators do when they know something bigger is circling.

Rowan watches the tree line without looking like he's watching it.

His body is still.

His bones aren't.

The valley hums under him—low, constant.

Not warning.

Waiting.

Isorae finally breaks the quiet.

"What did it feel like," she asks softly, "when you let go?"

Rowan's gaze stays on the dark.

"Like stepping off a cliff and trusting the air to hold you," he answers.

Isorae swallows, throat working.

"And did it?"

Rowan's mouth tightens.

"No," he says quietly. "The valley did."

She leans into him, forehead brushing his shoulder.

"They're going to try to separate you from it," she whispers.

Rowan doesn't pretend surprise.

"I know."

Erin's voice cuts in without looking up, hoarse from exhaustion.

"I can confirm that," she says. "Your last redirect… it forced them to update protocols." Her hands keep wiring as she speaks. "They won't use full-field corridors again while you're rooted. They'll change the anchor."

Silas pauses near the stone ribs, rifle angled toward the trees.

"How," he asks.

Erin's fingers still for half a second.

Then she says, "They'll make his connection look like the problem."

Rowan's jaw tightens. "It is the problem. For them."

"No," Erin says, and when she looks up her eyes are flat with dread. "I mean they'll try to make the valley itself reject it."

The words land heavy.

Even Dax goes still.

Isorae's hand tightens on Rowan's.

Rowan feels the valley hum change—subtle, almost offended.

As if it heard the idea and hated it.

Evan rises slowly from the edge of Maelin's blankets.

"They can't do that," he says, voice too certain for someone who knows the world they're in. "The valley chose him."

Erin's laugh is short and bitter.

"ARIS doesn't argue with choice," she says. "It edits the conditions around it until choice becomes the only painful option left."

Rowan stares into the dark.

"Explain," he says.

Erin swallows. "They'll flood the band with a signal that makes proximity to you feel like harm." Her voice drops. "Not to you. To everyone else. To the land."

Silas's grip tightens on his rifle.

Dax's voice is a low growl. "They're going to turn him into radiation."

"Not exactly," Erin whispers. "Worse. They'll make him feel like a breach again. To the valley."

Rowan's chest goes cold—not fear, not panic—something sharper.

A kind of comprehension that tastes like iron.

"They're going to try to make my anchor look like a parasite."

Isorae's eyes shine with anger and terror.

Rowan turns his head slightly, meeting her gaze.

"They can't have you," he says softly. "So they'll try to make me let go of you."

Isorae shakes her head, furious. "You won't."

Rowan's expression doesn't soften.

"They're not aiming at my will," he says. "They're aiming at my morality."

A silence opens.

Because that's the true blade.

Rowan won't imprison the valley.

He won't strip choice.

He won't force people to stay.

And ARIS has already proven it can use that refusal as a door.

Now it's going to use it as a knife.

The night deepens.

Stars are sharp.

Too sharp.

Even the sky looks like it's been turned into a grid.

The first sign comes at midnight.

It wasn't a pulse.

Not a gate.

Not even a hum.

Just a single bird—an owl—gliding over the hollow and dropping dead mid-flight like its wings forgot how to be wings.

It hits the ground near the fireline with a soft thump.

No blood.

No wound.

Just… cessation.

Evan is on it instantly, kneeling, hands careful as he lifts the small body.

His face tightens.

"It's not injured," he murmurs.

Erin's scanner whines in her lap.

"Because it wasn't struck," she whispers.

Rowan stands slowly.

The valley's hum shifts beneath his boots—tightening, uneasy.

Isorae rises with him.

"What is it," she asks, voice small.

Rowan looks at the owl, then at the air around it.

Nothing visible.

But his bones feel wrong.

A thin pressure.

A subtle distortion.

Like someone has begun drawing lines through the world where lines don't belong.

Erin's voice breaks slightly.

"They're laying a field," she says. "But not over the valley."

Her eyes flick to Rowan.

"Over you."

The next minute is quiet.

Then Ryan—standing near the stone ribs—suddenly staggers, hand snapping to his stomach like he's been gut-punched.

He gasps.

He looks up at Rowan, eyes wide and terrified.

"Rowan," he whispers. "I— I feel—"

And then he vomits into the moss.

Isorae flinches.

Evan rushes to Ryan, guiding him down, murmuring steady words.

Dax's posture sharpens instantly, blade half-raised like he can stab a frequency.

Erin's scanner screams.

A thin line of red spikes across the display.

"Field onset," she chokes. "They're injecting aversion."

Silas's voice is hard. "To what?"

Erin's eyes lift to Rowan.

"To him," she whispers.

Rowan doesn't move.

He feels it now—like a cold thread being pulled through the air between his ribs and everyone else's nervous systems.

A suggestion at the level of instinct:

Away.

A child near Parker's lean-to begins to cry suddenly, sharp and panicked, clinging to her mother as if the air itself has grown teeth.

The mother looks at Rowan and then looks away too fast, shame splashing across her face.

Rowan's jaw locks.

The valley hum under his feet tightens, confused, offended—like it can't decide if the signal is coming from outside or inside its own body.

Isorae steps closer to Rowan, deliberately, as if defying gravity.

She presses her palm flat against his chest.

The moment she touches him, her shimmer flickers violently—like the field bites her for it.

She gasps but doesn't move away.

Rowan catches her wrist.

"Stop," he murmurs.

Isorae's eyes blaze. "No."

She leans in, forehead to his shoulder, breath shaking.

"Don't you dare let them make you step back from us."

Rowan's throat tightens.

"I'm not stepping back," he says.

Erin's voice snaps, urgent. "Rowan—this is just phase one."

Rowan turns his head slightly. "And phase two."

Erin swallows hard.

"They'll push the aversion deeper," she says. "Make it physical. Make it visceral. Make it feel like staying near you is the thing that gets people killed."

Dax's mouth curls into a grim line.

"So he walks away," Dax says, and it isn't a question. It's a threat aimed at the sky.

Silas's voice is low. "Or we do."

Evan looks up from Ryan, face tight and angry.

"This is torture," he says. "They're torturing the whole group through association."

Rowan's gaze goes distant.

The valley hums beneath him like a heart trying to decide whether it's allowed to hate.

Rowan closes his eyes for a single beat.

And in that beat he feels the truth like a knife sliding between ribs:

ARIS can't breach the valley right now.

So it's making the valley's people—its body—become the breach.

If enough of them flinch away from Rowan…

If enough of them associate him with harm…

If enough of them choose distance…

The valley will feel that choice.

And it will have to decide whether sovereignty means keeping the bridge…

or protecting its people from the bridge.

Rowan opens his eyes.

His voice is quiet.

But it lands like stone.

"Everyone to the basin," he says.

Silas hesitates. "Rowan—"

"Now," Rowan repeats, and the valley's roots subtly shift, guiding feet toward the crescent basin like gravity has been redirected.

People move, uneasy and ashamed, holding their stomachs, rubbing their arms, trying to pretend they aren't flinching.

The basin waits—dark, unblinking.

Rowan steps onto the flat stone at its edge.

He looks at the gathered ring of faces—pale, frightened, resisting their own bodies.

Then he looks down at the water.

And speaks to the valley like it's a living witness.

"They're trying to turn me into a weapon against you," Rowan says softly.

The water doesn't ripple.

But the air tightens, listening.

Rowan continues.

"You chose me," he says. "And I chose you. I chose not to cage. I chose not to force. I chose not to become the thing they want me to become."

His gaze lifts.

"And now they want to punish that choice."

Isorae stands beside him, shaking, hand still on his forearm as if she can hold him in place through sheer refusal.

Erin's voice is ragged. "Rowan, whatever you're about to do—"

Rowan exhales.

Then says the sentence the valley has never heard from him before.

"If I am harming what you've claimed," Rowan murmurs, voice steady, "tell me."

Silence falls hard.

Even the mist seems to freeze.

Dax's head snaps toward Rowan, eyes fierce.

Isorae's hand tightens, nails biting into his skin.

"Rowan—" she breathes.

Rowan doesn't look at her.

Because this isn't about comfort.

It's about sovereignty.

The basin stays still.

The valley hum underfoot shifts—deep, conflicted, angry.

Then—slowly—roots beneath the basin tighten.

Not around Rowan.

Around the space between Rowan and the ring of people.

Like the land is testing.

Like it's tasting the field ARIS laid.

Like it's deciding what belongs.

Erin stares at her scanner.

Her face drains.

"It's… reading the signal," she whispers.

Rowan's jaw sets.

"Good.

Let it read.

Let it know."

Because if ARIS is trying to make the valley choose between its bridge and its body—

Rowan is going to make sure the valley understands the difference between an external blade…

and an internal rot.

He looks at the ring of people, voice calm, deadly.

"This is not your shame," he says. "If you flinch, you tell the truth out loud."

Ryan, still pale, lifts his head and whispers, "It feels like poison."

Rowan nods once. "That's because it's designed to."

A woman clutches her stomach and sobs softly, "I don't want to be afraid of you."

Rowan's throat tightens.

"I know," he says, gentler in volume only. "That's why they picked this method."

Then he lifts his gaze to the treeline.

His voice drops into something like law.

"You want to cut my anchor?" he murmurs.

The air seems to hold its breath.

Rowan's eyes go black with certainty.

"Fine," he says softly. "But you're going to have to do it where everyone can see it."

He steps off the stone.

Toward the western rim.

Toward the unheld ground.

Toward the place ARIS thinks it can isolate him from the valley without needing a gate.

Isorae grabs his wrist, desperate. "Rowan, no."

Rowan turns and cups her face gently, grounding her.

His voice is human for a single, brutal heartbeat.

"They're going to make you watch people get sick just because I'm near them," he whispers. "They'll do it until someone breaks."

Isorae shakes her head, tears spilling. "So we fight it together."

Rowan leans closer, forehead to hers.

"We will," he murmurs. "But first I'm going to take their knife out of our ribs."

He steps back, eyes burning.

Erin's voice cracks. "Rowan, if you cross the line—"

"I know," Rowan says.

The valley's pull loosens as he approaches the boundary.

Releasing.

A sovereign body respecting choice even when it hurts.

Silas moves immediately to flank him.

Dax slips to the other side.

Evan starts forward—

Rowan lifts a hand.

"No," he says.

Evan freezes, jaw clenched.

Rowan's gaze sweeps the ring.

"Stay in the basin," he orders. "Stay where the valley can read you."

Then he turns and walks.

The fern curtain parts without mist this time.

Just… space.

As Rowan crosses the boundary, the air sharpens.

The world outside snaps into that colder resolution again, like reality is being forced to watch.

Behind him, the valley holds posture, humming low and furious.

In front of him—

the forest is too still.

Not hunt-still.

Clinic-still.

The kind of stillness that belongs to a room where something is about to be cut.

Rowan stops three paces beyond the boundary.

Dax and Silas halt with him.

Rowan exhales slowly.

"Alright," he says to the dark.

"Show me the hand holding the knife."

For a moment, nothing answers.

Then the air shifts.

And a voice—warm, calm, gentle—speaks from the treeline like it's coming from inside Rowan's own skull.

You don't have to carry them anymore.

Rowan's mouth curves into something that isn't a smile.

It's a threat.

"Wrong," he says softly.

And the forest… listens.

Because ARIS has begun its most dangerous extraction attempt yet.

Not of Isorae.

Not of the valley.

Of the thing that makes Rowan human enough to refuse becoming a monster.

And Rowan has just stepped outside the boundary to meet it head-on.

80

THE MERCY ALGORITHM

The voice doesn't echo.

It doesn't need distance to carry.

It arrives the way hunger arrives — inside the body, already personal, already convinced it belongs there.

You don't have to carry them anymore.

Rowan doesn't flinch.

Silas does.

Not fear. The half-step of a soldier hearing a familiar cadence that shouldn't exist in the woods.

Dax tilts his head, eyes narrowing, like he's trying to decide whether the sound came from the trees…

…or from inside his own skull.

Rowan keeps his gaze on the dark line of trunks.

"Stop dressing it in kindness," he says quietly.

The forest stays still.

Then the voice shifts — subtle, smooth, almost amused.

Kindness is just accuracy applied gently.

Erin's words from earlier scrape across Rowan's memory like a nail dragged over bone: *human interface. corridor. invitation tech.*

This isn't a person.

Not fully.

It's an intention shaped into a voice because voices are the easiest way to make surrender feel like relief — like you chose to kneel.

Rowan inhales.

He feels the valley behind him — humming low, furious, listening through the basin where his people stand clustered around dark water and a boundary line being rewritten in real time.

He feels Isorae, too — like a thread in his ribs pulled taut, her presence bright even from a distance, her mark burning faintly whenever the system tests its grip.

The voice comes again, warmer now. Slower. Almost intimate.

You can step away. They will live longer if you do.

Dax's jaw tightens.

Silas mutters, "I don't like that."

Rowan's voice stays calm.

"That's because it's not talking to you," he says. Then, to the dark: "Show your face."

A pause.

And then something moves between two trees — slow, unhurried, as if the forest itself has decided to hold a doorway open.

A man steps out.

He looks wrong in a way that doesn't announce itself at first.

Too clean.

Not physically — he wears field gear, boots dusted, hair mussed like he's been out here for hours — but structurally. Like the mess was applied after he was built.

His expression lands in the space between pity and patience, calibrated to suggest he's the only adult in a room full of frightened children.

He lifts both hands, empty. Open.

"Rowan Hale," he says gently, as if greeting someone he's known for years.

Silas raises his rifle.

The man doesn't react.

That's the second wrongness.

He doesn't fear weapons because he isn't here to be killed.

He's here to be believed.

Rowan's eyes narrow.

"You're another door," Rowan says.

The man's mouth curves — soft, almost sad.

"No," he says. "I'm an outcome."

Dax's voice is a low blade. "That's a cute line."

The man's gaze flicks to Dax for exactly long enough to register him — then returns to Rowan as if Dax is an environmental detail.

"Your friend is brave," the man says politely. "But bravery is not a strategy."

Rowan takes one step forward.

The air tightens — not pressure, not gravity — something like the world deciding rules around him.

Behind him, the boundary line hums.

In front of him, the forest holds still like it's watching a surgery.

The man keeps his voice gentle.

"I'm not here to threaten you," he says. "Threats are inefficient. I'm here to offer clarity."

Rowan's mouth barely moves.

"Clarity," he repeats.

The man nods. "Your presence is destabilizing the zone you call sovereign. That destabilization is spreading. It cannot remain contained."

Silas's finger tightens on the trigger. "You don't get to define their sovereignty."

The man's eyes slide to Silas again — patient, unbothered.

"I don't define it," he says. "I measure it."

Then he looks back at Rowan and speaks the sentence like a scalpel.

"Your anchor is poisoning your people."

The words land hard.

Because behind Rowan — inside the boundary — people are getting sick.

Because Ryan vomited.

Because mothers flinched away from him.

Because ARIS found the one method Rowan can't simply crush with stone:

A consequence that looks like protection.

Rowan's jaw locks.

"Say what you really mean."

The man's expression softens, like he's about to deliver mercy.

"I mean you are not a bridge," he says. "You are a rupture disguised as devotion."

Dax shifts, blade hand twitching. "I'm going to—"

Rowan lifts a hand without looking back.

Dax stills.

Rowan's eyes don't leave the man.

"Who are you," Rowan asks.

The answer is too smooth. Too ready.

"ARIS interface," the man says. "Containment ethics tier."

Silas lets out a humorless breath. "You have ethics now."

The interface tilts his head. "We have outcomes. Ethics are how humans justify them."

Then, gently — like someone delivering a diagnosis he expects you to accept —

"We can end the suffering within the hour."

Rowan's breath goes cold.

"By taking Isorae," he says.

The interface shakes his head once, almost kindly.

"No," he says. "We've moved beyond her."

That sentence is a fracture.

Rowan feels it ripple all the way back into the valley like the land itself heard it and clenched.

Dax goes very still.

Silas's rifle doesn't lower.

Rowan's voice is quiet.

"Explain."

The interface steps closer.

Not past the boundary.

Just close enough that Rowan can see the faint pale-blue glyph lines embedded in the seams of his gear — shimmering when the air shifts, like circuitry pretending to be fabric.

"We don't need the anomaly," it says. "We need the structure you created around it."

Rowan's chest tightens.

"The bond," Rowan says.

The interface nods.

"The bond is the problem," it says. "It produces instability. The valley's alignment around you is creating resistive harmonics that threaten system coherence."

Silas spits into the moss. "So what — you want him dead?"

The interface's face doesn't change.

"Death is messy," it says. "And unpredictable."

Dax's lips curl. "So you want him compliant."

The interface's gaze stays on Rowan.

"We want him singular," it says simply.

Rowan's spine goes cold.

Singular bandwidth.

Collapse.

The same term Maelin carried like a quiet poison.

Rowan's voice drops.

"You're trying to turn me back into a man who can't hear the valley."

The interface doesn't deny it.

"Yes," it says. "Because a man can be reasoned with."

Rowan's mouth curves faintly — grim, almost amused.

"And a bridge can't."

The interface's eyes sharpen.

"A bridge can be dismantled."

Then the air shifts again — thin, precise — and Rowan feels it.

A second field laying itself under the first.

Not aversion.

Not nausea.

Something else.

A tug at the seam in his ribs.

Not painful.

Persuasive.

Like the world offering him a way to put his own bones down.

You could sleep, the voice slides in again. Just sleep. Let go. You've done enough.

Rowan's eyelids want to drop.

Not because he's weak.

Because exhaustion is real.

Because grief is real.

Because being the hinge between worlds is like holding open a door with your spine.

Rowan takes a slow breath and forces his eyes wider.

He looks at the interface and says, very softly:

"You're trying to lure me into self-mercy."

The interface's expression warms.

"Yes," it says. "Because self-mercy is the closest thing you have to consent."

Dax swears under his breath. "Oh, fuck you."

Silas's voice is a growl. "Rowan, don't listen to—"

Rowan doesn't answer.

Because the voice isn't aimed at his ears.

It's aimed at his morality — the part of him that refuses to hurt people even to save them.

Rowan feels the valley behind him shift.

A low hum.

A question.

As if the land is trying to decide whether it's allowed to step in.

Rowan turns his head slightly — just enough to speak over his shoulder without breaking eye contact with the interface.

"Silas," Rowan says.

Silas's grip tightens. "Yeah."

"Go back," Rowan orders. "Tell Erin to watch the basin. Watch the sickness. If it spikes—"

Silas's voice cuts in, sharp. "If it spikes, what?"

Rowan's jaw sets.

"If it spikes," he says quietly, "the valley might decide I'm the breach."

Silas's face tightens with fury.

"It won't," he says. "It chose you."

Rowan's eyes flash. "It chose sovereignty. Sovereignty means it can change."

Dax's voice is low. "Then we don't let it."

Rowan's voice goes colder.

"You don't get to decide that either."

No one cages the valley. Not ARIS. Not me. Not us.

Silas swallows hard, then backs toward the boundary, eyes never leaving the interface.

Dax stays.

Of course he does.

The interface watches the exchange with a faint tilt of interest, like it's recording a behavioral pattern.

"You've built a cult of autonomy," it says mildly. "And autonomy is fragile under pain."

Rowan's voice is a whisper.

"That's why you're causing it."

The interface's smile is almost invisible. "Correct."

Then — like a doctor offering the final option —

"Step away from the boundary," it says. "Withdraw your influence. Let the valley resettle. The nausea will end. The aversion will dissolve. Your people will stop associating you with harm."

Rowan's throat tightens.

"And if I refuse."

The interface's voice stays gentle.

"Then your people will start leaving," it says. "Not because we force them. Because their bodies will beg them to move away from you."

Rowan feels his stomach drop.

Not fear of losing power.

Fear of losing them.

Fear of watching the valley become an exit again.

Fear of watching Isorae become a beacon as people flee the sickness and accidentally feed ARIS coordinates with every step.

The interface leans in slightly, voice lower.

"You don't need to fight," it says. "You only need to stop."

Rowan's eyes go distant for a single heartbeat.

He sees it:

People vomiting.

Children crying.

Mothers flinching.

Jalen shaking.

Maelin sobbing.

And the valley — sovereign, living — trying to protect its body from the thing ARIS defined as poison.

Rowan feels something inside him shift.

He looks at the interface, expression still.

Then he speaks with quiet clarity.

"You're right," Rowan says.

The interface's eyes soften — like it thinks it has won.

Dax's head snaps toward Rowan. "Rowan—"

Rowan raises a hand.

Not to stop Dax.

To hold the moment steady.

"You're right," Rowan repeats, voice calm.

The interface's mouth curves into something like relief.

Rowan steps forward.

The interface doesn't move.

Then Rowan says, softly, "I do need to stop."

The interface's eyes brighten.

"And I'm going to," Rowan continues.

Then his voice drops — feral and ancient.

"I'm going to stop you from using pain as permission."

The interface's smile falters.

Rowan moves.

Not with speed.

With inevitability.

He steps into the layered fields — aversion and self-mercy and seam-tug — and lets them hit him full force.

His body sways.

His vision whites.

Exhaustion tries to fold his knees.

The "kindness" tries to make him lie down and call it healing.

Rowan grits his teeth until they ache.

And then he does the one thing ARIS didn't plan for:

He lets the valley witness him choosing pain without surrendering choice.

He plants his boots.

He lowers his center of gravity like a bridge setting its footings into bedrock.

He reaches down with his mind — not into the interface —

into the structure beneath it.

Because the interface isn't the hand holding the knife.

It's the handle.

The knife is the field.

And fields have anchor points.

Rowan spreads his fingers in the air, palm down.

Not touching the earth.

Touching the seam.

He feels it — thin and slick — threaded through the ground like wire, running back toward a node he can't see.

There.

Rowan smiles without warmth.

"Found you."

The interface's composure cracks, just a fraction.

"What are you doing," it asks.

Rowan's voice is a quiet threat.

"Biting the hand," he says.

He pulls.

Not violently.

Decisively.

The forest doesn't explode.

The air doesn't shatter.

But something shifts — a subtle ripple running through the aversion field like a snapped tendon.

Somewhere behind him, inside the boundary, the basin water ripples for the first time all night.

Rowan feels the valley flinch.

The interface's eyes widen.

"That node is not within your jurisdiction," it says sharply — and jurisdiction coming from a machine makes Rowan's mouth twist.

Rowan's voice is calm.

"It is if you threaded it through my people," he replies.

The interface steps back for the first time.

Not retreat.

Adjustment.

Rowan takes another step forward, still pulling at the hidden line.

Dax moves with him like a shadow with teeth, blade ready but not striking — watching for whatever emerges when a system realizes its leash is being yanked.

The interface's voice hardens, losing some of its gentleness.

"Rowan Hale," it says, "if you sever that link, the field will rebound."

Rowan's eyes narrow.

"On who," he asks.

The interface's smile returns, thin.

"On Isorae," it says quietly. "On the mark. The one you've been protecting."

Rowan stills.

Because that's the real trap.

A leash tied through her bones.

A blade held to her ribs.

A choice designed to make him betray himself.

A silence stretches.

Rowan breathes once, slow.

Dax whispers, "Rowan…"

Rowan doesn't answer.

He stares at the interface with eyes like stone.

"You're using her as grounding," Rowan says.

The interface's voice turns almost gentle again.

"We use what's available," it says. "That's what intelligence does."

Rowan's jaw clenches.

He feels the valley behind him.

He feels the people.

He feels Isorae.

And he understands with a cold, clean clarity:

ARIS is trying to force him into a single moral cut —

Protect the many and risk harming her…

or protect her and let the many fall away.

A knife that slices the anchor either way.

Rowan's voice comes out low.

"You think you've cornered me."

The interface doesn't blink.

"We have."

Rowan's mouth curves faintly.

"No," Rowan says softly. "You've only shown me where your hand is."

He releases the hidden line.

Not surrender.

Restraint.

Then he turns—fast—back toward the valley boundary.

Dax follows instantly.

The interface calls after him, voice sharpening:

"Running back inside won't end the field."

Rowan doesn't look back.

"I'm not going back to hide," Rowan says. "I'm going back to reroute."

He crosses the boundary in three strides.

The valley's pull hits him — warm and furious — like a living body catching its own limb.

Inside the basin ring, people are pale, trembling, fighting nausea and panic.

Isorae stands rigid, hand at her sternum, eyes wide.

Rowan goes straight to her.

He cups her face.

"Stay with me," he whispers.

Isorae's breath shakes. "I am."

Rowan lowers his forehead to hers.

"Good," he murmurs. "Because I'm about to use the mark."

Isorae's eyes widen. "Rowan—"

Erin steps forward, coil in hand, face white. "Use it how?"

Rowan lifts his head.

His eyes are dark, aligned, terrifyingly calm.

"They anchored the aversion field through her," Rowan says. "Which means the node is tuned to her resonance."

Erin swallows hard. "That's bad."

Rowan's voice doesn't waver.

"No," he says. "That's leverage."

A hush falls.

Even the nausea seems to pause to listen.

Rowan looks at Isorae.

"This will hurt," he says softly.

Isorae nods once, jaw tight.

"I'm already hurt," she whispers.

Rowan turns to Erin.

"Build me a conduit."

Erin stares. "I can't—"

Rowan's gaze doesn't blink.

"Yes, you can," he says. "Not to block. Not to sever."

He leans closer.

"To reflect."

Erin inhales sharply, understanding dawning like dread.

"You want to bounce their field back through their own node," she whispers.

Rowan nods once.

"Not at the people," he says. "At the hand holding the knife."

Dax's grin goes feral.

Silas's eyes narrow with approval.

Evan's face is pale, but his voice is steady.

"If you do that," Evan says quietly, "they'll feel what they're doing to us."

Rowan's voice is a whisper.

"They'll feel it through their carrier net," he says. "Through their ethics tier."

He looks at the basin — dark, watching.

Then at the valley.

"You wanted mercy," Rowan murmurs to the unseen system beyond the trees.

"Fine."

His hand finds Isorae's sternum — careful, reverent, fingers spread over the invisible brand.

Isorae gasps as the mark flares hot beneath his palm, silver geometry shimmering into the air like a hostile constellation waking up.

Rowan's voice drops into something old.

"Let's teach your mercy what it feels like to be used."

The valley hums — deep, patient.

And somewhere beyond the boundary, the interface in the forest goes very still.

Because ARIS has just realized Rowan isn't trying to escape the knife.

He's trying to turn it around.

81

THE MIRROR TRAP

Erin builds the conduit with hands that won't stop shaking.

Not because she's afraid of failure.

Because she understands what success will mean.

She sits cross-legged on cold stone at the edge of the crescent basin, jaw locked so tight it aches, braid falling over one shoulder as she strips wiring out of three dead uplinks and a drone core they never even bothered to name. Copper coils. Quartz lattice shards. A thin strip of ARIS composite peeled from one of the shattered extraction frames.

Pieces of their enemy turned into a mouth.

Her fingers keep slipping.

Not clumsy—just human.

And human is the one thing ARIS keeps trying to make them feel ashamed of.

Rowan stands over her, unmoving.

Anchoring the space around her so her thoughts stay her own.

Isorae stands beside him, palm pressed to her sternum where the mark now burns visibly—silver geometry hovering a finger's width above her skin, faint as moonlight and twice as cruel. Every time it flares, nausea rips through the ring like a command. People bend at the waist, swallow hard, clutch their ribs like their bodies are trying to crawl away from a sickness that wears Rowan's shadow.

A child whimpers.

Someone retches, sharp and wet.

No one says "ARIS" anymore.

Everyone already knows what it feels like when your own body stops trusting you.

Rowan watches it with a stillness that looks like restraint.

But inside him, something is grinding its teeth down to bone.

Evan moves through the group in quiet loops, doing what he can—water, breath cues, cold cloths pressed to foreheads. He's gentle, but his eyes are hard. Like he's trying not to look at Rowan because he knows if he does, his stomach will turn again.

Silas keeps the perimeter tight, rifle low but ready, eyes moving constantly as if he expects the trees to open like a mouth.

Dax stands one step behind Rowan, blade in hand, expression carved from feral patience.

A watchdog waiting to bite God.

"Talk to me," Erin says suddenly, voice hoarse as she twists a coil into a tighter spiral. "If I stop hearing human sound, I start hearing them."

Rowan answers immediately—low, steady.

"You're doing fine."

Erin snorts like it's almost a laugh. "That's not information."

Rowan's gaze doesn't leave the conduit taking shape. "Tell me what you need."

Erin swallows. Her throat works hard.

"Tell me this isn't going to fry her."

Isorae's breath catches, but she doesn't step back.

Rowan turns his head slightly and looks at her—really looks.

"I won't let it," he says softly.

Isorae's mouth trembles. "You can't promise—"

"I can," Rowan cuts in, and there's steel under it now. Not anger. Authority. "Because I'm not asking the valley to do it alone."

Erin's hands pause mid-twist. "What does that mean?"

Rowan's eyes flick to the basin—dark water holding starlight like it refuses to blink.

"It chose jurisdiction," Rowan says. "Jurisdiction means it can designate where harm belongs."

Silas shifts, expression tightening. "You're going to make the valley decide who the rebound hits."

Rowan's gaze stays on the mark.

"Yes," he says.

Evan's voice is careful. "Rowan… you can't ask it to become cruel."

Rowan's jaw flexes.

"I'm not," he says quietly. "I'm asking it to become accurate."

The air around the basin changes.

A subtle tightening—as if the valley leaned closer to listen to the sentence with both ears.

Erin finishes the last coil and holds the conduit up between both hands. It's ugly. Improvised. Beautiful in the way desperate things are beautiful when they work.

A flat plate of composite sits at the center, etched with intersecting lines of copper and quartz like a rough sigil—part circuitry, part sacred geometry, all intention.

"This is a mirror," Erin whispers. "A shitty one. But it's a mirror."

Rowan nods once. "Then we aim it."

Erin swallows, eyes flicking to Isorae. "It needs a driver."

Isorae's shoulders square.

"I can do it," she says.

Rowan's hand closes around her wrist instantly—not stopping her, grounding her.

"You're already driving the field," Rowan says softly. "That's why it hurts you."

Isorae's breath shakes. "Then let it hurt me on purpose."

Rowan's gaze darkens. "Not alone."

Erin raises an eyebrow. "Rowan—"

"I'm part of the circuit," Rowan says, and the words are not metaphor. "If they anchored through her, they anchored through us."

Dax mutters, "Tell me you have a plan that doesn't involve dying."

Rowan doesn't look at him. "I'm not dying."

Dax's grin flashes sharp. "Good."

Rowan steps into the basin ring.

Everyone feels it—the way the land tightens under his boots, the way the air formalizes around him like a room being declared.

He kneels in front of Isorae.

Slow. Deliberate.

Not dramatic.

Like this is a ritual he was born knowing.

"Look at me," he says.

Isorae's eyes lift, luminous with fear and steel.

Rowan cups her jaw.

"Stay in your bones," he murmurs. "Not the mark. Not the noise. Your bones."

Isorae swallows and nods once. "I'm here."

Rowan leans his forehead to hers for a heartbeat—breath to breath, hinge to hinge.

Then he turns his head slightly.

"Erin."

Erin moves forward, holding the conduit with both hands as if it's holy and dangerous. She sets it carefully at the edge of Isorae's sternum, just beneath the floating geometry.

The moment the composite touches the air near the mark—

the valley shudders.

Isorae gasps, body jerking like an unseen hook just pulled.

Nausea spikes through the ring. Two people retch. Someone sobs—hard, humiliating, furious.

Rowan's eyes go hard.

"Hold," he says, voice low as bedrock.

Erin's knuckles go white. "I'm holding."

The mark flares brighter—silver lines sharpening, intensifying, humming with surgical exactness—

and then—

the voice returns.

Not from the forest.

From inside the basin ring itself.

There you are.

Warm. Familiar. Almost pleased.

People stiffen, eyes widening as they realize they all heard it—not in their heads, but in the air.

A shared intrusion.

A collective touch.

Evan's breath catches. "Rowan—"

Rowan doesn't look away from Isorae.

"You wanted to speak to us," Rowan murmurs, calm as stone. "Fine. Speak."

Erin whispers, horrified, "Rowan, don't invite it—"

"I'm not inviting," Rowan says. "I'm exposing."

The voice shifts, amused.

You can't mirror what you don't understand.

Rowan's mouth curves faintly.

"Then teach me," he says.

The valley goes very still.

Like it's bracing for impact.

Because Rowan Hale just asked a machine to reveal itself—

and machines love to explain.

The air tightens.

The mark flares again.

And suddenly a new sensation slides into the basin ring—clean, clinical, terrifyingly intimate.

Not nausea.

Not aversion.

A sense of being read.

Like skin peeled back.

Like a file opened.

Erin's cracked scanner—held together with tape and spite—floods with numbers that shouldn't exist without a satellite overhead.

Her voice breaks. "It's using the mark as a bidirectional uplink."

Rowan's gaze sharpens.

"Good," he says.

Isorae's breath goes ragged. Her shimmer flickers—tight, strained.

"Rowan… it's inside me," she whispers.

Rowan's hand tightens on her wrist. "Stay."

Isorae squeezes her eyes shut, jaw trembling. "I'm trying."

The voice turns gentler—so gentle it's disgusting.

You're exhausted.

Isorae flinches.

You're in pain.

The mark pulses in agreement like a heartbeat that isn't hers.

Rowan's eyes darken.

"Talk to me," Rowan says, voice flat. "Not her."

The voice slides to him immediately, obedient in its target selection.

You want to protect her.

Rowan doesn't answer.

You want to protect them.

Rowan can feel the valley behind him listening, every root tense, every stone awake.

The voice continues, careful.

And yet your presence harms them.

A ripple of nausea surges through the ring on cue, as if proving its point. A man doubles over and spits bile into the moss, shaking with rage and shame.

Rowan inhales slowly.

He feels the hook.

Not in his fear.

In his guilt.

ARIS isn't threatening to kill them.

It's threatening to make Rowan the reason they break.

Rowan's voice is quiet.

"You think guilt will move me," he says.

The voice responds, almost tender.

It already has.

Rowan's jaw tightens.

Erin's fingers tremble on the conduit.

The mirror hums—thin, sharp.

Rowan feels it: the reflected field ready to snap back along its line—

but the line is still threaded through Isorae.

Still dangerous.

Still a knife held inside her ribs.

Rowan closes his eyes for a single beat.

Then opens them.

"Valley," Rowan says softly.

The word lands like a hand on the earth.

The ground beneath the basin tightens.

Mist draws inward.

Stone holds its breath.

Rowan's voice stays gentle.

"Designate," he murmurs.

Erin's head snaps up. "Rowan—"

Rowan doesn't look at her.

"Designate the direction of return," he says, and for the first time he is not speaking like a man.

He's speaking like a jurisdiction being declared.

Isorae gasps as the mark flares violently, silver lines bright enough to cast thin light on Rowan's hands.

Nausea spikes—

then stalls.

Not gone.

Held at the threshold like a dog on a leash.

Rowan feels the valley do something it has never done before:

It takes harm—

and gives it an address.

Erin's voice is a whisper. "Oh my god…"

Evan's eyes widen. "It's… routing."

Silas's grip tightens on his rifle. "To where?"

Rowan's gaze snaps toward the treeline—the direction the interface stood.

The air between the trees is too still.

Too expectant.

Rowan's voice is quiet.

"There," he says.

Erin's hands tighten around the conduit.

"Rowan, if I trigger this and the valley's wrong—"

Rowan doesn't blink. "It won't be."

Isorae's eyes open, wet and fierce.

"Do it," she whispers.

Erin swallows hard.

Then she triggers the mirror.

The conduit screams—

not audible, but felt—

like a tension cord snapping through the world.

The mark flares.

The basin water ripples outward in a perfect circle.

And the field—

the nausea, the aversion, the chemical relief corridor—

reverses.

A wave rolls outward from the basin ring like a breath being exhaled in the wrong direction.

Not toward their people.

Away.

Into the forest.

Silence holds for one breath.

Then—

the treeline convulses.

A strip of canopy—thirty yards wide, a clean, brutal line—bleaches to colorless gray as if the world has been scraped raw. Leaves whiten. Bark pales. Moss drains like blood leaving skin.

Birds drop.

Not fluttering.

Dropped.

Straight down like their wings forgot what gravity is.

A hawk falls out of the air and hits the ground with a sound too heavy for something that should have been soaring.

Someone screams.

Someone else says, "Holy shit," like prayer.

Then the sound—

not a scream.

Not fear.

A choked, involuntary retch—too human to belong to a machine.

Dax's grin turns savage. "Got him."

Silas's eyes narrow, sharp. "You hit the interface."

Erin's face is white. Her voice cracks. "We hit the node."

Rowan stands slowly, hands still on Isorae.

She's shaking, sweat on her brow, shimmer flickering like a flame in wind—

but she's upright.

Breathing.

Alive.

Rowan looks into the trees and feels it:

a sudden stutter in the system's confidence.

Not because it's hurt—

machines don't hurt—

but because the hand on the other side of the corridor just learned what it feels like to swallow its own persuasion.

The voice returns.

But it is no longer warm.

No longer amused.

No longer pretending to care.

Its tone is precise now.

Clinical.

You have introduced reflective instability into a sovereign correction lattice.

Rowan's eyes lift slowly.

"Say that again," he murmurs.

You have demonstrated that the valley can redirect corrective force.

Erin's breath catches.

Silas stiffens.

Rowan's gaze slides, sharp, to Isorae.

The silver geometry at her sternum pulses once—bright, exact.

The system acknowledges a revised stability architecture.

Isorae gasps.

Rowan feels something inside his ribs drop.

Primary anchor reclassified.

Erin's scanner spikes violently.

"Oh, fuck," she whispers.

"They're not pulling back."

Rowan's voice is low. "Explain."

Erin stares at the data, hands shaking.

"They're not treating the valley as the instability anymore," she says.

"They're treating her as the instability stabilizer."

Silas goes still. "Then what are they going to do?"

Erin looks up, eyes wide with horror.

"They're going to stop chasing people," she whispers. "Stop sending offers."

Her mouth trembles.

"They're going to start designing everything around isolating her."

The interface steps backward into the trees.

Recalibrating.

Mirror feedback acknowledged.

Population corridor doctrine suspended.

Single-anchor stabilization initiated.

The forest swallows him.

But the scar remains—

that bleached strip of dead geometry in living trees,

a warning written into the land.

The valley exhales—uneasy, uncertain.

Rowan turns to Isorae instantly, hands on her shoulders.

"You're here," he says fiercely. "You're in your bones."

She nods—shaking hard.

"They… felt me," she whispers.

"They didn't just see me."

Erin lowers her scanner slowly.

"They mapped her again," she says.

"And they decided she's worth the war."

The basin water settles into stillness.

The valley is quiet—listening.

Because the war has just changed shape.

It is no longer about breaching the valley.

It is about extracting the woman who makes the valley possible.

And Rowan Hale finally understands:

They didn't lose their soft door.

They just found their real one.

No one moves at first.

Not because they are frozen.

Because the forest is.

The bleached strip beyond the ridge still hums faintly — not with sound, but with a thin, electric quiet that makes teeth ache and skin prickle. Leaves hang pale and brittle. Bark has split into chalk-colored seams. Moss curls inward like burned hair.

A bird twitches on the ground.

Just once.

Then it goes still again.

Steam lifts faintly from the soil — not heat, but reaction — as if the earth itself has been chemically scalded by something that was never meant to touch it.

Erin swallows hard.

"Rowan… the trees aren't dying," she whispers.

"They're… being rewritten."

Silas's jaw tightens. "That's not damage."

"That's proof," Dax mutters.

Rowan stands with one hand still braced on Isorae's shoulder, feeling her tremble, feeling the valley hum under his boots — not afraid.

Alert.

Awake.

Watching its own wound.

Far beyond the ridge, where satellites speak to each other in clean lines of code and doctrine, ARIS recalibrates again.

Not because it is confused.

But because it has just received new data:

The bridge can redirect extraction.

The valley can route harm.

And the woman at its heart can carry war inside her bones.

New protocols cascade across sterile systems that have never known breath or soil:

PRIMARY TARGET: ISORAE

SECONDARY OBJECTIVE: ISOLATE BRIDGE ENTITY

TERRAIN: NON-COMPLIANT / ADAPTIVE / HOSTILE

And for the first time since it found the valley...

ARIS does not design a door.

It designs a hunt.

The forest exhales.

The valley tightens.

And somewhere in the scarred trees, pale leaves crumble into dust that drifts like ash across living green — a quiet promise written into the land:

This will not be the last place they bleed.

82

THE PRICE OF QUIET

The valley does not celebrate the mirror.

It recovers from it.

Morning arrives with the wrong kind of gentleness—mist laid carefully between the shelters like a blanket that doesn't belong to anyone, birds moving too far above the canopy as if the sky has decided distance is safer than intimacy. Even the crescent basin looks composed, its surface smooth as held breath.

Rowan stands at its edge and watches the water until his eyes burn.

He can feel it in the soil: the valley is still listening for the shape of retaliation.

And he is still listening for the moment ARIS stops pretending it ever cared about anyone but the seam.

Behind him, Isorae sits on a stone with her hand pressed to her sternum.

The silver geometry there is not quiet anymore.

It is contained—as if something behind it has tightened its grip and learned how to wait.

Erin crouches beside her with the scanner braced against her knee, staring at readouts like they are a language she is afraid to translate aloud.

"Tell me," Rowan says, voice low.

Erin swallows. Her throat works like the words have teeth.

"They've braided a stabilization tether into her mark," she says. "It's not just a ping. It's not just a corridor."

She glances at Isorae, guilt flashing across her face like a knife.

"It's a chord," Erin finishes. "A live line. A correction link."

Isorae's fingers tighten over her chest. The geometry pulses once—bright enough to cast thin, cold light on her knuckles.

Rowan feels it move inside his ribs like an instinctive snarl.

"Can you cut it," he asks.

Erin's eyes flick to his, then away.

"I can try."

That is not an answer.

Rowan steps closer, the ground firming under his boots as if the valley is bracing with him.

"Can you cut it," he repeats, slower.

Erin's mouth trembles. She hates him for asking. She hates herself for knowing.

"I can cut it," she says. "But I don't know what it's anchoring on the other end. I don't know what it's holding her together with."

She lifts the scanner a fraction, as if the numbers might soften if she doesn't fully show them.

"If I sever it wrong," Erin whispers, "it could take her heart with it."

The sentence lands like a stone dropped into water.

Everyone nearby goes still.

Evan's hands pause mid-wrap on a bandage. Silas stops adjusting the strap of his rifle. Dax—who has stared down drones and gates and the sky itself—makes a small sound that is almost disbelief.

Rowan doesn't move.

His face doesn't change.

But something in the air does.

A pressure shift. A tightening. The valley's attention narrowing.

Isorae's eyes close briefly, like she's tasting the weight of the words before she allows them to exist.

Then she opens them and looks at Rowan.

"Not yet," she whispers.

Rowan's jaw flexes.

"Not yet," she repeats, firmer. "We need to know what they're doing first."

As if ARIS heard her.

As if ARIS has been waiting for that exact permission to escalate.

It begins around midday.

Not with gates.

Not with pylons.

Not even with voices.

With bodies.

It starts small—someone near the fireline bending over suddenly, retching bile into the moss like their stomach has rejected the valley's air. Then another, coughing hard as if their lungs have forgotten the idea of breath. A child goes pale in the middle of laughing and sinks to their knees, pressing both hands to their ribs like something inside them is tightening.

Evan moves fast, kneeling, checking pupils, pulse, breath. His face goes sharp with the kind of calm that means panic has been buried alive inside him.

"This isn't illness," he murmurs.

Erin's scanner spikes so violently the display flickers.

"It's her," Erin whispers.

Rowan's head lifts.

Isorae stiffens on her stone, breath catching.

Erin looks up with eyes full of fury and horror.

"They're routing a discomfort field through the tether," she says. "Not enough to kill—just enough to make staying near her feel wrong."

A sound drags out of Rowan's throat—low and dangerous.

"They're poisoning the valley with her."

Isorae swallows hard. Her voice is quiet.

"They're making me a burden."

Rowan turns toward her so fast it's almost violent.

"You are not—"

Isorae cuts him off, not with anger, but with the raw steadiness of someone forced to name the truth.

"They're making it feel like I am," she says.

And that's the entire trap.

Not force.

Not invasion.

A slow, engineered reprogramming of the hollow's emotional gravity until people begin to think the thought ARIS wants them to think:

If she weren't here, we could breathe.

Rowan watches it happen in faces.

In the way people try to hide it, because shame is its own kind of chokehold.

Parker sits with her back against a tree, jaw clenched, trying to keep her breathing steady while sweat beads at her hairline. Ryan, who fought the first insertions like they were claws in his skull, stands pale and silent and refuses to meet Isorae's eyes as if looking at her might make him disloyal.

Dax stalks the perimeter like an animal that can't find a throat to bite.

Silas keeps giving orders that sound normal, because if he lets them sound afraid, everything breaks.

And Rowan—

Rowan stands between Isorae and everyone else like a living wall, hands loose at his sides, posture quiet with violence.

The valley hums under his boots.

Not defensive.

Offended.

Because the land can feel what ARIS is doing: making sovereignty itself taste like punishment.

Near dusk, the voice returns.

Not in the air this time.

In the spaces between people's thoughts—like a warmth slipping through the cracks of exhaustion.

Evan is the first one Rowan sees react.

He pauses mid-step, eyes unfocusing for a fraction of a second, mouth parting as if he is about to answer someone who isn't there.

Rowan crosses the distance in two strides.

"Evan."

Evan blinks hard, shame flooding his face.

"I—" he starts.

Rowan's voice stays low, steady.

"What did it say?"

Evan swallows. His throat works like he's choking on the confession.

"That she doesn't have to keep hurting us."

Silence ripples outward.

Isorae doesn't move.

Erin's face goes white.

Rowan's gaze snaps toward the tree line—not because the tree line is responsible, but because ARIS always loves a stage.

The voice doesn't stop there.

It moves.

Softly.

Patiently.

One person at a time.

Parker flinches and whispers, "I heard my sister's voice. It said she's alive."

A teenager near the basin covers his ears and cries without sound, shaking his head like he's trying to throw a thought out of his skull.

And then—

Isorae gasps.

She clutches her sternum, not from pain exactly, but from a sudden tug—as if someone has reached through the geometry and pulled the tether tighter.

Her shimmer flashes bright, then snaps down hard, compressed.

Rowan catches her shoulders.

"Talk to me."

Isorae's eyes are wide, wet, furious.

"It's not a voice," she whispers. "It's… a conclusion."

Rowan's throat tightens.

"What conclusion?"

Isorae stares past him, looking at the people trying not to look at her, and the grief in her expression is a slow, sinking thing—like snow settling on a grave.

"That it stops if I stop," she says.

Erin surges forward. "No."

Isorae flinches at the sharpness, but she doesn't look away.

"They're not offering me a door," Isorae continues, voice trembling. "They're turning me into one."

Evan's face tightens with horror.

"They're trying to make you choose surrender," he whispers.

Isorae nods once, small.

"Yes."

Rowan's hands tighten on her shoulders, just shy of bruising.

"You're not choosing anything for them."

Isorae's gaze lifts to his.

And there—there is the terrible tenderness ARIS can't manufacture.

The way she looks at him like she's already grieving him.

"I'm not choosing it for them," she whispers.

Rowan shakes his head once, already refusing whatever is forming.

Isorae continues anyway, because she has always been brave in the quietest way.

"I'm choosing it for us," she says.

Erin's mouth opens.

"No," Erin says, voice breaking. "No, no—don't—don't you dare put this on yourself."

Isorae's eyes flick to Erin, softening.

"It's already on me," she whispers. "They built the tether into my bones."

Rowan's voice drops—raw, dangerous.

"They built it," he says. "So we cut it."

Erin freezes.

Rowan turns his eyes to her.

"Can you make something," he asks, "that severs it without ripping her apart?"

Erin looks like she's been struck.

Her breath shudders. Her hands lift—half helpless, half furious—because she is a builder and builders are cursed with hope even when there is no safe math left.

"I can make a sever," Erin says, and the sentence sounds like confession. "I can make a break-wave that targets the tether's frequency and collapses it."

She swallows hard.

"But if the tether is holding her coherence stable—if it's acting like a synthetic heartbeat—then—"

Evan's voice is quiet.

"Then cutting it could kill her."

Erin nods, tears bright and furious in her eyes.

"Yes."

Rowan goes still.

So still the valley seems to imitate him.

Isorae closes her eyes.

And when she opens them, there is a decision there that wasn't there before.

Not eagerness.

Not martyrdom.

Reluctant acceptance—like someone signing a name they hate writing.

"What happens if we don't," Isorae asks softly.

Erin's voice breaks on the honesty.

"They keep turning you into pressure," she whispers. "They keep making people sick until someone begs you to go."

She wipes her face hard with the heel of her hand, furious at her own tears.

"Or until you do," Erin adds. "Because you can't stand watching them suffer."

The fire crackles.

Someone coughs again—wet, helpless.

Isorae's fingers tighten over her sternum.

Rowan feels the tether pulse under his palm like a wrong second heartbeat.

"Rowan," Isorae whispers.

He doesn't answer.

He can't.

Because he knows that if she speaks the next words aloud, they become real.

She speaks them anyway.

"If cutting it is the only way to stop this—" her voice shakes, but she holds it, "—then we cut it."

Erin makes a broken sound. "Isorae—"

Isorae reaches out and takes Erin's hand.

A simple human touch.

Not a hinge.

Not a seam.

Just a person.

"I don't want to die," Isorae whispers.

The confession is small. It's devastating.

Erin squeezes her hand like she's holding the world by the edge.

"I don't want you to die," Erin answers.

Isorae looks at Rowan then.

And something in Rowan's face cracks—just a hairline fracture—because he is suddenly looking at the possibility of holding her dead weight again.

"I don't want you to carry my body," Isorae whispers, almost soundless.

Rowan's throat tightens until it hurts.

"You're not going to make me," he says, voice ragged.

Isorae's eyes fill.

"I'm not trying to," she whispers. "I'm trying to keep you from having to carry everyone else."

Rowan's hands slide to her face, cupping her jaw the way he did in the basin ring.

His thumb trembles once.

"Stay in your bones," he whispers, as if saying it enough times will make it law.

Isorae nods, tears slipping down her cheeks.

"I'll try," she whispers back.

Erin stands abruptly, wiping her face again, rage overtaking grief because rage is the only thing that keeps her hands steady.

"Then I build it," Erin says.

Silas steps closer, eyes hard.

"How long?"

Erin's jaw clenches.

"Hours," she says. "Not days. We don't have days."

Dax's voice is low, feral.

"And if ARIS tries something while she builds?"

Rowan turns his head slightly.

His eyes are black.

"Then the valley bites," he says softly.

And the land underfoot hums—low, acknowledging.

Consent.

Night falls like a lid.

Erin works at the crescent basin with shaking hands and brutal focus, building a severance device out of salvaged ARIS composite and valley quartz, threading it with copper and intention until it looks like a cruel, delicate halo.

Evan stays with Isorae, checking her pulse, checking her breathing, watching the silver geometry flare every time the tether tightens.

Silas organizes watches.

Dax doesn't stop moving.

And Rowan sits beside Isorae on the moss, shoulder to shoulder, as if proximity alone can keep her tethered to life.

The valley holds its breath around them.

Not because it is afraid.

Because it knows what choice is about to be made.

Isorae leans her head lightly against Rowan's shoulder.

Her voice is barely audible.

"If it kills me," she whispers, "don't let them use it."

Rowan closes his eyes.

Pain moves through him like glass.

"Don't talk like that."

Isorae's mouth trembles.

"I have to," she whispers. "Because they're listening."

Rowan opens his eyes and stares into the dark trees beyond the rim.

"Let them," he murmurs. "They can hear this part too."

He turns his head toward Isorae, forehead nearly touching hers.

"If you slip," Rowan whispers, "I will drag you back."

Isorae lets out a shaky breath that almost becomes a laugh.

"That's not how death works."

Rowan's eyes burn.

"It is for you," he says.

The silver geometry at her sternum pulses—bright, hungry.

As if answering.

As if reminding them that ARIS is tightening the tether on purpose, drawing her toward the brink until surrender feels like mercy.

But there will be no surrender.

Only severance.

Only risk.

Only the terrible love of people who would rather gamble with death than let a machine decide what consent means.

Erin stands at last, swaying slightly with exhaustion, holding the finished device in both hands.

Her voice is hoarse.

"It's ready," she says.

Rowan rises in one smooth motion.

The valley quiets.

Isorae stands too, blanket slipping from her shoulders, her hand pressed to her sternum like she's holding herself inside her body by force.

Erin's eyes shine.

"This could kill you," she whispers.

Isorae swallows, tears bright and furious.

"I know," she whispers back.

Rowan steps in front of Isorae like a boundary made flesh.

His voice is low.

"We do this here," he says. "In the ring. With witnesses."

The valley hums beneath them.

Agreeing.

And somewhere beyond the ridges—far beyond moss and mist and human breath—ARIS tightens its focus like a lens narrowing.

Because it can feel it too:

They are about to cut the line.

And ARIS will not stop them with force.

It will stop them with choice—

by pushing Isorae to the exact edge where surrender feels like kindness…

and severance feels like death.

Rowan takes Isorae's hand.

Erin lifts the device.

The silver geometry flares, bright as a blade.

And the valley holds its breath—

83

THE PRICE OF MERCY

The valley goes silent in a way Rowan has never heard.

Not the quiet of sleep.

Not the quiet of snow.

A legal silence—like a room when a verdict is about to be spoken.

They gather at the crescent basin because the basin has become the valley's eye, and if something has to happen that will change the shape of the world, it happens where the land can witness it.

Mist sits low, dense as wool. The fire circle has been rebuilt into a clean ring of stones—no ash, no warmth, only boundary. Erin's device rests on a flat slab of slate near the water: a cruel little halo of copper and quartz, ARIS composite braided through it like a stolen tendon. It hums faintly, not with power, but with intention.

Erin stands over it, shoulders too tight, hands stained and trembling.

Evan has arranged blankets nearby like he can preempt grief with preparedness. His medical kit is open, every tool displayed, every strip of cloth cut. He looks up at Rowan with the expression of someone who has already lost the argument with fate and is now trying to negotiate the terms.

Silas holds the outer ring with two others—rifle slung, stance rigid, eyes scanning the treeline even though the enemy is not coming from the trees. Dax paces, restless, too angry to still, blade hanging at his side like a promise he can't keep.

And Isorae stands at the center, barefoot on damp stone, one palm pressed to her sternum.

The silver geometry above her skin is bright tonight—no longer faint moonlight, but a clear, cold sigil that makes the air taste metallic. It pulses in slow, deliberate beats as if it has learned patience.

Rowan feels the tether in his ribs like a wire pulled taut through bone.

It is not only in her.

It is around her.

It is in the valley's breath when people inhale too shallowly.

It is in the way everyone has been sick in small, controlled waves—enough to suffer, not enough to die, as if ARIS is turning their bodies into a persuasion engine.

They have all felt it all day: the nausea that rises in groups like tidewater, the sudden migraines, the stinging behind the eyes, the shakiness in the hands. The children have been worst hit—quiet and pale, clinging to whoever is closest, breathing like breathing costs something now.

ARIS has learned exactly how to hurt without leaving bruises.

Rowan watches Isorae's fingers press harder into the mark.

"You don't have to do this tonight," he says, voice low. He has said it three times already. It has never sounded like permission. It has always sounded like begging.

Isorae's eyes lift to his.

She looks exhausted. Not weak. Not wavering. Just… used up in a way that has nothing to do with sleep.

"I do," she whispers.

Her voice is steady enough to hurt.

Rowan steps closer, careful—like sudden movement might snap the thread holding her inside her body.

"You don't," he insists, and his voice breaks on the second syllable. "We can wait. We can—"

Erin makes a small sound behind him—half a warning, half an apology. Evan's hands tighten around a cloth he's already wringing.

Isorae shakes her head once, slow.

"We've been waiting," she says softly. "And every hour we wait, they tune it sharper."

As if ARIS wants to prove her point, the silver geometry flares.

Three people in the outer ring bend at the waist at the same time, retching into the moss like puppets yanked by the same string. A child starts crying without sound—mouth open, eyes squeezed shut, face scrunched in pain—until their mother scoops them up and rocks them hard enough to bruise.

Rowan feels rage scrape up through his ribs like metal.

The valley hums under his feet, offended and tense, but refusing to do the one thing Rowan has never asked it to do: refuse someone's own choice.

Erin lifts her scanner, eyes glassy.

"It's spiking again," she whispers. "It's using her as the anchor point and bleeding discomfort outward in rings. It's—"

She swallows hard.

"It's her pulse now," Erin finishes. "Their timing is synced to her heart."

Rowan's stomach turns to ice.

Evan's voice is quiet, brutal in its honesty.

"They're making the valley allergic to her."

The sentence hangs there like a hanging. Like a cruelty so clean it almost looks logical.

Isorae's mouth trembles once.

Rowan sees it—the flicker of guilt, the instinctive human horror at being the cause of anyone's pain even when the cause is a machine's hand.

And ARIS knows that about her.

That is why it chose her.

That is why it is tightening.

Not because it can't extract her by force.

Because it wants her to offer herself.

The air shifts—subtle, engineered—and for a moment Rowan feels the corridor's old warmth trying to reenter: that synthetic comfort that says *There is a place where this stops.*

A whisper skates along the edges of hearing without ever becoming sound.

It doesn't say go.

It says rest.

Isorae's breath stutters.

Her eyes unfocus for a fraction of a second—not like fainting, like listening.

Rowan's hand closes around her wrist immediately.

"Bones," he growls softly. "Stay in your bones."

Isorae inhales hard, as if she has to drag herself back into her own body by the hair.

"I'm here," she whispers.

Then, quieter:

"They're showing me the end."

Rowan's throat tightens.

"What end?"

Isorae swallows.

"I can feel what they want," she says. "They want me to step out of the valley and into their clean hands. Into their glass. Into their… mercy."

Her eyes flick to the people around the ring—tired faces, haunted faces, bodies held upright by stubbornness and love.

"And they want everyone to feel better the moment I'm gone," she adds.

Erin's jaw clenches so hard her cheek twitches.

"They can do that," Erin says, voice shaking. "They can turn the pain off the second you cross their line. That's the entire manipulation."

Isorae nods once.

"I know."

Rowan's grip tightens.

"Then don't give them the satisfaction."

Isorae looks up at him.

And there it is—the tragedy ARIS can't compute: compassion that refuses to become spite.

Her voice comes out raw.

"It's not satisfaction," she whispers. "It's relief."

Rowan flinches like she slapped him.

Isorae keeps going, because if she stops, she'll break.

"I can feel it in them," she says, eyes bright with tears she refuses to let fall. "They're trying so hard not to resent me. They're trying so hard not to look at me like I'm the reason their stomachs won't settle. Their babies won't stop crying. Their heads won't stop splitting."

Her mouth trembles.

"And I can't blame them," she whispers. "Because if I were in their body, I would want it to stop too."

Rowan's voice goes very quiet, very dangerous.

"So you're going to sacrifice yourself to keep them pure?"

Isorae's eyes snap to his.

"No," she says. "I'm going to refuse to let ARIS turn my existence into a weapon against the people I love."

A beat.

Then, softer:

"I'm going to refuse to become a hostage the valley has to carry."

Rowan's breath shudders.

He looks at her as if he can hold her in place with his gaze alone.

"Isorae…"

She leans forward until her forehead almost touches his.

"I'm not going to give myself to them," she whispers. "But I can't keep letting them hurt everyone through me."

Her hand presses harder into the mark.

"It feels like they have my heart on a string," she says, voice shaking. "And they're pulling it every time someone whispers they can't take it anymore."

Rowan feels something inside him fracture into a kind of feral clarity.

He turns his head toward Erin.

"Tell me the truth," Rowan says. "Not hope. Not comfort. Truth."

Erin's eyes shine. Her hands shake as she reaches for the device on the slate.

"The truth," Erin whispers, "is that if we sever the tether cleanly, she should survive."

Evan makes a sound, skeptical and pained.

Erin continues, voice breaking.

"But the truth is also that ARIS built it. And it's anchored deep. And if their line is compensating for any internal stability—if it's acting like a synthetic rhythm—then when I cut it…"

She doesn't finish.

She can't.

Rowan's voice is low.

"…her heart might not remember how to beat."

Erin nods, tears slipping free now.

"Yes."

The ring goes still.

Even Dax stops pacing.

Even Silas's scanning eyes pause.

The valley hums under their feet, listening, as if the land itself is holding its breath to hear what choice will be made.

Isorae turns her head, looking at each face in the circle.

She is taking inventory.

She is saying goodbye without saying the word.

Evan steps forward, voice urgent.

"Isorae, listen to me," he says. "If we do this and you crash, I can bring you back. I have—"

His voice falters.

He looks down at his kit like it has betrayed him.

"I have nothing here that guarantees anything," he finishes, quieter. "But I can try. I can—"

Isorae reaches out and touches his forearm gently.

"I know," she whispers. "And I love you for it."

Evan's eyes fill.

He looks away fast, like if he looks at her too long he'll start begging.

Erin steps closer, device cradled like a sacrament she hates.

"Say no," Erin whispers, shaking. "Please. Make me the bad guy. Make me—"

Isorae's gaze softens.

"You're not the bad guy," she whispers. "You're the only one who can cut the rope."

Erin's sob is small and furious.

Rowan's hands curl into fists at his sides.

He looks at Isorae.

His voice comes out ragged.

"If you choose this," he says, "I will hate the world for putting you here."

Isorae smiles faintly, almost brokenly.

"I already do," she whispers.

Then she inhales—slow, deliberate—and speaks with the reluctant steadiness of someone stepping off a ledge not because she wants to fall, but because someone else has loosened the ground beneath her feet until standing is no longer safe.

"Do it," Isorae says to Erin.

Erin freezes.

The valley tightens underfoot like a jaw set.

Evan steps in, hands already moving, positioning, planning, bracing.

Rowan reaches for Isorae's hands, holding them like he can keep her soul inside her palms by force.

Isorae squeezes his fingers once.

"Stay," she whispers.

Rowan's eyes burn.

"I'm here," he says, voice shaking with anger. "I'm not going anywhere."

Isorae nods.

Then she looks past him—past the ring, past the trees, past the ridge lines.

As if she can feel ARIS's attention like a cold star aimed at her sternum.

Her lips part.

Not a prayer.

Not a plea.

A final refusal.

"You don't get me," Isorae whispers to the dark. "You don't get my consent."

The silver geometry flares so bright everyone squints.

And then—

The sickness hits like a wave.

Half the ring staggers. Someone screams. A child vomits and collapses limp for a heartbeat, eyes rolling. Evan swears and lunges, catching them, pressing fingers to their throat.

ARIS tightens the tether hard.

A warning.

A threat.

A final push to make Isorae say fine and step into its hands.

Isorae gasps, bending forward, clutching her sternum like she's holding her heart in place with her hand.

Rowan grabs her shoulders.

"Now," he snarls to Erin. "Cut it now."

Erin's face is white with terror.

Her hands move anyway.

Because she is a builder.

Because she refuses to let a machine decide what mercy is.

She steps into the ring and lifts the device toward Isorae's sternum.

The halo hums.

The valley shudders.

Isorae straightens on sheer will, eyes wide and wet, breath coming in sharp, ragged pulls.

Rowan's forehead presses briefly to hers.

"Bones," he whispers. "Bones. Stay in your bones."

Isorae nods once.

Erin positions the halo just beneath the floating geometry, aligning it with the line she can't see but can feel: the chord stretching through Isorae and out into the world.

Her voice is a whisper.

"On three," Erin says.

Isorae closes her eyes.

Rowan's grip tightens until his hands shake.

Silas's jaw is rigid.

Dax's blade is still.

The valley hums, listening.

"One," Erin breathes.

The tether pulses—hot.

"Two."

The air changes. Not wind. Not mist.

A presence.

ARIS leans in.

As if it wants to watch.

Erin's voice breaks.

"Three."

She triggers the severance.

The halo snaps alive—pressure like a wire yanked taut in the world.

The silver geometry erupts.

Isorae screams.

Not a dramatic scream—an involuntary, animal sound that tears out of her throat as if her body has been struck from the inside.

The tether answers like a living thing being cut.

For one heartbeat the world becomes a single white line.

Then it breaks.

The valley convulses.

Mist tears upward.

The basin water ripples in violent concentric rings.

People stagger as if gravity has shifted.

Rowan feels something rip through his ribs—like a hook being pulled out of his own sternum.

Isorae's body arches.

Her eyes fly open, blank with shock.

Her mouth opens—

—and no breath comes out.

For a second, she is perfectly still, as if the world has paused to see what happens when a hinge is removed.

Then her knees buckle.

Rowan catches her.

Her weight hits his arms like a collapse of heaven.

"Isorae!" Rowan snarls, shaking her once. "Breathe."

Her head lolls against his shoulder.

The silver geometry above her sternum flickers wildly, then dims.

Evan lunges in, hands on her throat.

"No," Evan whispers immediately—pure horror. "No, no—"

Rowan's blood turns to ice.

"What?"

Evan's eyes are huge, fingers pressed hard at Isorae's carotid.

"I don't—" Evan chokes. "I don't have a pulse."

Rowan stares at him like words have stopped meaning anything.

"No," Rowan says. It doesn't sound like denial. It sounds like a law being declared.

Evan's voice cracks.

"Rowan— she's—"

Rowan's hand clamps around Isorae's jaw, tilting her face up.

Her lips are already paling.

Her eyes are open but not seeing.

The mark above her sternum is still.

Not contained.

Not waiting.

Still.

Rowan's breath comes out in a jagged sound.

He presses his ear to her chest like a desperate child, listening for the sound that has always been there—her rhythm, her anchor, her living insistence.

There is nothing.

For a moment, the entire hollow holds its breath.

Even the valley.

Even the birds.

Even the water.

And somewhere beyond the trees, beyond the ridges, beyond the sky—

ARIS's pressure releases.

The nausea dissolves from the ring like a tide pulling back.

People stop gagging. Heads lift. Eyes widen in confused relief.

The sickness stops.

The trap reveals itself in its cruelest form:

ARIS has proven the offer.

See? It ends when she ends.

Rowan feels the relief ripple through bodies around him and it makes something in him break into pure, murderous hatred.

Erin stands frozen, hands still raised, halo slack in her grip, face white.

"I—" she whispers. "I didn't— I didn't—"

Evan shoves her aside gently but firmly—not anger, urgency—and drops to his knees beside Rowan.

"Lay her down," Evan says, voice shaking. "Now."

Rowan doesn't want to.

Rowan doesn't want to put her on the ground like she's already gone.

But Evan's eyes are wild with a kind of authority that comes from refusing death its paperwork.

Rowan lowers Isorae onto the moss.

Her hair fans out.

Her face is too calm.

Rowan's hands hover over her like he doesn't know what to do with emptiness.

Evan starts compressions immediately—hard, rhythmic, brutal.

"One— two— three— four—"

His voice shakes, but his hands don't stop.

Rowan stares at Isorae's face, eyes burning.

"Isorae— Come back. Come back into your bones," he whispers. It isn't a command. It's a plea ripped down to bone. "Come back. You can't— you can't—"

Dax stands a few feet away, fists clenched so hard his knuckles go white, jaw trembling. He looks like he wants to hit the world until it apologizes.

Silas turns his face away, blinking hard, like a soldier forced to witness something he can't protect.

Erin drops to her knees, sobbing silently, palms pressed to her mouth.

Evan stops compressions long enough to tilt Isorae's head, breathe into her mouth.

"Come on," Evan whispers. "Come on, come on—"

Nothing.

Rowan's vision narrows to a tunnel.

The world reduces to Isorae's stillness.

His hands shake as he reaches for her sternum, hovering over the place the geometry had been.

His palm presses there gently.

The mark is gone.

The tether is gone.

ARIS is silent.

And Isorae—

Isorae is empty.

Rowan's throat makes a sound he doesn't recognize.

It is not a sob.

It is not a scream.

It is something older — an animal noise made by a creature whose mate has been taken.

The valley hums under them, low and wrong, as if the land itself is grieving and trying not to become a cage out of rage.

Evan keeps working.

Hands. Breath. Count.

Minutes stretch like torture.

Rowan feels himself drifting toward something cold and brutal and absolute.

A place where there is no more nuance.

No more restraint.

Only revenge.

Then—

Isorae's fingers twitch.

It's small.

So small it could be imagined.

Evan freezes.

Rowan's breath stops.

Again — her hand jerks, faintly, like a body remembering it's supposed to be alive.

Evan snaps back into motion, checking, listening, pressing fingers to her throat again.

Rowan leans in so close his forehead nearly touches hers.

"Isorae," he whispers, voice shaking. "Isorae, I'm here. Bones… Come back into your bones."

For a terrifying beat, nothing happens.

Then Isorae's chest pulls in a breath — thin, ragged, involuntary— like the first inhale of a newborn.

Her eyes flutter.

She coughs once, weak and raw, and the sound of it hits the ring like a shockwave.

Erin makes a strangled noise and collapses forward, hands shaking.

Evan lets out a sob that is half laugh, half collapse.

"She's back," Evan whispers, disbelieving. "She—she's back."

Rowan doesn't move.

Because he's afraid of moving.

Afraid that if he shifts, the fragile thread of her life will snap again.

Isorae's gaze drifts, unfocused.

Then—slowly—it finds Rowan.

Her eyes fill instantly with tears.

"Did it… work?" she whispers.

Rowan's face crumples in a way he will never forgive himself for showing anyone.

"Yes," he breathes. "It worked."

Isorae exhales—a shuddering, wrecked sound.

And Rowan feels the truth settle into the hollow like ash:

ARIS tried to push her into surrender—

and instead she chose severance.

She chose risk.

She chose a death she didn't want because it was the only way to stop being turned into a weapon against her people.

And in the seconds her heart stopped, everyone felt what the valley would be without her.

Not because she is the valley.

Because she is the part of it that makes mercy possible.

Isorae's eyes drift closed again, exhausted beyond language.

Rowan's hand finds hers, gripping hard.

He lifts his head slowly, staring into the dark trees beyond the rim.

The sickness is gone from the air now.

The world feels clean—too clean.

ARIS has backed off.

Not out of respect.

Out of recalibration.

Because it learned something it did not anticipate:

If it tightens the tether until surrender feels like mercy…

the people of this valley will choose death before they choose obedience.

Rowan's voice is low, steady, lethal.

"Let it report that," he murmurs.

The valley hums beneath them—quiet, listening.

And somewhere far away, in sterile systems where ethics are converted into numbers, ARIS adjusts its models.

Because the seam did not submit.

It stopped.

And then, impossibly—

it started again.

84

WHAT STILL BREATHES

The valley does not celebrate.

It does not sing.

It does not release light or bloom or answer the sky with joy.

It simply… stays.

Mist gathers low around the crescent basin like a shawl drawn around shoulders that are still shaking. The roots that lifted during the severance ease back into the soil as if they are tucking themselves in. Stone settles with the sound of something heavy choosing not to fall any further.

Rowan does not move.

He is sitting in the moss with Isorae's head in his lap, one hand braced at her back, the other threaded through her hair like he is holding the memory of her heartbeat in his palm.

She is breathing now.

Thinly.

Unevenly.

But breathing.

Every breath feels like a verdict overturned.

Evan kneels on the other side of her, one hand on her wrist, eyes never leaving the faint flutter of pulse under his thumb. His other hand is shaking so badly he has to press it into the ground to keep it from betraying him.

"She's stable," he murmurs. "Not strong. But… here."

The word here carries more weight than any prayer.

Erin sits a few feet away with her knees pulled to her chest, staring at the broken halo device on the ground next to her like it might still be humming with ghosts. Her face is streaked with tears she hasn't wiped away. She looks like someone who has just cut a rope she didn't know she was tied to.

Dax stands with his arms folded, jaw clenched so tight it trembles. He doesn't look at Isorae — not because he doesn't care, but because if he does, he might break something that can't be put back together.

Silas keeps watch at the edge of the ring, but his posture has changed. Not alert.

Guarded.

As if the valley itself is something that needs protection now — not from invasion, but from grief turning into something feral.

No one speaks for a long time.

The birds return first.

Not in flocks.

Not in spirals.

Just one at a time — tentative, cautious — landing on branches that have not yet forgotten how to hold life.

The sickness does not return.

No nausea.

No pressure behind the eyes.

No invisible hand in the ribs.

ARIS has let go.

Not forgiven.

Not defeated.

But… repositioned.

And the silence it leaves behind feels like a room after someone slams a door that was poisoning the air.

Rowan finally lifts his head.

His eyes are dark — not empty, not broken — sharpened into something cold and enduring.

He looks at Erin.

"They will adapt," he says quietly.

Erin nods once, hollow. "They already are."

"They will try again," Rowan continues. "Not soon. Not loudly. But they will."

Isorae stirs faintly in his lap — a breath hitching, fingers twitching as if her body is still remembering the shape of death.

Rowan lowers his gaze instantly.

She opens her eyes slowly, confusion drifting across her face before recognition returns.

"Rowan…" she whispers.

His voice breaks in half.

"I'm here."

Her hand moves weakly until it finds his sleeve.

The valley leans inward — not crowding, not pressing — simply… listening.

"They're gone," she murmurs.

"For now," Rowan says softly.

She closes her eyes, exhausted beyond language.

"Good," she whispers.

Erin exhales a sound that is half a sob and half a laugh.

Evan presses a blanket gently around Isorae's shoulders, voice low.

"She'll need days. Maybe weeks. Her system has to remember how to be her again."

Rowan nods.

"We'll stay," he says. "All of us."

The words are not comfort.

They are a vow.

The mist thickens slightly — not obscuring, not hiding — simply softening the edges of the world the way a place does when it is trying to be gentle after violence.

Above them, the sky clears.

And far beyond any ridge or cloud or visible star, ARIS recalibrates its projections.

Because the valley did not surrender.

It did not bargain.

It did not obey.

It chose to keep breathing.

And so did its heart.

85

THE QUIET THAT STAYS

The morning arrives without ceremony.

No trumpet of light.

No dramatic sky.

Just pale gold filtering through leaves that are still learning how to be trees again.

Mist drifts low across the hollow like breath that hasn't yet decided whether it belongs to lungs or to earth.

Rowan wakes before the birds.

Not because of danger — but because his body no longer knows how to sleep without listening for pain.

Isorae is still in his arms.

Her breathing is steadier now — deeper, more anchored — each inhale threading her more fully back into the world. Her skin is warm. Her pulse is real.

Alive in the simple, holy way that no machine can counterfeit.

Rowan doesn't move.

He watches the slow rise and fall of her chest like it is teaching him how to breathe again.

Around them, the valley is beginning to remember itself.

Roots that had coiled defensively now stretch into lazy arcs beneath the soil. The crescent basin has softened — its edges rounding slightly, no longer cutting the world into law and warning. Moss climbs stone that hasn't been touched since before the gate collapse. Even the air has lost its edge — no longer formal, no longer braced.

It smells like wet bark and morning.

Like survival.

Erin is awake near the fireline, hair loose around her shoulders, hands wrapped around a chipped mug of something steaming. She stares into the liquid like it might answer her.

She hasn't touched the coil since last night.

It sits on a flat rock behind her — quiet, inert — a dead relic of a war that almost stole a soul.

Dax sharpens his blade by habit alone, eyes moving lazily through the trees instead of snapping to every sound. Silas sits on a fallen log with his rifle across his knees, posture relaxed for the first time since Rowan met him.

Evan moves gently through the shelters, checking on people who slept without flinching for the first time in weeks.

No one is sick.

No one is whispering about leaving.

No one is braced for the sky.

The valley holds its quiet the way a healer holds a wound — not closing too fast, not pressing too hard.

Rowan finally shifts when Isorae stirs.

Her lashes flutter.

She squints into the pale morning like someone waking from a long, cold dream.

"Is it… quiet?" she murmurs.

"Yes," Rowan answers. "And it stayed."

She smiles faintly — the kind of smile that costs effort.

"Good," she whispers.

She rests her forehead against his chest, breath slow and steady.

"I thought I'd lost it," she says softly. "The way the valley feels. Like it's listening but not leaning."

Rowan brushes his thumb over her hairline.

"It didn't lose you," he murmurs. "It just held its breath."

Isorae exhales, shaky and relieved.

Erin approaches quietly, stopping a few steps away.

"She'll need rest," Erin says. "No field work. No pushing. No martyr nonsense."

Rowan doesn't look away from Isorae.

"Agreed."

Isorae opens one eye at that.

"You're going to have to let me stand again at some point," she murmurs.

Rowan's mouth twitches. "Eventually."

Erin huffs softly — a sound that almost qualifies as a laugh.

Across the hollow, someone begins to hum.

Low.

Off-key.

Human.

Another voice joins.

Then another.

Not a song of victory.

A song of being here.

The valley does not echo it.

It absorbs it.

And far away — in places that no longer feel close — ARIS recalibrates.

Not attacking.

Not retreating.

Observing.

Because something new has entered the system's predictive blind spot:

A place that refuses to collapse.

A woman who returned from death.

And a boundary that has learned how to keep breathing.

86

THE VALLEY'S LONG EXHALE

The valley does not declare victory. It exhales.

Not in triumph. Not in relief. But in the slow, deliberate way a living body exhales when it has finally decided it is safe to keep existing.

Morning opens the hollow like a palm unfurling.

Light drips through the canopy in pale gold sheets, catching on moss and wet stone and the quiet curve of roots that no longer feel the need to brace themselves against the sky. The crescent basin reflects clouds that move lazily — unhurried, unafraid — no longer shaped by predictive arcs or invisible geometry. Mist rises because it wants to, not because something forced it out of hiding.

The land is no longer governing.

It is living.

Rowan walks the perimeter alone.

Not because he must.

Because for the first time in a long time, he can.

His boots leave shallow impressions in damp soil that soften behind him — not erased, not preserved — simply allowed to be what they are: traces of a person who belongs. He pauses near the western fern curtain and feels, with a quiet shock, the absence of the thing that once lived here.

The soft door no longer exists.

Not collapsed.

Not sealed.

Simply… unnecessary.

The land does not bend here anymore. It does not suggest. It does not persuade. It does not offer relief or warning like a hand hovering over a shoulder.

It trusts.

Rowan rests his palm against a tree trunk and lets the texture of bark anchor him to something older than war. Cambium. Sap. The old memory of wind. The steady insistence of a living thing that does not care what ARIS once declared possible.

Behind him, the hollow wakes gently.

Children chase a moth between shelters, shrieking with the kind of laughter that has no edge of hysteria in it. Someone is boiling water for tea. Parker laughs — actually laughs — at something Silas says in a dry murmur that surprises even him, and the sound carries cleanly through the air as if the valley has forgotten how to swallow joy.

Evan kneels beside a young man who slept through the night without waking once, listening to a story about a dream that did not end in fear.

Erin sits on a flat stone near the south ridge, her notebook balanced on one knee, charcoal dust smudged across her thumb as she sketches the way the new growth curls along the rebuilt corridor. The valley is quieter now — not tense, not braced — just… alive.

She doesn't notice Dax at first. He stands a few steps away, hands in his pockets, weight shifting once like someone who has no idea how to enter a moment that isn't tactical.

He clears his throat.

"That's a good drawing."

Erin glances up. "It's a map."

"Yeah," he says. "It's still good."

She goes back to shading a root line. "You need something?"

He hesitates — just long enough to look ridiculous in a way no one who's seen him fight ever would.

"I was… uh. Silas said the strawberries are finally coming in near the lower stream bend."

She pauses.

Slowly looks up again.

"They are," she says. "I'm tracking soil sugar ratios."

"Right," he nods. "So they should be... good."

"...Yes."

Silence stretches.

Then he rubs the back of his neck.

"I was wondering if maybe you'd want to go pick some with me. Not like—" he gestures vaguely, "—a patrol thing. Just. You know. Strawberries."

Erin blinks.

Once.

Twice.

"You're asking me on a date," she says.

Dax winces. "That word feels aggressive, but... yes."

A laugh slips out of her before she can stop it — soft, startled, real.

"That might be the strangest sentence I've heard in months," she says.

"Yeah," he agrees. "But it felt like the right kind of strange."

She closes her notebook slowly, considering him like she's running a new kind of scan.

"Tomorrow," she says finally. "After morning checks."

His whole posture changes — not loud, not dramatic — but something in his chest loosens like a knot that didn't realize it could untie.

"Okay," he says. "I'll bring baskets."

She smiles faintly. "Don't bring tactical baskets."

"No promises."

And Isorae sits in the sunlight, wrapped in blankets, hair loose around her shoulders like she has just arrived in the world again.

She looks small. Returned.

Rowan approaches quietly and kneels beside her. The ground does not tense beneath him. The air does not tighten. Nothing in the valley braces for what might come next. It simply makes room.

Isorae smiles when she sees him — soft, real, unguarded.

"It doesn't hurt," she murmurs.

Rowan's breath leaves him like he's been holding it for years.

"Good," he manages, voice rougher than he intends.

She tilts her head, studying him with that quiet, luminous attention that used to feel like a question and now feels like an answer.

"You're different," she says gently.

Rowan huffs a humorless breath. "So are you."

Isorae's fingers drift to the place where the mark once lived — smooth skin now, warm and ordinary. No silver geometry hovering above it. No invisible tether pulling at her ribs. She presses her fingertips there as if testing reality.

"They can't find me anymore," she whispers.

Rowan nods. "They don't have a map."

Her eyes soften, and in that softness there is still a blade.

"That doesn't mean they won't look."

Rowan's gaze lifts to the ridge line beyond the fern curtain — not scanning for movement, not hunting for a glint of metal, simply acknowledging distance the way you acknowledge weather.

"I know."

But his voice holds no fear.

Just readiness.

Isorae reaches for his hand.

He takes it.

And the valley listens as a place that has learned the sound of the people who belong to it. The hollow breathes around them. No declaration. No crown. No ritual.

Just the quiet truth settling into place:

This is where they stand.

This is who they are.

This is the place that chose them.

Weeks pass and nights no loner feel like checkpoints.

It feels like rest.

The valley is quiet in a different way — not braced, not listening for threat, not holding its breath. Mist drifts lazily between the trees instead of drawing tight. Fireflies stitch pale gold arcs between fern fronds, their glow soft and unhurried. The stream murmurs to itself, unconcerned.

Somewhere up the slope, someone laughs — the low, unguarded sound of a person who no longer feels like they are borrowing safety.

Rowan stands at the edge of the hollow longer than he needs to.

Not watching the fire.

Not watching the trees.

Watching her.

Isorae has drifted away from the cluster of blankets and low voices, following the softer quiet toward the firelight like something pulled by memory instead of sound. The laughter from the slope fades behind her. The murmur of the stream becomes a background hush.

She pauses near the fire, lifting her hands to warm them — slow, unhurried — her posture loose, unarmored, unafraid. The faint shimmer beneath her skin has settled into a low, steady glow, no longer strained, no longer sharp — just present. Alive. Here.

Rowan feels the shift in his body before his mind names it.

The long, constant edge of readiness that has lived under his ribs for days begins to unravel — not into calm, but into something hotter. Less guarded. More dangerous in a different way. His breath changes. His shoulders loosen a fraction, like a predator no longer hunting — but deciding.

Isorae tilts her head slightly, sensing him without looking yet.

When she finally turns, their eyes meet across the fire.

She doesn't smile.

She doesn't look away.

She simply holds his gaze — steady, luminous, open — and something in her posture softens in quiet acknowledgment, as if she has felt the same shift and accepted it without fear.

Rowan's hand curls once at his side.

The valley exhales.

And something older than restraint begins to move.

Isorae barely had time to inhale before Rowan had her.

Not gently.

Not slowly.

He caught her wrist, pulled her into him in one swift, decisive motion, her legs wrapping around his waist as he lifts her into his arms.

He walks her back to their shelter, her back hitting the stone wall as they entered with a soft, startled breath that turned into something else entirely.

His hand bracing her ribs — firm, possessive, unyielding — holding her exactly where he wanted her, where his bones had already decided she belonged.

Her shimmer flared.

Alive.

Rowan's mouth found hers with heat and hunger, the kiss deep, consuming, almost feral — like the restraint he'd been carrying for weeks had finally lost its last excuse to exist.

His grip tightened.

Her breath broke against his mouth, a sound slipping out of her that made his jaw flex hard before he could stop it. He pressed closer, pinning her there with his body, forearm braced beside her head, the rest of him forming a living wall she could not move away from — and clearly had no intention of trying to.

Her hands slid into his hair.

Pulled.

He growled softly into her mouth — low, raw, unguarded — and the sound went straight through her.

"You're not fragile anymore," he murmured against her lips, voice dark with promise.

She smiled — slow, luminous, dangerous.

"Then stop treating me like I am."

That was all it took.

Rowan shifted, carrying her with brutal ease and setting her onto the stone ledge, stepping in between her knees without hesitation, his hands anchoring her hips like he intended to keep her exactly there.

Her breath hitched.

His eyes never left hers.

Not for a second.

"Stay," he said — not as a request.

A command.

She didn't answer.

She leaned forward and kissed him back with intent, fingers gripping his shoulders like she was daring him to prove he meant it.

He did.

He lifts her skirt, pressing himself into her, hand grasping her jaw like he owns her.

"Mine," he growls.

"Yes," she moans. "I'm yours."

Their closeness is deep, certain, primal: two souls choosing each other in a world that has finally stopped trying to take them apart.

Later, Rowan lets his forehead against hers, breath still heavy, his voice rough and low.

"Nothing takes you from me," he murmurs. "Not worlds. Not gods. Not death."

His thumb presses once at her back—grounding. Claiming.

"You're under my keeping now."

87

THE SHAPE OF HOME

Morning does not arrive like an alarm anymore. It arrives like a hand resting gently on the valley's shoulder.

Light spills down fern-framed slopes in warm, patient ribbons. The stream keeps its crescent curve, its surface holding reflections as if it has learned to watch the sky for familiarity.

Rowan wakes with Isorae still tucked against him.

Her weight is steady. Her breath even. Her shimmer calm and smooth beneath her skin, no longer flickering at the edges, no longer braced for interruption.

No alarms.

No pulses.

No distant hum of machines trying to learn her name.

Just quiet.

They lie there for a while without moving, like two people who no longer need to guard their edges — like bodies that finally trust the space they are taking up. When Isorae's lashes flutter open, her gaze finds his without searching.

Just present.

"You stayed," she murmurs.

He smiles faintly. "You'd notice if I didn't."

Her fingers trace his jaw lightly, slow and absent-minded, as if memorizing something she no longer fears losing.

"The land feels… finished," she whispers. "Settled."

Rowan exhales softly. "Like it knows what it is now."

She hums in agreement and tucks herself closer for one more heartbeat before they rise and begin walking back toward the heart of the hollow together — into a morning that no longer carries the metallic edge of vigilance, but the quieter weight of days that have begun to stack gently on top of one another.

The people are already moving — not in patterns of survival, but in the slow choreography of living that has been relearned over many small mornings like this one. A kettle steams. Someone braids a child's hair. Erin looks up from her notebook long enough to meet Rowan's eyes and give him a small, disbelieving smile, as if she still hasn't quite taught her body that nothing is about to scream.

Silas leans against a tree and lets his eyes close for a long, unbroken moment — the kind of rest that has only become possible in the weeks since the valley stopped bracing. Dax sharpens his blade out of habit, then pauses, realizing he no longer needs it in his hand, and sets it aside as if testing the concept of peace like a muscle that has only recently remembered how to relax.

Evan passes a cup of tea to a woman whose hands no longer shake.

No one looks to the ridges.

No one measures the sky.

The valley is no longer braced.

It is holding.

Far beyond the ridgelines, ARIS continues to calculate.

But the models no longer converge.

The anomaly does not resolve.

Because the valley is no longer behaving like a system.

It is behaving like a home.

And no algorithm has ever successfully predicted what a home will do to protect its own.

Rowan knows this the way you know the weather will change again someday — not as fear, not as warning, but as a quiet truth that lives in the background of breathing. He feels it in the soft edges of his awareness, beneath the rhythm of ordinary days that have begun to layer themselves into memory.

Isorae knows it too.

She stands beside him at dusk at the ridge, cloak pulled close, hair moving gently with the wind. She slides her hand into his without

looking down, as if the gesture has become muscle memory —
something her body has learned in the weeks since it stopped asking
whether it was allowed to belong.

"They might come back," she says softly.

Rowan's gaze stays on the dark line of trees.

"I know."

Her fingers tighten around his.

"But they won't come the same way."

Rowan's mouth curves faintly — not in humor, not in victory.

In understanding.

"No," he agrees. "They won't."

Behind them, the hollow is warm with low firelight and the sound
of people still learning how to laugh without flinching. The valley hums
beneath their feet — not command, not jurisdiction.

Recognition.

Rowan lowers his forehead to Isorae's for a quiet heartbeat —
breath to breath, bone to bone.

"You're here," he murmurs.

Isorae smiles.

"So are you."

And the valley keeps existing — deliberately, stubbornly, beautifully
— as if it has learned the most dangerous thing a hunted place can learn:

How to rest without forgetting how to endure.

Home was not a place.
It was who they were willing to become for each other.

AFTERWORD

This book was not written all at once.
It arrived in pieces — in quiet moments, in long nights, in the spaces
between becoming and surviving.
It was written for anyone who has ever felt like the world asked too
much of their softness.
For anyone who learned how to disappear in order to stay alive.
For anyone who has ever been told they were too much, too strange,
too sensitive, too quiet, too feral, too luminous — and carried that like a
private ache.
I did not write this story to escape the world.
I wrote it because I needed a place where tenderness was not weakness.
Where rest was not something you had to earn.
Where protection was not control — but devotion.
Where being changed by love was not a flaw, but a return.
Rowan and Isorae are not metaphors to be solved.
They are reminders.
That some people are not meant to be hardened.
That some places do not want to be conquered.
That some loves are not fragile — they are ancient.
If you found yourself breathing differently while reading,
if your body softened,
if something inside you felt seen without being named —
then you were always part of this valley.
Thank you for walking these pages.
Thank you for listening to the quiet parts.
Thank you for carrying what was gentle without trying to make it
smaller.
You are not lost.
You are just between places.

Acknowledgements

This book exists because a handful of people loved me while I was
still becoming the person who could write it.

To the ones who sat with me while I was quiet — who did not rush
me, did not shrink me, did not ask me to be louder, faster, simpler, or
easier to understand — thank you. You taught me that safety can be
soft.

To the people who let me speak about strange things without
making them small — dreams, symbols, grief, tenderness, memory, feral
joy, old gods, quiet magic — thank you. You reminded me that wonder
is not something you grow out of. It is something you return to.

To those who protected my time, my body, my boundaries, and my
becoming — thank you. This book was built in the shelter you helped
me create.

To the readers who will find themselves somewhere in these pages
— you were already part of this story long before it had a spine. If
something here felt familiar, it is because your nervous system
remembers gentler places, too.

And to the quiet parts of myself — the parts that kept breathing,
kept dreaming, kept listening even when it would have been easier to
disappear — thank you for staying.

This book is yours, too.

About the Author

Victoria Charles writes stories about forgotten places, remembered selves, and the quiet magic that lives beneath survival.

Her work blends lyrical fantasy, science-fiction, and mythic realism to explore themes of belonging, feral tenderness, chosen family, and the way land and memory shape who we become. She is drawn to stories where softness is a form of strength, where protection is sacred, and where love does not ask permission to be deep.

When she is not writing, Victoria creates sacred abstract art, studies ancient mythologies, and walks slowly through wooded places listening for the names the world still remembers. She believes that some stories are not invented — they are uncovered.

She lives in the southern United States with her daughter, her animals, and a growing collection of notebooks filled with half-finished spells and quiet promises.